Praise for _Fr..._

"No one blends the ancient with ... ...
His _From Sun to Sun_ is an entertaining, thought provoking
exploration of women struggling to overcome against great odds."
—Reed Farrel Coleman, _New York Times_
bestselling author of _Sleepless City_

"By turns evocative, provocative, lyrical, visceral, tender, and
brutal—but always engaging and fascinating—_From Sun to Sun_
is a tour de force by a master story-teller at the top of his form.
In recounting the respective quests of two ethnic minority
women, Wishnia provides a story from radically different
perspectives that nevertheless makes a powerful case for the
power of humanity and courage in the face of bigotry and
the shameless abuse of power. Lots of times, a good book is
praised because the reader can't put it down in the thrall of
its relentless pace. But this book, which is no less relentless,
will cause the reader to periodically stop and think and feel,
savoring not only the thrilling ride, but also its deep wisdom."
—James Lincoln Warren, Black Orchid Novella
Award–winning author of "Inner Fire"

"In _From Sun to Sun_, author Kenneth Wishnia nimbly vaults
across time and space to create a lively correlation between
two fierce young women, Ruth and Felicity, living millennia
apart in disparate social hierarchies. It's a story of defiance and
accommodation, an immigrant's story of biblical Ruth and her
dizygotic twin Felicity, native born but treated as an outsider,
whose worth is constantly judged and evaluated by men. It's
a crime story, plus it's a feminist story of women forced into
servility by custom and circumstance. Last but never least, it's
a love story. Woven throughout is a searing social critique,
filled with exposés of New York's building codes, the Persian
conquest, scholarly debates, and tribal squabbles during
the Iron Age. Wishnia delivers with humor and aplomb."
—Summer Brenner, author of _Nearly Nowhere, I-5_, and _Dust: A Memoir_

Praise for *The Fifth Servant*

"A gripping page-turner."
—*Publishers Weekly* (starred review)

"Powerful ... A densely philosophical yet
surprisingly witty historical mystery."
—*Booklist*

"Works nicely on at least three levels: as
history, mystery, and theology."
—*Kirkus*

"This fast-paced historical combines scholarly
details that bring the sixteenth century alive with
believable characters and a compelling mystery."
—*Library Journal* (starred review)

"Brilliant, intense, and well researched ... I eagerly await
his next venture into any period of Jewish history."
—*Jewish Book World*

Praise for the Filomena Buscarsela series

"Riveting circumstances, a strongly focused plot, and
ably described settings make this essential reading."
—*Library Journal*

"Great fun ... Fil is a hyperbolic character, spewing enough
acerbic opinions to fill half a dozen average mysteries."
—*Publishers Weekly*

"Wishnia writes with brio, energy, rage, passion,
and humor. Brash, sassy and indomitable,
Filomena is purely a force of nature."
—*Booklist*

From Sun to Sun

by
Kenneth Wishnia

From Sun to Sun
© 2024 Kenneth Wishnia
This edition © 2024 PM Press

ISBN: 979-8-88744-035-4 (paperback)
ISBN: 979-8-88744-045-3 (ebook)
Library of Congress Control Number: 2023944310

Cover by John Yates / www.stealworks.com
Interior design by briandesign

10 9 8 7 6 5 4 3 2 1

PM Press
PO Box 23912
Oakland, CA 94623
www.pmpress.org

Printed in the USA.

Enjoy happiness with a woman you love all the fleeting days of life that have been granted to you under the sun—all your fleeting days. For that alone is what you can get out of life.
—Ecclesiastes 9:9

For all the wanderers who are still
searching for a place in this world

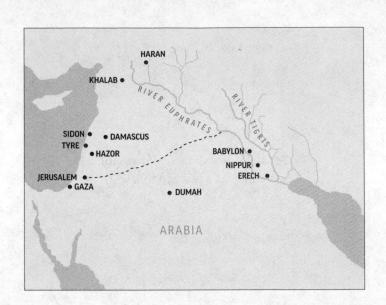

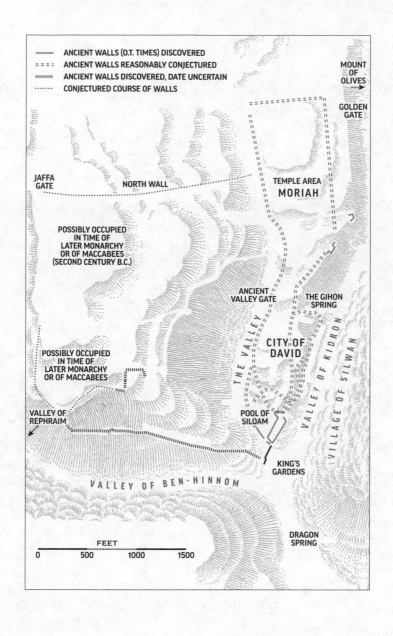

ANCIENT WALLS (O.T. TIMES) DISCOVERED
ANCIENT WALLS REASONABLY CONJECTURED
ANCIENT WALLS DISCOVERED, DATE UNCERTAIN
CONJECTURED COURSE OF WALLS

MOUNT
OF
OLIVES →

GOLDEN
GATE

JAFFA
GATE   NORTH WALL

TEMPLE AREA
MORIAH

POSSIBLY OCCUPIED
IN TIME OF
LATER MONARCHY
OR OF MACCABEES
(SECOND CENTURY B.C.)

ANCIENT
VALLEY GATE   THE GIHON
SPRING

CITY OF
DAVID

POSSIBLY OCCUPIED
IN TIME OF
LATER MONARCHY
OR OF MACCABEES

VALLEY OF
REPHRAIM

POOL OF
SILOAM

KING'S
GARDENS

VALLEY OF BEN-HINNOM

DRAGON
SPRING

FEET
0   500   1000   1500

"*Parasite.*" She spat the word after the fleeing rodent. "We have to fix that hole. Anything can come crawling through it. Snakes, scorpions, venomous spiders—"

"All right, I'll take a look at it tomorrow."

"Listen to my big warrior man sounding like he's ready to settle down to a life of domestic bliss," she said, softening a bit.

"I wouldn't say that," he said, caressing her cheek with the tips of his fingers. His hands were too rough and abrasive for such tenderness, but his young wife didn't seem to mind. She took his hand and pressed it to her face, closing her eyes, as if to enhance the sensation of his ruggedness.

"But no more wandering as a man of the sword for a while," he said. "We can be ourselves here."

He ran his hand through her long, loose hair—a bit coarse from years of punishing heat and wind—and marveled at her tan skin, pockmarked here and there by flying cinders, which only made her more desirable in his eyes.

"First we must honor my mother's wishes," he said.

Ruth nodded, wondering which wishes he meant.

"The last few years have been rough on Naomi," he admitted. "She's still mourning my father, Elimelekh, may his soul be at peace, even though it's been more than a year since he walked this earth."

Ruth bowed her head as a sign of shared mourning, though she had never met Makhlon's father. She gently squeezed her husband's hand.

"They agonized for months about uprooting the family and trekking through the wilderness to come here," he said. "But there's so much more opportunity in the Land between the Rivers. We can put down stakes, stop living hand-to-mouth, make something of ourselves. The *rabonim* are even talking about opening an academy for Torah study—"

"The who?"

"The teachers," he explained.

"What do they teach?"

"That we can't just live on fried bread and onions, that we also need the wisdom of the Torah."

She eyed him quizzically. "The big scroll you always read on *yom Shabbat*?"

"Right. The big scroll. Maybe I should put down the sword long enough to teach my unpolished bride the rules for being a good wife and daughter-in-law of the tribe of the Yehudim."

"And while you're at it, we could put a business."

"You mean start a business."

"*Start* a business," she corrected.

"What kind of business?"

"You're joking, right?" She tugged playfully at his beard. "I know how to forge weapons. You know a legion of mercenaries who need weapons. If we can—"

"I don't know if people are ready—"

"Sure, it'll be hard at first, but I know what it takes to run a metalsmithing business, trust me."

"For a woman to—"

"We could start off making household utensils, tools, and weapons, and if word gets around that we can make or repair anything from iron-tipped javelins to cast-iron cooking pots, maybe someday build our own foundry."

"That would certainly tie us down."

Ruth fell silent under her husband's penetrating gaze, awaiting his verdict, his judgment.

"Got it all figured out, haven't you?" he said, forcing a smile. "What about children?"

Ruth had no special gift for the rearing of children.

"I'm praying for a whole brood of children to please your mother."

A genuine smile spread across his face this time, despite his thick, curly beard. He took her by the shoulders and admired the glow of her hair in the lamplight, the way she straddled him. Forceful and determined.

"Now let's make that grandson for Naomi."

~

I love to pray at sunrise, when the day is young, the world is new, and all things are possible.

Ruth bowed to Jerusalem, five hundred miles to the west, and said a brief blessing, for the elders had decreed that the fourth day of the Babylonian New Year festival was the best time to begin the journey to the land of their fathers.

She washed her hands in the manner of the Yehudim and rolled out a measure of dough, stoked the fire, poured a bit of oil into the blackened pan, and set the flat, misshapen bread to toast in it. She chopped up an onion and tossed the oversized chunks into the oil around the edges of the heavy iron pan.

She glanced at the bed—a mat on the floor, really. Makhlon was still sleeping off last night's marital revels, his lips warm and wet, floating in a sea of curly black hair as he snored open-mouthed.

He always wanted something sweet in the morning. Ruth reached for the jar of dried dates and nearly dropped it when a green-and-black speckled lizard slithered out of the jar's mouth and scurried along her arm. She swatted it off before it slipped down her back, and chased it outside with the broom. At least it wasn't a scorpion this time.

Her slumbering warrior must have been too distracted to put the stopper on tight last night.

Breakfast was sizzling as she swept the dust into the street. The dull yellow cloud flew into the air and dispersed, as her own people had been scattered by the winds of time and the cruelty of men. The roads were under Persian control now, yet a cold thrill of fear tickled the soles of her feet as she considered the potential risks of following the Great River upstream to the northwestern edge of the old Assyrian Empire, now the Persian province of Damascus, then down through Galilee and Samaria to the province of Yehudah: nearly nine hundred miles on foot.

She set up the wooden stools that had somehow gotten knocked over the night before, scraping her palms on the rough wood.

As the first trumpet blasts atop the immense walls of the Babylonian capital heralded the awakening of the gods, a shadow fell across the threshold. Ruth's sister-in-law Orpah stood in the doorway, her onyx-black eyes shining from her own sensual midnight feast with Makhlon's younger brother, Khilyon.

"What are you burning now, O Ruth the Moabite?"

"Don't call me that," Ruth said, grabbing a rag and pulling the pan off the fire before the bread was completely blackened.

"Why not? They're a proud people."

And sworn enemies of the Yehudim.

"Besides, a little charcoal is good for the digestion," Ruth replied, rescuing the charred bread from the pan.

"Forget about that. Want to go watch the festivities?"

Ruth's eyes flitted to her husband's muscular chest, gently rising and falling under the faded coverlet.

"They won't be up for a couple of hours, and you already made his breakfast—after your own unique fashion." Orpah's voice grew seductive: "Come on, they're reenacting the sacred marriage ceremony today."

Ruth felt the pull of her domestic duties yielding to a deeper longing. Surely Makhlon would understand.

"If we hurry we can beat the heat and get back before they even notice we're gone," Orpah said with a conspiratorial smile.

They locked gazes. Ruth tossed her apron aside and reached for a small blue jar on the shelf.

"What are you doing?"

"Rubbing on a little oil first—"

"We'll be back before the sun gets too hot. Come on, let's go!"

Ruth grabbed a headscarf and they took off, raising their skirts just below their knees to run faster, the silver amulet swinging from Orpah's neck as they giggled like young girls.

"And you shouldn't use date pits for cooking fuel," Orpah said as they trotted along, leaving a cloud of dust in their wake.

"Why not?"

"They make the fire burn too hot."

"And that's bad?"

"You're frying bread, not smelting copper."

They dodged a couple of emaciated dogs rummaging through a pile of rubbish.

The authorities had decreed a festival day for slaves as well, so nobody was knee-deep in the canal cutting reeds or dredging the silt that constantly clogged the sacred waters, so central to the life of the city that defiling the river in any way—even spitting in it—carried grave consequences.

The flow of people slowed to a crawl as families of all tribes—Arabians, Medes, Yehudim, even a few far-flung Egyptians—converged on the narrow bridge and squeezed through the gate to Zabara Street. The stonemasons' chisels were silent after many days of chipping away at the monumental reliefs, removing the names of the great kings of Babylon while leaving their images intact. For what power could the images have over men's souls once the names had been erased and replaced with those of their Persian conquerors?

Bodies pressed closer on all sides, and as the sweat formed on the back of her neck, Ruth felt the soft stab of someone's manhood against her thigh. They shouldn't have come without their men. But their men wouldn't have let them attend the pagan rites.

Ruth felt a twitch of anticipation as the tangle of humanity pushed closer to the Processional Way, and the spectacle of the Babylonian gods parading through the streets produced a collective gasp from the crowd as the towering figures seemed to come alive. Mounted on sacred animals, they bobbed about with their right arms raised, bestowing their blessings on the people. The idols had full square beards carved in the Babylonian style, and elaborate cylindrical headgear that added two feet to their height.

And when the sun rose above the city's massive fortifications, and its rays kissed the silver crescent moon crowning Ishtar, the goddess of love and war, called Inanna by the Akkadians and Asherah by the Yehudim, Ruth resolved to say a prayer to Ishtar to help her carry on the family name after the death of Naomi's husband Elimelekh on the battlefield, months before Ruth had married into the family.

"Come with me," Ruth said, grabbing her sister-in-law's hand and pulling her through the mob of gawkers blocking the intersection while a pair of Persian sentries kept a wary eye on the festivities.

When the heavens above were yet unnamed
And no dwelling beneath was called by a name

The priests began to recite the Creation story, and the people stood transfixed before Esagil, the soaring temple that had been the House of Marduk since before King Hammurabi laid down the law more than a thousand years before.

On a raised platform, a chosen couple reenacted the marriage of Marduk and Ishtar, the groom pouring perfume over the bride's head while his relatives laid fine linens and provisions at her feet. A dozen slave girls in flowing white robes supported the train of the bride's dress as the couple ascended to the chambers atop the temple, known as the House of the Mystery of Heaven and Earth, where they would enact a ritual they were forbidden to reveal, although Ruth had a pretty good idea of what they would be doing up there.

A hawker offered the women roasted locusts on skewers,

but they kept moving past the vast open space separating the profane world from the seven-story Etemenanki, the Foundation of Heaven and Earth, a mountainous structure reaching nearly two hundred cubits upward, like a giant stairway to the gods.

The procession reached the Temple of Ishtar, bursting forth in full celebratory swirl. Couples caroused freely, sweat glistening on their bodies, weaving a path between mothers nursing newborns and grandmothers feeding toddlers honey cakes. Ruth had to block it all out as she prayed to Ishtar—that is, to Asherah—to listen to her pleas, to take pity on her, to soften the hearts of the gods and open her womb.

She knew what she was doing would be denounced as *sheketz*, an abomination, that the God of Israel had commanded Moses to smash the altars and cut down the sacred posts of those who worshiped the goddess Asherah. But she couldn't help it. It was the way of the world. The way of the seed and the soil. There was no Enlil without Inanna. No Baal without Astarte. No El without Elath. And no Yahaweh without Asherah. How could you believe in the god and not the goddess?

Purple-robed attendants carried the gilded gods into the House of the New Year Festival, where they would remain for three days while the Gates of Ruin flew open, unleashing the forces of chaos on the world until the gods emerged once again to restore order to a grateful world.

"We'd better be getting back to our husbands," Ruth said, a strange uneasiness gnawing at her stomach. She thought she heard the plaintive wail of the *shofar* in the distance.

"Don't worry, sweetie," said a gruff voice, creeping up from behind. "*I'll* open your womb for you."

"Leave us alone," said Orpah, as the man clutched his member, boasting of his prowess.

Ruth faced him, summoning the legendary harshness of her mother's tribe, and told him right where to stick it. Orpah had to grab Ruth and steer her back toward the southeast gate while the man told everyone within earshot what he thought about the morals of two married women going to the New Year's festival without their husbands.

His taunts were drowned out by silver trumpets announcing the entrance of King Cyrus and his retinue. The Persian army took over the parade ground at the foot of Esagil with a dazzling display of drums and colors, and the new king promised that his first act after reestablishing the throne of the one true god, Marduk, would be to release all those who were unjustly imprisoned by the disgraced former Babylonian ruler, King Nabu-naid.

The people hissed upon hearing the name of their weak, defeated king, the son of a priestess who served the moon god Sinn. A half-naked prisoner was dragged through the streets, his dark-ringed eyes blinking in the sunlight, and the people cried out the names of their sins while the guards reddened the prisoner's back with lash strokes and beat him about the head, his matted red hair sending up puffs of yellowish dust at every blow. It was the price of his freedom: to absorb the blows and absolve the Babylonians of all their sins over the past year.

And soon the city officials, and the princes, governors, and military leaders of Sumer and Akkad were called upon to bow to the new monarch and kiss his feet. The Babylonians stood on their tiptoes to catch a glimpse of this remarkable spectacle, their bodies swaying like reeds.

A call went out from the center of the city that reverberated down the street:

Let us now purify his temple and his city

Sacrificial lambs squirming beneath the blades squealed in terror as pious men of god prepared to slit their throats. Muscular men occupied the shadows under the eaves on virtually every street corner, gripping sacrificial animals by the scruff of the neck, the sun growing hotter with each breath. The slaughterers stepped into the blinding sunlight, wrestling with their unwilling victims. Orpah tried to get Ruth to slow down, but she plunged ahead as if an evil wind pursued her.

The slaughterers raised their sparkling blades high. Ruth covered her ears as the crowd roared, and the priests drained the lambs' blood and presented the severed heads to Marduk.

Ruth nearly doubled over as she bumped into a Yehudi slave girl.

"Lilah! What are you doing here?"

"I was sent to look for you."

"By whom? Why?"

"By my master. He says to come quickly. Your husbands have been struck by the hand of Yahaweh."

CHAPTER TWO

Ruth

The Babylonians made *kuppuru* with the bodies of the slaughtered rams, spattering the walls of the city with their blood. They dragged the carcasses to the water's edge while the priests carried their dripping-red heads and threw them into the river.

Ruth barely saw the new blood washing away the sins of the old, barely felt her breathless body barreling down the dusty lanes toward the mud-brick houses along the canal where she and Makhlon lived among his people, grasping at the slim thread of hope that it was a case of mistaken identity, that someone's else's husband lay in the marriage bed gasping and choking on thick clots of blood.

And now his blood was on her hands, her hands were on his cloak, and his cloak was full of blood and bile issuing from his nose and mouth. She prayed to Yahaweh to destroy the hostile spirit that had invaded his body, to cast out the one who devours and is not filled, the one who drinks and is not satisfied, offering to make any sacrifice to keep his spirit from crossing over to the land of Mot. But Yahaweh did not answer.

The piercing cries of the *shofar* rent the air as the high-born Yehudim celebrated their imminent departure from the land of exile.

Ruth pleaded with the Redeemer of Israel. She prayed to Him using every name He was known by or might respond to. She prayed to Shaddai, to Elohim, to Yah, to El Elyon, to the God of Abraham, Isaac, and Jacob. She prayed for strength, for knowledge, and when that didn't work she begged Asherah, mother of the gods, to intercede on her behalf.

But Makhlon kept slipping from her grasp. His blood-red eyes did not see, his tortured tongue could not speak her name as his body pitched from side to side. Then a foul whitish-gray ooze dribbled from his nostrils and the man who had taught her to worship the God of his fathers unleashed the inarticulate howl of a wounded jackal dying in the wilderness.

Then his body went limp.

Alaley!

Ruth lifted her voice and wept.

For his spirit was condemned to wander in the shadowy netherworld until he had a son to carry on his name. Unless she was already pregnant with his seed, how could that happen now, without the aid of God or His messengers?

Outside in the public square, King Cyrus's much-anticipated decree was proclaimed under the blazing sun:

> *Thus says Cyrus, king of Persia*
> *All the kingdoms of the earth has*
> *Yahaweh God of heaven given me*
> *And charged me with building Him a House*
> *In Jerusalem which is in Yehudah*

She smashed the jar of dates into a hundred pieces. She clawed at herself until she drew blood. She grabbed a knife to gash herself and suddenly a dozen hands were upon her to stop her from shaming herself in this way, but not before the blood was streaming down her arms. They dragged her into the daylight, but she twisted loose and writhed around in the dust as if she were trying to smother the flames of her grief.

> *Whoever is among you of all His people*
> *Let Yahaweh his God be with him*
> *And let him go up!*

Joyful noises filled the air.

Blood mingled with the dust and dirt as Ruth and Orpah stood clinging to each other, unable to loosen their grips even for a moment, for her Khilyon had met the same horrible fate.

Orpah's words spilled hotly into Ruth's ear: "You don't think—?"

"No, no," Ruth replied, her voice steadying. "I don't care what the prophets say, *nobody* deserves to die like that."

But surely something was amiss.

How could they both die the same way? Ruth darted over to a hole in the mudbrick wall's exterior, probed it with her fingers, and came out with traces of a slimy residue that could have been left by a venomous snake. She shifted her attention to the abutting wall, scanning its base until she found what she was looking for: a second hole leading to Khilyon and Orpah's bedroom, a faint shimmer on the dull clods of baked earth confirming her worst fears.

Voices surrounded them:

"It must be some kind of punishment."

"It must be God's will."

How could this be God's will?

It felt more like someone had put the Evil Eye on them. But who? Ruth scanned the faces in the crowd, wondering which of those leering hypocrites could be the guilty one.

"It was vengeful beings, jealous of their happiness."

Orpah spoke through tears, her voice strained, nearly gagging on the wetness of the words: "Are our few bits of happiness so much as to make a god jealous?"

Love is as fierce as death, says the Song of Songs.

So the answer was yes, love is something that God cannot control, so He had chosen to destroy it.

Ruth was seized by the sudden urge to vomit. She pushed Orpah away and collapsed in the dust, her body convulsing with dry heaves because she hadn't eaten anything yet that day.

"Look at this so-called breakfast she left out for him. Burnt lumps of bread and soggy onions."

She felt like a cracked storage jar, empty and useless. The sweat on the back of her neck turned dry and stiff as the heat clung to her like hot tar.

Her tongue tasted bitter.

The elders announced that King Cyrus of Persia had returned the treasures looted by Nebuchadnezzar, may his bones be ground to dust, from the House of Yahaweh in Jerusalem. And the community of returning exiles cheered the glittering display of thirty golden bowls and utensils, four hundred ten silver bowls and utensils, twenty-nine slaughtering knives, and the grand oversized menorah that would require a cart all to itself and six full-time attendants to ensure that it was transported safely to God's House in Yehudah.

A young man with the unkempt hair and beard of the prophets of old climbed onto the back of a cart and praised King Cyrus as *ha-mashiakh*, the anointed one, and led the gathering tribes in a dry-throated rendition of a song of Yah:

> *Let the name of Yahaweh be blessed now and forever*
> *From the rising of the sun to its setting*

> *The same Yahaweh who had taken her beloved Makhlon and turned his brains to mush,* Ruth thought acidly.

But the young prophet's eyes burned with conviction, and his words plumbed her soul like an iron-tipped spear hitting home:

> *He comforts the childless woman*
> *And makes her a joyful mother of children*
> *Hallelu-yah!*

So there it was. The vengeful God of the Israelites had taken everything from her, and she would have to make the journey to His House in Yehudah to get it back.

Eyes widened and fingers pointed as Ruth found the strength to rise on shaky legs and return to the place of death to wash and prepare Makhlon's body for burial. Some praised God, and some praised the nameless prophet. They didn't know that by going in, Ruth hoped to die by the same hand that had taken her husband.

~

She carefully wrapped the corners of the shroud around Makhlon's feet as if swaddling a newborn baby, then threw her remaining valuables into a sack. She took all the surplus wealth she had in the world—a few sacks of barley—and gave them to a local merchant in exchange for his promise to sustain the dead man's spirit with meal offerings for as long as the supply lasted.

"And fresh water," she said. "You must put out fresh water at the appointed times, or his—" She stopped herself from saying *or his spirit will return to haunt you.*

"Yes, yes, I understand," the merchant assured her.

The volunteer burial committee took hold of the flimsy palm-frond bier, but she stopped them with a shout:

"Wait! Don't—"

The men awaited further instructions.

Khilyon's body was already in the ground, awaiting his brother and companion for all eternity.

"I must ..." Ruth gently lifted the shroud from her husband's face.

The blood must have flowed again after she washed him, and the sight of fresh carnage caused her mother-in-law Naomi's strength to fail. The professional women mourners rushed in to support the grieving mother on both sides, raising their voices to the skies in anguish.

While everyone was distracted, Ruth slipped a coin into her dead husband's mouth so he could pay the ferryman to take him across the River of Death. She removed his Shield

of David necklace and hung it around her own neck so she
would have some part of him close to her, always.

She placed a kiss on his forehead, the only part of his
face that wasn't defiled with dried blood, a last moment of
human contact before he departed on his journey to the land
that lies west of the sun. She knew better than to suggest that
they send his spirit upward by means of the carrion birds,
which the Yehudim believed to be *tamey*, unclean.

Makhlon's body was lowered, and as the volunteers
befouled his pristine shroud with the first shovelfuls of
sand and earth, Ruth wrapped herself in his bloodstained
cloak—yes, even in this heat she wrapped herself in his
cloak—and knelt to pray to the God of his fathers to bless
her departed husband and redeemer, and to make His face
shine upon him and grant him peace. She asked the God of
Israel to comfort Naomi, who was beyond such wailing and
keening. Poor Naomi was completely broken, silent as the
stones that littered the ground beneath their feet. Having
lost her husband and both sons, she had no standing at all
among the people of her tribe according to the ways of the
Yehudim—no wealth or property to her name, no identity at
all unless some male relative was willing to claim her and
redeem her standing within the community.

Some distance away, at the head of the caravan, the
elders brought out a first-born ram to sanctify their imminent departure, and when Ruth opened her eyes, they sliced
its throat and poured the blood out onto the sand.

She shuddered and drew the cloak closer around herself,
though the sun was radiating the kind of heat that bakes
mud into bricks, and the cloak was beginning to smell like
the rotting corpse of a dead animal. She insisted on rooting
around in the sand to gather stones to mark her husband's
grave and keep his soul from wandering the earth. One of
the mercenaries hired to protect the caravan—a muscular man named Yedidyah with the long, flowing hair of a

Nazirite—stepped in to lift her up, but she kept at it despite torn and bleeding fingertips, until the mercenary extracted a promise from a stonemason with a patchy gray beard to carve an appropriate testament to the deceased's piety and worthiness.

But Ruth said, "No empty praises. Save your praise for King Cyrus of Persia."

"It's got to say *something*," said the stonemason. "Even just a few words—"

"Just put what you always put—*Here lies Makhlon, son of Elimelekh, who died on the fourth day of Nisannu in the first year of the reign of Cyrus king of Persia. Peace be upon him.* What else is there to say?"

Unless it should include a curse on anyone who disturbed his bones, but Ruth wasn't sure how the Yehudim would react to that.

"And I want you to carve it in black basalt."

"You sure? Most folks go with limestone or Assyrian sandstone—"

"I said use basalt. It lasts longer."

"All right, but it's going to cost you."

Ruth flailed about for the sack she had thrown together, and pulled out a polished ax-head.

The stonemason examined it closely, or pretended to, since any man with eyes in his head could see its true value the instant she took it out of the sack: the flawless iron blade was razor-sharp and so artfully made it appeared to issue from the jaws of a creature with saber-like teeth that glinted brightly in the sun. This formidable weapon had clearly been wrought by a world-class artisan over the course of many long hours at fantastically high temperatures.

"Where on earth did you—?"

"It's a Luristan blade. The best there is."

A group of merchants standing in a circle eyed each other.

"Then maybe you should hold on to it."

"I've got others. Well, not like that one. But—"

"No, not like this one. Clearly not." The stonemason took a breath or two, then nodded and accepted the ax-head as payment.

Three sharp blasts of the *shofar* announced that the caravan was ready to depart. They were supposed to be ready at the first light of dawn, but with all the delays the sun was now directly overhead, sapping the exiles' enthusiasm and punishing the beasts of burden.

The young prophet tried to revive their spirits: "Come on, people! We're supposed to leave Babylon filled with joy! Even the road will sing with joy beneath our sandals! Every hill and mountain will cheer us on, and all the trees of the field will applaud our passing!"

But people can't eat prophecies, no matter how cleverly fashioned, so the young prophet had to run around trying to convince anyone who would listen that since King Cyrus had appointed one of their own, Prince Sheshbazzar, as governor of the province of Yehudah, the returning exiles were being granted the right of self-rule.

A few of the famously stiff-necked children of Israel responded with half-hearted whoops and faint praises for Ezra the Scribe and Nehemiah the military engineer, who had been appointed to supervise the rebuilding of the Temple of Yahaweh in Jerusalem.

But as the last saddlebag was secured, the last leather straps drawn tight, and the Yehudim were saying their final goodbyes, beneath the fine speeches, Naomi heard murmurings against the women who were less than pure, women whose men had clearly died because of a curse or some immensely evil act that would bring bad luck to any man foolish enough to draw near them.

And she went up to her daughters-in-law, their faces still streaked with dirt and tears, Ruth still wearing the cloak that smelled like a butcher's apron, apparently oblivious to the odor, and said, "Go back, each of you, to your mother's house."

Ruth and Orpah were stunned.

Naomi tried to kiss them goodbye, but Ruth stiff-armed her: "What are you talking about? We're going with you."

"I've always admired your determination, Ruth. But go back, my daughters. You have lost your husbands, but you can still find happiness and security with a man. I have lost my husband *and* my sons. Even if I were to find a husband tonight, and give birth to sons, would you wait for them to grow up?"

Orpah lowered her head and stared at the shifting sands.

Naomi nodded. "Yahaweh has hidden His face from me, and the line of Elimelekh of Beit-lekhem is ended."

She put her hands on Orpah's shoulders and hugged her close, tears forming once again in the corners of their eyes.

Then Orpah undid the clasp on the silver chain hanging from her neck and put it on Ruth and repeated what Khilyon had whispered to her while caressing the amulet housing a tiny scroll bearing the words: "May your days be prolonged and may you be satisfied. May you be blessed by Yahaweh of Shomeron and his Asherah."

"You're going? You're really going?"

Orpah nodded, her eyes flooding with tears.

Ruth went blank. There were no words to express her feelings in a language that her sister-in-law would understand. All she could think of saying was, "I'm going to miss the taste of your red lentil stew."

"I'll give you the recipe."

"It won't be the same."

And they raised their voices and wept.

Then Orpah turned and walked away.

Ruth fixed her eyes on the curve of bare skin on the back of her sister-in-law's neck, slightly lighter than the surrounding skin, where the silver chain and amulet had hung for so many moons. Under this oppressive sun, the distinctive band of lighter skin would disappear in a matter of days.

She felt the desert wind howling through the canyons of her body.

The wagons bearing the ruling elite of Yehudah set off, followed by the pack animals, and those returning on foot were already mobilizing.

"I have to go now," Naomi said.

But Ruth clung to her like a possessive demon: "*Don't!*"

Naomi looked around to make sure no one was watching.

"I mean, don't make me abandon you like this."

"Listen, my daughter, you have done much kindness for my son, and I'm grateful. But I've released you from your obligation. You're free to go."

"I didn't know I needed to be freed."

"Let me go. See? Hasn't your sister-in-law returned to her people and her gods? And so you are free to return to your mother's house."

"No," Ruth said. "Your son paid the bride-price for me. He gave his last ounce of silver to buy my freedom. He could have made me his slave or his concubine. He made me his *wife*. He made me his *equal*."

She was too overcome with grief and confusion to make sense of all that had happened, but *something* was off about the manner of their husbands' deaths. She recognized the signs of snakebite poisoning in both men, but their nearly simultaneous deaths aroused her suspicion, and surely the answer lay here in Babylon. But she thought of her husband's words, *too much bad blood and petty grudges*, and sensed that the true answer would be found in Jerusalem.

"I owe him a debt that can never be repaid," she said. "But I can repay it by going with *you* to Jerusalem to marry my husband's nearest kinsman and produce a son to carry on the dead man's name."

"Listen—"

"No, you listen. I'm a widow now and no one can disavow what I'm about to say: I'm going with you. Your people are my people. Your god is my god. May Yahaweh do *this* to me—" She drew her finger across her throat in a quick slicing motion.

"—if I ever turn my face from you."

"But this road passes through the land of the Hatti," Naomi said, ignoring the weight of Ruth's words. "The hills are full of lions, panthers, and wolves—"

"If you can face them, so can I."

Naomi's voice grew bitter: "Listen, you stubborn pagan woman from beyond the sea, don't you understand? There's nothing left for me—here or anywhere. I have no heir, and without an heir, *I have no redeemer*."

"Then we'll find one."

Naomi was ready with an acerbic reply, but when she saw how resolute Ruth was, she stopped arguing with her.

They fell in step behind the caravan of exiles, when a pair of mercenaries with short pointy beards trimmed in the Persian style stopped them with outstretched arms, their loins girded with battle-scarred swords.

"No Moabites."

Naomi aimed an accusing look at Ruth, who had to explain for the thousandth time since marrying into the tribe of Yehudah that she had only spent a couple of seasons working as a servant girl for an itinerant metallurgist at the copper mines near the southeastern coast of the Salt Sea in what was once Moab, but that she was *not* a Moabite.

"Then what are you?" said the one named Hezkiyah.

"I am the widow of Makhlon, son of Elimelekh of Beit-lekhem."

"Who the hell is *that*?"

Ruth hesitated.

"She's as dark as a Moabite," said the one named Mesha, who was shorter and definitely the nastier of the two.

"I'm no darker than the people of your land."

"You mean you're one of the people of the land? Those dirty peasants?"

"Say something in Moabite," Hezkiyah goaded her.

She thought of something to say in Moabite, but kept it to herself.

"Anyway, the Law couldn't be clearer: *No Moabite shall enter the— the—*" Mesha snapped his fingers trying to remember the rest.

A man's authoritative voice interrupted the dispute: "You mean, *No Ammonite or Moabite shall be admitted into the congregation of Yahaweh.*"

The mercenaries spun toward the commanding voice, but relaxed when they saw it was only that scrawny prophet with the threadbare cloak.

"But if you study the Law closely," the prophet went on, "you will find that the prohibition only covers males. There is no law forbidding a Moabite *female* from marrying a Yehudi. So they are permitted."

"And who the hell are you?" said Hezkiyah.

"I am a disciple of the prophet Isaiah the Elder, may his name be—"

"There are no more prophets."

"*In the land of exile.* But we are returning to Yehudah, where prophecy will flourish once again."

That settled the matter, for now at least. The mercenaries grumbled into their beards and jogged toward the front of the caravan.

Ruth thanked the would-be prophet and asked his name.

"Whatever I do, I do in the name of the great prophet Isaiah," he said, "whose spirit still walks the very streets of Jerusalem. Therefore you may call me Ben-Isaiah."

She thanked him again for his kindness, then this self-professed Son-of-Isaiah scurried on ahead to strengthen the spirits of the other anxious exiles.

And so Ruth and Naomi set out for the land of the

Yehudim in what was now the Persian protectorate of Beyond-the-River. Naomi only spoke up once during the long, thirsty hours before they stopped and camped for the night.

"One thing, my daughter."

"Yes?"

"At least take that foul cloak off."

CHAPTER THREE

Felicity

The megaphone's scratchy electronics turn the police sergeant's voice into something machine-made: *You can't walk there! Get back on the sidewalk! You're blocking the street!*

The NYPD are setting up barricades to keep the media and mobs of protesters away from the courthouse entrance, struggling to hold the line against middle-aged women with yellow ribbons pinned over their hearts carrying posters of combat vets stuck in bureaucratic limbo, some dying while they wait for a hospital bed from the VA. Jobless victims of the economic slump are milling about with dollar bills taped over their mouths, while a vocal minority raise their fists in solidarity, demanding jobs, accountability, and free weed—according to one sign, anyway. A group of activists is even trying to convince the police that this is *their* struggle, too, since the city just tried to cut police pensions. They're shouting *Join us!*—the lettering on their signs mottled with moisture, the ink dripping like blood from a wound as the first snowflakes of the year swirl around us, even though there are still five weeks to go before the official start of winter.

"You can't film here!"

The cops snatch a photographer's camera and start deleting photos, threatening to arrest her despite the clearly visible press credentials hanging from her neck.

I have to worm and wheedle my way past the line of occupiers, find an opening, and negotiate safe passage through a cordon of riot cops in lightweight tactical gear just to reach the security clearance area, where they order me to empty my pockets and place everything in the plastic bins. I surrender my briefcase and get in line for the metal detector.

"Hey! Take those shoes off!"

"Are you serious?"

They pull me aside, and I explain as politely as I can that there's already a thin layer of slush on the sidewalk, and I am *not* taking my shoes off.

Also, the shoes are a size too big and they're being held in place with duct tape because my thoughtless boyfriend left the bathroom scale in the middle of the floor for me to trip over, forcing me to hunt down the only other pair of shoes that match my Expert Witness outfit because my toe swelled up so much. But the matching shoes were so big my feet kept sliding around in them like a kid playing dress-up, which is how I ended up with two strips of gray duct tape on the balls of my feet holding my otherwise sensible shoes in place.

"Stand there!"

I plant my awkwardly shod feet on the yellow outline of a man's size-16 shoes and raise my arms above my head for the head-to-toe wand swipe. A bomb-sniffing dog jabs his snout into my crotch with military efficiency, and I instinctively move to protect myself.

"Arms in the air!" barks the guard swiping me with the wand, incensed by my refusal to follow a simple command. Then he gets to my shoes and the wand starts beeping and wailing like a Roman candle on the Fourth of July.

The security guard's look hardens, as if he'd like to ship me off to a secret location eight time zones away so I can spend the next six months in an underground cell handcuffed to a set of electrified bedsprings.

They confiscate the duct tape.

There's a bright flash as a uniformed cop takes my photo, then I'm prodded toward the metal chute.

Always arrive cold, wet, and miserable, that's my motto.

~

"Welcome to the hospitality suite," says a smiling young lawyer in a skinny gray suit.

"What the hell is going on here?" I say, looking around at the battered gray lockers, the water-stained drop ceiling and the dented Korean War–era metal wastebaskets strategically placed to catch dripping water and soggy clumps of ceiling tile. The cheap fluorescent fixtures hum and flicker, providing very little illumination. At least sixty people are crammed into this dreary bunker, prepping for court in a room that was built to hold less than half that number.

"They're overwhelmed," he explains.

"I'll say."

"You here to testify?"

No, I'm here to mop the floors and put in new ceiling tiles, asshole.

"You're not a reporter, are you?"

I hand him my card.

"*You're* Felicity Ortega?"

"No, I'm Felicity Ortega Pérez. Why?"

"'Cause you look just like that hot chick on the *10 O'Clock News.*"

Right. Another light-skinned Latina with dark hair and eyebrows. Otherwise I look *nothing* like her.

"I'm with Reedman, Wyler, and Marx," he says, flashing a hundred-watt smile and handing me a card. "Maybe I could get you some work with the firm."

Pretty smooth talk for a guy who looks like he had his first legal drink about three weeks ago.

I tell him, "That's Cole Reedman, Kip Wyler, and Harry 'Harpo' Marx, right? I've done some work for them."

"Cool. So what case you working?"

I hesitate to share this information with a complete stranger.

A brash lawyer is holding court under the rusty carcass of a nonfunctioning air conditioner, staying loose by busting the opposition's balls with off-color jokes. Masculine laughter fills the musty air in this decommissioned fallout shelter.

"People versus Grimes," I say.

He whistles. "Big case. Which side you on?"

"The DA's office hired me."

"So you're working for Fishman, huh? He's sharp. I just hope you got paid in advance, because he takes *forever* to pay."

Great.

I tell him I've got to go over my notes, then I turn away before he gets the chance to keep the conversation going, and I nearly topple over when my left heel slips out from under me. I recover in time to claim the only empty seat in the place, a ten-inch-wide slice of real estate on a splintery bench crisscrossed with mystical symbols carved into the wood or scrawled in indelible marker by the previous inmates of the bowels of the justice system.

I text Fishman's assistant Gary Phillips to let him know I made it past the gauntlet and into the building. He answers immediately:

Grt. Whr R U?

I'm typing *I think I'm in the dungeon* while balancing the briefcase on my knees when the guy next to me suddenly comes alive, swearing into a tiny Bluetooth device I didn't realize he was wearing: "Tell her to stay put till I get there! And for God's sake tell her to keep her damn mouth shut." He gets up, smooths out the creases in his pants, and departs, giving me a bit of room to finish reviewing my notes with a stubby number 2 pencil. But my brief moment of comfort is cut short when another guy in a blue suit wearing a ton of cheap cologne crams himself into the same spot and the industrial smell of fake lavender washes over me.

Most people don't know there's a small dent in my skull from when a neighborhood kid hit me in the head with the business end of a heavy metal rake, teeth first, when I was four years old, and it's starting to throb when I realize I made a mistake. I flip the pencil around to correct it, but—*Oh, crap*—it's one of those hard old erasers that leaves an ugly orange-brown streak on the paper, making it look like someone ate a whole pumpkin pie and wiped their ass with my documents.

"Yeah, I gotta talk to the personnel director about that," the brash lawyer by the rusty AC unit says at full volume. Frat-house guffaws bounce off the concrete walls as my phone *pings* with a text: *ur up nxt!*

Jesus—this is *not* how it's supposed to be done.

I riffle through my files one last time to make sure they're in order and squeeze through the bodies blocking the path to the doorway.

I lurch toward the stairs, the pressure building in my temples as I mount the steps in these ill-fitting shoes, *clomp clomp clomp*, my hands deadened and senseless, all background noise fading to a distant hum. I might as well be trapped under two hundred feet of water with every sound compressed to the sonic pulses of a nuclear submarine patrolling the inky blackness under the North Pole.

The hallway outside the courtroom is jammed with concerned citizens hoping to get a ringside seat, TV reporters fanning themselves to keep their makeup from running under the hot lights, bored camera operators waiting for a recess, a lunch break, or anything filmable, and court officers keeping an eye on the two slabs of Welsh bluestone in matching suits and turtlenecks who've apparently been hired to stand around and intimidate everybody else in the place.

"Sir? You can't block the door like that—"

"My orders are not to move from this spot," says the first hunk of bluestone.

"Sir—"

The other private security guard tries to block my path with his arm: "Can't go in there, miss."

I ignore him and address the proper authorities: "Officer, I'm testifying on behalf of the People this morning. I need to get in, if these two rock stars don't object."

The court officers scrutinize my paperwork and allow me to enter the courtroom.

The rock star bit would have been a great exit line if I didn't suddenly find myself teetering on the newly waxed floor and grabbing the wooden railing to steady myself in these ill-fitting shoes. Dignity more or less intact, I straighten up and step slowly and purposefully toward the seating area behind the prosecution team, and let the big guy know that I'm ready.

The stately patrician on the witness stand, elegantly attired in a pearl-gray suit, is none other than Winthrop D. Chase III, VP of Greystoke-Prescott Enterprises. The defense attorney, Theo Krebs, a balding middleweight in a light-brown suit that surely contains at least *some* polyester, is cross-examining Chase about a little matter of defrauding the Department of Defense of around $80 million.

"Some waste is inevitable, but it's a necessary expense," says Chase. "After all, where would we be without our military?"

That's easy: we'd have national health care, fully funded Social Security, and bridges that don't collapse.

My capillaries are constricting, robbing my brain of much-needed oxygen, and I might as well be lip-reading as Krebs mouths the words *No further questions* and the bailiff rises and calls my name.

My sensible shoes feel like a pair of cross-country skis as I do my best to take the stand without wiping out in front of all these people. They make me swear a perfunctory oath to the goddess of Justice, then I get to sit in the hardest seat in the house. Fishman actually coached me not to cross my legs or look too comfortable up here—as if *that's* a possibility.

Pesach Fishman's a big guy, a little over 6′2″, with a high forehead, a big Jewish schnoz and slicked-back curly-wavy hair that belongs in a black-and-white ad for Brylcreem from 1952, yet somehow it works on him. He begins by asking me to identify myself and to describe the results of my investigation. Good thing I've gone over this so many times I can do it on autopilot. I explain how internal documents, interviews with coworkers, and a review of security camera footage clearly demonstrate that the defendant, William Grimes, in his capacity as chief expediter of Greystoke-Prescott's largest shipping operation, knowingly and repeatedly defrauded the Department of Defense by replacing high-performance parts and equipment with generic parts bought at Home Depot, and that he subsequently billed the DOD at highly inflated prices and pocketed the difference.

Now comes the million-dollar question: "Did you uncover any evidence of complicity on the part of Mr. Grimes's superiors at Greystoke-Prescott Enterprises?"

"No, I did not."

There's a palpable shift in the room, an excitement at this revelation, and I can actually hear the print journalists flipping their notepad pages and scribbling furiously. Some of the pressure eases inside my skull.

"In other words, you found no evidence that the management at Greystoke-Prescott Enterprises had any knowledge of the defendant's fraudulent activities?"

"That is correct." Though Lord knows I tried to.

"Thank you. No further questions."

Grimes is sitting with his team of lawyers, radiating cold waves of desperation. He's got thinning hair, pallid features with the greasy sheen of wet dough, and a permanent slouch. He spends the whole time staring at me open-mouthed and practically drooling, so help me, doing his best to look like a serial child molester.

Then his boy Theo Krebs goes to work on me.

"Ms. Ortega, you describe yourself as a certified document examiner and forensic accountant."

Yeah, just like you describe yourself as a defense attorney.

He goes on: "So would it be fair to say that your job relies heavily on your powers of observation?"

"Yes, but—"

He spins around and faces the courtroom.

"Then would you mind telling the court what color my tie is?"

I stifle a chuckle. Not *that* old gag.

I tell the court: "It's a yellow paisley pattern dotted with little pink-and-black ponies."

The court stenographer clears her throat, and a rustle of movement suggests that Grimes's defense team is not pleased with this tactic. I allow myself to breathe a little, my headache leveling off at around 8.5 on a scale of 1 to 10.

Krebs keeps his back turned to me. "Without looking, would you please tell the court which flag is displayed over your right shoulder?"

"The American flag."

"And is there anything special that you can tell us about this particular flag?"

"Without looking at it?"

"Yes. After all, this is a test of your *observational* skills."

I ignore the tone of that statement. *Don't let him get to you, girl.*

"Well, for one thing, the golden eagle on top of the flagpole is missing one of its wings."

Krebs turns to look at the flagpole, his face betraying a more than a hint of surprise. That gets some audible chuckles from the print reporters for the *Indypendent* and the *Brooklyn Hipster.*

"I can't believe what I just heard," says Krebs, feigning indignation. "Are you making fun of *patriotism*?"

My eyes flit to Fishman to see if he's planning to object to any of this. Nothing doing.

"No, I'm making fun of masculine pomposity."

Fishman's perky assistant gives me thumbs up, then turns back to his smart device. I think he's actually live-blogging this. Or else he's Googling the term "pomposity."

Krebs switches tactics: "Ms. Ortega, were you born in this country?"

What?

My eyes widen, my face aflame. "I sure was. You want to see where they stamped MADE IN AMERICA on the back of my neck?"

"That won't be necessary," he says, his cockiness flooding back like a shot of Viagra because I let him see how easy it was to get under my skin.

He picks up a packet of photos from the exhibit table and spends the next few minutes hammering away at my weak spot, trying to provoke another emotional outburst, but I've figured out his game and that's all he's going to get out of me.

Finally, he says, "Tell me, Ms. Ortega, would other experts agree with your conclusions based on the same evidence?"

Instead of going with *How the fuck should I know, you bigoted asshole?* I take a moment to breathe and get it right this time: "If presented with the same evidence, I would expect experts with the appropriate background and training to reach a similar conclusion."

He presses a bit, blustering about how "There's reasonable doubts all over the place about this case," then a predatory flash of teeth tells me he's hit on something.

"Isn't it true that you were hired by the district attorney's office to do this work?"

"Yes."

"So District Attorney Fishman *paid* you for the work you did analyzing these documents, right?"

"Not yet he hasn't," I say, glaring right at Fishman. And that cracks it wide open. Even the cynical freelance reporters are laughing out loud at that one. The judge bangs his gavel and tells Krebs to move on, but he keeps weaseling away at me, spending so much time trying to piss all over me that when it's over, I feel like standing up and saying, "Hey, you missed a spot."

~

On the subway heading back to Queens, I'm contemplating the promise I forcibly extracted from Fishman to pay me before the first of the month, which means that we might actually be able to eat out tonight without having to count the change in my purse first. I've got some big money clients lined up, which is good because Jhimmy and I are hoping to get married once we save up enough.

We've been together for three years now. So if the first anniversary is paper, and the second is cotton, what's the third?

Tin foil, I believe.

I rub my temples and do my best to ignore the files that I should be reviewing in favor of flipping through a copy of *UrbanGrrl* magazine that some righteous sistah abandoned on the bench next to me.

The cover trumpets a feature story: WHAT MEN CRAVE IN OCTOBER. Answer: *The same thing they crave in August and September, bitches!*

There's also an article revealing how major retailers have finally discovered that fifty million US Latinos actually shop for stuff, and some celebrity gossip about the pros and cons of seventeen-year-old former child star Sheza Hogg's recent video, in which that skinny little white girl rides bareback on a giant inflatable hot dog dripping with mayonnaise and baby oil.

Why do all these teen pop stars always try to show how they've *matured* by displaying their freshly waxed booty? Why don't they do some Shakespeare in the Park or something, instead of this corporate kiddie porn?

Talk about screwed-up priorities.

I get off at 103rd Street and Roosevelt Avenue and stop

at the corner bodega to warm myself up with a café con leche before crossing the street to my office.

The Number 7 train rumbles overhead, rattling the windows of Mi Patria, the Ecuadorian restaurant on the street level of this mixed-use building, and the smell of garlic simmering in olive oil and of deep-fried *yuca* and *plátano* follows me up the narrow wooden stairs to my cramped second-floor office. The lettering on the door uses the Spanish version of my name: FELICIDAD ORTEGA PÉREZ— INVESTIGACIONES followed by a bilingual version of the company motto: DE TOTAL CONFIANZA—ALWAYS RELIABLE.

The phone's ringing and the radio's blaring the latest traffic report, but my priority is washing up in the tiny bathroom and taking off my cold, damp stockings. I've got a pair of emergency stockings in the bottom drawer of my desk just in case, but first I need to kick off the offending shoes and set up a space heater for my frozen toes.

The radio's telling me that if I call in right now, I can win two free tickets to the Who. Great. Does it come with a time machine so I can go back to 1970 and see them when they were good?

The phone message is from Fishman's assistant Gary, thanking me for helping them nail the case shut, and gushing about the prospects of a favorable outcome.

My only regret is that *mi mami* isn't here to see what a success her little girl has become.

She smiles down on me from the faded photo tacked to the wall above the computer, frozen forever with one hand blocking part of her face. Never a sharp image—the wind was blowing her hair into her eyes and she moved as my dad clicked the shutter—now the edges are curling, the emulsion cracking.

I refresh my alert system, which automatically forwards selected messages to all my devices, mainly because of my brother and my dad, for reasons I'll explain later.

I open my inbox, and find a message from Caine Construction, which was about to hire me to examine a set of false documents provided by dozens of workers. Their goal is for me to provide expert testimony that the documents in question are of such high quality that the company should *not* be held liable for hundreds of thousands of dollars in fines for "knowingly hiring undocumented workers." Now they're writing to tell me the case has been delayed for at least three months.

Then there's a cryptic message from Battle Creek, Inc., a civilian contractor fighting charges that their shoddy workmanship led to the electrocution of US Army private while he was taking a shower in Baghdad's Green Zone. They were planning to hire me full time to go over the records—blueprints, contracts, bills of lading—to show that this job was subcontracted out to Bighorn Industries, a subsidiary of Silver Bullet Security, an unrelated company, and that any potential liability lies with them.

I call Battle Creek for clarification, but I've already got a queasy feeling about this, and sure enough, they tell me they're "not going forward with that aspect of the case" because they're negotiating an out-of-court settlement that will likely save them millions of dollars in litigation fees.

¡Cónchale! That case would have paid my rent for the next two months. So much for my big plans to eat out tonight.

I've got other cases pending, but the local clients are all working-class immigrants and day laborers who need to stretch the payments for a $150 invoice into a dozen weekly installments of $12.50 each, and even then I've got to practically squeeze the money out of them, which I don't particularly enjoy.

"Knock knock."

I look up. A big guy in a damp trench coat is standing in the doorway wiping the slush from his polished brown brogues on my ancient welcome mat. Damn—I was in such a rush I must have left the door unlocked, a definite no-no in this business. And here I am set up like an invalid with my little pink toesies waving at him, making a terrific first impression.

"Miss Felly-see-dad Puh-*rez*?" he says, mangling my name.

"That's me," I say, shutting off the space heater. Not much point in putting on the emergency stockings now. I feel my face flushing, and I know it's showing, too. I turn the radio down to a low murmur.

"Mind if I sit down?"

"Sure—" I push the swivel chair toward him and jam my feet back into my shoes, which are still damp.

"How's the foot?" he asks, setting down his briefcase, taking off the trench coat and dropping heavily into the chair. He doesn't look like he misses too many meals. Big ruddy face with a lot of broken capillaries, suggesting he hasn't missed out on the drinks, either, and a thinning mop of white hair that's been blown about by the elements. I can smell the cocky attitude of an ex-cop turned private security consultant from ten feet away.

"Much better, thanks," I say, my face still warm. "What can I do for you?"

"This is your lucky day, Miss Puh-*rez*." He hands me a business card that says he's Frank Gustella, lead investigator for Cadmium Solutions. "We were very impressed with your performance in court this morning, and we'd like you to do some work for us."

You were watching that shit show? Oh, Jesus . . .

"What sort of work?"

"You ever heard of a company called Silver Bullet Security?"

"Sure, they're private contractors who supplied—" I stop and look closely at the business card.

Gustella sits there with a twisted smile on his lips like he's played this joke on a dozen other PIs and I'm the first one to get it.

"They're a subsidiary of Cadmium Solutions, aren't they?"

He sits there waiting for more.

"Didn't they used to be Morse Techtonics?"

"They sure did. We're rebranding."

"And you need me to—"

"We need you do some background checks and other investigative work to help us exonerate the company for alleged wrongdoing by a contract worker named Kristel Santos we employed in Iraq during the drawdown."

"Any idea where she is right now?"

He looks at me like maybe I'm not the right person for this job after all.

"That's what you want me to find out, isn't it?"

"There you go," he says, reaching into his briefcase and pulling out a thick file folder.

"So what's the alleged wrongdoing?"

"Our personnel are being accused of unauthorized removal of valuable antiquities from the National Museum in Baghdad."

"What kind of stuff?"

"Mostly trinkets, cylinder seals, a few bracelets, stuff like that," he says, leafing absently through the first few pages of the file. "The more stuff you can chase down, the more resources we'll be able to devote to helping the contractors who were wounded or disabled in the line of duty."

I'm jarred by this declaration, but he's removing a Post-it from one of the pages and he doesn't appear to notice.

"Then why do you need a documents examiner?"

"One of the missing items is a rare Hebrew scroll."

"I don't know anything about ancient Hebrew manuscripts—"

"What's to know? Treat it like any other stolen property." He crumples up the Post-it and stuffs it into his jacket pocket. "I don't need to tell you that some very powerful people are interested in the outcome of this case."

"If it's so important, why aren't you using a bigger firm with a more experienced legal team?"

"Think about it for a second, huh? We can't mobilize an army of forensic investigators without attracting attention. And we need this taken care of discreetly before the media gets hold of it. You've already shown us that you're good under pressure, and you know how to handle yourself in a tough situation. You're a young, bright, and articulate Spanish girl, which is just what we need in this case."

The subsonic tremors of an approaching subway train mask my moment of intense annoyance. At this point, the only reason I'm still listening to this jerk is that grumbling in my stomach and the prospect of having to go out and trap sewer rats for dinner.

"So you want me to find a former employee named Kristel Santos *and* the missing scroll?"

"The scroll's more important—"

"This seems like more of a case for my cousin Filomena," I say, reaching for the laminated binder full of business cards.

"We already asked her. She told us to go fuck ourselves."

"That sounds like cousin Filomena all right."

"You said it, babe." Someone opens the downstairs door, letting in a fresh wave of *bachata* music from the street. "We need a trained professional who understands the need for finesse, and we think you're the gal for the job. How soon can you start?"

I look up at the dry-erase calendar, which still has the next few weeks filled up with work for Caine Construction and Battle Creek, Inc.

"We'll beat whatever they're paying you by twenty percent if you can start right away on this," he says. "The trial's scheduled to start in thirty days, so we don't have much time."

Just in time for the holidays, and all the care packages I'm expected to ship to the extended family back in Ecuador.

"I guess I can get them to hold off for a month or so."

"There you go," he says with a grin. He drops the heavy file on my desk and hands me another card. "First I need you to call this number to get fingerprinted."

"What for?"

"Routine background check, but it's gotta get done since you're going to need a company car on this case. Some of these people live pretty far out in the boonies, you know." The wheels on his chair squeak as he shifts his weight. "And while you're at it, you should look into cleaning up your online profile. A quick search turned up your name as *Velocity Ortega Perez*. What's that about?"

"Oh, that," I say, my eye drawn back to the thick folder full of potentially incriminating evidence. "It's like that on my birth certificate. No one in the Town Clerk's office knew Spanish back then, so they misspelled my name when my mother told them it was Felicidad. They put down *Velocidad* by mistake, and once in a while it still turns up like that on some documents. I still get junk mail for her."

That's my name: misspelled happiness.

"I should call you Speedy Gonzalez," he says, with a chuckle.

"Please don't."

"That's your name, isn't it? Speedy?"

I pick up the eraser and wipe away the big ticket calendar entries for the next four weeks, reducing their names to a cloud of gray and black streaks. Then I write in CADMIUM SOLUTIONS in bold black marker and circle the day the trial is supposed to start: December 15.

Gustella's attention fixes on the snapshot tacked up next to the calendar of a dark-haired soldier in dusty fatigues leaning on the hood of a damaged Humvee, smiling stiffly as the desert sun glints off his shades.

"That your boyfriend?"

"My brother."

Specialist Jeremías Ortega Pérez, Babil Province, Iraq. He enlisted the minute he turned eighteen, but when it was my turn, I chose a different path. I'm not the military type. I could barely deal with the regimentation level of ninth grade gym class.

"Good-looking guy. I'm sure you're proud of him."

The floorboards begin to shake as the Number 7 train rolls by on its way to Jackson Heights.

I open a computer file and print out a copy of my basic contract in English for Gustella to sign. He seems to get a chuckle out of my company slogan: ALWAYS RELIABLE.

"Just reliable? Not responsible?"

I open my mouth to answer.

"Good," he says, cutting me off. "Because that's just what we need." He gets up with a groan as if his knees are getting rusty and shakes a few excess water droplets from his trench coat. "I need you to study that file tonight and report to our offices on the eleventh floor of the Schneerson Building tomorrow morning at 8:30 a.m. sharp."

He picks up his briefcase and leaves, the stairs creaking under his heavy tread as he descends to street level.

I kick off the offending shoes and pad over to the grimy window in time to watch Gustella step onto the busy sidewalk and hail a green-and-black-checkered cab back to Manhattan. It's nearly 3:00 p.m., and I can already feel the last few hours of the day slipping through my fingers. But at least the sun's coming out and it looks like the slush is finally melting. The tantalizing aroma of *pargo frito* wafts up from restaurant below, reminding me how much I like fried fish.

I'd better get started on that file.

Cadmium Solutions. Silver Bullet Security. Battle Creek, Inc.

There isn't a file folder big enough to hold all the sins those companies have committed while the watchdogs were getting their budgets downsized.

Grievous sins.

Deadly sins.

My eyes linger on the photo of the fine young warrior in his oil-stained camos.

I'm no dewy-eyed heroine whose innocence will be shattered when she discovers that the world is hopelessly corrupt and full of evil. I've looked evil in the face so many times I could pick it out of a lineup. Except that you never really know what you're getting into with these corporate types, or how far they'll go to set a new low for crass depravity and greed.

Cadmium Solutions and its subsidiaries loom large on the list of private security firms that scuttled the mission in Iraq with their reckless shoot-from-the-hip practices, which turned every one of my brothers and sisters in uniform into moving targets.

But there's nothing but a few lonesome dollar coins rattling around in the cash box, so I keep up a running monologue with myself about how it's only a short-term contract that'll pad my résumé while I wait for something better to come along, because when the rent check is due, I'm going to need something on there besides the fact that I can type 65 words per minute with a good tailwind.

And here it comes again, flying down Roosevelt Avenue from the beating heart of this borough's Chinatown by way of Flushing Meadows Park.

I am the Number 7 train.

Hear me roar.

CHAPTER FOUR

Ruth

Ruth drew a curved dagger from her sack and set to work lopping off hunks of hair, slicing away her sun-damaged locks, intent on making herself repellent to other men for three full cycles of the moon before she could be considered an eligible bride. Soon her hair lay in ruins, her scalp scratched and bleeding from her overzealous hacking.

A stocky man wearing a long-sleeved tunic approached with the timid gait of a supplicant walking across hot coals.

He said his name was Ga'al. Ruth warned him that she was unclean, but he dismissed her concerns with a wave of his hand, and Ruth permitted him to help her up. Her blood-smeared fingers gripped his sleeve, pulling on it and exposing a Hebrew phrase tattooed in the Babylonian fashion on the underside of his wrist: *l'yshyu*.

Property of Yoshiyahu.

It meant he was not a free man.

"Where is your master, Yoshiyahu?"

"Oh, he's up front with the rest of the wealthy folk," Ga'al said, pulling his sleeve down to cover the mark. "Now, come on, don't sit by yourselves. Join us."

~

They offered Ruth and Naomi a simple mourner's meal of toasted flatbread and lentils. Ruth grimly chewed her food, using a double-edged dagger to trim her nails. Then she used the dagger to pry the clots of dried blood from her husband's cloak and let the flakes fall into the amulet Orpah had given her, blanketing the tiny scroll with the essence of his spirit. She snapped the lid closed and pressed it to her lips, seeking communion with the vestiges of her husband's spirit, squeezing it along with the sharply pointed star, the sweet pain transporting her to the day Makhlon first spotted her treading the wineskins feeding air to the forge where the warriors got their weapons repaired, how he approached her and vowed to free her from bondage, and how he always treated her with grace and kindness, which he called *khesed*.

The same word Naomi had used when trying to send Ruth back to her "mother's house," a place that didn't exist. *Khesed*. Caring for others. It wasn't her strongest attribute, until she learned what it is to belong to a family. And now the family was gone, except for two widowed women. Ruth glanced at Naomi, saw the tears running down her sunken cheeks, the orange streaks reflecting the firelight. Ruth nudged closer, put her free arm around the grieving mother and held her, squeezing.

She blinked away a bit of wetness that might have dropped from her eyes in a more fertile climate. But in this blasted wilderness, so hot and dry, even one's tears evaporated before they got a chance to fall.

A pair of Yehudi mercenaries with pointed beards in the Persian style stepped into the firelight. Ga'al excused himself to go see if his master needed anything as the mercenaries stood there kicking the sand out of their sandals and staring at Ruth through the flames. She tried to blend in with the shadows, but with her head shaved clean as a river rock she stood out like a panther among swans. The mercenaries looked at the others around the fire and continued on their rounds, their weather-beaten sandals kicking up dust behind them.

No wonder the Babylonians overran them. How did they expect those flimsy sandals to compete against greased leather boots that add three inches to a warrior's height?

A woman named Yiskah, who was heavy with child, stared at Ruth, the firelight flickering across her face. "Don't let What's-His-Name the prophet catch you doing that."

Ruth's heart jumped. "What do you mean?"

"*That*," Yiskah said, indicating the amulet holding the last dry flecks of Makhlon's blood. "This is not our way. At least put on some sackcloth. That is our way."

"Sackcloth?"

"Dark cloth, widow's weeds, the mourner's garments you should have been wearing since your husband's death."

"Oh," Ruth said. "Do you have any?"

Yiskah shrank from her. "Don't touch me! You've been in contact with a dead man and you haven't immersed in a *mikweh* yet!"

Right. Got to think of the baby. Ruth understood. But it was going to be awfully hard to immerse herself in a ritual bath in the middle of the wilderness.

"Do I look like I wear clothes made of coarse haircloth?" Yiskah's tirade continued. "You'll have to ask around. And don't forget to be humble," she called after Ruth.

~

Ruth wandered about the camp, taking care not to intrude, speak out of turn, or look directly at a man while enduring the tantalizing aromas of fresh goat meat simmering in garlic, coriander and, in one case, a pinch of saffron.

The fires were dying down by the time a Persian Yehudite named Miryam took pity, told her to wait a moment, and after fishing around in her moth-eaten saddlebags, offered Ruth a sleeveless tunic made of undyed sheep's wool.

"But it's white as snow," Ruth protested.

"White as *what*?" Miryam said, her headful of black wavy hair shining in the firelight.

"She means white as pure lamb's wool," said Ga'al, returning from his errand with a jug of wine in the crook of his arm. "She needs a garment made of dark goat's hair, as is appropriate for mourning."

"Ah." Miryam's big dark eyes grew sad. "I have just the thing."

～

Ga'al led Ruth through the maze of tent ropes and flickering shadows cast by the arms of the giant lampstand.

"Cheer up," he said, offering her a cup of wine.

"I don't drink wine."

"Oh. What about beer?"

"I don't drink beer, either."

"No intoxicants at all then, eh?"

"I didn't say that."

His brow wrinkled as if he were puzzling out a mathematical problem, then smoothed. It was getting late, and his questions could wait.

The campfire was cold by the time they returned to the circle of cooking stones.

"Who's there?" a male voice demanded. A tent flap flew open and a man lunged at them, his mouth twisted with suspicion. "Oh, it's you." His mouth relaxed.

Ga'al introduced him as Yiskah's husband, Hanokh, whose skin was so fair there was a tinge of red in his short, unruly hair. His eyes were puffy with sleeplessness.

Ruth had seen those haunted eyes and slave's haircut before, and after a moment recognized him as the prisoner who had been dragged, whipped, and beaten through the streets of Babylon before being set free as part of the New Year's celebrations.

"In that coat of black wool, you blend in with the night," Hanokh said, by way of an explanation.

"She is quite a sight," Ga'al agreed. "As hairless as a she-demon," he added, running a thick hand over her naked skull. Ruth ducked away from his touch.

"How long were you in prison?" Ruth asked.

The bluntness of her words blindsided the men. "Uh ... six months," Hanokh murmured.

Ruth nodded, satisfied with his explanation of the dubious arithmetic of his wife's pregnancy.

Nervous laughter followed, then goodnight wishes.

Ruth stepped around the blackened cooking stones, took off her sandals, and lay down for the night, the coat of sackcloth serving as her bed and blanket.

Ga'al spread his cloak on a nearby stretch of sand, his knees cracking as he lay down a little closer than was proper. He propped himself up on his elbow and faced her.

Ruth kept her gaze fixed on the heavens, her left hand silently closing around the handle of the double-edged dagger. But he kept staring at her, so she tilted her face toward him.

"What?"

"What do you mean?"

"Oh, good Lord." She raised herself up on her elbows. "What on earth are you thinking?"

His eyes traveled the length of her body like a military strategist scouting the terrain before an attack.

"I'm thinking that maybe some of us aren't so much heading to Jerusalem as they are running away from Babylon."

"You mean like how you're a runaway slave?"

Ga'al recoiled as if he'd been slapped. "What are you—?"

"If your master Yoshiyahu was really up front with the rest of the wealthy folk, you'd be traveling with him. But don't worry, I won't give you away."

"How can I be sure of that?" He glanced nervously around the encampment.

"Because it's a commandment from God handed down at the Mountain of the Moon in Sinai. *You shall not give up to his master a slave who seeks refuge with you.* That's why."

His intentions were written across his face as plainly as ink on parchment.

"And back off or my husband's vengeful spirit will follow you to the ends of the earth and pour out his wrath upon you."

So much for keeping humble.

It took him a while to digest her words, but soon he stopped fidgeting and brightened to the idea that she wasn't going to raise the alarm.

He tried to be playful about it: "Seems like quite a few of us left something behind in Babylon that we'd rather keep buried."

"Amen to that," she said, lying back down.

❧

But sleep did not come easily. The great warrior-heroes of old knew how to sleep with one eye open and their hands on their weapons, but she could not.

Their legendary prowess kindled Ruth's sensory recollections of when her mighty warrior returned from the field of battle, dirty and sore and ravenous for a woman's touch, his voice raspy as he took her in his arms and whispered that her body was like a slice of heaven, an earthly goddess that he, a mere mortal, got to touch, his mouth upon her neck. And then lower. How he purred like a tiger as he buried his face in her, deep-throated and feral. There was something so primal about it, something bottomless and uncontrollable. Those deep rumbling growls elicited a response so turbulent that even now the memories stirred within her body, as a creature of the deep responds to the bullish roars of the male rippling through the water and exciting her, almost against her will.

It was going to be a long night.

❧

Makhlon's shade came to her, behind a thick green veil, reaching out to her, trying to speak, to tell her something, to warn her of some earthly danger, but a shiny beryl-green serpent was coiling around his neck, constricting his breath. His mouth opened soundlessly, and Ruth seized the glistening reptile but it just hissed at her and slipped through her fingers.

Ruth awoke with the six-pointed star stabbing her skin and an ache in her soul, a premonition that some evil force had been set loose, and that it was up to her to seek justice and heal the wound, somehow. She shook off the sands of sleep determined to know the cause of this unnamed treachery, and if called for, to exact revenge.

~

"I want my baby born in Yehudah."

That's all she said, the merest trickle of words, but Yiskah's words left princes and military engineers scratching their heads, until a Persian guard named Manukka, a Commander of Ten, came forward and claimed that he knew a shortcut. The full caravan transporting the majestic lampstand to God's House in Yehudah should keep to the route following the winding river north to the city of Khalab, but a little-used crossroads ten *parsas* to the north could be reached by the following evening. From there it would be a journey of four hundred miles westward to Jerusalem across some of the harshest terrain in all creation. Ezra the Scribe spoke in favor of taking the shortcut, since it would get them to the Jerusalem in time for the wheat harvest, but others cautioned that the desert route was too dangerous for the women and children in their care.

All eyes turned to Prince Sheshbazzar, who stroked his long white beard and agreed that there weren't enough provisions for the entire caravan to cross the wilderness. Still, he ruled that a small group of exiles could take their chances.

But when the caravan of exiles reached the western trail the next afternoon, a shrill wind howling out of the wasteland made their faces cloud over, and terrors from beyond the grave swept through their bodies as the wind whipped their cloaks about their faces.

"If the way is too dangerous and you want to go back, I will not argue with you," Naomi said.

"I can't go back. Not now," Ruth said, utterly dismayed. "I made a vow to the God of the Yehudim to provide you with a male heir to carry on your husband's name."

Naomi let out a short, bitter laugh. "With you looking like a prisoner of war?"

"My hair will grow back by the time we reach Jerusalem."

"How much? An inch? The men of Yehudah like a woman whose hair is like *a flock of goats streaming down the mountainside in Gilead.*"

"I can't go back after marrying a Yehudi."

Naomi threw up her hands in complete exasperation.

"Stop acting like you've made *such* a sacrifice by coming with me," she sputtered. "Why are you so *mit'ametzet?*"

An unfamiliar word, but Ruth got the gist: *Why are you so stubborn?* She spread her fingers, flexing them, and said, "Because you are the mother of my husband, and these hands will close your eyes someday."

Naomi's cheeks drained of color, as if Ruth had put the *ayin ha-ra'ah* on her.

Ruth instantly regretted her words. Naomi had lost everything to Mot, the insatiable God of Death, whose name Ruth hadn't even known when she joined the tribe of the Yehudim. She saw herself sweeping Naomi's kitchen, the morning sun beaming through the east window, as Naomi patiently taught her uncivilized daughter-in-law the names of pots and pans and other domestic objects in the tongue of Aram. It was tough going, as the languages shared no words or even some basic concepts. To stave off any cause for resentment, Ruth was determined to be a quick study, practicing vocabulary words and verb tenses as they washed and hung the freshly shorn lamb's wool to dry, for the men's tunics. She remembered Naomi's congratulatory hug and heartfelt praise when Ruth said her first full, complete sentence in Aramite.

Ruth heard the low buzzing of male voices questioning if she should be treated like a shameless wandering woman, who, according to ancient Babylonian Law, Section 132, is to be thrown into the sacred river so her fate can be decided by the river god.

A strong male voice cut through the chatter: "They're going to need protection as they cross the wilderness," said Manukka, stepping out of formation. "I'll need two more volunteers. Who's with me?"

"Here, Commander!" cried a Persian guard named Rashda, his upraised hand aimed defiantly at the Yehudi leaders.

"Who else is with me?" said Commander Manukka. "I need one more man."

Ezra the Scribe fought off the urge to curse them all. The last thing we need is a group of foreign-born idolaters splintering off, especially if it means they'll arrive in Jerusalem before we do.

"One more man," Manukka said, scrutinizing the ranks of mercenaries, trying to shame them into action.

Finally, Yedidyah, the kindly Nazirite who had helped Ruth haggle with the stone carver, looped his thumbs through his belt, stepped forward and nodded at the commander, his long, kinky hair trailing in the wind like a lion's mane.

A strange feeling of pride rippled through the crowd when two more Yehudi mercenaries, Mesha and Hezkiyah, fell in behind him.

The would-be prophet pushed to the front and practically kissed the mercenaries' feet, hugging them and anointing their beards with sweet-smelling oil as he shared his vision that a road would appear in the desert, a straight road, a sacred road offering favorable passage to all, that waters would burst forth in the desert, no wild animal would approach them, and no traveler would go astray.

"Turn away from all that is unclean," the prophet insisted.

"Keep pure as you set out, avoid contact with anything *tamey*, for the God of Israel is leading us on a new Exodus through the wilderness."

What a bunch of riffraff, Ezra thought. But now, looking over these lowly undesirables of mixed race, a new feeling came over him. *Fine, let them go across the wilderness.* Maybe they would all die out there.

CHAPTER FIVE

Felicity

"You're doing *what*?"

"It's just short term, Jhimmy." The pot of rice is bubbling away, the cover rattling as steam escapes. I lower the flame and go back to peeling the shells off a half pound of shrimp, the tips of my fingers still stained with faded fingerprint ink residue. "And it's a good line to have on my résumé."

"What, working for those corporate assholes?" he says, flicking his long dark hair out of his eyes.

"Do you know how much I had to spend this year on database fees alone?"

"Yeah, so you could service the wealthy by checking up on the help," he says, heading for the pantry.

Oh, come on. That's a low blow. He *knows* I was volunteering once a week at the local community center until the economy took a dive into a giant vat of pig shit.

I'm pulling the stringy gut glop out of the shrimp and washing it down the drain.

"Jhimmy, it's money."

"What about that opening at the courthouse for a Spanish interpreter?" he yells from the other room.

"That's strictly per diem."

"What about your other cases?"

"They'll keep."

Our kitchen is so tiny, the pantry is out in the living room. The spaghetti squash is simmering in a pan that takes up half the narrow stove. I toss in the shrimp and stir.

"Where is this place, anyway?" he says, his voice muffled, and I can tell he's rummaging around in the pantry.

"Near the corner of Wall Street and Pearl."

"That's rich white man's territory."

"Jhimmy, the whole freaking country is rich white man's territory," I say, sprinkling salt and *achiote* on the shrimp.

"Yeah, but it was literally a slave market back in the 1700s." I hear him pushing cans and jars aside, the crinkle of plastic packaging.

"You could rent a slave by the day or week." His words come out all thick and sloppy, like he's talking with his mouth full.

I'm washing a bunch of fresh cilantro when my distracted brain finally makes the connection. I walk to the archway. Jhimmy's at the table, typing away on his laptop while eating a banana and handfuls of mixed nuts straight from the bag.

"You're having a snack ten minutes before dinner?"

"How am I supposed to know when dinner's gonna be ready?"

"You could try asking me."

"Okay, fine, but I'm organizing a vigil at Gracie Mansion and we need at least a hundred fifty people to show up or the media won't take us seriously."

"A candlelight vigil?"

"No, they told us not to bring candles. For security reasons."

"So what are you doing?"

"Telling everyone to bring a flashlight."

∽

"I'd have gotten more shrimp, but this was all they had left," I say, digging into my dieter's delight.

"Hey, the Bock Brewery is up for sale," says Jhimmy, stuffing my spicy concoction of shrimp and spaghetti squash into his mouth while checking the news feed on his laptop. "Got $850 million?"

"Hell, if I had that kind of money I'd just cut out the middleman and buy my own senator. Now that's a *guaranteed* money maker."

"I don't know. In this economy, it might be better to start small, with a city councilman."

"What if I can't afford a city council member?" I say, pleading with him like a damsel in distress.

"Just bribe a meter maid or a crossing guard and work your way up."

He gets up and takes his plate to the kitchen. But instead of putting his plate in the sink, he's getting seconds.

"Don't take too much or there won't be enough for lunch tomorrow."

"Hey, there's shrimp in here," he says, sounding very much like he just noticed.

I stare at the small portion of stringy orange textures occupying my dish.

He comes back to the table, his plate piled high.

"Is there anything left in the pot?" I ask.

"Not much," he says. "You should have bought more."

I put my fork down and gaze at the back of his computer screen. I can tell without looking that he's scanning the international news, which reports that Secretary of State Angela Sheehan is in China trying to convince them that there's a difference between capitalism and slave labor.

They're still trying to convince me of that, too.

～

I gather up the dishes and steamroll into the kitchen. I drop the dishes into the sink hard enough to produce a nice, satisfying crash, but they stubbornly refuse to break. There's rice on Jhimmy's plate that I have to scrape into the garbage, and there are rice grains stuck in the tines of his fork that I have to get out with a paper towel. And there's practically nothing left over in the pot. I toss the little bit that's left into a pint-sized plastic container and slam the door to the fridge. Then I pull on the latex-free gloves and start running the hot water. As it steams up, I call out:

"When you get back, can you help me move the bookcase with all the computer stuff in it?"

No response. I peer around the archway.

"Did you hear me?"

"I heard *computer*," he answers, zipping up his winter coat. I repeat my request.

"I'm gonna be back late." He wraps a faded Andean scarf around his neck. "And I promised the collective I'd go to the office first thing tomorrow and help organize the files."

"That's going to take you all day." I go back to scrubbing the pot with steel wool and soap.

"It's gonna take me all day," he says, shutting the door and leaving me alone with my thoughts—and all the unfinished chores. This despite all my efforts to get him to recognize that, like his other volunteer labors, taking out the garbage is just another way of chipping away at the oppressive power of the state.

But dismantling the patriarchal system will have to wait. I've got a big file to go through and a lot of preparation to do for tomorrow.

～

Jhimmy actually got up before me, made himself eggs and toast, and left without saying goodbye or, you know, something supportive like *Good luck at the new job*. He also left the eggs, bread, and butter out on the counter. But at least he remembered to set the toaster oven to *stun* this time. The first time he tried to toast a croissant in there he set the dial to *destroy*, and the buttery pastry went up in flames and charred the whole interior, filling the kitchen with smoke. I brought the ruined toaster oven back to the store, and the apathetic teenager at the customer service counter said, *What's wrong with it?* I mumbled something about how it was all messed up inside and she just gave me that *okay, whatever* deal and let me exchange it for a brand new one.

So don't knock apathetic teenagers.

Jhimmy's family was worse off than mine economically when he was growing up, but at least he had a stable home, and it's pretty clear that his mom took care of all things domestic. His recipe for fried eggs evidently includes the instructions: Be sure to spatter the *entire* stove top with butter when frying, and leave it for someone else to clean up.

I wipe up the mess and put the kettle on. He also took yesterday's leftovers with him, leaving me the gleanings from the *seco de pollo* I made two nights ago, so I wash some carrots and an apple to stretch the rations, put the filter cone on the coffee pot and reach for the coffee beans and and and—

Where the hell is the coffee grinder?

I check all the kitchen surfaces, on top of the fridge, open the cabinets. *Oh, crap. Where's the fucking coffee grinder?* I don't have time for this right now. I dig out the emergency bag of preground coffee and dump in enough espresso to wake the dead.

I'm already feeling a stress headache coming on, so I press my hands to my face and apply finger pressure at the trigger points and breathe deeply, but it's a long way to the Financial District and I need to get ready. I also need to pluck the thick black bristles of my Frida Kahlo unibrow, but when I get to the bathroom I have to wipe the toothpaste spatter off the mirror just to get a good look at myself. With all the overtime I've been putting in lately, my skin is getting so pale I could almost pass for white. Or at least whitish.

I reach for a towel and stop short in time to avoid another calamity.

He did it again: he moved the bathroom scale away from the wall to weigh himself and left it there for me to trip over. At least I'm ready for it this time.

I've asked him to put the scale back when he's done using it, especially when I'm groping around in the predawn darkness in the dead of winter, but that would require him to use his executive cognitive skills. *Yes, it's called remembering*, I explained. *It's like planning for the future, only backwards.*

I'm running late and I hear the mating call of the Number 7 train, but as soon as I hit the street one of our neighbors, Mrs. Perel, an elderly immigrant from Eastern Europe, calls out to me from her stoop.

"You shouldn't be out in this cold dressed in your housecoat," I tell her.

She dismisses my concern with a curt wave of her hand. "*Pff!* You have any idea how cold is winter in Poland? Now tell me please, what is this?"

She's holding a postcard addressed to Mrs. Sharona Perel, and it says *Notice: Vehicle Warranty Expiration: Immediate Response Required*, and gives an 800 number for the National Vehicle Headquarters in Missouri.

"I buy car for my daughter at Robby Robby's place and he give me five-year extended warranty, so I—"

"It's a scam," I say, interrupting her. "There is no such thing as the National Vehicle Headquarters in Missouri. The DMV is state-by-state, and a warranty expiration notice would come from the dealer or the manufacturer's corporate offices."

"So, is okay if I ignore this?"

"Yes. Unless you want me to call the 800 number and curse them out in my bitchiest Spanish."

"Between Yiddish and Polish, curses I have enough."

"I bet you do."

The wind picks up, kicking up grit and wrapping fast food wrappers around my ankles. I don't know how she can stand it out here in that housecoat and slippers. My fingers and toes are already going numb. Still, I take a moment to warn her about a rise in mortgage refinance scams targeting seniors and tell her to be suspicious of anyone claiming to be a "mortgage consultant" or a "foreclosure specialist" or anything like that.

I hurry to the 103rd Street station trying to get my circulation going again. The Flushing line stays above ground for a dozen stops while I catch up on the news. The lead story is about two brothers, Luis and Eduardo Valdés, who were washing the windows at a luxury steel-and-glass tower on East 66th Street when one of the cables supporting the scaffold snapped, and they plunged forty-seven stories to the street. Forty-seven stories of sleek, curved glass, the cool corporate look, with nothing to grab on to if you slip. By some miracle Luis survived.

Despite a boom in construction, the city has slashed spending for building inspectors, who might have spotted the faulty cable installation in time to avert this latest disaster, and their big plan for closing a $5 billion hole in the budget is building a Golden Fleece Casino at the old Aqueduct Raceway.

I transfer to the IRT at Grand Central and take it down to Wall Street, the train packed tighter than a carton of tax-free cigarettes. And as the stream of humanity converges on the stairs to the street, my nose is assailed by a strong pissy odor that elicits a loud *Oh, Jesus!* from me that draws some stares from the cynical New Yorkers.

The area around the subway exit is crawling with hard-hatted construction workers scurrying about high above the asphalt canyons, raising up slabs of concrete and steel for the new temples of trade and laying the foundation for the altar to the Great Bull of Hedge Funds while their overlords strut around in their pinstriped suits, whips at the ready.

Both ends of Wall Street are barricaded against street traffic and patrolled by cops in black helmets clutching high-powered rifles, with black knitted NYPD-issued vests stretched over their bulky body armor. Deli deliveries are being treated like fissionable material, with clerks and secretaries dutifully handing over their egg salad sandwiches to be X-rayed.

"What's your destination?" says one of the gatekeepers.

"The Schneerson Building, just down the block."

"I know where it is. What company?"

"Cadmium Solutions."

"Got a company ID?"

"Not yet. It's my first day," I say, handing over one of my business cards.

"You mean you work for this guy?" he asks, tapping the card.

"No, I am that guy. That's my name on the card."

"Oh." He squints at the card some more. "I'm going to have to call ahead."

"No problem."

Maybe I should have used a bigger font. Or at least put the phrase YES, I'M A WOMAN under it.

~

"*You're* Felicity Perez?" says a beefy security guard with a shaved head and a bushy goatee, comparing my face to the ID photo in the system.

"No, I'm Felicity *Ortega* Pérez."

"You look much darker in the photo."

"Is that a problem?"

"We need accurate likenesses of all employees and subcontractors. Come with me."

I made it to the eleventh floor on time, only to be stopped at the gates. The guard leads me to a frigid alcove where they've set up a camera on a tripod with a neutral backdrop. He takes a series of flash pictures, jacking up the luminosity of the flash after each photo till my already pale skin is blanched white as alabaster. My optic nerves are still recovering as he slow-walks me through the steps required to punch in and out using their biometric time and attendance system.

When I have to lean forward to place my right thumb on the photosensitive screen, he makes such a supreme effort not to stare at my boobs his neck muscles stand out like he's deadlifting a half ton of iron at the summer Olympics.

No duct tape to hang me up this time when I go through the metal detector. I take off my watch and necklace, but I keep setting off the alarm, so they run the handheld detector over me, back and front, until it zeros in on my underwire bra. You'd think that would be the end of the matter, but they instruct me to go to the public ladies' room and remove the bra so they can pass it through the X-ray machine.

I go to the ladies' room, hang my winter coat and dark-blue blazer on a hook, set my overburdened briefcase on the sink, unbutton my white satin blouse, and unhook the offending bra. Mission accomplished, I'm buttoning back up when the briefcase tips over and falls into sink, and the automatic faucet comes on and drenches it in a torrent of water. ¡Puta *madre!* I'm righting my waterlogged briefcase and wrestling with the tightfisted paper towel dispenser to blot up the excess water when the bra slips from my hands and the faucet turns on and soaks my bra through and through.

Argh! Who cares about the coming AI robot apocalypse when an automatic faucet can ruin my day?

I wring out the bra and hold it under the hand drier, but the spongy material remains saturated while the underwire quickly heats up to within a few degrees of the melting point of its Spandex-Polyester sheathing. Thank God for the blue blazer, because it feels like they've got the AC on full-blast in the middle of this cold snap.

I get back in line again, and the security team handles my padded bra with their light blue latex gloves, squeezing it and eyeing me suspiciously as water drips through their fingers into the plastic bin.

They send it through the machine, then they make me take off the blazer and send that through the machine, and but for the grace of a thin layer of creamy-white satin, my virtue would be severely compromised.

I cross the bulletproof Plexiglas threshold into the silicone heart of this giant data collection, processing, and storage facility taking up the entire eleventh floor of the building.

There's a constant buzz of low-level indignation coming from the flat-screen TVs mounted every twenty feet or so and perpetually tuned to WWTF, the All Outrage All the Time network.

"Are you the new legal assistant?" asks the smiling young receptionist, looking up from her computer screen. She's got a light café-au-lait complexion and impossibly bright greenish-blue eyes. It takes me a moment to spot the faint rings around her irises, indicating that she's wearing tinted contacts.

I give her my name, and she checks her screen and says I need to see Ms. Velda Renko.

"Not Frank Gustella?" I say, and there's a sudden drop in the cabin pressure as a skinny fiftyish woman in a tight black jacket and lace-up mini skirt freezes in her tracks.

"All new personnel are required to see *me* for preliminary training, *not* Mr. Gustella," says Ms. Renko.

"Training? What training?"

And I can tell by the way she cocks her head at me with a swish of her asymmetrical slash of copper-tinted hair that there's a mental list in her head, and she just scratched me off it.

"Follow me," she says, her face a tight white mask.

Great. I've been on the job less than two minutes and I've already made an enemy.

A team of harried technicians is zipping about with thick bundles of electrical cable, setting up TV lights in a luxurious conference room in front of a big blue backdrop with the slogan PLAN FOR VICTORY repeated over and over like some kind of evil behaviorist experiment, but we breeze right by it.

Ms. Renko directs me past rows of tiny airless cubicles to the tiniest, most airless cubicle in the place and begins a litany of workplace protocols that you might need to spell out to a teenage intern with the office skills of a Hostess Twinkie: Keep the photo ID lanyard around your neck at *all* times when you are in the building. Shred all scrap and log off the network every night without fail. Regarding phone inquiries, say we are "business consultants." Give out *no other information* over the phone.

"I'm sorry, but am I expected to field *inquiries*? I thought I was hired to—"

"I know exactly who hired you and why. Skip tracing some mentally defective head case who tried to sabotage our mission is a little below their pay grade."

Then she leans in and whispers something nasty, brutish, and short about my braless unprofessional dress.

And there's an office meeting at 10:00 a.m. sharp. We expect you to be there.

"I'll be there with bells on," I say.

"What?" she says, as if she's never heard someone use a figure of speech before.

"Seriously, it's a condition of parole."

She looks as if she'd like to slay me with one swish of her copper-tipped hair, then she spins around and marches away with a *rat-a-tat-tat* of her stiletto heels.

Pity her, my children, for she was born without smile muscles.

I open my briefcase, remove the soggy file folder, and spend my first twenty minutes on the clock carefully peeling the pages apart and laying them out to dry. I find a box of magnets in the desk and use them to plaster the walls of the cubicle with more damp pages, then I hang my mishandled bra near the air vent in the hope that it will dry in time for the meeting.

I got a head start on the case last night, looking for the

missing subject, Kristel Santos, age twenty-six years, in the usual places. First I checked to make sure she's still alive, or at least not known to be dead. A Social Security trace brought up an address in Elmhurst, Queens, but the case file states that Cadmium's in-house investigator, retired NYPD detective (*told ya!*) Frank Gustella already checked that address and found that the subject had moved. No indication that he actually went to the address and questioned the neighbors or whoever's living there now, so that might be worth following up in person, especially since, like so many ex-law enforcement guys who exchange their badges for a PI's license, Gustella's report is riddled with awkward phrasing and spelling errors like "Pakastan International Airlines," "answering maching," and a two-for-one: "Sargant Esquobar."

That would be Sergeant Diogenes Escobar, the Iraq War vet who commanded a group of thirty Silver Bullet contractors, including Kristel Santos; a guy whom I desperately need to speak with. Except that he's currently training counterinsurgents in the tribal regions of Balochistan Province, our ally in the standoff with neighboring Zabul Province.

I also checked state and federal prison records, and did a county-by-county search of criminal records in the tri-state area as well, and came up empty. No property holdings in the area, either. Military records: zilch, making her the only one on her team at Silver Bullet who wasn't ex-military. That must have been rough on her. I wonder why she signed up? Probably for three square meals a day. Though I did manage to find a defunct cable TV account under Ms. Santos's name at the Elmhurst address indicating that the bill was last paid as recently as three months ago. She took down her FriendSpace page around the same time and had it completely expunged, and no one seems to have tagged her in the intervening months, either, though I didn't have time to do an exhaustive search of social media.

The case file included a copy of her fingerprints but no

driver's license. I'm hoping the Personnel office has a copy of her license on file, since they asked me for one.

I'm having trouble logging on to the office computer when a major leakage of testosterone floods the area.

"—met with their new manager yesterday."

"She hot?"

"No, but her assistant is."

"Like the man said, you go to bed with the pussy you have, not the pussy you might want or wish to have at a later time."

"Excuse me," I say, stepping out of the cubicle. "Can either of you gents show me how to log on to the company computer system?"

Detective Gustella's features reveal nothing as he swaggers into my cubicle to fiddle with the keyboard and mouse. At least the younger guy looks a bit embarrassed, his bright pink skin glistening like freshly peeled chicken meat. But not for long.

"You the new girl?" he asks, studying me as if he's grading me like a USDA meat inspector.

Only now do I realize that my bra is dangling in full view of anyone standing in front of my cubicle.

He notices it and checks me out again, pursing his lips and nodding slightly as if reappraising the merchandise.

Gustella pushes the chair back abruptly.

"Sorry, can't help you," he says. "You gotta get a username and password from Ms. Renko."

Oh, great.

~

I dash to the women's room a few minutes before the office meeting in a last-ditch effort to resuscitate my ill-fated bra and, apparently, my professional reputation. The office bathroom on this side of the bulletproof Plexiglas is even fancier than the one outside, with polished marble surfaces, brass fixtures, and the heavily sweetened scent of synthetic air freshener emanating from an automatic dispenser stuck on the wall up near the ceiling.

The overpowering chemical smell adheres to my clothes and nasal membranes as I hustle to join the office staff filing into the cramped, windowless conference room, since the main conference room is being set up for some kind of product launch.

"Have a seat, Ms. Perez," says J.T. Haggard, the executive running the meeting. He's a milk-white WASP with ice-blue eyes, fabulous cheekbones, and perfectly blond, windblown hair that's beginning to thin on top.

The reception I get from the rest of the staff is so chilly I feel a sudden urge to wrap myself in a woolen blanket and cuddle up with a mug of hot chocolate.

"I believe you've already met Detective Gustella."

In walks the big guy with the gynecological vocabulary, his shock of white hair pointing in all directions.

"Ms. Perez is going to help us prove that the trouble in Escobar's unit was limited to one or two individuals," Haggard informs the staff. "Just a couple of bad apples, am I right?"

The question is directed at me, and he seems to expect an answer, so I nod and say, "Absolutely, sir."

"All right, then. Let's get right to it. Detective Gustella?"

"Thank you, Vice President Haggard." Detective Gustella's report on cybersecurity includes a trick from long before the digital era, describing how he circumvented the law that makes it a federal crime to get financial information from insurance companies and credit rating companies using pretexts, or false pretenses—something I've had to do myself on occasion—by calling up a stock brokerage firm with his old police scanner squawking away on a desk next to the phone. Did he *say* he was a police detective investigating a case? Absolutely not. Did they *believe* he was a police detective investigating a case? Who can say? But they gave him the information he wanted.

Detective Gustella looks directly at me, trying to gauge my reaction. I give a little nod to show I'm impressed.

~

"You sure know your stuff, Detective. I bet you know way more about insider trading and stock manipulation scams than some of the MBAs in this place."

"Those puppies? Their idea of legal research is binge-watching three seasons of *Law and Order*."

I laugh effusively, accompanied by the merry tinkle of my necklace jiggling. "Oh, that's a good one."

That's right, I'm stroking his ego. You know a better way to get a man to do you a favor, leave your name and number with my secretary and I'll get back to you.

I've got a ton of questions about his involvement in the Santos case, but most of them are adversarial, so I need to keep it on the down-low for a while.

"So, Detective, can you please ask Personnel to send me a copy of Kristel Santos's driver's license?"

"Shouldn't be a problem."

"I also need to see a copy of the original contract for her services."

"That's classified."

"I still need to see it."

"Why?"

"Okay, two reasons. One, I need to see the terms of the contract to determine the extent of Cadmium's potential liability if the subject's alleged culpability is not substantiated."

"There's no *alleged*. This isn't a courtroom. She's off the grid and we need you to find her."

"And I'd probably be able to find her more quickly if I could see the original contract."

"How so?"

"Because it might give me a better idea about why she disappeared."

"How do you figure that?"

"Because I might see things other people missed. I am a certified document examiner—that's why they hired me."

"They hired you because—" He stops himself.

"Because what?"

"I thought you said you read the file. You're so smart, you figure it out. I gotta go deal with another headache right now."

He wheels around and in two quick strides puts me several feet behind him. I've got to chase after him, which is probably just what he wants.

"Detective, please, let me explain."

He stops and faces me. "Make it quick, Speedy."

"Give me a second, okay?" I take a breath. People are looking at us. I don't have time to reprimand him for the nickname thing. "Can we talk somewhere else?"

"No. Out with it."

I make every effort not to roll my eyes.

"Okay, let me give you an example. One time I was working a case involving harassment, extortion, and—this is the reason I was called in—threatening letters?"

Jesus, why did I just make that sound like a question? *Ponte pilas, chica.* Keep it professional.

"Now these letters were double-spaced typed pages, one-inch margins all around, standard twelve-point Courier font, produced on a brand new laser-jet printer, so they can't be easily traced to a particular machine, right?"

He nods.

"No fingerprints or saliva on the letters or envelopes," I say. "And they're out of ideas, so they come to me. I go through the usual preliminaries, checking for typos, idiosyncratic word usage, regionalisms, then at my insistence they let me examine the original documents. I'm pulling on the vinyl examination gloves when I realize I'm picking up the faintest trace of a weird smell. The paper stock is porous enough to absorb ambient odors, and I lean in close and get a subtle but unmistakable whiff of cigarette smoke and the harsh disinfectant they use in cheap hotel rooms. I told them to check on anyone who reserved a smoking room in one of the roach motels near the crime scene. There were only three. I practically led the cops to the guy's doorstep. And that's why I need to see the original contract, not a copy. Because I'm willing to bet you I'll find something the MBAs missed."

Detective Gustella makes a show of considering my words, rubbing his chin and eventually giving me a nod. "You should really promote your skills more in that area."

"Yeah, right. Try putting that on a résumé: *I smell things other people might miss.*"

"Sometimes you just have to go with your gut."

"No, my gut tells me some pretty weird things sometimes. Now what's going on with that headache you have to deal with?"

"Oh, *that* bullshit," he says. "There's a big trade show next week at the Hartley Hotel in Midtown. We got three trunks full of display materials, and they're telling us to bring it to the loading dock, meaning we gotta pay a couple thousand bucks in drayage fees just to have them roll the stuff into the freight elevator and bring it up two flights to the showroom. I've been trying to Jew them down, but they won't budge."

"Sounds like it would be cheaper to just book a room and bring the freight in the front door. Prices for a single room at the Midtown Hartley start at $150 a night."

I won't say his jaw drops, because that would be an exaggeration. It's more like he opens his mouth to say something and the words slip out the back window and down the fire escape.

Take your time, Detective.

Finally, he says, "I'll be back," and directs his mass of unruly white hair toward the front office.

Time to get back to work.

But seriously: *Jew them down?*

~

Once you get away from the flashy reception area with its polished chrome, bulletproof façade, and all-marble bathroom, the place is pretty drab and monotonous. The break room is so shabby even the fake plastic plants are faded and covered with grayish dust. And the other employees are giving me cold stares as if I'm some creature from their nightmares come to snatch their children.

I have to visit the ladies' room again, and this time the cloyingly sweet chemical smell is so overwhelming I nearly gag. Or rather, I nearly *vomit*. That does it. I break into the janitor's supply closet, get out the step stool and drag it into position. I step on it, reach up, and try to yank the plastic facing off the automatic dispenser, but it won't budge. So I retrieve a lipstick tube from my purse and a nail file to wedge between the plastic tabs, and use the principle of the lever to pry the facing off.

The dispenser's guts are pretty simple: a clear plastic container holding the vile smelling liquid sits beneath a tiny fan that directs the noxious fumes toward the innocent victims within the five-meter "kill zone." This is chemical warfare, people, and all's fair. I don't see a battery, so it must be hardwired to the electrical system. Hmm. I don't really want to get caught destroying company property my first day on the job, but a closer look reveals that the wires lead to a metal contact plate that delivers the juice to the fan's tiny motor.

I head back to the supply closet, grab a carton of paper towels and tear off a piece of cardboard. I climb back on the stool and slip a thin strip of cardboard between the motor's lead wires and the contact plate and voilà. *Chemical weapons system disabled, sir.*

Nice work, soldier.

I'm snapping the plastic facing back on when the

bathroom door swings open and a woman with skin the color of powdered nutmeg comes in pushing a cart full of cleaning supplies. For a split second my mind flails about for the best way to talk my way out of this, then the woman, whose name, MAYLITA, is stitched on her light-blue janitor's smock, says, "*Gracias, señorita. Siempre he detestado ese olor.*"

Thanks, miss. I've always hated that smell.

~

I head back to my desk, flapping my clothes to get the smell of cheap air freshener out of them.

I'm going through the case file again, finding gaps and inconsistencies, deciphering notations in Gustella's crabby handwriting, and flagging trouble spots where I think I may be able to provide a fresh perspective, when Detective Gustella knocks on the partition, steps inside, and hands me a photocopy of Kristel Santos's driver's license.

"Thanks, Detective," I tell him, my eyes drawn to the inch-wide high contrast image of her face, the shadows on her cheeks greatly exaggerated by the black-and-white photocopying process, which makes healthy flesh look gray and turns the hollows of her eyes into bottomless pools of jet-black ink. I'd say her face looks haunted, but I don't look that great on my driver's license, either.

"This license only expired a month ago," I say. "It still lists that address in Elmhurst."

Detective Gustella nods and turns to leave. I wake the computer from its slumber and prepare to dive into the DMV records.

"Oh, there is one more thing," he says. He drops a file folder on my desk. I open it and glance at the first page.

The original copies of Kristel Santos's employment contract.

~

Jesus, look at this stuff.

Kristel Santos was supposed to be part of a "force protection" unit that was responsible for guarding military installations, deploying and maintaining armored vehicles supplied by US taxpayers, among other duties. But somebody screwed up and left a copy of the contract's original boilerplate language in the file, complete with emendations, deletions, and Post-it notes filled with scribbled suggestions for further changes. No wonder they didn't want anyone to see this. Most damning is the deletion of the word *armored* from the phrase *armored vehicles*, which must have saved the parent company millions in reduced costs while putting the contractors in very real danger of being ripped apart by machine guns, road-side bombs, and rocket-propelled grenades.

Kristel Santos was still a teenager when she signed up for this.

"Find anything yet?" says Detective Gustella.

"Jesus, do you have to hang over my shoulder like that?"

"Company policy, honey. Who watches the watchmen, right?" he says, parking his weight on the edge of the desk.

"Touché, Detective."

I'm flipping through two sets of pages, comparing the original contract with the revised version. I can't believe they left all these Post-its in the file, especially since they contain exemplary specimens of three different people's handwriting that are as unique and identifiable as fingerprints.

"So, you getting any special vibes from this or what?"

Yeah—they're not as smart as they think they are.

"I'm just wondering what other changes they considered but never put in writing."

"Why, you got a crystal ball in that briefcase of yours?"

"No, but I can get access to the latest electrostatic-detection devices, which is almost as good."

"Another reason you need to work with the original copies," he says.

"I'll make a convert out of you yet, Detective."

He pushes off from the desk and brushes some imaginary wrinkles out of his suit.

"I better get that file back to Personnel before they notice it's missing," he says, holding out his hand.

I close the Santos file and hand it over. "One thing I don't get is the need for *force protection*. This is the US Army we're talking about. What kind of protection do they need?"

"It might sound crazy now, but you gotta realize that when the war got rolling there just weren't enough troops to get the job done, so private contractors filled the need."

I nod and pretend I'm agreeing with him. "But you have to wonder how some big, strapping Marine felt about being *protected* by a nineteen-year-old girl with no military experience."

"A nineteen-year-old with skin so tight you could play a drumroll on it? He probably couldn't wait to get into her pants."

"How nice for her."

I turn back to the computer to run the ID number on the driver's license. Detective Gustella's about to leave but stops when I blurt out, "Well, whadaya know."

"What? Whadaya got?"

"Kristel Santos renewed her driver's license three weeks ago at the DMV on Ninety-First Avenue in Jamaica, Queens."

"That's the most recent activity anybody's seen from her," he says, checking the screen to see for himself.

"Time for me to check out that address in Elmhurst."

"You don't need to leave the office. Just call them."

There he goes again, telling me what I need and don't need to do.

"Look, Detective, you said it yourself. I was hired because of my rapport with the Latino community. And let's just say that a lot of my people are more comfortable on their own turf, where they can look you in the eye and try to figure out where you were born from the way you speak Spanish. And even if they do pick up the phone when the caller ID shows an unfamiliar Anglo-American name, most of them will say whatever they think it takes to get rid of you."

"I think I can see through a dodge like that," he says, puffing himself up.

"Sure you can, Detective Gustella. You're an old pro at this. But how many times did one of your subordinates move on to the next name on the list because somebody said, *No speak English* with a heavy accent? Did they know that over ninety percent of second- and third-generation Latinos speak English fluently?"

His brow furrows, his chest deflating a bit, and he does a great job of at least *looking* like he's considering my words.

"I don't know if the company will pay for surveillance at this point," he says. "Not until we're reasonably sure we've located the subject."

"Who said anything about surveillance? I'm going to knock on doors in broad daylight and talk to people who knew her, or might know her, or once stood behind her at the local bodega."

"Rick's not going to like it."

"Rick who?"

"Rick Fursten, the CEO."

"You've got to clear this with the CEO? It's basic fieldwork. This is *Private Investigation for Dummies*."

"He doesn't like the investigative staff going out in the field. He wants them to stay in the office and comb through the databases."

"Well, we can go to his office right now so I can explain that there's a lot of information that doesn't turn up in the databases."

"Like what?"

"Aside from the smell of smoke and cleanser? Okay, I see that you ran a credit check on Kristel Santos back in

September." I turn to the second-to-last page of his most recent report, which is full of handwritten additions and corrections.

"Yeah, she's dead broke."

"Right, but a credit report isn't going to tell you *why*. It's not going to tell you that maybe she spent her last thousand dollars on a motorized wheelchair for her cousin who got shot in the chest because some gangbanger mistook him for a rival gang member. It's not going to tell you that maybe she had mental health issues but *no health insurance* and the medical bills kept piling up and with nowhere else to turn, she's on the run and she's *pissed* about it."

He opens his mouth and I stop him with an upraised palm.

"And while we're at it we can tell your boss that no database is *ever* going to be fully up to date, especially if the subject is on the move and doesn't want to be found, which seems to be the case here. Then you're much better off talking to friends and relatives *in person*, not over the phone, and I'm sure you remember that from your time on the job, Detective. Now, if nobody minds, I need to run a quick check on Kristel Santos's neighbors in Elmhurst so I know what I'm getting into. You don't want to walk into a potentially hostile interview unprepared."

I figure we're done here, that he's got a million other things to do. But he fetches a chair from another cubicle, rolls it into my narrow workspace, and plops himself down close enough to engulf me in a puff of air that's a complex bouquet of knockoff Dolce & Gabbana aftershave with a hint of hazelnut coffee and a dash of rug shampoo. I concentrate on his latest report.

"Missing from the case file is any kind of description of the scroll itself," I say.

"What scroll?"

"The rare Hebrew scroll that the subject allegedly stole."

"Stop saying *allegedly*. There's nothing *alleged* about it. We got five witnesses who saw her shoving it into her duffel bag before she shipped home."

"What is it—encrusted with a king's ransom in jewels or something?"

"Just find her, all right? Soldiers take home all kinds of crazy souvenirs from a war zone, you know."

"Yeah, including shards of shrapnel embedded in their skulls. Now what can you tell me about this scroll?"

He makes a big deal of leaning in close again and thumbing through his old reports, licking his thumb with his thick, wet tongue before turning each and every page, and practically pinning me against the desk with his elbows before he agrees to share some "classified" intelligence I could have gotten in three seconds on Wikipedia.

"The week our troops marched into Baghdad, one of the first buildings they secured was the HQ of Saddam's intelligence unit. So they head to the basement looking for WMDs, and they find thousands of books and documents under three feet of water. A lot of the stuff looks like it's in ancient Hebrew or something, so somebody orders them to salvage what they can. Can you imagine? Saving soggy old books in the middle of an invasion?"

He stabs the report with a thick finger.

"So they rescue the stuff, but some of it gets lost in the shuffle. The fog of war and all that. Fast forward ten years. Silver Bullet's teams are clearing out a safe house on Baghdad's west side that's a known insurgent hangout, going floor by floor, nervous as fuck, and they kick down a door, expecting to find a cache of ammo or something. They find a storage room full of Torah scrolls, among them, the missing scroll in question. Whadaya think of that?"

Not so remarkable, considering we also managed to lose track of thousands of high-tech weapons, small arms, explosives, and around $10 billion in cash.

Oh, and our humanity.

"So it's a Torah scroll?" At least I have a vague idea what one of those is.

"Something like that. You want more info, you're gonna have to talk to the surviving members of the team."

"Thanks, I'll do that. What happened to the others?"

"What others?"

"You said the *surviving members* of the team."

He rolls his chair away from me and stands up.

"I gotta go see if I can get approval for your trip to Queens." And he leaves without saying another word.

Only now do I realize that was a slip. Something else that isn't in the file.

I decide not to press it. I'm going to get the story eventually from the team anyway. There are red flags popping up all over this case, big flashing red railroad crossing lights screaming WARNING: DANGER AHEAD! THIS WAY LIES PERDITION! I'D TURN BACK IF I WERE YOU!

I ignore the warnings.

It kind of runs in the family.

CHAPTER SIX

Ruth

The women caring for Yiskah offered Hanokh a dish of lentil stew with a hardboiled egg and a portion of bread, as Commander Manukka did his best to reassure the exiles that King Cyrus had personally guaranteed safe passage to all.

Ga'al set up his own circle of stones some distance away, and lit a heap of dry brush to heat the stones while he threw together the ingredients to make his own bread. When everything was ready, he swept the glowing embers aside and purposefully laid the flat disks of raw dough directly onto the hot stones.

"It comes out better when baked in an oven, but this will have to do," said Ga'al, offering Ruth a portion.

"So you were a house slave," said Ruth, biting into a perfectly toasted piece of lentil-barley bread.

Ga'al's arm froze, the bread halfway to his mouth.

Ruth took his hand and gave it a reassuring squeeze. His eyes dropped to the unyielding sands of the desert floor.

She spoke with a quiet confidence: "I told you before, you have nothing to fear from me."

Ga'al looked up, cleared his throat and said, "Did anyone ever tell you that your hair is like a flock of goats streaming down from Gilead?"

Ruth pulled her hand away and ran it through the prickly ball of fuzz on her head.

"Don't worry, it'll grow back," he assured her.

"So I've heard. Enough talk. I'm starving."

~

Yiskah lay on the birthing mat, red-faced and sweating, the contractions so protracted and painful that when she called God's name it sounded like her soul was leaving her body. The attending women feared that she would die in this place and that her spirit would haunt the barren wilderness for a thousand generations.

Naomi called for an iron sword to be placed next to the agonizing woman to give her strength and keep the demons at bay. Yedidyah the Nazirite offered his sword and stepped away, for such God-wrestlings were better left to women. Naomi cracked open an alabaster vial, poured out the thick, oily salve and rubbed it on Yiskah's abdomen. Ruth wondered how long Naomi had waited to use the ointment in that vial.

Yiskah took a couple of shallow breaths before her renewed entreaties to God turned into drawn-out cries of agony. Even the meddling prophet knew enough to keep quiet when Naomi called directly upon Yahaweh to help Yiskah with her labor.

Hanokh was sitting outside the circle with a white-knuckle grip on a small ram's horn when Yiskah clawed the air and screamed, "B'asherah!"

And then it was all naked and bare and wallowing in blood and they spread a cloak over it and cut the cord with a crude flint dagger and bathed it in water, and a baby boy emerged as they washed the blood off him and anointed him with fragrant oil, then they rubbed his glistening body with salt and wrapped him in faded red cloth to keep away the envious spirits, and hung sparkling pieces of silver on the swaddling near his ears, mouth, and nose.

A newborn child. A first-born son.

And Ruth thought, *Aren't they going to pass him back and forth over the fire to give him strength, as iron ore is tempered by the flames? Or at least pass him through the rising smoke to protect him from the demon-wind.*

Mesha and Hezkiyah broke the seal on a jug of wine and passed it around, pouring huge servings for themselves. Hanokh blew the ram's horn while others smashed earthenware plates to fool the local spirits into thinking that it was a sad occasion.

And in the middle of all the clamor the prophet asked Yiskah, What did you say? Did you call on Asherah? And she said No, he must have heard wrong. She had named the boy Asher.

And they held Asher up and paraded him around and Naomi went pale for a moment as if the stress had gotten to her, or perhaps she had seen a vision from beyond the borders of life, which has been known to happen under extreme conditions if the Lord wills it.

~

The campfires burned brightly, defying the vast emptiness of the Assyrian desert and chasing away the spirits that dwell in the shadows. The men chose the best of the underfed calves and butchered it so the women could prepare a stew for the celebration of Asher's birth.

The exiles scrounged up some linen cloth for swaddling clothes and a crude rattle as gifts. Hanokh thanked them for their kindness but worried that there was no gift for their Persian protectors. His breath caught when Ruth unrolled a strip of frayed burlap and spread out a set of arrowheads before the Persian commander's eyes. Six gleaming arrowheads of polished iron, whose points were sharp enough to punch through a warrior's shield and still inflict a mortal wound, made even deadlier by a pair of long, angled indentations from base to tip that would open an unstanchable wound, with a reinforcing spine running halfway up the head to counteract any weakness created by the indentations.

She heard some grumbling from the exiles about the folly of offering such fine weaponry to their Persian overlords.

But Commander Manukka eyed the lethal arrowheads shining brilliantly in the firelight and grinned.

~

Commander Manukka held up a disk of fresh-baked flatbread and ripped it in two, his heart merry with newfound companionship as he tore off a chunk of his half with his teeth and passed the other half around the campfire to be shared with the others.

"No city dweller's feast could ever taste like a meal cooked under the stars," he declared. "Not even in the palace of the king himself."

The men wagged their beards in agreement as they passed around a wineskin. Ruth refused it when it got to her.

"Do you curse all those who build houses as well?" asked Manukka.

"I do not, Commander," Ruth answered out of obligation, but the question unsettled her.

"You test me with the riddle of your true kinship," he said. "For you have sojourned among the clans of skilled metallurgists, and you refuse wine as they do, yet you do not proscribe house building, else I would take you for one of the Rekhavim."

Ruth's head jerked up to meet his gaze. "What do you mean?"

Manukka smiled assuredly as he brushed away the bits of breadcrumb stuck in his beard.

"You show your forehead proudly, yet something about you bears the telltale mark of the chariot yoke."

Ruth's heart nearly seized, and she realized her hand was clutching her chest, though she didn't remember putting it there. She let it drop back into her lap.

"Maybe she wants some of *this*—" Mesha said, drunkenly

shoving a cup full of lamb's blood in her face and spilling a few drops on her widow's garment. "You want me to mix in some milk for you—?"

She smacked the cup out of his hand, sending the blood splattering across the sand.

"All right, leave her alone," Manukka said, taking Mesha aside. After a few quiet words, the Persian commander turned back to Ruth. "Is that true? Your people still drink blood?"

"I have lost my taste for it, Commander."

"Then your husband's name shall surely be redeemed, for you are truly becoming like the Yehudim."

A furtive smile slipped past the guardian of her lips, pushing aside her memories of gorging on the warm blood of freshly slaughtered prey, and of bathing naked in the blood to absorb its power and to ward off evil, just as the Israelites did on *pesakh*, splashing their doorposts with blood. Now the thought of drinking lamb's blood turned her stomach, for the god of the Yehudim forbade them from consuming it.

Howls of laughter disrupted her thoughts. A crowd of men gathered in a circle, hooting and cheering a friendly wrestling match between Hezkiyah the Yehudi and the Persians' chosen champion, Rashda. Both men had stripped to their loincloths, their chests glistening with sweat.

Manukka leapt to his feet and let out a full-throated war cry, praising the display of skill as the tribal elders engaged in the distinctly male pleasure of watching two men wrangle with each other.

"That's how it should be done," said Manukka, directing his comments at the women by the fire. "Two men facing each other without weapons of iron or bronze, each warrior standing or falling by his own hand."

But Ruth had no taste for such sport. She knew what it led to before she even had her first blood, when she was working the open-faced copper mines below the plains of Moab, separating ore from dross. It was hard, heavy work for a slim young girl, breathing in clouds of noxious smoke and facing down waves of searing heat that left blisters on her hands and parched her skin till the worst patches looked like the cracked mud at the bottom of a ravine. And the men would come out of the earth after their dawn-to-dusk shifts and stare at her as if they hadn't seen a female in weeks. She knew all about that look in men's eyes. She had seen it in the eyes of the weary soldiers streaming away from the battle-fields who gaped at her as if she was an unfamiliar animal a thousand miles from its natural habitat. And they would tell her that she had the legs of a gazelle.

And as she grew like a stalk of barley and her breasts became firm and her hair sprouted, she had to cover her naked legs, and they no longer compared her to a gazelle but to an endless and bewildering variety of small, furry creatures.

Raucous screams and shouts broke into her rumination. The wrestlers had shown equal prowess, defending them-selves bravely, and the match was declared a draw. The sound of brotherly backslapping reverberated around the campfires.

Ruth turned away from the spectacle and sought the company of the women cleaning up from the feast, gathering the communal serving dishes and spooning the remaining food into the central cooking pot, which was swinging over the low fire.

"Help me with this," Miryam said.

Together they lifted the heavy pot off the hook and set it on the ground to cool, then they hung a pot of water to warm over the glowing embers. Miryam knelt and covered the mouth of the cooking pot with a piece of oilcloth and stretched it tight while Ruth emptied the dishes of salt into a large storage jar.

Miryam lowered her voice. "Where did you learn to make weapons like that? The Saka Paradraya region?"

"They wouldn't let me make them. I just assisted."

"Well, the man you assisted was a real master," she said, securing the oilcloth in place with a length of hemp.

"My training began with studying his rubrics in the gardens of Luristan," Ruth said.

Then came the years of itinerant desert living, trekking to wherever the veins were rich, then moving on when the veins were depleted, always feeding the fires and manning the blow pipes and hawking the wares and being the pretty girl behind the counter who attracted the customers while the master closed the deals, then hauling the cart across the sands to start all over again somewhere else. And every spring, when it was the season of war, following the armies and sharpening their weapons, repairing their weapons, and when the time was right, supplying them with newer and better weapons.

But always wandering.

~

The next thing she knew the iron collar was around her neck, the jagged coupling digging into her flesh even as the cross bar pressed against her shoulder blades, the relentless friction ripping open her scar until the heavy iron chains running down her back were wet with blood.

Her hand flew to her throat, and relief flooded her limbs as she felt the amulet and six-pointed star dangling from a tiny chain against her own smooth skin. No iron collar dug into her flesh. No shackles encircled her wrists. No bloody chains hung across her back. The horror of being enslaved was just a dream. Surely malevolent spirits inhabiting the area had inflicted these night terrors on her. They fed on fear and panic, and she needed to guard against providing them with anything else to feed on.

She knew better than to speak his name out loud, so she conjured it up in her heart. *O, Pazuzu, demon of the southwest wind, I call on you to protect Yiskah wife of Hanokh and her newborn son Asher, for the child will not bear the mark of the Covenant until seven days have passed. Speak to me on the wind, Pazuzu. Speak to me.*

She repeated the incantation not once or twice but again and again until she sensed a shift in the air.

Yes, he was out there. She could feel two sets of leathery wings stirring up the ether and smell his foul breath upon the wind. She could almost taste the venom seeping from his scorpion's tail and the snake head issuing from between his legs. She flinched at a vision of his horned skull with the wide-toothed grin, but she had to go through with it. They were in the middle of the vast uninhabited wilderness, in a dead zone between the land of Marduk and the land of Yahaweh, and neither god was coming forward and making his presence known.

~

Breakfast was last night's lentil-barley bread softened with a few precious drops of water, while the mercenaries stumbled around, headachy and irritable, yelling at everyone to jump to it already.

Nobody needed to be told twice.

The sky was a sheet of dull bronze casting a pall over the land, making people's faces look gray and giving their eyes a yellowish tinge.

By midday they came upon a boundary stone carved with ominous pictographs of giant birds of prey, double-headed lions, archers with thick scorpion-bodies wielding compound bows, and a giant snake slithering up to the sky either to serve as a bridge to the heavens or else to engulf the sun, the moon, and the stars. The symbolism wasn't terribly clear and there were no written words to help decipher it.

Ga'al tried to shrug it off. "Well, that's encouraging, isn't it?"

But Ruth was already sniffing evil in the air.

Someone shouted and pointed to the north. A thin trail

of smoke was spreading skyward. Then a crack formed on the horizon, like a fireball at the center of a whirlwind. Perhaps it was the signal fires at the head of another caravan trying to get through a sandstorm. But Rashda said there were no caravan routes in that area. Maybe the caravan got lost, someone said. Or maybe they had been lost for centuries, said another.

With no other way to signal them, the Persians set fire to a couple of staves pried from the old wooden cart and waved them from side to side like torches, but the wind kissed the bright flames, and behold, the fires turned blue, a sure sign that there were spirits on the wing, and closing in fast.

~

The northern sky darkened to a sheet of beaten lead, bearing down on them like a giant battering ram. They tied down the animals and pitched their tents, doubling the ropes, and prayed that they could ride out the storm.

And it came to pass in the middle of the night, when the thunder came rumbling over them like the wheels of a giant chariot, the voice of the prophet Ben-Isaiah rang out:

"Help us! The day of the Lord is near!"

The storm-winds whipped through the encampment. The voice of the demon-wind hurled loose objects into the air, clattering like the consonants in a language that was old the day that Yahaweh subdued the forces of chaos and separated the light from the darkness.

Shhhutuuuushhhhaduuuuuimshuhhuuuuuashamshatuuuuuu...

It came upon her suddenly, unwished-for, in a flash of recognition. The unmistakable *swoosh* of the airborne-she-demon, Lamashtu, the one who flits from house to house, from street to street, from town to town, across the expansive wilderness, ever on the prowl for the enticing scent of unprotected newborns to snatch away from their weakened and distracted mothers.

Ruth sprang to her feet and shouted over the wailing wind. She tore aside the red cloth separating her from the group and ordered the cowering Yehudim to make noise, to strike the mortar with the iron pestle, to hold hands and form a protective ring around the mother and child. But they wouldn't listen to the ravings of an unclean woman whose strange ways had angered their God.

She heard the wind-spirits approaching, the beating of their wings whooshing through the air and thrumming through her body until it matched the rhythm of her pounding heart, doubling in strength as Lamashtu-She-Who-Roams led a swarm of harpies from the depths of the underworld on a wild flight into the heart of the maelstrom.

She turned to the prophet and told him to chant that antidemonic psalm.

"Which one do you mean?"

Which one? A wild-haired she-demon was coming for the child, and she was supposed to remember *which* psalm might keep her and her cohorts at bay?

"The one that goes, *For He will save you from the plague-demon that walks in darkness, and the destroyer who ravages at noon.*"

"Oh, you mean *Yosheiv b'seither elyon*, He who dwells in the shelter of the Most High."

"Yes, yes, that one." Ruth stifled the urge to yell, *Just start chanting, you idiot!*

They had to act quickly, before Lamashtu called upon her limitless reserves and broke open the gates of She'ol, raising the dead to overrun the earth and feast upon the living, for the dead easily outnumber the living.

Omar l'Yahaweh makhsi umtsudothi elohey evtakh-bo.

I say of Yahaweh, He is my refuge and stronghold, my God in whom I trust.

Some say she is a vampire-witch, an airborne bloodsucker who lives on the sweet fresh blood of newborn children.

Ki-atoh Yahaweh makhsi.

For you have proclaimed, Yahaweh is my refuge.

Some call her Kheba, the wife of the Storm-God who rides into battle naked on a lion's back and causes the earth to reel to and fro like a drunkard.

Al-shakhal wofethen tidrokh, tirmos kefir wethanin.

You will tread upon lions and snakes, you will trample the lion cub and the serpent.

Ruth could feel the dreadful pounding of the lion's paws in the wilderness, rattling the crockery and shattering the cups.

The child! They had to circumcise the child. The only way to protect him was to shed some of his blood.

"No, it's too soon!" the Yehudim protested. "You have to wait until the eighth day."

"If we don't act now he won't live to see the eighth day."

"God forbid!"

"Only cutting a covenant of blood will keep back the demon-wind," Ruth insisted.

The wind shook the tent ropes so fiercely it sounded like they might snap at any moment. So Ben-Isaiah took up the flint stone dagger and performed the deed, spilling a few drops of the child's blood in the process. Ruth swiped her finger through the bright-red drops of innocent blood and smeared it on the child's forehead as protection against the Destroyer.

Hanokh fell ill from the sight of it.

And still the giants danced and the earth shook and the harpies threw their heads back and cackled at Ruth and Ben-Isaiah's pitiful efforts to save the boy from being devoured by the insatiable jaws of Hell.

The boundary stone had forewarned them of this. Had it also contained a clue as to what charm or spell or formula could counter these evil powers, and she was too blind to see it?

The blood was supposed to fool the demons into thinking that the child was already mortally wounded and turn them away. Why wasn't it working?

The voice of Yiskah droned on, endlessly repeating her plea: *Save him please God please heal him please save him please God please please save him please save him please God please please please* . . .

Hanokh groaned, as the walls of the tent pushed toward him, reaching for him. Reaching for *him*.

Ruth spun on him and pointed at his pale, sickly face.

"It's *you* they're after! Not your son."

Hanokh could barely raise his hand against the shadows pressing so heavily against him on all sides.

"It's *you* who needs to be cut, isn't it?"

He tried to deny it, waving his arm weakly, his head lolling from side to side.

"Or else it's you who bears the bloodguilt," she persisted.

Everyone was stunned when Ruth lunged at him, skidded to her knees and grabbed the hem of his garment. He tried to hold her off but she overpowered him, uncovering his legs and grabbing the waistband of his loincloth.

"Do you want to die out here?" she berated him. "Do you want your life to end in this barren wilderness with no one to mourn you?"

The men broke free of their torpor and rushed forward to stop her from committing an unpardonable transgression, but they were too late. Ruth yanked on the loincloth with both hands and ripped it loose in one clean motion.

And there, exposed before the eyes of the whole community, lay the flaccid, incontrovertible proof that Hanokh did not bear the mark of the Covenant.

And the voice of the whirlwind lit up the night, spitting fire and flame.

Ruth grabbed the flint dagger but Hanokh batted it away. It smacked against a stone and the blade snapped in two.

"You're not coming near me with that bloody flint knife," he said, his fighting spirit reviving.

"You're right, it's too brittle." She reached inside the folds of her skirt and drew out a short-bladed dagger with an ivory handle in the shape of the goddess of love and war, the copper haft bearing an ancient wedge-word inscription to Nin-agal, Lord Strong-Arm, the patron god of smiths.

The mercenaries tried to stay her hand, but she flashed the dagger at them and said, "Stay away from me. Unless you've got a better idea."

We are calling on Yahaweh to protect us, they answered, but they kept out of striking range.

"Well, He doesn't appear to be answering the call." And with that, Ruth leaned in, the gleaming blade hovering in the air over the paradox of Hanokh's true identity.

A powerful gust of wind nudged the blade off course and threatened to rip the tent in two, to uproot the whole flimsy structure, ropes and all, and suck everyone into the voluminous updraft, scattering their bodies throughout the length and breadth of the wilderness to become food for the crows and jackals.

The wind receded, slightly. It remained strong but steady now, and Ruth set to work.

"Aah!" Hanokh cringed in pain, and every male in the room winced as if their own manhood was going under the knife.

"Stop squirming! You think I've never seen a man's flesh before?" It wasn't easy carving a slit in the foreskin without some kind of salve, but there was no time for such luxuries.

A column of cloud had arisen between the earth and the sky, a darkness swirling so thickly that no light escaped it, destroying everything in its path and tormenting the air with a crackling roar that no mortal ears have heard and lived to tell the tale. The voice of the demon-wind, whose breath unleashes ten thousand plagues.

"Hold still!" Ruth said. "Almost done."

Hanokh kept his head turned to the side, his eyes squeezed shut.

"Try to breathe normally."

Hanokh let out a sharp burst of air that might have been a strangled laugh, but he forced himself to keep still.

"There!" Ruth sliced through the last bit of dangling foreskin and touched it to his inner thighs, leaving two streaks of blood dripping toward the nexus of his loins.

She smoothed out his garment and covered him up, then she leaned back on her heels and dropped the bloody piece of flesh between his legs.

She turned to face her detractors, who were paralyzed with shock.

"Now I am truly a bride of blood to your people," Ruth said, dusting off her knees as she stood up.

Before she could wipe the blood off the dagger, they heard scrub trees exploding as the dark swirling cloud touched down nearby.

In the name of Heaven! Was it still not enough? What more could she do? Would this giant twisting snake swallow everything in its path? Then it hit her, bubbling up from the churning face of the deep: The archers' images carved into the boundary stone.

The scorpion-men with their compound bows firing into the sun.

Face the demon-wind head on with an iron weapon that can cut through the whirlwind.

"You!" Ruth turned to face the Persian guards. "Manukka, Commander of Ten. I trust your arrowheads are made of tempered iron?"

Manukka practically chuckled. "They're not for decoration, if that's what you mean."

"Grab your bow and follow me."

A few devilish smirks skittered across the men's faces.

But the smirks vanished, wiped clean away when Ruth ran her fingers along the flat edge of the bloody knife blade and smeared the blood on her upper lip.

"Your word *pesakh* means protection, right?" she asked, blood dripping from the corners of her mouth.

A couple of the men nodded, dumbfounded.

"Then let us hope the Destroyer is satisfied with his portion and will turn away from us."

Manukka shouldered his bow and quiver and fell in behind Ruth. The tent flaps wafted open, beckoning.

Ben-Isaiah threw himself in front of them, blocking the way to the threshold. "You must stop what you're doing and await Yahaweh's intervention."

Another tree exploded in the distance.

Ruth said, "This dry and empty land is *mawat*, a dead spot between Babel and Yehudah. And your living god is not in this place."

"But your actions will render you unclean."

"I'm already unclean," she said, her lips glistening with blood.

And with that, she and Manukka slid through the narrow slit and out into the tempest.

Gale-force winds battered the two of them as they braved the sandstorm, leaning so far forward they were practically crawling along the ground.

"Where are we going?" Manukka shouted above the squall.

"To select a goat," Ruth shouted back.

"Why?"

"These local gods can be pretty unpredictable," Ruth said, crawling toward the animal pen. "But a fresh sacrifice can't hurt."

"More blood? I don't like it."

"Then why don't you show the demon-wind that guarantee of safe passage from the king and see if that works?"

Manukka had nothing to say to that.

Ruth pulled the double-edged dagger from her waistband and started sawing away at one of the ropes tethering a group of petrified goats together. She pointed at a scrawny young goat with the tip of her blade.

"How many damn weapons have you got in there?" Manukka said, throwing his meaty arms around the unlucky goat to keep it from bolting as Ruth severed the rope.

He held on tightly as Ruth retied the ropes to secure the rest of the animals.

"Who's going to repay the owner for this?" he said, as they dragged the reluctant animal headlong into the raging wind.

"When did you become such a jokester?"

"When I realized I may not live through the night."

Ruth nodded, though the gesture might have been missed as they squinted to avoid being blinded by the wind-propelled sand biting into their faces.

They advanced about thirty paces north of the encampment, when Ruth stopped so abruptly that Manukka fell on top of her, arrows spilling out of his quiver and scattering across the sand.

Manukka cursed in Persian and left Ruth holding the rope while he scrambled frantically to gather up his arrows. He must have felt foolish with the wind twisting his cloak around his legs and tripping him up, and no man wants to look foolish in front of a woman. When he finally flopped down next to her, clutching his arrows, she apologized.

"Sorry, that was my fault."

"No argument there. Now what?"

"Get ready to launch those arrows."

Her fingers fumbled for the amulet around her neck. She brought it to her lips and kissed it, closed her eyes and prayed fervently: *O Yahaweh, god of Yehudah, god of my husband, forgive me for what I am about to do.*

She squared herself and rose to her feet, wobbling slightly as the wind raged about her.

She called on Yahaweh again, but He refused to answer, so she called on Marduk, who created the seven evil winds who dance in the dust—the tempest, the whirlwind, the tornado, and the four winds whose names she dared not speak. But Marduk was getting old these days, old and senile and hard of hearing, and he didn't answer either, so she called on the winds themselves.

O En-Lil, Lord of the Winds, O Lil-itu, Lady of the Winds, listen to your servant! she cried. And the storm winds rose, knocking her back a few steps.

"May the gods serve as my witnesses," she said, facing directly into the mouth of the north wind. "As I cut this covenant with you. Turn aside your wrath and let these people pass safely through your land, grant safe passage to them and to the child born to them, and you can take me as payment if you wish."

Manukka positioned himself low to the ground, as Ruth instructed him, with his weight on his right knee and his left foot planted squarely in front of him, his right foot trailing behind like a tail. With his bow stretched back, and his arrow notched, he really did look a bit like a giant scorpion.

She seized the goat by the scruff of the neck and raised the dagger, holding it there to give the wind-gods time to gather around. The double-edged iron blade was sharp and glistening, enough to scare off myriads of lesser spirits, even under this heavily overcast sky. She let the blade hang in the air just a little longer. She wanted the wind-gods holding their breath in anticipation. She raised the dagger another inch. Aaannd—

"Now!"

She sliced open the goat's neck as Manukka launched the first of his arrows into the heart of the whirlwind. Ruth held the pitiful animal as its lifeblood gushed out onto the sand.

While he was distracting the wind-gods with the remaining arrows, Ruth laid the goat's dripping carcass on the ground from east to west, perpendicular to the direction of the wind, and proceeded to cut its body in two. Slicing through the entrails was easy, but the backbone was tough to cut through and she had to lean on the handle with both hands, putting all her weight into it, blood and entrails sluicing into the crease. Finally it gave, and the blade went clean through.

Manukka regarded her, transfixed, as she dragged the two halves of the goat's carcass in opposite directions, leaving three cubits of blood-soaked sand between them.

She turned and held out her hand to him, an unspoken invitation to join her, but he shook his head. She nodded and turned her face to the wind.

Then she raised her voice and called out across the vast expanse of the wasteland: *May this and more happen to me if I violate the terms of this covenant.*

As she placed the tip of her sandal on the edge of the blood-gorged sand, the winds came up again, flinging sheets of sand into their faces.

Manukka pressed his face against the earth, eyes clamped shut. He covered his head with his hands as sand and other debris sailed past. First twigs and pebbles, then heavier branches and stones skittered by, bouncing off his back, nicking his elbows and grazing his knuckles, then the whole desert floor seemed to writhe beneath him. No sooner were the words of an end-of-life prayer forming on his lips when the storm winds died down, the fist-size stones rolled to a stop, the barrage of pebbles and sand dwindled to a light sprinkle, then everything fell silent. He felt the warmth of the sun's rays on the back of his neck, and when he dared to open his eyes he was astonished to behold that the storm clouds had parted to reveal a miraculous bright-blue sky ringed by dark clouds, as if the all-seeing Eye of God was peering directly into his very soul.

Ruth lay motionless, her prostrate form surrounded by twigs and stones and other detritus, her clothing torn and smeared, a long gash in her forehead, her razor-chopped hair floating in a pool of blood. He hoped it was the goat's blood.

The air was completely still. Not a single dangling thread stirred in the breeze, not a loose hair fluttered in the wind, not a single carrion bird circled overhead. No wolves prowled the edges of the zone of destruction. The lambs didn't baa, the goats didn't whinny. Earth and sky were without sound or movement, as if the wandering stars themselves had dropped from their courses and the music of the spheres fallen silent.

Another line of clouds drifted southward toward them, but they were outliers, camp-followers, ordinary clouds presenting no threat, no menace, like the afterbirth that comes sliding out easily after a strenuous and life-threatening delivery.

The air was so clear he could pick out his arrows strewn about an area of sandblasted scrubland about a hundred paces to the north. He'd have to come back for them later.

Manukka gathered Ruth in his arms and carried her back to the encampment.

CHAPTER SEVEN

Felicity

The TV monitor explodes with a burst of red, white, and blue, obliterating the rapid-fire rage-fest of the regular programming. A surge of cheering emanates from every TV screen in the office, coming at me from all directions. Placards take flight as supporters wave them in an orgy of adoration, bearing the messages FURSTEN FIRST and PUTTING PEOPLE FIRST in huge red letters.

They turn down the lights in the conference room and crank up the bass-heavy theme music, and the wall-sized screen lights up with a giant advertisement for Cadmium Solutions: tank treads roll across desert sands, choppers disgorge aggressive assault teams, men with the bodies of professional wrestlers grit their teeth and kick down doors, a detachment of mercenaries in this private army comes to attention, the company-issued unit patches stitched clean and sharp on their uniforms.

I try to focus on my work, but the quaking soundtrack and flashy images are too disruptive. Who needs a meaningful discussion of the issues when you can just drown out the competition with the sheer size of your sound system?

Finally an on-screen limousine pulls away from an embassy protected by armored vehicles bearing the Cadmium logo: the camera zooms in on the big red *C* with a small golden *a* in its crosshairs and holds, letting it fill the screen while the music makes a running leap at the climax.

I do my best to block out the racket so I can run an asset search on the property in Elmhurst. I find out that it's owned by a single human being—not a corporation—named Lizzy Martínez, who lives on the premises and rents out the second floor and the basement. Sounds promising, if the information is current. A live-in landlord is going to know a lot more about her tenants than some absentee landlord based in New Jersey. Thank God she uses the name "Lizzy" on legal documents, which makes it relatively easy to find basic info about her. If the listing had been "L. Martínez," it would have taken a week to verify that I had the right person.

No indication of illegal or abusive practices, so the odds are good that she won't come after me with a sawed-off shotgun when I ring her doorbell. But you never know.

The lights come up in a blaze of glory, and a groundswell of applause erupts from the conference room as Cadmium's CEO Rick Fursten makes his grand entrance through an honor guard of hard-bodied *force protectors* in spotless dress uniforms covered with streamers and confetti. Fursten is fairly young, in his midthirties, with shiny black hair that's been gelled into a soft, wavy peak on the right side of his forehead. His manner and dress are unmistakably modern, but there's a certain retro look about the hair that I can't quite place.

He waves at the crowd, then gets a stranglehold on the microphone: "Today is the *day*, my friends! We've had en*ough* of Washington in*sider*s telling us what *to* do! And how *to* run our *bus*iness! Now I *have* a plan for *vic*tory!"

I sift through the readily available data on Lizzy Martínez's neighbors. Nothing jumps out at me. No outstanding warrants for violent crimes or major felonies, just petty stuff like parking violations, drinking in public, a summons for marijuana possession, and a couple of violations for disorderly conduct.

I keep poking around, ignoring the slashing syllables and dental plosives that keep piercing my concentration like daggers finding the chinks in my mental armor: "Cut *tax*es … *mi*litary spending … homeland se*cur*ity … talking about to*day*, and that's energy se*cur*ity."

I'm trapped in this office, the walls of this tiny cubicle pressing in on me, plugging away at the databases while everyone else is being seduced by the ritualistic display of leader worship when I feel an intuitive jolt: If all available staff members are attending the mandatory pep rally, there's a chance that some of the internal systems have been left open and unguarded so I can dig up some intelligence on the rest of Kristel Santos's ill-fated team.

"Big business needs living space!"

Hoo-boy. You might want to run a quick internet search of that phrase before using it in a speech.

The TV lights glisten off Fursten's gel-teased coiffure, which remains rigidly in place no matter what pose he strikes, and that's when I realize where I've seen it before: It's President Reagan's hairstyle. Or at least it's meant to evoke Reagan's hairstyle. They've updated it a bit, no doubt to suggest the seriousness of his ideas despite his youth.

"Now is the time to look forward, not back."

No luck with the internal systems. All hatches battened down and sealed, Captain.

"With the rise of globalization, we have to lead with a whole new way of doing business—the American way!"

It's a surefire applause line, but why is he talking about international trade issues if he's running for mayor?

Oh, shit...

My premonition becomes a reality, proving that my patented Bullshit Detector™ is still functioning properly, because the next thing I know he's announcing that he is officially kicking off his campaign to become the next president of the United States of America, and the true believers unleash a wave of hosannas.

I'm struggling to stay afloat in this sea of toxic waste when Detective Gustella returns and tells me they approved my expedition to the wilds of Queens. "But you gotta use a company car and phone to check in for all out-of-office travel, so—"

"So they can keep track of my movements with the GPS. Got it."

"Uh, yeah," he says, not quite knowing where to look.

"Detective Gustella, you're a breath of fresh air." I give him my brightest smile as I gather my notes and slip them into my briefcase along with the company tracking device and make a break for the exit. My Bullshit Detector™ is overheating and I need to get out of here before it blows.

Fursten is signing copies of his book, which I believe is called *When I Was a Kid Everything Was Great, Ice Cream Was Free, Blacks Knew Their Place, Gays Were in the Closet, and Women Were Subordinate to Pathetic White Men Like Me*, when a news flash breaks into the on-screen gabfest and WWTF News correspondent Dolores DeCabeza announces with a skillfully balanced combination of glee and gravitas that the Pentagon has confirmed that a Hellfire missile launched from a Predator drone has killed Al-Qahol's number-two man in Balochistan Province.

Talk about bad timing. That's going to push Fursten's campaign announcement right off the front pages and further down in the news cycle.

~

I start the car and get slammed by angry voices at earsplitting volume: *WHY* IS THIS MAN RUNNING FOR PRESIDENT? *WHY* IS HE HERE?

The assault's coming at me from all sides but the source is the satellite radio built into the instrument panel.

I'LL TELL YOU WHY! HE'S HERE BECAUSE *GOD* PUT HIM HERE! WE NEED A MAN LIKE RICK FURSTEN AT A TIME LIKE THIS!

I lunge instinctively for the volume control knob but *there isn't one*. Is it operated by remote? Voice command?

HE'S THE *ONLY* ONE WITH THE *GUTS* TO TAKE ON THE BIGGEST SPONSOR OF STATE TERRORISM IN THE WORLD!

I dive for the glove compartment while shouting voice commands as loudly as I can, but it's locked. The onboard computer responds: *I'm. sorry. your. voice. has. not. been. properly. entered. into. the. wireless. voice. command. system.*

WE'VE GOT TO TAKE OUT THE TERRORISTS IN ZABUL PROVINCE WHILE WE'VE GOT THE CHANCE OR IT'S GAME OVER!

Please. consult. the. operating. manual.

I'm screaming at the computer to *Shut the fuck up—*

Unrecognized. command.

—as I make a desperate grab for the keys and shut off the ignition.

Silence. Blessed silence. I sit there and breathe deeply for a couple of seconds.

I unlock the glove box and fumble around for the remote. Got it. Christ, my fingers are shaking. I point the remote at the radio, but of course nothing happens. The car has to be on for it to work.

I brace myself for another assault, slide the key into the ignition and turn it.

IT'S ALL GOING TO COME DOWN TO WHO BLINKS FIRST!

I press the remote's volume control, but nothing happens.

AND I TRUST RICK FURSTEN NOT TO BLINK FIRST!

I press the button again and again and it finally works, thank God, and lets me lower the volume:

AFTER ALL THEY STARTED IT!

That's as low as it goes. I try to change the station, but there doesn't appear to be a function that will allow me to do that, and there's no on/off button for the radio itself.

Ay, Dios mío. Driving from Manhattan to Queens is torturous enough without being forced to listen to WWTF News the whole time. I feel the radio's pebbled plastic underbelly for switches, dials, or a loose wire I can accidentally rip out. No such luck. I fiddle with it a bit more, then give up. I don't have time for this right now. But there's got to be a way, short of ripping the radio out with a crowbar.

WE NEED TO MAINTAIN AMERICAN CREDIBILITY IN THE REGION!

I may have to go back on my pledge not to destroy any company property my first day on the job.

Detective Gustella actually had the balls to tell me I should use the car for surveillance. Right. I'm supposed to sit in the car for five hours listening to a bunch of lunatics tell me that torture isn't torture if we're the ones doing it.

Unless there's a self-destruct switch on this thing.

THE PEOPLE OF ZABUL PROVINCE JUST DON'T GET IT!

I feel a *ping* and check my phone. It's my dad, inviting me over for dinner. I text him back: *Okay, see ya in a couple hours.*

~

My trip to Elmhurst is a bust. I couldn't turn up a single bit of useful information on Kristel Santos. The landlady hardly ever saw her or spoke to her, and she apparently had no friends or family in the area, which is really unusual for a Latina—we tend to come from large families (who will stigmatize you for moving into your own apartment, you whore), which suggests that she was already withdrawn and a bit of a loner *before* her term of service in Iraq, so God knows what state she's in now.

And I'm going to have to go back to Cadmium Solutions tomorrow morning and spend the day scouring every database known to humanity.

~

In these uncertain times, I suppose I should find it reassuring that my family hasn't lost the ability to drive me completely nuts.

My dad invited me over for dinner. You'd think that

means he's making dinner or something, right? But when I get there, he hasn't showered or changed yet, and his work clothes are still spattered with paint and spackle and covered with a thin layer of wallboard dust.

Turns out that not only is dinner *not* being made, but I'm expected to make it. Plus I have to go buy the ingredients, since there's nothing in the apartment to eat.

If I'm going food shopping, I might as well ask if he wants me to make anything special.

"*Bistec empanizado con yuca frita y frijoles negros*," he says, as if he's been planning this menu all afternoon. "Like your mother used to make," he adds, reciting the words like a blessing.

As if I needed to be reminded.

A triptych of cardboard-framed studio photos has kept watch over the living room from a place of honor above the TV for as long as I can remember. Color photos of my brother and me at ages eight and four, respectively, dressed in stiff formal outfits, flanking a brittle black-and-white photo of our parents on their wedding day, José Ortega Mendieta and María Pérez Espinoza, my dad looking trim and fit, my mom tall and gorgeous, her dark wavy hair hanging nearly to her elbows.

Gone these twenty years, her ashes scattered on the waters of Flushing Bay, she might have survived if she'd been up here, a few blocks from a clinic run by Mount Sinai Hospital. But she was visiting relatives in the Peruvian highlands, and by the time the pickup truck made it down the bumpy dirt road to the paved highway, it was too late. She's the reason I insist on using both of my last names professionally, keeping her name alive, because one of us has to.

I phone Jhimmy from the bitterly cold sidewalk to ask if he wants to eat with us, but he's putting in overtime at the community center, painting signs and printing fliers for tomorrow's big protest. I promise to save him some leftovers.

I squeeze through the narrow aisles of the corner bodega, picking up breadcrumbs, cooking oil, *yuca*, onions, fresh cilantro (a must), a five-pound sack of rice, and some canned beans.

Damn, this basket is getting heavy. Where's a big strong man when you need one?

They ring me up, stacking the provisions in separate plastic bags at my request so I can distribute the weight evenly. I carry my purchases down the block so I can wait in line at the butcher shop, the straps on the heavy plastic bags digging into my palms.

How the hell did this get to be women's work?

To be fair, my dad tried, at first. But I remember a lot of dinners of spaghetti and ketchup, so I learned to cook for my father and brother before I was tall enough to see all the way over the counter. They got me a stepstool. Soon I was cooking for my uncles and my forty-two cousins and every other male relative who stayed with us for a couple of months when they first got to this country, until my father found them off-the-books jobs and they were able to move out and start their own families, because I was born here and they weren't, and that made all the difference.

I turned down my first marriage proposal when I was fourteen.

I ask the butcher for a pound and a half of meat sliced so thin you can practically see through it, enough for lunch and dinner for five and then some.

When I get back, I hear male laughter coming from inside the apartment in tenor and baritone registers.

My dad and his buddy Eloy Sucushñay are working their way through a six-pack of Tecate and watching *Los tres chiflados* on TV, a classic featuring the original Curly, my dad's second favorite comedy show after the old black-and-white series *La tremenda corte*. I'm not sure which Three Stooges short it is, but it's the one where they hit each other a lot.

"Hey, *mira quién se asomó*," my dad says, nodding toward Eloy. Neither of them have changed out of their work clothes.

Eloy stands up and gives me a hug. He's bonier than my dad, with long dark hair tied back in a ponytail, reddish brown skin, and the sharp nose and brow that marks him as a native of the Ecuadorian Andes.

Anyone else dropping by? I wonder, as I head for the kitchen. Good thing I got extra food. An old habit. I set the bags on the kitchen counter and rest my weary arms. I'm rubbing my hands together, trying to get the feeling back into them, and I see that my dad has left a piece of *pan de San Antonio* over the doorway as an offering. Like God's too important to come down for a crust of bread, but you might get lucky with Saint Anthony.

I unpack the groceries and when everything's set out and ready, I sprinkle the meat with *ajo, comino y achiote*, then smother it with breadcrumbs. I lay the breaded meat into the frying pan and the smell soon entices my dad into the kitchen.

"You got *canned* beans?" he says, picking up a can and studying the label, as if he can't believe his daughter would betray her heritage in this way.

"*Papi*, real beans have to soak overnight and simmer all day. You know that. Don't worry, I'll dress them up like the real thing."

He looks at me skeptically, but he puts the can down and folds his paint-flecked arms so he can watch me chop up the onions for a dish called *moros y cristianos*, Moors and Christians, a mixture of black beans and white rice. Probably not the most politically correct name for a side dish. When it's evenly heated, I garnish it with fresh chopped cilantro, just to provide a nice green buffer between the opposing factions.

Now, peeling and slicing tough, tuberous yuca into french fry–sized pieces and deep frying it, *that's* work.

"So how's the new job?" he asks.

"It's okay." I poke the slices of yuca with a two-pronged kitchen fork, separating them so they'll fry evenly to a golden brown. "It would be a lot easier if they actually trusted me."

"What do you mean?" he says, the skin around his eyes crinkling up. He used to tower over me, but age has narrowed the difference to a couple of inches.

I tell him how they want me to find somebody without having access to any of the information that is typically provided in a case like this. They won't tell me when they learned of her disappearance or who reported it, plus they're giving me a hard time about visiting the locations she frequented prior to her disappearance, and they won't even let me interview her close associates at Silver Bullet.

"You should have gotten a job working for the city. Then you'd have some security—"

"*Papi*, there's no such thing as job security anymore. The city just laid off two thousand workers even though the unions offered a giveback."

"And Mayor Gatti rejected it!"

"Careful, *viejo*, you'll burst a blood vessel," says Eloy, leaning on the doorframe with a beer in one hand.

"Those Wall Street assholes make more money in five minutes than I do in a year, and the mayor has the nerve to say that public workers are the problem? That the *teachers unions* are too greedy?"

"No, that was Governor Christie of New Jersey."

"Another asshole."

"Make room, the yuca's done," I say, lifting the first batch from the hot oil with a strainer.

"It's bad enough that they make us sit through a weekly presentation by some jackass in a fancy suit who tells us that unions are nothing but a scam, and that voting for the union could cost us our jobs."

"How'd you like to dress the salad?" I say, concerned about my dad's blood pressure, an ongoing issue since the time he went off his meds and punched out a window to get into the apartment when he forgot his keys instead of doing something a bit more logical like, say, knocking and waiting for me to let him in.

"Sure," he says, opening the door to the fridge.

Eloy parks himself near me. "Meanwhile, we're there ten hours a day, six days a week, for seven hundred dollars cash. And it's dangerous work. But at least we're free on Sundays to go to church and pray for God's protection." He takes a long, contemplative sip of beer.

My dad's rooting around in the fridge, glass jars clanking against each other.

"Lord knows we need His protection," Eloy says, watching me turn the meat over in the pan. "Though I don't know how much time He spends on East Fifty-Third between Park and Lexington."

"How's that going?"

"*La construcción está en veremos,*" he says. It's in a state of we'll-see-how-it-goes. "There's plenty of work, *gracias a Dios,* but what the companies do now is they hire three guys with union cards to fool the inspectors, then they subcontract out the rest of the jobs to cheap nonunion day laborers who don't know what the hell they're doing. *Mi compadre* almost had to cancel his dinner plans when some *pendejo* nearly dropped a load of bricks on him from fifty feet up."

"*What?*" I nearly burn myself with spattering oil. "When did this happen? Today? Are you all right?"

My dad tells me to relax, *no pasó nada,* tomorrow's their last day on the job, and their next job is at a small site, a three-story building on Glenmore Avenue in East New York.

"Well, that's a relief," I say, sprinkling too much salt on the fried yuca. My dad likes it salty.

"*No te preocupes por tu papá,*" Eloy reassures me. "Your

dad has a guardian angel watching over him so closely that he could take a flying leap off the Fifty-Ninth Street Bridge blindfolded and there'd be a barge full of mattresses and feather pillows passing under the bridge at that exact moment."

"This guardian angel must belong to a damn good union," I say.

That makes him laugh.

"Salad's ready," my dad announces.

Oh, Christ. He's completely slathered the lettuce with a heavy mayonnaise-based dressing.

Leave it to my dad to find a way to make salad unhealthy.

~

"*Dios bendiga a esta mesa, y a quienes no tienen que comer. Amén.*"

"Amen."

My dad takes a few bites, then winks at me and nods his approval.

The men sit there talking about how *los* Mets *y los* Yankees are going to do next year, and what a shame it is that they're tearing down both stadiums, no, more than a shame, it's a crime against all that is holy.

Then my dad tells me, "Before you go, I need you to help me program the new thermostat's digital display."

"It didn't come with bilingual instructions?"

"Sure it did. Everything comes with instructions now. They've got programmable refrigerators, dishwashers, washing machines—who the hell has time to read all these damn instruction manuals? And learn all seventy-eight functions that the new microwave oven has to offer?"

This is how it is for me. Not only am I expected to perform all the tasks traditionally assigned to women like shopping, cooking, and cleaning, but I'm also supposed to fill the traditional male role of translating technical verbiage into a language my dad can understand.

"And how's that boyfriend of yours?"

"We're fine, Dad."

"Then what's bugging you?"

That's kind of a trick question, since something is *always* bugging me. But it gives me a chance to tell them about my trip to Elmhurst, and about Kristel Santos's apparent loneliness and isolation.

The men nod, acknowledging this sad state of affairs.

"How could she have no family?" says Eloy. "Unless she left them behind and sneaked across the border by herself, or they all died while trying to cross the desert."

"Neither. She was born here."

My father seizes on this and blames American society for making her feel lonely and alienated.

"The gringos can be so cold with us, you know? When we do a job for *la gente de nuestra tierra*, one of our people, they always introduce themselves, call us by name, offer us a little café con leche or something. Whenever we show up at some gringo's house, they treat us like the help, they point us toward the boiler room and tell us what the problem is and then they either disappear or else they stand over us the whole time to keep an eye on us because they think we're going to steal their rusty boiler screws."

He gets so worked up he starts coughing, a gooey wet smoker's hack that doesn't stop till he gets up and spits something gross into the sink.

He never smoked a cigarette in his life. But he spent three weeks on the pile at Ground Zero, sifting through the debris by hand in those first few hours, which became days, when they were still hoping to find survivors, until all the good intentions dissipated and settled over the site like a layer of fine white dust. And the long arm of death continues to cast its shadow across the intervening years, revealing and concealing itself like a showgirl's teasing sleight-of-hand, pulling off a deceptive vanishing act from the collective consciousness only to reappear the day my dad's demolition crew found bone fragments on the roof of the Deutsche Bank four and a half years after the towers collapsed in a holocaust of dust and ashes.

I'm packing two dinners when my dad says there's some leftover cake in the fridge, and he proceeds to take out the cake and cut it into two pieces, horizontally. Did I mention that my dad has a crazy streak? Who cuts a layer cake in half *horizontally*?

I know he loves the Three Stooges, but I've told him time and again that they're *not* instructional videos.

Another photo, another frozen sliver of time, held to the fridge with magnets. Dad and me on either side of my brother Jeremías with our arms around him on the day he shipped out, reminding me that I've got someone else to visit.

~

Slow down. Small pieces. Chew chew chew. Good. No, that's too big! Cut the meat into small pieces. Yes, like that. Take your time. No wonder you gained so much weight. Good. Chew chew chew.

Don't steal food. If you want more, just ask.

You want some juice? Orange or apple?

A-puh.

Okay, good asking.

Doh-ee.

Yes, don't eat anything that isn't food.

No, don't pull hair! Be nice.

Ba-oo.

Bathroom? Okay, let's go.

Stand closer. And aim for the bowl. Come on, you know how to do this. All right, wipe it up. Don't use so much toilet paper!

Ca-ca.

Okay. Boy, those blueberries went right through you,

didn't they? You really have to start chewing your food better. Now wipe.

Wi.

Yes, wipe. Good wiping. Now wash hands.

Sho-wah.

You want to shower? Okay, I'll run the water. Is that warm enough? How's that? No? How's that? Okay, get in. Get in. Get in already. Okay, soap soap soap. Good. Put your face in. Wash wash wash. Turn around and I'll do your back.

Okay, now do your underarms.

Buh.

Colder? How's that? More? Okay. *Límpiate la nalgita.* Okay, good. Don't eat soap! No. Come on, put it down. Put it down. Good listening. Okay, rinse rinse rinse. Rinse rinse rinse. Good.

Dry dry dry.

Tee.

Okay, where'd they put the floss picks?

Wow, you really build up a lot of tartar, especially on the upper teeth. I see you had corn for lunch. Hold on, almost done.

Bu-tee.

Time for new bristles on this thing, huh? Okay, good. Spit out. Good.

Gargle gargle gargle. Okay, rinse and spit. Good.

Wa-kuh.

Walk? Oh, it's too late now. Next time, okay? Next time.

Don't bunch the pads up like that. Spread them out. Like this. Yes. Good.

Wee-buh.

Read a book? Okay, which one? *The Wheels on the Bus?* Okay.

The wheels on the bus go round and round
Round and round, round and round
The wheels on the bus go round and round

All through the town.
Again? Okay.

My brother, the human beanbag chair.

Miss Ortega?
Yes?
May I remind you that we have a very strict policy regarding food from the outside? No plastic sandwich bags, no glass bottles, no toothpicks, nothing with bones. All meat must be cut into pieces no larger than one inch square. Plain peanut butter sandwiches are not permitted. If you make a peanut butter sandwich, please apply extra jelly.
Oh, and Miss Ortega?
Yes?
We're going to need more diapers.

CHAPTER EIGHT

Felicity

Junk mail, Christmas catalogs, gas and electric bills, a fund-raising letter from Magen Abot, an Israeli ambulance corps (how on earth did I get on *that* mailing list?), and a letter from my health insurance company, which always fills me with dread because no matter how many times I read the fine print—and remember, I'm a certified document examiner—I never know if the letter is going to say something benign like *Please remit your $50 copay* or something heart-stopping like *This procedure is not covered. Please remit $17,000. You mean you thought your brother's physical therapy was covered?*

Sucker.

I hear the clatter of roulette wheel spinning wildly as I tear open the envelope and remove the letter. *No more bets, no more cancellations.* Aaand … the magic number is fifty dollars. We have a winner, ladies and gentlemen. Disaster averted. God be praised.

I put away the leftovers from tonight's dinner. Jhimmy must have come home and gone out again, because the sink is full of dirty dishes that I don't feel like cleaning up. Maybe I'll just pretend I'm a PI in one of those best-selling novels and have a glass of white wine and go jogging on the beach. Oh, right. I live in New York, and it's the middle of November.

I open up Jhimmy's lunch containers, releasing a feculent cloud of vapor. *Blecch!* Shrimp residue in a sealed container will turn lethal in a couple of hours. I almost barf in the sink but manage to hold my breath, squirt some dishwashing liquid into the containers, and fill them with hot water and soap bubbles. I lurch into the hall, breathing heavily, and head to the shower to wash off a layer or two of filth.

By the time I step out of the bathroom wrapped in a towel, he's busy at our combination dining table and workspace. He looks up, flicks his hair out of his eyes, and temporarily forgets about whatever's on the computer screen, coming over for a close hug. And a kiss. One hand stays high as he presses against me, massaging the back of my neck, while the other slides down and squeezes my ass through the damp terrycloth.

"So, should we have sex now, or immediately?" he asks.

"If you have the energy …"

"Just let me finish posting this message."

He breaks away and goes back to his electronic mistress.

"Did you see this video clip on the *Nation*'s website?" he asks.

"You mean there's a video on the internet that *isn't* porn?"

"They're saying that the NYPD has been assigning undercover cops to infiltrate the peace movement under the pretext of *rooting out potential terrorist activity*."

"What? That's ridiculous."

"Yeah, why don't they just come out and say that it's meant to intimidate and harass us? It would be a lot closer to the truth," he says.

My ass is getting cold out here. I scoot toward the bedroom when I remember.

"Oh, yeah. Have you seen the coffee grinder?"

He's already completely absorbed in the story.

"Jhimmy." Nothing. "*Jhimmy!*"

"Jesus! What?"

"Where's the coffee grinder?"

"Oh, that. *Mi compañero* Bernardo needed to borrow it."

"You going to ask for it back?"

"Don't be telling me what to do—"

"It's not like borrowing a hammer to put up a picture. We use it every day."

"Look, this is between me and Bernardo, okay? You know, bros before hos."

What? Did you just call me—?

"Kidding! Jesus, can't you take a joke?"

"No, I can't. Not right now. I'm not in the mood."

"Wait—"

~

And then it's all okay, for a while.

"No, really, what's bugging you?" he says, his neck salty-sweet from our lovemaking.

I let out a long breath of air. "These two guys at work keep making sexist comments about women."

"So you threw them in a headlock till they begged for mercy, right?" he says, fingertips caressing my eyes, nose, and lips.

"They're too smart to say it to my face."

"What kind of stuff?"

"I'm trying to find an ex-contractor before the company can make her the scapegoat for all their screw-ups, and this twerp keeps talking about how he once knew this girl who was so skinny she had *no* tits and no ass. *But she sure knew how to use her mouth and cunt*, he says. And I have to listen to this."

"Compensation, I think it's called," Jhimmy says. "Like when a blind person develops really good hearing."

I crack up in spite of myself.

"Great, now I feel guilty for laughing at a misogynistic joke."

"Don't worry, your secret's safe with me," he says, toying with my brown sugary nipples. "It just sounds like the #MeToo movement hasn't made it up to the eleventh floor of the Schneerson Building yet."

I lie back and stare at the ceiling. "I just feel like no matter how much I do, it's never enough. Between my father and my brother and—" *You.* "—working for The Man ... I could use more support from you."

"Hmm."

"*Hmm?* What's that mean?"

"It means don't spoil the mood."

"Okay, I won't."

Not now, anyway.

~

"Oh, man, you shoulda seen her. This gorgeous redhead in a bright-green sweater on the steps of the Stock Exchange, with a set of honkers so round and smooth they looked like they were just out of the box. I'm talking mint condition."

Ah, I see that the morning shipment of testosterone has arrived.

The one substantial lead I have is that Kristel Santos, or someone purporting to be her, renewed her driver's license three weeks ago. But after coming up with nothing else, I spend the better part of the morning doing a state-by-state search of driving records and other computer-searchable information, and there is no simple, idiot-proof way for a PI to run a national criminal records check. It can make for some *reeeally* tedious searches. State by state. County by county. Precinct by precinct, if need be.

I need to talk to the people who knew Kristel Santos, but I've got to find them first.

I sit and face the computer screen.

Ah, internet: bottomless pit of information, quasi-information, and complete horseshit.

I hold my nose and dive in.

The standard databases yield nothing, but the file on Santos indicates that she graduated from John Adams High School in South Ozone Park less than a decade ago, so there might still be traces of her presence on social media. She couldn't have been *that* much of a loner, or expunged her records that far back. Even if it's some popular girl who hated her, I ought to be able to find *something*.

I log on to FriendSpace, and I'm narrowing the search to Kristel Santos's junior and senior years in high school when a distinctly angular female shadow looms over me.

"I don't believe the company is paying you to update your status on FriendSpace," says Velda Renko. She thrusts her face toward my computer screen, nearly poking out my eye with the tips of her metallic hairdo. "*Popular girls at John Adams High School?* Really!"

"So the company is aware of everything I do on this computer, is that it?"

"Let me give you a friendly piece of advice, Ms. Ortega. Just stay in your cubicle and do what you were hired to do."

"That's what I'm trying to do. Let me show you—"

"Any further infractions will be noted in my records. And no fraternizing with the other employees. Is that clear?"

"Except for Detective Gustella, right?"

A disgusted sound emanates from deep inside her esophagus as she nearly drills a hole in the floor with those stiletto heels.

What next? A blood test for endorphins to see if I'm having too much fun on the job?

"How's this for an answer, Ms. Renko? I promise you a lead by the end of the day if you would just—" *Shut the fuck up.* Uh, I mean "—stop berating me every time I cross an invisible line and let me do the job I was hired to do."

"That's exactly what I've been telling you to do."

Right.

"Then let me show you something."

Ms. Renko keeps a polite distance and remains at the entrance of my smooth-walled cell as Detective Gustella shows up and crams himself into my workspace, pressing about as close to me as a slab of form-fitting packing foam as I explain that I'm using social media for the legitimate purpose of locating the subject's friends and family members.

"Certain platforms allow for highly specific searches. So, let's say I put in the following terms—"

I type in: *gorgeous redhead in green sweater on steps of NY Stock Exchange 8:50 a.m.* Nothing on FriendSpace, but it directs me to a link to a photo on SnitFlit. I click on it.

"Is that her?"

Detective Gustella leans in close enough to inhale the pixels right off the screen. "I'll be damned. That's her all right."

"Give me fifteen minutes and I could probably tell you where she works, what she's looking for in a relationship, and if she's addicted to online poker. But that wouldn't be nearly as much fun as hunting down Kristel Santos's old high school classmates on FriendSpace."

I look up, but Ms. Renko is gone. I guess that means I've bought myself a few hours of uninterrupted work. Detective Gustella hovers over me for forty-five stressful minutes while I scroll through whichever circle of Hell is reserved for the unfiltered gossip, rumors, and backbiting of culturally deprived teenage girls living in the shadows of JFK International Airport and the old racetrack. It's a long, hard slog, until I find a girl who tagged a friend who tagged a friend who tagged a friend who—

Bingo. It's a seven-year-old photo of a coy, half-smiling teenage version of the face in the driver's license photo, posted by a friend named Kelly Tran. The teen Kristel Santos is wearing a light-brown tank top and squinting into the sun in front of a plastic kiddie pool in someone's yard. But the photo's real value lies in the fuzzy but recognizable tattoo on her left arm, just below the shoulder: a radiant cross superimposed on a sacred heart pierced by a thousand daggers.

That wasn't in her file.

"That tattoo is going to make her a lot easier to identify," says Detective Gustella. "Good work. Now see what you can dig up on this friend of hers," he says.

"Thanks. I'll do that."

He straightens up, yawning and stretching, his joints cracking, and he finally leaves me alone so I can breathe something besides his aggressively cheap aftershave. I take a screen-grab of the photo and send a copy to my smart-phone. Now that I've got something to go on, it's relatively easy to find Ms. Tran: after high school, she put in four years at Queens College CUNY, graduating with honors, then snagged an MA in occupational therapy from the La Guardia Institute of Technology, and currently works at the Calamari Nursing Home in Long Island City, where if there's any justice in the world, she's working her way up to depart-ment head.

But there is precious little justice in the world.

I'm chasing down a thread of communications between Ms. Tran and her college friends when I smack right into a brief flurry of messages between her and Kristel Santos on a now-defunct Flitter account discussing Kristel's plans to enroll in the fall semester at Triboro Community College.

By midafternoon I've got that lead I promised: Kristel Santos registered as a full-time student at Triboro on August 27. That's some reasonably long-distance planning on her part, suggesting that she intended to stick around more than seven weeks into the semester, at which point she disappeared.

"Big deal" is Detective Gustella's response to my discovery.

"She registered for four classes, so she must have a hundred classmates I could go talk to."

"*If* she ever showed up for class. But there's no way to know that, and we're not going to pay you to drive all the way out to Flushing to interview a hundred college kids."

"Then I'll talk to her professors."

"Just find her, okay?"

"How?"

"What do you mean, *how*?"

"How am I supposed to find her when you people won't let me do the job properly?"

"I thought you were supposed to be good at this."

Yeah, but I can't work miracles.

Droplets of sweat are forming in the hollows of my underarms despite the air conditioning, as the sleeping dragon inside me looses its hot breath and threatens to break free of its chains, the sharp ridges of its tail scraping against my spine as the beast claws at the base of my skull.

"Okay, Detective, okay," I manage to say. "There are two avenues to pursue here. *You* choose. And then turn me loose, goddamn it, and stop blocking my every move with all this *need to know* bullshit."

He's briefly distracted by the flashing images on the TV monitor hanging over my head, then he turns his attention to me. "Okay, shoot."

"Either you let me drive to Triboro Community College first thing tomorrow to interview anyone who might have known the subject, or you give me the names of the other people in her unit and I go and interview *them*."

His eyes flit back to the TV. "And in the meantime you keep scrolling through the databases till you come up with something better for me, all right?"

"Yeah, sure, fine."

"Let me see what I can do for you," he says, his eyes glued to the TV monitor. He peels himself away and heads for the front office.

What is so damn interesting on the TV? It's just some talking head, right?

I turn and look up. It's Detective Gustella's former boss, Police Commissioner John Patrick Mackey, the closed-caption text spooling out his words in thick black bars: BASICALLY SPOILED RICH KIDS COMING DOWN TO TRY TO PROVOKE YOU.

Provoke what? What's he talking about? Only now do I realize that the sound has been muted on every TV unit in the office for the last few minutes. The cameras cut to a line of riot police in full battle gear—body armor, NYPD vests, helmets, gas masks—carrying three-foot-long nightsticks, plastic cuffs, and what sure as hell look like rifles.

Their target: A swirl of humanity taking over Lower Broadway. I wonder where Jhimmy is in all this. He said he'd be there, handing out leaflets and getting people to sign up for the community center's e-newsletter before the rally's permit expires at 4:00 p.m.

The numbers on the screen click over to 4:01 p.m. EST as the riot police charge the crowd like thoroughbreds out of the starting gate, firing heavy rubber projectiles at the protesters on the front lines who go jackknifing to the ground regardless of age or gender. My heart lurches sideways. I look around the office helplessly as the mayhem rolls silently across the banks of TV screens, and I'm here, taking it all in, utterly powerless to help. Not a condition I'm used to. I scramble for my phone, dig it out of my purse, and send a text: *Jhimmy, get out of there*.

The riot squad casts its orange plastic nets across the human sea to ensnare the protesters, forcing them to their knees. After snapping on the plastic cuffs, the police blind the marchers with pepper spray just to show them who's boss, I guess, because no one's offering any serious resistance. And in an eyeblink it transforms into the violent repression in Chile in 1973, or the crackdown on Arab Spring protests in Cairo in 2011 or Tehran a decade later, as huge black shadows pass over the crowd, then solidify into attack helicopters hovering over the kneeling mass of people, and there must be some mistake because the helicopter doors slide open and police sharpshooters move into position aiming rifles at the crowd to intimidate anyone who somehow hasn't gotten the message yet.

This can't be happening. It must be an ad for an

action-adventure movie, and those are stuntmen and extras, and any minute a pumped-up movie star is going to lumber into view and entice us to come see the latest installment in the franchise.

But there is no mistake. This really is happening. The police really are rounding up a group of activists armed with little more than FOOD NOT BOMBS T-shirts and defiant attitudes for what the arresting officer tells us is the crime of FEEDING THE MARCHERS WITHOUT A PERMIT.

"If you care so much about these scumbags, why aren't you at the protest?" says Detective Gustella, stealing up behind me.

I turn to face him. "I don't have the luxury of spending the day protesting." I step back a bit to put some distance between us. "Or of getting strip-searched in a cell, which has become standard practice in some precincts."

Detective Gustella laughs, open-mouthed and freely, like a guy who's got a couple of cruise missiles in his arsenal while I'm standing there flat-footed, fiddling with a spitball and a plastic straw.

He informs me that his superiors have authorized my excursion to Flushing first thing tomorrow to interview Kristel Santos's professors. Depending on how that goes, and anything else I can bring to the table by the closing bell tomorrow, they'll decide what further duties to assign to me. Then he leans in and pretends to whisper in my ear words to the effect that, never mind what his superiors say, *he* still expects me to bring in a solid lead by the end of the day *as promised*, even if it takes me till midnight.

~

No reply from Jhimmy, which could mean either the police confiscated his phone, he's too busy counseling his fellow detainees about their legal rights, or he simply hasn't bothered to check his messages yet. I send another text anyway, telling him I have to work late tonight, but text me if you need me.

The TV monitors roar back to life with President Kinney's emphatic declaration that we're not invading Zabul Province yet, we're just mobilizing the troops because now is not the time to show weakness.

Six o'clock flies by in a streamlined blur. Seven o'clock zips by without even bothering to wave. Eight o'clock trudges by hauling a barge full of pig iron while the Red Army Chorus sings the "Song of the Volga Boatmen." By the time ten o'clock crawls in, ragged and emaciated, its parched lips begging for water, I can barely focus on the most basic information on the college's website about the professors I'll be interviewing tomorrow—their office locations, emails, phone numbers, and brief bios—but I still haven't found any solid evidence that Kristel Santos actually attended any classes there.

When in doubt, go through the file one more time. Maybe I missed something. I rub my eyes and check it page by page, looking for any details that might help pinpoint the specific time frame for the event that led to her dropping off the grid, if indeed any single "event" is responsible for her apparent breakdown. The available data, plus a dash of intuition on my part, suggest that whatever happened must have taken place just two to three weeks before she was sent home from Iraq.

A whiff of ammonia-based cleaning fluid curls up my nose and jolts me to full alertness. *Where am I? What time is it?* I look up. Maylita is pushing a cart full of cleaning supplies through the narrow space between the rows of cubicles, wiping scuff marks off the featureless cubicle walls and emptying trash cans.

"*¿Qué está haciendo aquí?*" she asks. What are you doing here?

"*Parece que las dos estamos trabajando tarde esta noche.*" Seems like we're both working late tonight. We keep talking in Spanish.

"No, I mean what are you doing with all those papers?"

"Oh. I guess you don't see too many people studying printed documents in this office, do you?"

"None at all, señorita Ortega."

"Please, call me Felicidad."

I give her a brief rundown of the thrilling world of forensic accounting and document examination, but instead of helping, I sense that I'm making her feel inadequate in some way, so I try another tack. Her cart has receptacles for three separate trash bags: one for food garbage, another for recyclable metal and plastic, another for paper. I reach into the bin full of crumpled papers, pull out a couple of handfuls, and spread them out on my desktop.

"Where did these papers come from?" I ask, sifting through the discarded memos and yellow sheets of legal paper.

"The executive conference room."

"Okay, well, here's an unusual item." I gather up the hand-ripped pieces of several sheets of brown bag paper, some with partially torn receipts still stapled to them, and the two of us easily put a couple of these crude jigsaw puzzles back together. It's a week's worth of lunch orders from a takeout deli, written in blue ballpoint pen.

"Okay, what do you see?" I ask.

She stands there fidgeting, then shrugs.

"Go ahead, tell me what you see."

"I don't see anything besides what they ordered for lunch this week." She's already collecting the memos and papers in her vinyl-gloved hands and stuffing them back into the correct receptacle.

"All right, let me show you something," I say, holding up the deli receipt with today's date. "One: we know there were at least seven different people at today's meeting, and we've got handwriting samples from each of them."

"Oh. Yes. ¿Y *qué?*"

"So that could come in very handy if we ever want to

compare writing samples and determine if a signature is genuine or a forgery. Two: We know they were there long enough to have lunch."

She nods, though it seems like an obvious statement to her.

"Three: They can all *write*."

She's a bit taken aback by this observation.

"I do a lot of work with less-than-fully-legal immigrants, Maylita, and some of them are functionally *analfabetos*, especially in English. Never take anything for granted. Remember, I wasn't there, but I can say with reasonable confidence that at least seven fairly well-educated people were present at today's meeting, and stayed long enough to eat lunch. Right?"

"Not *highly* educated?"

"Look at their food choices. Ordering out for deli sandwiches. These guys are middle management, not top execs."

She's starting to get the idea.

"Okay, so on Monday this guy ordered a Number Thirty-one with lettuce, tomato, onions, and hot peppers. The next day he asked for liverwurst on a poppy seed bagel with lettuce, tomato, onions, and hot mustard. What does that tell you?"

"He likes things spicy."

"Okay, what else can you tell me?"

She studies the handwritten menus, her eyes flitting back and forth from one day to the next.

She says, "The same person ordered tuna salad on wheat with tomato on Monday, Tuesday, and Wednesday?"

"How can you tell?"

"It looks like the same handwriting to me."

"Very good. What else?"

"And this guy is going to have a heart attack someday from all that cholesterol. He ordered the Belly Buster with everything four days in a row."

She stifles a tiny giggle at this glimpse of her bosses' all-too-human frailties.

I can't help smiling as well. "You've got what it takes to be a first-rate investigator, Maylita. You're observant, you're a fast learner, and believe me, no one would ever suspect that the cleaning woman is the one spying on them. They wouldn't even notice you."

She locks eyes with me, giving me a deep, troubled look that says her invisibility is a rather sensitive matter.

"I'm sorry, but believe me, that's an asset in this business," I tell her. "And you know how to talk to people. That's important, too. You want people to be comfortable around you, especially during an interview, unless you're taking a deposition or something."

"What's that?"

I explain that's when you take a formal written statement from a witness in a location other than a courtroom, often in exchange for the promise that by doing so, they won't have to testify in open court.

She says my parents must be very proud of me, but when I turn it around on her she smiles sadly and says it's too late for her to start a new career. She's already working extra shifts and making all kinds of sacrifices to put her kids through college so at least *they* can become professionals just like me, and that we educated young Latinas are a credit to *la raza*, helping our people move up in this country, which may be more than my shoulders can bear at the moment, but I appreciate the sentiment.

"Thanks for the kind words," I say. Some days, a few kind words is all I have to go on.

And since the next generation of Latinos are experienced in more than one language and culture, they understand the world better than the average American, she says. "Look at this garbage on the American TV news. You want to find out what's *really* going on in the world, you have to watch Univision or BBC Español."

I nod in agreement. I remember my dad telling me that

when the US invaded Panama back in the late 1980s, he had to watch the Spanish news to find out that the air strikes aimed at General Noriega's compound also leveled the neighborhood around it and killed at least a thousand civilians whose only crime was being from Panama. The mainstream US networks never mentioned this. We saw the damage they never showed you. We saw a different war.

Maylita says she'd better finish up, and I say sure, my mind already racing toward endlessly branching avenues of investigation. I hop on the computer and rev it up like an outlaw on a customized Harley-Davidson tearing through the Mojave Desert on a wild ride to Tijuana. I stay off the main highways, far from the glow of the neon signs and the speed traps, keeping to the back roads, gullies, and arroyos where you can still cross paths with farmers who grow their own vegetables and reporters who will actually describe what they witnessed in all its horrific and tragic glory instead of hiding behind the claim that their job is simply to report what Senator X said at such-and-such committee meeting, not comment on it or analyze it or run it through the Bullshit Detector™ as if cutting and pasting the official press release word for word into the first three paragraphs of your story is the ultimate sign of journalistic integrity and objectivity rather than merely phoning it in, you fucking bunch of wankers.

I ignore the NO ENTRY signs, roar past the tollbooths, and ram through the crossing gates, my tailpipes screaming far into the night.

Until I find it, in a deeply archived Spanish-language news source called Noticiero-Zaragoza.com, buried under layers of seaweed and silt. The details of what happened the night a fanatical splinter group of nationalist insurgents stormed the top three floors of the Ishtar Hartley Hotel, three blocks from the banks of the Tigris River in Baghdad, and launched a deadly attack on a six-person team of Silver

Bullet *force protectors* who were standing near their vehicle in the hotel parking lot. One member apparently fled to safety while the five remaining team members took up defensive positions behind the vehicle and returned fire. But the vehicle was lightly armored and easily perforated by heavy-caliber machine-gun fire, resulting in the deaths of two male team members, names not given, leaving two women and one man. The man, Thomas Ard, age twenty-eight, survived by rolling behind a concrete traffic barrier, which was targeted by several RPGs, or possibly a Russian Katyusha rocket according to some reports, but somehow Ard survived. One of the women, name not given, apparently panicked and abandoned her post, leaving the last two members of the team vulnerable to enemy fire. The other woman, Megan Bishop, age twenty-two, remained behind the heavily damaged vehicle and continued to return fire, emptying two twenty-round clips despite being seriously wounded by flying shrapnel, with multiple fractures in both arms, until she ran out of ammunition. Ard then dashed across open ground under heavy fire and rescued Bishop, carrying her to safety and radioing for an ambulance, which arrived within minutes and rushed Ard and Bishop to an Iraqi-run medical facility once called Saddam Hussein Hospital, where Ard threatened the surgeons with his weapon if they didn't save his wounded comrade.

That's one hell of a story.

It all revolves around three people.

And if I can't find at least two of those people in the next couple of days, I don't deserve to call myself an investigator.

CHAPTER NINE

Ruth

She was still clutching the double-edged dagger when the women laid her out to wash her clean. The dagger was practically fused to her hand under a thick layer of dried blood, but most of it turned out to be goat's blood. Her upper body was covered with scratches and bruises, with a nasty gash above her right temple, but they all agreed that she had been very lucky.

And now they were trekking west again, the storm clouds gone, as if they had never existed. The clear blue sky stretched from horizon to horizon, and the sun was beating down, baking their senses like flatbread on hot stones.

Ruth trudged along as Miryam explained that they had used up the last of Ruth's water supply washing the blood out of her clothes and hair, but that Yedidyah the Nazirite and the two Persian guards had donated a portion of their water rations to her.

She nodded to Rashda on her right, who responded with a quick nod of his own, then to Manukka on her left, who seemed to be keeping closer watch on her than usual, his eyes exploring the gaps in her loose-fitting garment of black goat hair.

Hanokh tramped alongside Yiskah and his newborn son, the only members of this new exodus riding in a cart instead of walking. Aside from a little soreness, Hanokh seemed to be recovering from Ruth's impromptu surgery. She caught him peeking at her, but he quickly looked away.

Yedidyah the Nazirite was somewhere near the front of the troop. And Naomi was ... where *was* Naomi?

She begged Asherah for strength and guidance as Manukka tried to keep her engaged with riddles.

Ben-Isaiah wedged himself between Ruth and Manukka. "I don't know why you persist in calling on this female god, but if we don't watch our mouths the God of Yehudah will send us back to the land of Mitzrayim to be sold as slaves."

Ruth stumbled and nearly dropped her water-skins. The two men on either side grabbed her to keep her from falling.

"Careful," said the prophet. "We had a hell of a time purifying you in the middle of the desert with so little water."

"I didn't realize I needed to be purified."

Most men would have given up by now, but the prophet clearly relished the challenge of instructing this headstrong female in the ways of the Yehudim.

"All weapons of war are unclean," the prophet explained.

"*What?*" Ruth exclaimed. "Why didn't anybody tell me—?"

"The sword, the knife, the dagger, the spear—"

"How about arrows?" said Manukka, unable to keep the sarcasm out of his voice.

"The shaft is clean but the head is unclean."

Rashda burst out laughing at the prophet's words. "So it's all right for her to handle the shaft but not the head?"

"Correct." The prophet turned back to Ruth, ignoring Rashda's fit of snickering. "But for now, you have been purged of uncleanliness."

"Then why is everybody looking at me sideways?" she said, her fingers seeking the handle of her dagger for reassurance.

"Because when the Persian guard returned with you to the camp, you were covered with unclean blood."

Ruth strained to recall the details, the fresh wound on her forehead throbbing until she remembered something.

"There was a goat. Where's the rest of the goat?"

"We left it there," Manukka said.

"But the storm-gods only feed on the blood. We could have eaten the rest—"

"*Absolutely not*," the prophet said. "You defiled it by offering it to the Babylonian storm-gods."

"Yet you are still walking beside me."

"Because saving a life outweighs all other laws."

"And she saved *twenty* lives," said Manukka, casting an admiring glance at Ruth's many cuts and bruises.

~

When darkness spread its wings over the land once more, the women took turns tending the oil lamp burning near the new mother and her newborn son to keep the hostile desert-spirits at bay.

Ruth chose the middle watch, the loneliest and darkest time of the night. And Ben-Isaiah elected to sit with her so that he could prattle on about the land of milk and honey and sing the praises of his namesake.

When she felt reasonably sure they were safe from prying eyes and ears, she asked him to explain the legal standing of childless widows under Yehudi law.

Ben-Isaiah fiddled with the fringes of his garment, and Ruth knew it meant bad news. For whenever he spoke about going up to Jerusalem and following in the footsteps of his idol, the great prophet Isaiah, which he pronounced *Yeshayahu*, his voice filled with glory and shook with emotion, and his eyes sparkled.

But now the words came out flat and colorless, as if he were summarizing a monthly expense report for the king's tax collectors: When a woman marries she becomes part of her husband's household. If the man dies childless, his widow must marry her late husband's brother in order to produce a son to carry on his name. If he has no living brothers, the widow must marry her husband's nearest kinsman, and so on. If no kinsman can be found, the widow is left without legal standing of any kind, like a piece of unclaimed furniture, although she is permitted to glean the leftovers from a rich man's field to keep from starving.

In other words, childless widows were one rung above beggars and whores on the social ladder, unless they could find a man to latch on to.

See what comes of having no priestesses? Ruth thought. *Every other tribe has them. But I married into the tribe of Yehudah.*

And she had worried what Naomi's response would be when Makhlon brought her home and presented his pagan wild woman of a bride to her, but Naomi gave her a big smile and threw her arms around Ruth, genuinely thrilled that her son had found a strong young woman to provide her with grandsons. There was surely some disappointment that he hadn't chosen a nice, modest Yehudi girl, but when you lived in the greatest crossroads in the world, the crucible of nations, what did you expect? When you came from a miniscule and easily outnumbered tribe that had needed to adapt to alien customs or perish many times in its long and troubled history, some cross-cultural drift was inevitable. And frankly, the tribe of the Yehudim was in need of fresh blood.

The shadows of the oil lamp's flame danced across the baby's glowing cheeks, his tiny head rising and falling contentedly on his mother's chest.

Ruth knew that Yahaweh had an equally powerful female counterpart. How could He not? After all, what were men without women? A bunch of savages who would kill each other off in a matter of months, if not weeks.

One reason she loved her own Yehudi warrior and dreamed of him still was because he enjoyed her in all her states—fresh and clean straight from the *mikweh*, yes, yet something visibly came over him when he took her before she had washed the sweat of fanning the cooking fires from her body, excited by the rank animal smell of a sweaty female, something that went deeper than all the rules set down in writing, because it was older than writing, older than clothing and pottery, older than speech itself.

~

She was startled awake by the pressure of a man's arm across her chest, pinning her down so he could press his loins against her face. There was only one layer of cloth between the man's fully aroused penis and her lips, and it was about to slip off. She grabbed his rigid flesh before he could uncover her nakedness, and reached for her dagger, her hand closing around—*nothing*. The dagger was gone, the space empty, and the oil lamp's flame was out so she couldn't see who it was or see his free arm swinging through the night to smack her hard against the temple so he could retreat into the safety of the shadows.

~

At the first light of dawn, Ruth grabbed her sack and marched to the edge of the camp, the metal clattering around her ankles. She dropped the sack with a loud clank, squatted in the dust, and went through it, taking inventory. Two of her daggers were missing, the double-edged one and the one with the goddess-shaped handle. Only two weapons remained, along with a pair of finely wrought ax-heads, a set of old utensils, and a bag of dried date pits.

Damn it! Where are my daggers?

Sleepers arose, tent flaps opened, heavy-lidded eyes turned somnolently in her direction to see what the ruckus was about.

She threw sharp glances back at every damn one of them, but could not read their hearts.

Modesty be damned, who the hell was it? Which one of you—?

She still possessed a deadly arsenal that would enable her to hack her way through four or five men and mutilate a dozen more before the mercenaries put an end to her rampage, because whoever stole her precious daggers had somehow left the curved dagger and short stabbing sword behind.

She had a good mind to strap on the sword and unleash such fury that, many years hence, men would still speak in hushed tones of her wading into the encampment and massacring every soul within reach until she was ankle-deep in blood.

How's that for unclean, you sons of Belial?

All of you who piss against a wall, may your right eye be darkened. May you go down alive into She'ol, every last one of you.

~

The exiles finished loading the pack animals and set off. Ruth followed at a distance, but she could still hear them gossiping about her, their words carried along on the prevailing wind: *She just grabbed his dick, the shameless hussy. I know, what is she, dick crazy or something? First Hanokh, now this . . .*

She stopped in her tracks, counted out a hundred and fifty paces, and followed at a great distance, and no one in the group dared to come near her, her anger burned so.

~

The signs were there, if you knew how to read them.

A few sparse blades of grass bending in the breeze. A few scattered patches of green dotting the otherwise featureless landscape, clinging brazenly to the windblown rocks.

The land was rising, slowly.

Ruth got up and stretched her tired bones and reached for her sack.

It felt heavier than the last time she handled it. She tested it a few times just to make sure. It was definitely heavier.

She gently lowered the sack and knelt beside it, loosening the drawstring. Her eyes flitted this way and that to check if anyone was spying on her, and when she was ready, she pulled it open.

Someone had returned her double-edged dagger.

She wondered whether they had done it out of remorse or fear of what she might do if she ever found out who had taken it so he could assault her like the lowest kind of slave girl.

Not that it mattered.

If she ever discovered her assailant's identity, no matter who it was, he'd learn a thing or two about what a woman can do with a knife.

~

After three more days of hiking through the wilderness, the exiles gathered in the pale green shade of a gurgling spring, drew water and poured it out before Yahaweh, and said *We have sinned*, though no one within earshot confessed to attempted rape.

"All who are thirsty, come and drink!" cried the prophet. "See how the God of Heaven provides for his children, and opens his hand to the stranger! Come and drink your fill! And when we go up to Jerusalem, the God of all the earth will provide bread and wine and milk in abundance, even for the widow, the stranger, and for all those who return to the House of God."

But Ruth wasn't returning; she was going there for the first time. So did the prophet's words apply to her or not?

The rugged landscape rose steeply, thickening into dry forest as they snaked through the narrow passes and ascended the mountains of Moab, following in the footsteps of Moses himself.

The young prophet insisted on teaching Ruth the Torah from the very beginning.

"Adam was a bit of a wild man, at first," he explained. "So God created Khava, the first woman, as an *'ezer k'negdo* for him."

"As a strong partner for him?" Ruth said.

"No no no, *'ezer* means a *helper*."

"But *'az* means *strong* in the tongues of Aram and Tyre, and even among the Moabites. The proof of Khava's strength is that she's the one who seeks knowledge from the forbidden fruit."

Miryam nodded enthusiastically while the prophet shook his head.

Toward nightfall they reached a plateau at the site of an abandoned fortress from the days of King Solomon. The corners of the stone towers rose squarely toward a deep-blue sky, still sharply defined after centuries of exposure to the wind and sand, far more durable than bricks of baked clay.

Surely such a structure contained a sanctuary, the prophet insisted. But when they entered the inner recesses, they found a pair of standing stones of slightly different sizes whose features had been erased by the ravages of time. The prophet tried to explain them away as unclean images from the days of the wicked kings who did evil in the eyes of the Lord, but it was obvious to anyone who bothered to look that they represented Yahaweh and his Asherah.

The next morning they drew near the base of Mount Nebo, where Moses is buried in an unmarked grave, and the prophet pointed, his voice quavering with excitement. "There it is! The King's Highway leading north to Damascus. Once we cross it, we will be perched upon the highest ridge of Gilead, and you will truly feel the presence of the Lord."

The prophet wasn't exaggerating this time. By midday Mount Nebo was behind them and they had reached the eastern ridge, overlooking the hundred-mile-long trench of the Arabah Valley and the fertile plains of Moab, two thousand feet below. The Salt Sea sparkled in the sun like a scroll of silver inscribed with letters of molten gold. The hill country of Yehudah rose up to greet them on the other side of the valley, less than twenty miles away, and the air was so clear they could just make out the hazy skyline of Jerusalem in the distance.

The exiles pushed and shoved to get a glimpse of the glorious sight, but the few remaining goats and sheep were getting nervous, straining against their ropes.

"Look at all that water!" said Miryam, enraptured by the sight of the wide river feeding into the expansive sea.

But the waters of the Salt Sea are too bitter to drink, Yedidyah the Nazirite explained, looking south toward the site of the ruined city of Ar, once the capital of the Moabite kingdom.

"It's God's way of reminding us that the Ammonites and the Moabites did not meet us with food and water when we came out of the land of Mitzrayim," the prophet said.

"And the Moabites were allied with the Assyrians in the last war, remember?" Mesha said.

"Take care where you tread, my friend," said Ben-Isaiah. "For Moses himself teaches us that the stranger may live anywhere he chooses among the settlements in our midst, and that we must not ill-treat or oppress him."

"Maybe you didn't hear me right," said Mesha, stepping closer, his hand on the hilt of his sword. Miryam let out a little yelp. "I said they were allied with the Assyrians who invaded the kingdom of Israel, raped and murdered our cousins, and scattered the surviving population throughout their empire."

The frayed rope finally gave way and the panicking goats scattered among the rocks and scrub trees, the sheep following blindly. Miryam ran to help the others chasing after them, the men cursing as they slipped and stumbled on the loose rocky soil.

Mesha confronted the so-called prophet: "Why are you defending this Moabite harlot?"

The scar over Ruth's right eye began to quiver.

"As a sojourner among us, she is entitled to the protection of the tribes who make up the covenant," the prophet said.

"You mean the *two tribes* that are left after *her people* wiped the other ones off the face of the earth!" Mesha said, nudging Ruth toward the edge of the cliff. "That's *ten* tribes gone!"

Ruth's eyes flitted across the rocky promontory, seeking a protector to come forward *right now* and make himself heard.

"The God of our fathers commands us not to hate the stranger," the prophet pleaded. "For we were strangers in the land of Mitzrayim."

Mesha edged close enough to shove Ruth into the abyss. Her Persian protectors were busy rounding up loose animals, wrestling with the skittish lambs and rolling in the dust, so Ruth reached into her sack and seized the first object her fingers closed around—a heavy iron chisel—as Mesha grabbed the sack and yanked it away from her.

"You better watch it. This chisel can split a stone in two," said Ruth, wielding the blunt instrument like a talisman, as if her tormentors were a pair of meddlesome demons who could be intimidated by a piece of man-made iron.

The mercenaries laughed as they unsheathed their swords.

"Keep away from me!" Ruth said, weighing whether she should swing the chisel at Mesha's head or his knees.

Yedidyah the Nazirite rushed toward them, his loose hair covered with dust. He tried to calm his comrades with gentle words, while Rashda and Manukka blocked the attack with the blunt ends of their spears.

Ben-Isaiah said, "Peace, brothers! You are profaning yourselves within sight of the holy city."

The Persian commander held his ground and challenged the Yehudite mercenaries directly: "You couldn't just put up with all this for another day or two, could you? No, you had to force me to declare in front of all these witnesses that whoever seeks the life of Ruth the Moabite must seek my life also."

"Of course you'd stick up for her, she's practically one of you!"

"What the *hevel* is going on here?" said Naomi, her voice cutting through the chaos.

Naomi who hadn't said two words to Ruth since the birth of Asher. Naomi who had plodded along for weeks unable to see beyond her own grief.

"What is this foolishness?" she said, the power of her words a marvel. "Have you no shame? Drawing your weapons on a defenseless widow."

"She doesn't look that defenseless to me," said Mesha, itching for blood.

But as Naomi reprimanded them in the name of Rachel, Leah, Bilhah and Zilpah, their swords seemed to wither in their hands and swing loosely toward the dust of the earth, their ardor fizzled.

For now.

~

The air grew warmer as they descended a narrow trail hugging the walls of a ravine. The rushing stream widened to a rolling river, and the rocky trail was soon enveloped by a canopy of succulent shrubs and young fruit trees in early bloom.

Ben-Isaiah and Manukka stayed close by Ruth, while Miryam chose to walk alongside Yedidyah the Nazirite after his daring heroics on the ridge.

"I've got a riddle for you," Manukka said. "I am a soaring bird—"

"Oh my God, are those *wildflowers*?"

Ruth rushed to the edge of the path and knelt before a patch of red and yellow flowers amid a sea of clover. She leaned closer to breathe in the sweetness and ran her hand over the lush green carpet, caressing the tiny flowers, awed by their delicacy and tenacity. She dug her fingers into the rich, dark soil and brought up a handful of crumbly loam and squeezed it in her fist, compressing it as hard as she could. She opened her palm, and the clod of earth stuck together, retaining its shape as it must have done when the goddess first formed a man of clay and breathed the breath of life into his nostrils. She wiggled her fingers and broke up the clod of dirt, releasing the mineral-rich scent of earthly fecundity, of eternal rejuvenation, and her eyes grew moist as she realized that whoever was blessed with the tillage of this land would never know hunger. The prophet's words about the Promised Land were true, and she had doubted him. And the moisture from her eyes reached down and kissed the moisture of the earth.

She wiped her eyes, inadvertently smearing her face with dirt.

While the others filled their water skins with the clear, refreshing waters of the river, Ruth clamped her eyes shut and erased the signs of weakness with her the sleeve of her cloak.

The strong-armed Persian commander helped her get to her feet.

"I can stand on my own, thanks," she said. "I just haven't seen such abundance in a long time."

"Wait till you see the pomegranate trees in the valley of Eshkol, heavy with fruit," the prophet said.

Manukka posed his riddle again: "I am a soaring bird that turns into a prison. What am I?"

Ruth gazed at the brave Persian warrior and the wise Yehudi prophet, her stalwart defenders. And she knew the answer.

"Love."

~

They reached the plains of Moab, the verdant basin at the northern edge of the Salt Sea, on the east bank of the meandering waters of the river Jordan.

Rashda and Yedidyah the Nazirite took the first shift at the head of the column.

The spring flood was long past, so it didn't take long to find a place to ford the river. When the exiles reached the banks of the Jordan, they washed their hands and prayed, for who so wades into a stream with unclean hands invites the wrath of God. And the cleansing waters of the Jordan washed around their ankles as they stepped into the current. They raised the hems of their cloaks and the Persian-style fringes of their garments, but Ruth welcomed the cooling waters flowing between her legs, pasting her skirt to her calves as she splashed between the sun-washed stones.

Ben-Isaiah pointed out the ruined walls of Jericho a few miles to the northwest, by a spring where the land begins to rise again up to the hill country of Ephrayim. With easy access to sweet water and bountiful farmland, it was easy to see why they had chosen to build their homes in the bottom of the valley, but those same factors also made them vulnerable to attack.

The northern stretch of the valley exhibited marvel after marvel, like the islands of asphalt—dark lumps of so-called Yehudite bitumen the size of headless bulls floating on the surface of the dead sea.

Rashda said, "Is that it? Is that the fabled oil called *naphtha*?"

"It's one of the ingredients," said Yedidyah the Nazirite.

"I've seen *naphtha* used on the field of battle," Rashda went on. "It clings to whatever it touches, and once ignited, it cannot be put out with water or any other liquid."

"Try using sand," said Ruth.

The two warriors stared at her.

"What? It works."

"Well, even a dose of flaming *naphtha* is better than one of the Ashkenazim's poisoned arrows," said Yedidyah.

"The who?" asked Rashda.

"The tribe of Ashkenaz. *Ash-ken-az*. What do you guys call them—the Sashkas?"

"Oh, God no, the Sakas—" Rashda shuddered. The tribe of the Saka possessed a secret recipe for a type of poison that was notoriously toxic. Every warrior feared their poison-tipped arrows—whether Assyrian, Persian, or Babylonian, even the Greek mercenaries feared them. A direct hit was fatal, excruciatingly so, and the slightest nick left a foul-smelling, festering wound that killed the victim slowly over the next several weeks.

Ruth stopped dead, thunderstruck, for they had just described Makhlon and Khilyon's deaths, which she thought was a tragic coincidence at the time, but now her suspicions awakened with a new fury: someone *could* have poisoned them in a manner that mimicked death by snakebite, and her first priority in the great city of Jerusalem was to unearth the rivalries he had spoken of. Were they enough to motivate the oldest crime?

The prophet stumbled into the dry streambed they would follow up to the hill country. He spread his arms in triumph as if wishing to encompass the entire band of returning exiles at once, filled his belly with the north wind and cried out, "Let us ascend this lofty mountain and bring tidings of joy to Zion!"

～

The higher they climbed, the stronger the wind blew, the same biting wind that had ground the stones of Jericho to dust and fed the flames of the smelting furnaces at Ir-nahash, the City of Coppersmiths, just visible on the eastern side of the valley twenty miles south of the Salt Sea. Ruth could tell they were still working the mines, though the men of Rekhab said the veins were dying out, the very mines that Moses had spoken of when he stood on the eastern ridge and proclaimed that the land that his children were about to enter possessed rocks of iron and hills where they could mine copper, but he forgot to mention the slave labor needed to do so.

The soil was much drier than in the fertile plains of Moab, and from this vantage point, the southern stretch of the Arabah Valley looked like a giant scar across the land, a great unhealed wound, with the enslaved laborers' walled enclosures dug into mountains whose lofty crags were as sharp as ogres' teeth.

They stopped for the night under a rocky outcropping, and set out the next morning, working their way up the patchy terrain, and it was all stones and sand, stones and sand, and occasionally a patch of grass for the sheep to gobble up or a bushy tree growing too low to the ground to offer even an inch of shade. And then the high plateau, with its ruined cities, their fortifications razed by the armies of King Nebuchadnezzar of Babylon, the lush greenery of the eastern slope a distant memory.

Then another deep valley in the parched highlands with a torturously steep rock face to negotiate.

The prophet scrambled on ahead, forgetting all else in his excitement. Others followed. After helping Miryam surmount the steepest part of the ascent, Yedidyah the Nazirite came sliding back down to carry one of the lambs on his shoulders. Yiskah strapped the baby to her back, and Hanokh pulled her up with him, straining but sure-footed as a mountain goat. Some of the men clambered up the steep slope as fast as they could, raining loose rocks and pebbles on those below.

Ruth and Naomi were left at the bottom.

There had to be an easier way. The group must have strayed from the main route, for the weak and elderly couldn't possibly make it up this leg of the climb without assistance.

Ruth held her hand out for Naomi. But the wind was in a jealous mood and a sharp gust sliced through the air between them, nudging them apart. Naomi gathered her strength against the forces swirling around them and gripped Ruth's hand, and together the two women scaled the rocky path toward the summit.

~

When they reached the top, they found grown men openly weeping at the sight of the ruined temple.

Great blocks of carved stones lay on their sides, unmoved from the spot where they had fallen on that fateful day nearly half a century before.

Stone lintels dangled at awkward angles, still bearing the scars of the all-devouring flames.

The burnt skeletons of houses, as yet unrisen.

The walls of the city decaying and useless against a foe.

And a buzzing, a yammering, a drawing in of breath, as the women of Jerusalem gaped at her mother-in-law's ragged cloak and her fraying sandals and her sun-withered skin and asked, "Can this be Naomi?"

And Ruth, looking beyond them to the jagged soot-smeared ruins, thinking, We came all this way for *this?*

CHAPTER TEN

Felicity

But first, a nice long scenic drive to Flushing, Queens. Once I'm clear of the cordon of traffic cops in blast-resistant armor controlling access to the ramps onto the bridge, I point the company car toward Queens Boulevard and the Long Island Expressway. I'm trying to make it to Triboro Community College in time to catch the professors between classes, so of course I end up in a snarl of traffic behind a cement mixer, a beer truck, and a rig hauling an oversized load of scrap metal. The only thing missing is the school bus.

By the time I reach the Triboro campus, the weather guys on WWTF are predicting a warm spell, although they take a moment to remind us that global warming is a complete and total hoax started by China to ruin our economy.

The main quad is a jumble of prefab modular units that looks more like a strip mall than a college campus, including a line of trailers that have been fitted with classrooms.

The first stop on my itinerary is Gibbings Hall, the crumbling brick-and-mortar structure where Professor Patricia Woolley is teaching an introductory course on the archaeology of the Ancient Near East.

I pulled her photo from the college website, but it's clearly out of date, showing a vivacious woman of around forty with straight dark hair who looks smart and sassy enough to make a four-thousand-year-old mummy sit up and take notice. But the ravages of time have reduced the aging professor in the darkened classroom to a dried-up husk, like something a spider left dangling in its web, her disheveled hair a puff of raw cotton.

I slip into the classroom and take a seat in the back as she brings up the next slide—an alabaster relief from the palace of King Sennacherib in Nineveh from around 680 BCE, depicting the aftermath of a bloody battle, with a couple of scribes in the foreground tallying up the body count by going through a big pile of severed heads.

The next slide is a Greek foot soldier's protective headgear, and all I can say is that you have to marvel at a culture that saw fit to carve *eyebrows* on a bronze war helmet. Professor Woolley switches to the subject of the Greek influence on ancient Israel during the Hellenistic period following Alexander the Great's conquest of Judea in 332 BCE, which put an end to Persian control of the region.

I squint reflexively when the cheap fluorescent lights come on, blinking against the coldness of the light as the students close their notebooks, pull out their phones, and shamble out past me.

Professor Woolley is gathering her notes, squaring the pages on the lectern so they'll fit neatly into a worn manila folder. I approach and tell her I'm looking for one of her students.

"I've got over three hundred students," she says, jamming the folder into an overstuffed tote bag. "Which one are you looking for?"

She flinches when I say *Kristel Santos* and tries to hide it by gathering her pens and whiteboard markers and snapping a thick rubber band around them, twice.

"She hasn't attended class since the second week of the semester," she says, keeping her eyes on the color-coded labels as she flips through the folders in her bag.

"Any idea why she dropped the class?"

"Students drop all the time without discussing their reasons with the faculty," she says, shuffling through the mismatched folders.

"Does anybody know where she went?"

She freezes, pretending to study a folder marked HUM 134: INTRODUCTION TO ARCHAEOLOGY.

"Look, this is a common problem," she says. "A lot of the vets simply stop coming."

"So you know she's a vet."

A rigidity comes over her features, a hardening of wrinkles. "Look, what is this about? Why are you looking for this particular student?"

I offer her one of my business cards.

"I'm working for Cadmium Solutions, and—"

"*Cadmium?* The company that got a $700 million contract to change the goddamn *lightbulbs* in the Green Zone while looters were smashing their way through five millennia of priceless artifacts less than a mile away at the National Museum in Baghdad?"

She shoulders her tote bag and marches past me, conversation ended.

I pursue her down the hall.

"Then you should appreciate that I'm trying to locate a former student of yours and recover a missing artifact."

I can tell I've struck a chord, but she keeps driving full steam ahead. "What kind of artifact?"

"A rare Hebrew scroll of some kind."

"Oh no, *please* don't tell me this is about the Baghdad Scroll." A tinkle of laughter falls from her lips.

"I don't really know that much about—"

"Because the *genuine* Baghdad Scroll is not indigenous to Iraq," she says, without turning around. "The material evidence firmly ties it to late-sixth-century-BCE Judea."

I'm close behind her.

"Then how did it get to Iraq?" I say, weaving through the crush of students heading to class.

"It didn't," she says. "Every now and then a 'lost' book surfaces on the antiquities market, and it always turns out to be a hoax. The so-called Baghdad Scroll in question is nothing but a modern forgery of no scholarly interest whatsoever."

"That's not what my sources are telling me."

She turns so abruptly a couple of students bump into us. "Listen! If you don't stop harassing me this instant, I will have you ejected from this campus by Public Safety. Is that clear?"

"Clear enough."

～

"You told her you're working for Cadmium Solutions? No wonder you got your ass handed to you. She hates that corporation almost as much as I do."

I'm on the phone with my older and more experienced cousin Filomena, who's telling me everything I did wrong.

"You should have gone to her under the pretext of being a student or something," she says.

"Why does she hate Cadmium so much?"

"Professor Patricia Woolley? Sounds like you didn't go too deep into the background check on this one, *prima*, unless—oh, that's right. This happened before you were born."

"What happened?"

I'm trying not to sound like a whiny child, and only partly succeeding.

She fills me in: "Back in the early '90s, Dr. Woolley was a promising assistant professor at Princeton surveying a stretch of the Iraqi desert when she stumbled upon a career-making discovery: the ruins of an entire city, untouched for millennia. Even the looters didn't know the place existed."

"This place have a name?"

"According to the artifacts unearthed at the site, it was called Mashkan-Shinar. A whole city, forgotten for centuries."

"So what happened?"

"A little thing called the Gulf War. And just like that, Iraq's archaeological sites were off limits for the next ten years. Then we invaded the place, and you know the rest."

Shit. I really did blow this one, didn't I?

"So she doesn't get tenure at Princeton, and ends up teaching at Triboro Community College," I say.

"And she blames Cadmium Solutions and all the other idiots who made a mess of the occupation."

"That's a pretty long list."

I try to imagine the unendurable frustration, no, the *agony* of finding an archaeological treasure, a lost city—a *real* lost city, not that Indiana Jones bullshit—and having it taken away from you, which is a bit like getting to hold the secret of immortality in your hands, only to have it snatched away by the treacherous serpent of our crude and all-consuming addiction to fossil fuels.

The saving grace of this campus is a spectacular view of Manhattan to the west, its jagged line of gleaming monoliths jutting skyward like a twenty-first-century Stonehenge. Framing the view is a bunch of repurposed trailers with utilitarian names like the C-1 Unit and the C-2 Unit. A young female student with dark, silky hair is sitting on a bench in front of the C-1 Unit, reading a copy of the self-help relationship book *Men Are Consonants, Women Are Vowels.* Maybe I should pick up a copy.

"So what do I do now?"

"Who's next on your list?"

I study the printout of Kristel Santos's class schedule, which some overpaid administrator has labeled the Interim Nonmatriculating Student Advisement Information Notice. The next entry reads: JDS 101 SHULEVITZ WH-109.

"Looks like my subject was pretty darn interested in the Ancient Near East. In addition to the archeology course, she was taking Introduction to Judaic Studies with Professor Shulevitz."

"Talk to him. And use a freaking pretext this time, *prima.*"

~

"Excuse me, which way is Wilson Hall?"

"You mean the Double-Wide Building?" says the Asian American student, looking up from her self-help book. She's got an old eyebrow piercing scar over her left eye, an increasingly common feature among the students in the city college system. She senses my confusion and explains, "Any structure that has *brake lights* on it doesn't get to call itself a Hall."

"Ah. Got it."

She nods to the east. "Just past the library."

"Thanks."

~

The hallway in this crummy prefab building feels more like the jetway connecting the passenger terminal with the airplane. I can feel the floor bending under my weight as I make my way to room 109, dodging the students shuttling between classes speaking seventeen different languages.

I spot Professor Shulevitz hurrying from the classroom followed by an irate student whose accent and attitude mark him as a local, Queens born and bred.

I must admit that I pictured a professor of Judaic Studies looking like one of those bearded dudes with the shaved heads and yarmulkes, sidelocks, and big bellies that make certain sects of Orthodox Jews look like bowling pins with wigs. This guy must be a newly minted PhD, because he's young and trim, with a headful of dark, curly hair and intense brown eyes burning behind horn-rimmed glasses.

"So, like, what's an eighty?" the student asks.

"An eighty is exactly what it's been since you were in third grade," says Professor Shulevitz, holding his briefcase in front of him so he can slip more easily through the crush of students.

"Like, what's that mean?"

"It means it's a B," he answers, clearly fighting back the urge to add, *you schmuck.*

"No way! I put a lot of work into this assignment. Why isn't this an A?" The student thrusts the paper in the professor's face.

"For one thing, you could use better examples—"

"I used examples, just like you told us," says the student, shoving the paper closer.

"Yes, but you need to use better examples—"

"What's *that* mean?"

Professor Shulevitz stops and takes the paper from the student, flipping to the second page.

"Here: I don't believe the death of Anna Nicole Smith is the best example of a major historical event."

"Well, that's just your opinion."

"No, it's my considered judgment as a scholar of history."

"Whatever."

Professor Shulevitz hands the paper back.

"Let's talk about this next week, all right?"

"What's wrong with right now?"

"After you've had a chance to reflect—"

"Look, I did everything you said—"

"I'm not going to argue with you about this."

"Hey! Don't walk away from me!" says the student, like some street punk who's got a rep to maintain.

Jesus. Talk about entitlement. I would never have dreamed of confronting a teacher like that—not even the lazy, third rate twaddlers who made us fill out boring worksheets all period instead of, you know, teaching us stuff.

Professor Shulevitz hurtles down the corridor and escapes, heading toward the C-2 Unit. I give him a little time to cool off while I come up with a strategy. He looks pretty sharp, with a low tolerance for bullshit, plus he's way too young to have had his career derailed by a war-hungry president with daddy issues. I decide to play it straight.

"Welcome to the holding cell," he says, pushing aside a mound of student papers to make room for the latest batch.

"Yeah, you know you're in trouble when your office space looks like the visitor's room in a minimum-security prison," I say, squeezing through the narrow doorway.

"So what can I do for you?" He's pulling a thick sheaf of homework assignments from his briefcase.

I hand him a business card and tell him I'm working for Cadmium Solutions.

"Really? That gang of mercenaries?"

"I suppose it wouldn't help if I told you they prefer the term *security solutions providers*."

He emits a cynical chuckle. "That's a little like trying to class-up a sleazy strip club by calling the bouncers *security personnel* and the strippers *exotic entertainers*."

"I happen to know some bouncers who are very particular about what they're called."

"So what are you doing with a student's INSAIN form?"

"I ... what?"

"This thing," he says, plucking the twice-folded form from my fingers. "The Interim Nonmatriculating Student Advisement Information Notice. And who's Kristel Santos?"

"I was hoping you could tell me something about her."

I'm five seconds into my prepared speech about recovering rare archaeological artifacts when three itinerant professors pile into this tiny office and ask Professor Shulevitz if he's finished using his section of the desk because they need it.

Professor Shulevitz begins packing up his students' assignments. "I'd love to help," he tells me, "but as you can see, I share this space with twenty other adjuncts."

"Twenty *exploited* adjuncts," the young blond professor corrects him. She looks like she just rolled off the graduate school assembly line in her crisp blue blazer, all brushed and polished and ready for the showroom, the chrome still gleaming. I notice she's wearing an Ivy League class ring as she lays out her English assignments on a precious sliver of desk space.

"Welcome to the academic gig economy," says the science professor, whose nametag—DR. PRAKASH—and accent indicate that she comes from somewhere in northern India. Her white lab coat has a couple of burn holes in it and she's clutching a pile of lab reports thick enough to choke a rhinoceros.

"We're the M*A*S*H unit of college professors," says Professor Shulevitz. "Our job is to stop the bleeding, sew up the worst of the wounds, and pray they survive the trip to a *real* hospital in Seoul."

"Well, if we can't talk here, is there a decent coffee shop nearby?" I ask. "My treat."

"You mean I get to sit down with a bright-eyed gal like you and have you pay rapt attention to my words?" says Professor Shulevitz. "Sure."

I decide not to mention that Cadmium Solutions is picking up the tab.

~

Professor Shulevitz takes me to one of those pretentious coffee shops where ponytailed baristas wear crisp white aprons with matching paper caps and a latte costs eight times what a Latino place would charge for the same thing under the name *café con leche*. I mean, this is Queens, so there's got to be a Latino place somewhere nearby.

And if that isn't enough, the place has a TV turned up full-blast, making it virtually impossible to have a conversation. I do my best to block it out.

"So what's it like teaching students who confuse arrogance with brilliance?" I ask, settling into my seat.

"It's like trying to make bricks without straw," says Professor Shulevitz, as he places his bulging briefcase on the empty seat beside him. "One of the problems with teaching these days is that I have to treat each student as if they're a potential mass murderer who might come to class with a gun if I say anything that upsets them."

"And it's your job to say things that might upset them."
I look into his silky brown eyes. "My mom always stressed the importance of education. She used to say that teachers are second to God."

"I don't know about that," he says, breaking eye contact to check out the offerings on a colorful chalkboard behind the counter. "I haven't seen too many demigods walking around the TCC campus, but education is so central to Jewish life that our idea of Hell is a place with no learning. As Ecclesiastes says, *For there is no reasoning, no learning, no wisdom in She'ol.*"

He grabs his top-heavy briefcase to keep it from toppling over as the waitress comes to take our orders. She nods approvingly as Professor Shulevitz rattles off an order for an *extra grande double-shot cappuccino half-soy half-skim no sugar powdered nutmeg supreme.* I ask for a regular café con leche.

"You mean a latte, right?"

"Right."

She checks off a box on the guest check pad and promises to return shortly with our coffees.

"Now, Professor Shulevitz—"

"Please, call me Aaron."

"Okay. Aaron Shulevitz, huh? Could your name get any more Jewish?"

He's not sure how to take that, so I turn it around: "I sort of have the opposite problem. People refuse to believe I'm Latina because I'm light-skinned and don't speak broken English."

He pauses to consider my words.

I ask him about Kristel Santos. He says he never met her. She was on the roster, but she never came to class.

"Not even once?"

"I take attendance every day, Ms. Ortega Pérez."

Wow. A white boy who actually says my name right.

"Can you tell me anything about the scroll that she allegedly stole?"

"I'm not a Dead Sea Scrolls scholar," he says.

"This scroll is much older, dating from the late sixth century BCE."

"Even worse. The historical records during the period of Persian rule are pretty spotty—"

"Dr. Woolley said it's also called the Baghdad Scroll."

"The Baghdad Scroll?" He scratches his chin, pondering the question. "That's not really my area of expertise. I can put you in touch with a couple of textual scholars, but if it's what I think it is, whoever stole it can't exactly sell it on eBay."

"So what is it?"

"It's supposed to be a variant text of the Book of Ruth."

"Meaning what, exactly?"

"It's rumored to be a longer version of the biblical tale of Ruth the Moabite."

"What's a Moabite?"

He pulls at the corners of his mouth, betraying a trace of annoyance with my limited knowledge of the subject.

The waitress brings two coffees. Mine comes in a heavy ceramic cup with just two ingredients, coffee and warm milk. His comes in a tall, tapering milkshake glass with three inches of whipped cream and powdered nutmeg on top.

I have a distinct feeling this is his lunch.

I take a sip of mine. It's warm and dark, the minimum essential criteria.

I let him luxuriate in the first few mouthfuls of his triple-decker parfait before I continue with my questions.

"What's so special about the Book of Ruth?"

He practically rolls his eyes at my ignorance. "If the Baghdad Scroll is ever authenticated as dating from the late sixth century BCE, it would be the oldest existing text of a biblical book, predating the Dead Sea Scrolls by roughly three centuries."

"No, I mean the actual plot of the Book of Ruth."

"The plot? You mean the narrative of events?" He licks some of the whipped cream off a long-stemmed spoon.

"Aside from the fact that Ruth makes a vow before the God of Israel to remain by her mother-in-law's side, which is a rare instance of female bonding in the Hebrew Bible, it's also considered the first example of a religious conversion that takes place *without* God's intercession."

I'm following him fine till then, but he senses some lack of understanding on my part and shifts into full Professor Mode:

"Two of the most important figures in the early books of the Bible, Abraham and Moses, convert when God calls on them directly. But Ruth converts out of loyalty, out of love, out of duty, out of a shared *human* experience, not because of divine intervention."

"Which makes her faith even greater than theirs."

"What?" He's thrown for a moment. "Oh, right, that whole Catholic thing about how much greater it is to have faith *without* having seen Jesus's wounds, *without* having seen that He is risen."

"Well, yeah. You just said that God speaks face-to-face with Abraham and Moses—"

"Literally, face-*in*-face, *panim bepanim*."

"Fo'real? You tellin' me God got all up in Moses' face?" I say, slipping into ghetto-speak as easily as flipping a switch.

"I suppose you could put it that way," he says, mildly amused.

I switch back to Standard English: "But Ruth acts without definitive proof of God's existence, so her faith is greater."

"Sure, but—"

He finally looks me right in the eye.

His gaze lingers there awhile.

"I guess I never looked at it that way," he says, breaking off and checking his watch.

"What else can you tell me about the scroll?"

"Well, there's some discussion among Bible scholars about whether the scroll was written by a woman."

"And what do you think?"

I take a swig of coffee, so my mouth is full when the waitress swoops by with a big, bright smile and asks, "How is everything?"

Everything is fine, we assure her.

"I think the Book of Ruth was included in the biblical canon as a deliberate counter to the xenophobic attitudes found in Ezra and Nehemiah," he continues. "She's a virtuous foreign woman who immigrates to the land of Israel and ends up giving birth to the line of King David. Her story challenges the nationalist narrative that foreign women are the root cause of all society's ills."

"All right," I say. "I'm not just sitting here so you can lecture me on background info like the French girl in *The Da Vinci Code*, but, how so?"

He toys with his spoon, then takes another sip of his poor man's power lunch.

"She's a foreign-born widow with no family of her own—no parents, no brothers or sisters, no cousins, no aunts or uncles. She has *no one*. She occupies the lowest level of the social strata in ancient Israelite society, which means that her very presence within that society could be regarded as a test of that society's worthiness in the eyes of God. And what does God command us to do?"

"*Thou shalt not reap the corners of thy field, thou shalt leave them for the poor*," I say, quoting a phrase that was drilled into my head in Catholic school.

"I was thinking more *Cursed be he who subverts the rights of the stranger, the fatherless, and the widow*, but close enough."

"Ooh, curses. Now you're talking. None of that prissy *Thou shalt not* stuff. Power to the oppressed people of Judea!" I say, pumping my fist in the air.

But he's unflappable: "The Book of Ruth begins with a famine in the land around Bethlehem, or *Beit-lekhem*, which means House of Bread. So it's ironic that there's no bread in the House of Bread."

"Now that you mention it, those pastries behind the counter are starting to look pretty tempting."

Back to Professor Mode: "Starvation was a real threat in biblical times. There are at least a dozen famines listed in the Hebrew Bible alone, and Ruth can't afford to let herself get too lean and hungry-looking or she won't be able to attract a man."

"Oh?" I say, my mouth opening like a cave.

"Don't shoot the messenger," he says. "These are Iron Age gender roles. Ruth is described throughout the book as a *na'arah mo'aviah*, a Moabite girl, so we know she's fairly young even after ten years of marriage. She's only called a woman, an *ishah*, when the community witnesses her second marriage to a local landowner. We don't know anything about what she looked like, but she's depicted in a couple of mid-twentieth-century historical novels as being *startlingly beautiful*, with *gleaming golden hair*."

That expectant look again, like he's challenging me to answer a question he hasn't asked.

"Okay, I give up. What are you trying to say?"

"Ruth? Blond hair? Seriously?" he says. "She's from the *land of the Moabites*, in what is now Jordan. How many blonds do you figure were walking around the hills of southwestern Jordan in 1000 BCE?"

I nod dutifully. "It says a lot about mid-twentieth-century stereotypes about feminine beauty."

"And the preconceptions about demure and deferential behavior."

I slurp up a mouthful of coffee.

"Say, isn't that your boss?" he says, glancing at the TV screen.

It's Rick Fursten all right, barking on about his company's performance in some of the world's most dangerous hot spots.

"Please don't call him my boss. It's hard enough working for them on a short-term contract—"

OUR MEN AND WOMEN HAVE *BEEN* DOING *GOD'S*
WORK, LIKE JEREMIAH REBUILDING THE TEMPLE WITH
A SWORD IN ONE HAND AND A SHOVEL IN THE OTHER!

"That idiot can't even tell the difference between Jeremiah and Nehemiah," Professor Shulevitz says, raising his too-sweet coffee to his full, shapely lips. "*Nehemiah's* the one who rebuilds with a tool in one hand and a weapon in the other," he explains, wiping his mouth with a paper napkin. "And he's rebuilding the defensive wall around Jerusalem, not the Temple."

"Some devout Christian," I say, watching Fursten's mouth move with machine-like precision.

Professor Shulevitz checks his watch again and gulps down the last of his syrupy coffee drink.

The waitress returns with the check and places it in the middle of the table, nudging it slightly closer to Professor Shulevitz. I reach for it while he gathers up his briefcase and jacket.

"Hold on," I say. "You can't leave without giving me the names of those Bible scholars you were telling me about."

He scribbles a couple of names on the back of my business card and hands it back to me so he can finish packing up.

"Gotta run," he says. "I've got a class at three."

"What's your rush? There's plenty of time."

"My 3:00 p.m. class isn't at TCC, it's at SUNY Old Westbury, forty-five minutes away in Nassau County. And thanks to you taking up my lunch hour, I'm going to have to grade these in the car," he says, hefting his overstuffed briefcase. "Thanks for the coffee. If you have any more questions after you talk to those two, let me know and we can meet again."

"Thanks. But next time I pick the place."

"Okay, sure. It's a date." He stands there for a second, then leans in and gives me an awkward, off-balance hug, his heavy briefcase pressing against my ribs.

He turns to go, riding off to combat ignorance and folly, one mind at a time, like the wandering heroes in our courtly romances and westerns.

I'm slipping the lunch receipt into the case file when I suddenly stop.

Wait. Did I just agree to go out on a date with him?

⌒

Whoever stole it can't exactly sell it on eBay.

I check anyway. No "Baghdad Scroll" for sale online, but somebody posted a listing for a metal-tipped ninetail "from the actual whip the Romans used on Jesus!" with a CUSTOMERS WHO BROWSED THIS ITEM ALSO BROWSED link to a piece of chewed-up wood from the doorway where Amadou Diallo, an unarmed West African immigrant, went down in hail of forty-one bullets, nineteen of which struck him, when the cops mistook his wallet for a deadly weapon.

And if Jesus ever comes back with that long, nappy hair of his, they'll probably put nineteen bullet holes in his body, too.

⌒

"You call this investigative reporting, you corporate media whores?"

Jhimmy is yelling at the computer again.

"What is it this time?" I call from the kitchen while stirring the *fanesca*.

"There's a cat trapped between two buildings on Hudson Street, and they've got correspondents from *five* different networks covering the story!"

Jhimmy's cranky because he didn't sleep well last night. I think there was a pea under the mattress.

"Do you believe this shit?" he says.

I ladle the *fanesca* into a couple of cobalt-blue ceramic bowls—my mother's favorite color—and put dinner on the table as the computer screen assails my eyes with a video clip of Sheza Hogg in a bath towel dry humping—uh, I mean twerking—with a male dancer, her hair damp, her back exposed, her face fixed in the kind of vacant stare that belongs in an AI-produced deepfake porn video, while the entertainment reporter praises her "post-erotic take on sexuality," whatever the fuck that means.

I savor the taste of *la madre patria* and try to ignore the news that Sheza Hogg just got a seven-figure advance for her memoirs, because she's got *sooo* much life experience and wisdom to share with us, like how to turn a drunk-driving conviction into a fashion event that gets over seven hundred million views on major media platforms.

"We have any mayo?" Jhimmy says, his eyes glued to the screen as I'm whipping the salad into submission.

"For what?"

"For the salad."

Ugh.

"There's a jar in the fridge."

He peels himself away from the computer screen and plods over to the kitchen, where he spends way too much time with the refrigerator door open, hunting for the mayo.

I tell him to check the top shelf, behind the hot sauce.

He leaves the fridge wide open while he hunts for something else, opening every drawer beneath the counter and slamming them shut.

"Where are the big serving spoons?" he shouts.

"Middle drawer, left side, next to the knives."

Jhimmy comes back with a perfectly spherical glob of mayonnaise sitting on top of the greens on his plate like the Dome of the Rock in Jerusalem. He mixes the thick eggy goop into his salad and grabs a pile of printout, munching away while he goes through the pages. I sit back and try to enjoy my salad.

The evening news begins with a clip of President Kinney

declaring that the latest intelligence reports contain absolute proof that Iran is sending arms to Zabul Province.

"I can't believe they're putting us through this again," I say, my fists clenching against my will.

"You just can't accept that Americans *like* war."

"No, they don't," I say, my jaw tightening. "They like what they *think* war is. They think it's all about guts and glory, not what it *really* is—"

My voice catches as I picture a healthy young man in a red-and-yellow *fútbol* jersey grinning with confidence as he hurtles through a line of defenders, scrambling through puddles and kicking dirty water in my face, the wetness splashing my cheeks.

Jhimmy's face darkens like a rotten apple. He tries to say something comforting, but all I hear is *So why'd he join up? Nobody put a gun to his head and forced him to enlist.*

My chair scrapes the hardwood as I push away from the table and head to the kitchen to make my lunch.

I need something to settle my nerves. Maybe some herb tea. That old standby. Better yet, how about some ice cream to go with it? Now you're talking, girl.

I get out a pint of double chocolate fudge and a tiny dessert bowl. Now where's the ice cream scoop? It should be here in the middle drawer. I open the other drawers and then I see it, lying in the sink, covered in mayonnaise and fish oil.

He left the jar of mayonnaise out on the counter, too.

And given his mood right now, I know that if I say anything, he'll just say that he was going to put it away but he got distracted and that I'm too hung up on bourgeois notions of cleanliness—you know, like cleaning up after yourself.

"You want to come to the meeting with me?" he says, gathering up his gear.

"Not tonight, I'm too tired."

"You never want to go to the meetings anymore. They're important, you know," he says, putting on his coat.

"I said I'm too tired from doing all the shopping, cooking, cleaning, and taking care of two generations of men in my family—"

"No, you're too tired because you spent all your time interviewing some revisionist professor—"

"Jhimmy, if the only way to participate in the collective decision-making process is to go to five-hour meetings every night of the week, then, no, I can't do it."

The door slams shut.

Okay, everybody. Deep, cleansing breath.

I grab the jar of mayonnaise and turn to open the fridge, but the jar slips from my hand, tumbling end over end in a stunning imitation of slow motion until it shatters in real time, spraying broken glass and gobs of mayonnaise all over the linoleum tiles and cabinets.

My fingers are still grasping the lid, because he left the jar on the counter without bothering to put the lid on right. *Fuck.*

Fuck fuck fuck fuck fuck fuck fuck fuck fuck fuck.

Repeat until the page is full, printer.

CHAPTER ELEVEN

Felicity

The Number 7 train plunges headlong into the bend over the train yards, whips around the curve and dives under the river, burrowing into the bedrock and piercing the tender flank of Midtown Manhattan till it reaches the heart of the city at Forty-Second Street. I switch to the Seventh Avenue local, where I'm actually able to get a signal and log on to a site for female investigators to get the benefit of their collective wisdom, until we lose power in the tunnel somewhere between Houston and Canal, leaving the gloomy interior of the subway car glowing with flat glass rectangles from all the handheld devices. It's like being trapped in a jar with a swarm of genetically modified fireflies.

My phone gives off enough light to read a smeared, secondhand copy of the *Amsterdam News* that some phantom passenger left on the seat beside me, open to a story about a pair of local landmarks struggling to keep their doors open: the Harlem Record Shack and Bobby's Happy House, which have kept people's toes a-tapping since the days of zoot suits and red-and-yellow DeSoto taxis. A spunky white girl who calls herself DJ Mobita is prowling the sidewalks, roping passersby into signing a petition to keep the stores from getting evicted by a greedy developer named Morton Fink, whose business model is based primarily on pushing working people out of trendy neighborhoods to make room for wealthier tenants, building settlements on illegally occupied land in the West Bank, and trading in blood diamonds from Angola.

I respect the effort to save the stores, but I suspect it's

a lost cause. In the past few months alone we've lost the Gotham Book Mart on East Forty-Sixth Street, stood by helplessly screaming as they pulled the plug on CBGB's storied reign at Bowery and Bleecker, and bowed our heads in shame as they shuttered the Funny Store at Forty-Fourth and Eighth, the renowned novelty and magic store that was the city's primary source of fake dog crap.

Okay, so I have mixed feelings about that last one.

But we all need a good laugh now and then, don't we? Especially after reading about *another* construction-related accident up in the Bronx involving an immigrant worker who was caught between a backhoe and an asphalt paver, the kind of thing that usually only happens when the boss is pressuring you to speed things up and not worry so much about safety. The victim was in his early thirties, a father of two, and had just come over from Kosovo seeking a better life.

Or the student from Bangladesh who was going to CUNY's College of Staten Island on a scholarship, whose version of the American dream abruptly ended on New Utrecht Avenue in Brooklyn, where he was beaten with a baseball bat and stabbed five times, and nobody came to his aid because someone called him a *terrorist*.

Or the trail of tears left by Buzutto Concrete, contractors at Trump Soho with a history of safety violations that contributed to the death of a worker from Ukraine, a big guy with an easy smile who fell forty-two stories when some shabby wood forms collapsed under the pressure of tons of wet concrete that went spilling across the catwalks.

The lights flicker on and the train lurches forward with a series of jolts before it settles into a groove and boogies into the station.

The conductor announces that we're being held due to signal problems at the Cortland Street–WTC station, so I get off and head up the stairs to the street. It's surprisingly warm today, heading into the sixties, so I get to walk downtown with my face open to the sky, not cocooned by the scarves and hats needed to survive the icy blasts coming off the Hudson River. I cut crosstown on Warren Street, a route that takes me past two bars, a conservative mosque trying not to draw too much attention to itself, another bar, and a bookshop with an old-fashioned sign twisting slowly in the breeze, with a deadly-looking dagger forming the T in MYSTERIOUS and an array of bleached skulls, Sherlock Holmes T-shirts and something called *printed books* on display in the shop's windows. I'll have to drop by sometime and see if they have any true crime books on securities fraud, a field I need to branch into.

My pace quickens as I swoop down Wall Street under the severe gaze of the quadrangular eagle reliefs embedded in the cornerstones of the monumental Depression-era buildings dominating the skyline in this district. I get slammed by the heavy crowds squeezing through the security barriers in front of a historic neo-Gothic skyscraper built in 1930 and bought in the mid-1990s by some rich prick who had nothing to do with planning or building the place, but he gets to slap his name over the entrance in three-foot-high gilded letters.

I wait my turn at the checkpoint behind a Black guy in jeans and a T-shirt with a heavy chain and padlock hanging across his chest *bandolera* style. He hands over his messenger bag as a youthful US Army reservist gives him a wide-eyed stare.

"Yore gunna hafta step aside, sir," says the reservist, with a poor-boy-long-way-from-home twang and an unblinking look in his eye that mystifies me until I realize it's probably because he's *never met a Black person* before.

I feel like saying, *Welcome to the real America, kid,* but I don't want to get pulled aside and have them discover that my light skin is just a ruse, that a DNA test will reveal my mixed-race origins.

～

"Office meeting in five minutes, babe," Detective Gustella says, peering into my cubicle on his way to the conference room.

"What? Really?"

"Surprised?" he says with a chuckle, enjoying the sight of me plowing through the stack of papers on the desk so I'll have something cogent to present to the bosses when they ask for a progress report.

There are so many new campaign staffers on the payroll it's standing room only in the conference room. So I'm forced to listen to some blowhard in a sharkskin suit laughing about what a bunch of sleazebags those private investigators are:

"They make it sound all official and stuff—*At 2300 hours on the date specified, our investigators visited the site and secured three large receptacles full of discarded evidence*—when all they did is go Dumpster diving, and they call that *securing* the evidence!"

He shares a laugh with everyone in the room, releasing a toxic plume of his fruity-scented cologne as Detective Gustella squeezes next to me, leaving very little wiggle room.

"We might as well get started," says J.T. Haggard, his voice snapping like a jib in a strong headwind. "Your report please, Ms. Perez."

Right. My report. Wait—where the hell's the executive summary? I swear I put it on top.

Just start talking.

Now.

"Thank you, Mr. Haggard. And to the rest of you ladies and gentlemen. After an exhaustive search of the databases, I was able to, um—"

Don't say 'secure.'

I'm standing there like a stork, frantically reshuffling pages on my raised knee when Detective Gustella takes over:

"At this time, we are pursuing numerous leads with regard to locating the subject's closest friends and acquaintances who may be able to assist us in locating the subject."

"Such as?" Haggard's left eyebrow shoots up like a Gothic arch.

Talk.

Just talk.

"I was able to gain access to the subject's phone records, and we obtained hundreds of numbers that we will be using for investigative purposes, contacting each number starting with the most recent—"

"Now hold on a minute," says a watery-eyed man with a sallow complexion. "Do you mean to tell me we're paying you to sit around all day and make telephone calls?"

"I intend to get in some fieldwork later today or first thing tomorrow—"

"So you're going to be cold-calling hundreds of numbers instead of checking the subject's criminal history in a nation-wide database?"

"Sir, private investigators don't have access—"

"Excuses, excuses," the old goat says.

Gustella cuts in: "Only law enforcement personnel can check criminal histories on a nationwide basis. Sorry, but that's the way it is. Most PIs are limited to searching state records, sometimes even just county records—unless you've got some friends in law enforcement who'll do it as a favor," he says with a wink.

The old goat gives a slight nod, his sinewy neck gnarling up like a shrunken tree root, but he appears to accept this explanation. Because a man said it, I suppose.

"What about credit reports?" he asks.

I respond, "Detective Gustella already obtained credit reports from the standard sources, and they didn't pan out—"

"Then perhaps you should try using some *nonstandard* sources? That is what we're paying you for, isn't it?"

"Yes, it is, sir. But the nature of the case—" My mind wavers, fluttering on the edge of going completely blank. "—might compel me to seek information using certain, um, pretexts—"

"She can't get info from a credit reporting agency under false pretenses," Gustella says. "It's a federal offense. Up to two years in the slammer."

I practically bow in deference to him. "Detective Gustella, I appreciate your input, but I can do my own—"

"Yes, what exactly *can* you do for us?" the old guy says.

Okay ... that hurt.

Just breathe.

Breathe.

"I will also be examining traffic records in Brooklyn, Nassau, and Suffolk Counties, since—"

"*Traffic* records? You mean *parking* tickets and such? What on earth for?"

"Mostly the accident reports," I reply.

"Well, out with it, girl. Get to the point."

"Yes sir," I say, the air around me going thin and cold. I feel like I should be wearing a fighter pilot's oxygen mask as I struggle to form the words: "Because combat veterans are involved in a higher proportion of car accidents than the general population, sir."

"I see. And how long will it take for this brilliant plan to yield meaningful results?" says my tormentor, the fibers of his voice standing up like freshly rosined horsehair.

Detective Gustella comes to my assistance, addressing the whole room: "It's a matter of due diligence, ladies and gentlemen. A rush job that produces incomplete data may suboptimize the accuracy of the reported information. We presume you want the most accurate results possible, correct?"

A curt nod from the boss suffices.

Gustella's not done: "Then it is my recommendation that the board allow Ms. Perez to proceed with her end of the investigation for another week or so, with regular daily reports, and a full review of her progress at the end of that time period."

"Very well, Detective," says Haggard.

The old guy glowers at me, his eyes the color of quarry silt. "Why is she still here?"

"Sorry, folks." I dip my head and bow out of the room.

～

I scurry to the bathroom and throw cold water on my face, not even waiting for it to get warm, the fruity chemical smell of that brash guy's cologne lodged in my nasal passages making me sick. I'm going to need a hot shower going full-blast when I get home to scrub the smell from my oversensitive skin.

"What the hell was that back there?" says Detective Gustella as I'm returning to my cubicle, drying my red, raw face with a paper towel.

"I believe I already told you that I have a highly developed sense of smell and a history of susceptibility—"

"You mean like panic attacks, right?"

"More like multiple chemical sensitivity, though I'm not qualified to make a professional diagnosis."

"Well, maybe you should talk to someone who *is* qualified to make a professional diagnosis."

"I'll take it under advisement, Detective," I say, tossing the wadded up paper towel into the wastebasket. "And thanks for bailing me out with that *suboptimize the accuracy* stuff. Where'd that come from?"

"Hey, we gotta watch each other's backs, right?"

I wait for more, because that sure sounded like the prelude to a *now-you-owe-me-one* proposition.

"Yeah, so …" he begins.

"So …?"

"So I was wondering if you could … help me unlock this phone."

He places a flat black slab on the desk. I don't need to know the details, I gather. It's a *flip* phone. I pick it up and open it. Dead, of course. There's a tiny hole for the AC adaptor, too small for standard American models. I have to hunt for a way to open the battery compartment, but finally it cracks open, revealing a rechargeable battery pack sheathed in green plastic insulation covered with rows of pictographic characters.

"That Japanese or Korean?" he says.

"It's Chinese, Detective."

The giant TVs overhead explode with patriotic colors as the words LIVE INTERVIEW WITH PRESIDENTIAL CANDIDATE RICK FURSTEN crawl across the bottom of the screens with disturbing synchronicity.

"Time for the Two Minutes Hate," I say, punching in my passcode and bringing up Kristel Santos's phone records.

Fursten starts off the interview with reporter Sarah Chen by blaming the media for dividing the country.

"Okay, what's it gonna cost me?" asks Detective Gustella.

Pressed by Ms. Chen, Fursten affirms his plan to make it a crime to offer material aid or assistance to illegal immigrants to "come or remain" in the US. So what I do routinely for my undocumented clients would be a crime punishable by imprisonment under President Fursten.

"You gonna make me stand here all day?" says Detective Gustella.

"Hold on a sec."

He opens his mouth to protest. I hold up a finger to silence him.

"He's already bashed immigrants and the media," I tell him. "I'm still waiting for him to slam the public employee unions."

Sarah Chen pivots to local issues: MR. FURSTEN, HOW DO YOU RESPOND TO BARBARA BOWEN, PRESIDENT OF CUNY'S TEACHERS UNION, WHO HAS CRITICIZED YOUR PLAN TO INSTALL ONE OF YOUR OWN CAMPAIGN DIRECTORS AS PRESIDENT OF HUNTER COLLEGE, EVEN THOUGH HE HAS NO EXPERIENCE IN ACADEMIC ADMINISTRATION?

Fursten replies: NOW, SARAH, THAT'S JUST WHAT WE HAVE COME *TO* EXPECT FROM A BUNCH OF ANTI-GOD *SECULARISTS* IN THE ACADEMIC WORLD!

"Yes! He nails the hat trick!" I say, punctuating my words with a fist pump.

"Will you just knock it off already and tell me what you want from me?"

I look Detective Gustella directly in the eye. "I want to see the complete expense reports for Silver Bullet Security's operations in the Green Zone covering the period when Kristel Santos was deployed on the ground in Iraq."

"Are you *nuts—*?"

"Irrelevant, Detective. We need to look at *anything* that could help us track down the subject, correct?"

Detective Gustella lets out a long, exasperated sigh. "Okay, deal."

He offers me a meaty hand, hairy knuckles and all, and we shake on it.

~

It takes me all morning to get past the first hurdle, but Detective Gustella is pleased.

"I think our guys can take it from here. Nice work, Speedy," he says, walking off with the boxy flip phone before I can tear into him for using that degrading nickname.

I spend the next couple of hours working my way down the list I gleaned from Kristel Santos's phone records, but I might as well be *buscando cinco pies al gato*—looking for a cat with five paws. Half the numbers are no longer in service, or people have moved, leaving me trying to establish a connection with total strangers like the woman who answered saying, "Speak Russian, no speak English. No." Then hung up.

There's a glimmer of hope when I spot a cluster of phone calls to a small town in Fauquier County, Virginia. But all I get is a gruff voice saying, "Nick's Place—we're closed."

Turns out it's a pay phone at a sandwich shop, and the guy sweeping the floors before the place fills up for lunch isn't terribly eager to share any information with me, no matter how nicely I ask. I'm sure I'd be able to squeeze something out of him in person, but not long distance, and not with a New York accent. So I call the local records office, and they tell me, "We don't do public record searches. You have to come in and search the records yourself." I try the courthouse, and they tell me they don't respond to requests by phone or fax, only those submitted in writing or in person, and there's a fifteen-dollar fee for each request, and they don't take checks. Cash only.

Ay, dios mío. Every county in this crazy patchwork quilt of a country is a tiny fiefdom unto itself, with different fees, different procedures, different quirks. And the good folks in Fauquier County should really consider changing the spelling of their name to Fawkyer County, since that's how they pronounce it.

The company's not going to send me to rural Virginia, but they might consider subcontracting the job to a local operative.

"No freaking way we're using subcontractors," says Detective Gustella when I present the idea to him. "There's always an excuse. Besides, I've got a feeling the subject hasn't left the area."

"I've got a feeling you're right about that, Detective."

Still, any serious investigation would be following up on the possible Virginia connection, or it would be if I were running the show.

"Any luck with the call list?" he asks.

"Nothing yet."

"What's taking so long?"

"I'm not a cop like you, Detective. Nobody's obligated to talk to me, especially when I'm cold-calling them. I've got to find common ground with someone before they'll open up to me."

"Sounds like you need a break from this call list stuff. Maybe this'll take your mind off it."

He hands me a couple of file folders—a slim file of monthly expense reports and a thick file folder full of loose receipts.

"Wow," I say, plucking a $3,000 invoice for HD cable from the jumble of loose papers and placing it on the desk. "Doing it the old-fashioned way."

"The monthly reports are all computerized, but, uh—"

"But they wouldn't authorize you to give me access to the electronic files."

"You know the drill, sweetie."

"Okay, just leave me alone with the files for a few hours."

He scratches his chin for a second as if he's considering a chess problem.

"It's a request, not an order, Detective."

"Yeah, yeah, no problem," he says, and strolls out of the cubicle.

My eyes drop to the invoice.

Holy fuck:

30 FT PREMIUM HD CABLE @ $100/ FT = $3,000

A *hundred dollars* a foot? What is it, gold plated? These days, cheap HD cable is just as good as the fancy stuff. Unless you're dangling from a bridge by it, cable is cable.

I open the thin file to go over the expense reports, glad to be finally looking at honest-to-goodness hard copy instead of straining my eyes on the computer screen, but the pages still carry the traces of Gustella's cheap cologne. I make a valiant effort to ignore it, but the smell is pretty darn invasive.

I'd ask for a fan, but they'd probably tell me I'm not authorized to interfere with the airflow patterns in the office.

~

I find the administrative assistant in charge of the case file archives—a young woman named Tori—and tell her I need to see any files on Silver Bullet Security relating to their subcontractors in Iraq.

"Which subcontractors?" she asks, blinking at me. I sense some hesitation.

"If I knew that I wouldn't be asking to see the files."

"Um, I'm not authorized to, um—"

"Mr. Haggard told you to cooperate with me on the Silver Bullet case, right? You want to run it by him first, be my guest."

"But he's in a *meeting*—"

"And you wouldn't want to interrupt him now, would you? So just get me the files, and you can clear it with him later."

File folders in hand, I head to my work station, slowing as I pass Fursten's office and get a glimpse of Velda Renko wearing a black pencil skirt and blouse with red accents to go with her killer heels—shiny stilettos with soles as red as freshly butchered meat—consulting with a couple of decorators who are planning to fill the boss's shelves with books that reflect his character and tastes.

"Does he just want to give a textural *accent* to the office, or does he want to make it to look like he's a thoughtful and cultured lifelong reader?" says Decorator Number One.

"Because we can fill the shelves with literary classics in vintage vellum bindings for about a hundred dollars a foot, if he doesn't mind a bunch of titles in German," says Decorator Number Two.

"No, no, they should look like books he might actually read," says Velda Renko.

"So a mixture of classic and popular works, including some paperbacks?" says Decorator Number One. "We can do that for around eighty dollars a foot."

"Make *sure* they're all in English," says Velda Renko.

"No problem."

I enter my solitary cell and start going through the Silver

Bullet files, trying to navigate a maze of contractors and subcontractors so legally dense and forbidding it's enough to make Ariadne drop her ball of thread and start climbing the walls.

It doesn't take long to uncover some serious gaps in the financial statements. One file appears to be missing several pages of itemized expenses, because some of the totals don't match the supporting documents.

To hell with Ariadne's thread. I'm going to need three hundred feet of bungee cord and a miner's helmet to get to the bottom of this. Inflated expense reports usually mean that somebody's siphoning off money, but in this case, the *absence* of such expenses is the curious occurrence.

They must have sent an underpaid assistant to do the job, because whoever did it forgot to remove three pages of spreadsheets that fill in some of the essentials. I'm closing in on something, I can feel it in my bones. Rows and columns, rows and columns, rows and—*there it is*: The heading for the Green Zone, and beneath it, itemized expenses for catering, vehicle maintenance, laundry services, *construction*.

The splashy BREAKING NEWS graphics and theme music jolt me out of my thoughts as the network switches to a press conference on Capitol Hill so House Speaker Jack Knobler can announce in his corn-fed Iowa accent that a drone strike has just killed Al-Qahol's number two man in Balochistan Province. Knobler defends the action, noting that the provincial government guarantees free speech and freedom of the press—except for anything that is deemed insulting to their culture, the region, or the royal family.

Yeah, you don't want to find out the hard way how touchy the Crown Prince is about his weight problem.

And suddenly there it is in fine print: Morton Fink's company, FinkBerg Incorporated, got a $70 million contract to design the barracks and attached sanitary facilities in the Green Zone. So *they* were the guys who installed the faulty wiring that electrocuted a serviceman while he was taking a shower. Why the hell would they use local slumlord for a high-stakes project like that?

Because he knows how to build things under adverse conditions in hostile territory.

See Blueprint File BZ12-04a.

"*Blueprints,*" I muse out loud, copying the file number onto a Post-it.

I feel a slight chill, as if I'm being watched by a bird of prey.

I look up. Velda Renko is blocking the entrance to my cubicle, fixing her eyes on me like she's trying to decide whether to accuse me of insubordination or make a meal out of me. Or do I detect a microscopic trace of approval beneath the diamond-tipped hardness? Is she impressed with the way I stood up to Gustella? Before I can put a name to it, she breaks the pose and darts off to prey on a nice, juicy administrative assistant.

I make copies of the spreadsheets and return the file to the fabulous Miss Tori. Then I go through the motions of asking her supervisor if I can examine the blueprints for the FinkBerg account, but of course the answer is no.

A good PI rarely takes no for an answer.

First I need to run another search of DMV records in case something turned up in the last couple of days. Nothing in the five boroughs, so I look east to Long Island, where I find that cash-strapped Nassau County has outsourced its records division to a private company that is currently upgrading their equipment and all records are offline for the foreseeable future. The Suffolk County DMV website is temporarily down as well.

"Nothing you can do about that," Detective Gustella says, checking on my progress. "Guess you have to go in person."

"To the Suffolk County DMV? No thanks."

"Then I guess you're stuck."

"No, I'm not. But it'll have to wait till the end of the day."

"Why's that?"

"Because I've still got several pages of phone numbers just aching for me to reach out and touch someone," I say, flipping through the printout on my desk.

He shakes his head and leaves me to my thankless task.

And so I call. And call. And call.

Pure drudge work, but sometimes even a drudge can find a pearl under a pile of garbage. This mindless repetitive task also helps me block out about two-thirds of the hazardous radiation leaking from the giant TV screens, but I can't help hearing that President Kinney just vetoed a bill to lift the ban on stem cell research on the grounds that all human life is sacred.

Unless those humans happen to live in a Middle Eastern country with big oil deposits. Then they're actually kind of expendable.

I'm reaching the end of the list for the past four months. Only about twenty numbers to go, unless I want chase down the calls Kristel Santos made back in June and July, and suddenly I'm jarred awake by a bitter, nasty voice on an answering machine: "If you ain't a friend of Tommy Ard's, you got the wrong fucking number." *Beeep.*

I run my finger down the page double-checking the date, time, and number called.

Data confirmed.

Kristel Santos placed a call to Thomas Ard, an ex-Silver Bullet teammate, less than twenty-four hours before a rash of calls to the Long Island area codes of 516 and 631. I do a quick reverse lookup and get a current address for Ard, Thomas J. on Jerusalem Avenue in Hicksville.

I flag the info and send it to my company-issued phone, then I run through the rest of the numbers. No more scorched-earth messages from tetchy combat veterans, but that girl sure got busy calling the VA Medical Center in Northport, the public library in Brentwood, a food pantry and a branch of the Salvation Army in West Babylon, and a couple of people in Bethpage and Wyandanch who posted rooms for rent on Craigslist. Sounds like Kristel Santos was looking to relocate to western Suffolk County just a few days before she blew off the fall semester at Triboro Community College.

Not that I blame her, after what she'd been through. And she doesn't appear to have had much of a support network.

No one should have to go through that kind of stuff alone.

It got so bad she reached out to a splenetic hard-ass like Ard. Sounds like she hit rock bottom to me.

Come on. Talk to me, Kristel. I know you're out there some-where. Don't give up on me. Not yet. Talk to me. Before they make you into a burnt offering.

I plug Ard's address into a travel app. Only about an hour from my current location according to the GPS-gods, which means I'll be using the company car, which means I *must* do something about the anti-immigrant ranting that assaults my ears every time I turn the ignition in that thing.

By the time I come up for air, the office is half-empty, the darkening sky pushing against the windows, reflecting my face in the oblong eyes of the night.

I head to the bathroom to wash up, and nearly trip over a pair of scuffed sneaker soles sticking out from the middle stall. The walls echo with the rhythm of breathless exertion, and my first instinct is to duck out and give the couple some privacy, but a second look confirms that this is not a furtive encounter. Maylita is on her hands and knees, scrubbing piss and filth off the plumbing fixtures. But the dominant smell is not disinfectant. It's . . . *silver polish?*

"*Oye, Maylita. ¿Qué estás haciendo allá?*"

"What does it look like I'm doing?" she says in Spanish. "I'm polishing the chrome in the restrooms. *All* of it. Señora Renko insisted."

She struggles to raise herself. I lend a hand, noting the

open jar of silver polish and dirty rags on the floor tiles beneath the gleaming pipes, shiny steel valves, and roundhead nuts.

"She told you to polish the plumbing?" I ask.

"What choice do I have? *El patrón* says he's going to deport people like me when he becomes president."

"I thought you were here legally," I whisper, even though no one's around and we're speaking the noble idiom of Lope de Vega and García Márquez.

The language of subversion.

"My children were born here, not me," she says, gathering up the rags. "But I met a lawyer who's going to help me apply for asylum."

"What do you mean, you *met* a lawyer?"

"He says it shouldn't cost more than three or four thousand dollars to get refugee status." She's fussing with the jar of polish. The lid's a bit corroded and it takes her several tries to screw it on properly.

"Hold it, hold it, hold it. How did you meet this lawyer? Because they don't grant asylum to—"

"He was handing out cards at the entrance to the subway the other day."

"Which day? Monday? Tuesday?"

"What difference does it make?" she says, stowing the rags and polish in her cart. "Monday, I guess."

"The day it was below freezing with a windchill factor of twenty degrees?"

"So?"

"Do you have it on you?"

"Do I have what?" she says, peeling off her blue vinyl gloves.

"His card."

She reaches into the folds of her light blue janitorial smock and hands me a cheap laser-printed business card on flimsy stock that says he's a "*notario licenciado.*"

"Don't give this asshole a penny," I caution her.

"*¿Cómo que no?*"

"Because he's a crook, Maylita. He probably makes a couple hundred thousand dollars a year scamming frightened immigrants like you."

"But—how?"

"Maybe back home, a *notario licenciado* means a licensed, practicing lawyer. But in the US *licenciado* just means he has a bachelor's degree—or at least he claims to have one. And you don't need advanced legal training or expertise to become a *notary*. It's not the same. You haven't paid him yet, have you?"

"Not yet."

"Good."

"But—I don't understand," she says, her eyes filling with panic.

"Just breathe easy and I'll walk you through it." I give her shoulder a squeeze, hoping to ease her fears.

"Here's how it works: This so-called lawyer asks you for a couple thousand up front, then he goes down to the offices of US Citizenship and Immigration Services and fills out an application for refugee status, even though you have virtually *no chance* of being classified as a refugee. But the office will provide a receipt verifying that the application has been submitted. He comes back with the receipt to convince you that your application is being processed. Then he hits you up for another couple of thousand for some more bogus paperwork, and this goes on for as long as he can string you along."

"But why would someone do such a terrible thing? And to his own people?"

Why does water freeze at zero degrees centigrade?

It just does.

"*Porque así es, Maylita.* Scammers can hack your phone and financial records, then call you up and say, *This is the Fraud Department at your bank. Please contact us regarding a problem with your account or we will have to place a hold on it.* You've got to be on your guard all the time against these leeches."

Maylita shakes her head at the iniquity of it all.

"I see our little device is still holding," I say, nodding at the automatic air freshener that we sabotaged.

A ghost of a smile flits across her face.

"You done for the day?" I ask.

"No, I still have to mop the floor in the storage room," she says, pulling out of set of keys, bright and shiny as a fistful of gold pieces.

"Wait," I say, my mind about three jumps ahead of my tongue. "You mean the storage room with all the oversized documents?"

She questions me with her eyes.

"Architectural drawings, elevations, blueprints?"

"Yes, but—" The keys jingle in her nervous hands.

"I need your help, Maylita."

"Oh, dear." She clutches the keys tightly to silence them. "I don't know, señorita Felicidad—"

Her eyes dart around, searching for listening devices.

"I need to examine what's in Blueprint File BZ12-04a."

She still needs convincing, so I promise to put her in touch with a *legitimate* immigration lawyer who might be able to do something for her. Of course, with a presidential campaign coming up, there are no guarantees. Ideals once considered unassailable are coming under attack. Hard-earned victories are being overturned. Everything's in play.

Fifteen minutes later I'm riding down to the lobby with unauthorized copies of the FinkBerg blueprints stuffed into my briefcase.

Now I've got to see a man about a car.

~

"Can you run a credit check for me?"

"Sure thing, kid, sure thing," says the cigar-chomping Lebanese immigrant, running his fingers through his gleaming dyed-black hair.

Good thing Robbie Robbie's used car lot stays open late on Wednesdays. I usually drop by a couple times a month to help him run asset searches and skip traces on buyers who try to weasel out of their monthly payments, and in exchange he sends me an occasional referral.

"You want a credit check, I'll give you a credit check, yes ma'am, yes ma'am," he says, repeating everything twice, which is how he got his nickname. He's wearing a grimy red plaid polyester blazer and matching tie, an outfit that just screams *used-car salesman*.

"Nice and warm today, huh? Nice and warm," he says, as he parks his butt in front of a desktop computer with a CRT monitor about a decade past its cutting-edge status.

"Maybe a little too warm. I was way overdressed this morning."

"No such thing, no such thing," he says, punching in the data with his stubby, nicotine-stained fingers.

A beat-up pickup truck pulls into the yard that Robbie Robbie unofficially shares with a scrap metal dealership, its creaky suspension groaning under a load of copper pipe of various lengths. The driver climbs out and stretches, working out the kinks. He's a huge guy with a bright-pink egg-shaped head, shaved bald except for a blond tuft that sticks up like a bird's nest.

"Whatcha got there, Tweety?"

The big guy turns around, a toothy grin blossoming on his big baby face when he recognizes me.

"Salvaged a whole buncha pipe from the projects," he says. "I'd a got more, but the crackheads beat me to it."

He says thieves make his job more dangerous by chipping away at load-bearing walls and ripping out pipes indiscriminately.

"Destabilizes the whole structure," he says. "Know what I mean?"

"Sure."

He grabs a fistful of tarnished copper pipes and yanks them out of the flatbed. I can't help noticing a length of shiny new half-inch copper cable sticking out from the pile of dented pipes, complete with an official government barcode affixed to the end.

That's not salvaged copper. It's stolen.

Tweety follows my line of sight, his big blue eyes hopeful, even pleading a little, as if asking, *Yeah. So? What are you gonna do about it?*

I shrug and head back inside.

Not my problem.

"Got a hit for you, Felicity baby, got a hit," says Robbie Robbie, ripping a sheet from the sprockets of his battle-scarred printer.

It sure isn't a credit report. I carry it over to the single naked lightbulb dangling overhead.

It's an accident report from last Tuesday.

"How'd you get this?"

He just smiles and says, "You have your tricks and I have mine, kiddo, I have mine."

At 2:53 p.m. last Tuesday, an iron-gray 1992 Toyota Corolla heading east on Jericho Turnpike in western Suffolk County ran a red light at Commack Road and clipped the left rear bumper of a brand-new Lexus LX.

Cause given: distracted driving.

The driver of the Corolla was identified as Ms. Kristel Santos of Elmhurst, Queens. The driver of the Lexus was identified as Mrs. Daniella Lowry of Dix Hills, NY. The Suffolk County DMV website is still down, but Mrs. Lowry's name gets me a solid gold hit: a recent address just off Vanderbilt Parkway in Dix Hills, Long Island.

I wonder if they exchanged contact information.

Please, God. Tell me they exchanged contact information.

I high-five Robbie Robbie and thank him for the favor. Now I've got a pair of leads and a place to start—and as

Archimedes once said, *Give me a pair of leads and a place to start, and I will move the earth.*

Or words to that effect.

~

"No, I don't want to connect a device to the port in the car's sound system. I want a completely separate system."

They practically laugh me out of the electronics store when I ask if they have any portable CD/cassette players.

"Nobody plays cassettes anymore. Don't you know that?"

"What do you mean? My dad's got a big collection."

"What's he play them on? A Victrola?"

"Okay, just the batteries, then."

"What kind?" Snicker.

"Eight D batteries." And save the laughter for someone else, you punks.

~

"Where's the *bacalao*? How can it be *fanesca* without *bacalao*?"

I let out a breath and tell him my inconsiderate boyfriend ate it all.

"*Esa buena para nada*," my dad snorts. "The big radical."

"Could we please just enjoy our nice, home-cooked meal?"

"I'm just worried about your reputation, *mija*," he says, tearing off a hunk of bread to sop up the last bit of thick bean soup coating the sides of his bowl.

"*Papi*, this is New York City. Nobody cares about a couple living together."

"*Claro que sí*," he says, stuffing the bread in his mouth. "Your room's ready whenever you want to come home."

"Don't talk with your mouth full, Dad."

"Ah," he says, a tender smile warming his features. "Now *that's* the voice of your mother talking."

It's a heartfelt sentiment, coming from him. But lately, whenever he talks about how I much remind him of his

María, it only throws into relief how much older he's gotten compared to his beautiful young wife, who has the benefit of being frozen and ageless in our minds. It's an unwelcome reminder that the same fate awaits him, eventually—a life crisis I haven't had to deal with yet. But it's out there, hovering in the wings, awaiting its cue.

"You want another beer?" I ask.

"Is the Pope still Catholic, or has he converted yet?"

I rise from the table and get another bottle of beer from the fridge.

"Where's *el señor* Sucushñay today?" I say, popping the top off and handing him the bottle.

"He wasn't feeling too good, so he went straight home."

"You're not ripping out any more asbestos for the Buzzuto brothers, are you?"

The pair of crooks whose specialty was underbidding the competition for state contracts for asbestos removal. After they won the bidding wars, they'd send a couple of trucks and a crew to the site, set up barriers and cover everything with plastic sheets. The crew would make a lot of noise, get plaster dust all over everything, but not actually remove any asbestos. The only thing that kept the Buzzutos out of jail was their annual tradition of sizeable contributions to Governor Fowler's reelection campaign and the army of cheap immigrant labor they hired to remove the asbestos right away, without proper equipment or training.

"No, but they all have their tricks," he says. "The building inspector came by last week and issued a stop-work order, and the bosses stood there wringing their hands and saying, *Yes sir, yes sir, right away, sir*, then—boom—we're back at work the next day."

"The inspector issued a stop-work order? For what? Safety violations?"

"Would you just relax a little? All I said was Eloy doesn't like working there. We're iron workers, not a demolitions crew. He's giving notice on Friday, then he's going to look for another job."

"And what about you?"

"I'll stick it out for another couple of weeks, maybe till after Christmas."

He tips the bottle into his mouth and takes a nice long pull. Then he sits back and opens the paper to the sports section, which is my cue to collect the dishes and take them to the sink.

When I come back for the glasses, the tabloid is flat on the table, open to a two-page spread of drab photos of a barren expanse of bulldozers and dirt near the original Yankee Stadium.

"I can't believe they're really doing it," he says. "They're tearing down Yankee Stadium. They're going to demolish the storage room near the batting cages where Lou Gehrig used to gather his strength before his final games. That's the closest thing to a holy relic we have in American sports! That's like tearing down St. Patrick's Cathedral to put up a fucking casino, God forgive me."

Dad is shaking his head in disgust. "Look what they did in Detroit, tearing down Tiger Stadium to build *Comerica Park*. What does a goddamn *commercial bank* have to do with *el beisbol*? They should have named it after one of their great players, like Hank Greenberg or Miguel Cabrera. And Fenway's still standing. You don't see *them* tearing down a hundred years of baseball history and replacing it with some giant corporate piece of shit. Now Boston gets to brag about having a better stadium than New York!"

An unthinkable situation for any diehard Yankees fan.

I try to steer him away from this volatile topic, which will only set him off and play havoc with his blood pressure.

"Where's that box of old sports memorabilia?"

"I'm not interested in selling my baseball card collection."

"I just want to look at it, okay?"

He takes another long swallow, then slaps the bottle down hard enough to raise foam on the last two ounces of beer.

"Top shelf in the front hall closet."

The closet smells vaguely of mothballs—an odor I truly detest, but at least my mom's old woolen coat and my dad's Sunday suit smell musty, not moldy. They just need a good airing.

The top shelf is a bit of a reach for me. If only some hunky knight-errant were here, he'd be able to do it one-handed. As for diminutive little me, I need to get out the stepstool.

I hear the scrape of the chair as my dad pushes away from the table, grabs the TV remote and flops down on the couch.

I gently ease the box toward me, making sure I don't trigger an avalanche. I slide it off the shelf with great care, revealing another layer of junk *behind* the first one that I don't remember being there. And right before my eyes is a water-stained cardboard box labeled RECUERDOS in faded red marker. A splash of water, long since dried, has caused some of the marker to run, leaving a trail of pale red drips running down the side of the box.

I set the box of *recuerdos* on the kitchen table, open it up, and stumble upon a time capsule of nearly thirty years of my mom's radicalism, from the late 1960s to the mid-1990s.

Buttons, bumper stickers and political pamphlets galore urging me to vote for Dick Gregory, Gus Hall, Angela Davis, Shirley Chisholm, Bella Abzug, demanding that we Free Huey, Free the Panther 21, Dump Nixon, Fight Apartheid, Boycott South African Products, Boycott Nestlé, Boycott Scab Lettuce, ERA YES, No Nukes, Stop the Draft, Stop the US War in Central America, Dump Reagan, Defeat Reagan, Impeach Reagan, *Silencio = Muerte*, No War For Oil, *El pueblo unido jamás será vencido! ¡Hasta la victoria siempre!* and a bunch of revolutionary literature from the days of the Shining Path movement in Peru. I also find some photos of a young María Pérez speaking at an antiwar rally in Union Square around 1979, judging from the fashions, protesting human rights abuses in front of the Salvadoran Embassy in the mid-1980s, and organizing a group of *indígenas* in the Peruvian high- lands where, no surprise, my mom's the whitest person in the photo.

Stoked with revolutionary fervor, I invade the privileged male space of the couch, liberate the TV remote from the grip of the oppressive patriarchy, and mute the sound.

"Why didn't you tell me about all this?"

He stares blankly at the mute actors gesticulating and mugging for the camera, their foreheads glistening under the bright lights of a Mexican *telenovela*, before he drags his eyes from the TV screen, peers at the dusty old box, and plunges in to explore it, his fingers sifting aimlessly through the keep- sakes my mother left behind.

He stops exploring when he pricks his finger on one of the old button pins. "*Chusa*," he says, sucking on the wound.

"Need a Band-Aid?"

"No, *gracias*," he says, lifting his hand to caress my cheek. "You know, when I first saw you in the ICU nurse's arms, I made a promise to myself that I would *never* slap this face."

I nod, though his work-roughened hands feel a bit like a piece of rusty iron dragging across my skin.

"I only did it once, when you were little and being *really* annoying. I don't even remember what you were doing. But oh, how María yelled at me. She really tore into me. And she ordered me *never* to do anything like that again. And I never did. So I broke my promise to myself, but kept my promise to your mother. She had that effect on people."

I blink, waiting for more.

His fingers drift away from my cheek and begin deli- cately stroking my hair.

"When you're young, you think you're going to have all

this time to share *so many* experiences with your kids," he says. "Then you end up working your ass off at one lousy job after another, and then in an eyeblink ..."

His hand drops.

"The pace of life in this crazy country doesn't give us time to breathe. My only comfort is knowing that as long as I have you, I've got someone to say a prayer for me when I die—"

"Papi, don't talk like that—"

"—and give me a proper Christian burial, not like some poor *chalado*."

He crosses himself.

"What's a *chalado*?"

"You don't know that word? *Eres muy gringa ¿tu sabes?* It means you're *un huerfano*, an *orphan*. From *chala*, the husk— you know, the part left over for the widows and orphans."

Them again. Seems like I've been hearing a lot about widows lately.

He stares at his hands, curled up like a pair of prehistoric mammals in his lap.

I don't really know where to go from here. So I slide my arm around his shoulders and hug him to me and tell him he did just fine. "In fact, I need your expertise on something."

"On what?"

"Something that came up at work," I say, unfolding my legs so I can get up and fish the FinkBerg blueprints out of my briefcase.

"*Ave María purísima*," he says, after a few minutes studying the plans for a $70 million construction project. "The walls aren't thick enough to support the roof safely, the support beams aren't spaced properly, and they're planning to use a *half inch* of concrete to lay down a floor that should be at least two inches thick. They got a permit to build this piece of crap? Why aren't these people in jail?"

Why, indeed? This is *exactly* the kind of incompetent cronyism that left my brother with severe brain injuries and astronomical health care costs, and nobody's investigating *that* crime against humanity.

So the next time someone asks you, *What does it profit a man to gain the world and lose his soul?* Just answer: *A helluva lot.*

~

Nu-tuh.

You want some nuts? Okay, here you go.

Chee.

Cheese? Okay. Small bites, small bites. Take small bites. And chew. Chew.

My, he certainly has an appetite, doesn't he?

Oh, there are foods he doesn't like, we just haven't discovered them yet.

Burp!

What do you say?

Coo me.

Yes, excuse me.

I kee.

Ice cream? Sure, we can go out and get some ice cream. It's pretty warm out tonight, we can walk through the park.

Wa-kuh.

Yes, we can take a walk.

What? It's okay, the dog's on a leash. See?

Hee hee hee.

Yes, I like the happy sounds.

Garbage! Don't touch that. Okay, throw it in the garbage.

Bu-vv.

What, now? Why didn't you tell me before? Okay, okay, do it in the bushes.

You don't have to stomp it out like that. You'll track mud into the rehab center.

I kee.

Yes, ice cream. It's on the other side of the park.

I kee.

Yes, ice cream.

I kee.

Yes.

I kee.

I said yes.

I kee.

Okay, you can stop saying ice cream.

I kee.

Stop saying ice cream.

I kee.

Jesus ...

I kee.

Yes, right over there.

I kee.

Oye, Felicidad y Jeremías. ¿Cómo van?

Todo bien, Enrique, todo bien.

I kee.

We have to wait a second. There's a little girl in front of us.

I kee!

No! Let go! Let go! That's not yours!

Aaah! Aaah! Aaaaah!!

Stop it! Let go!

Sorry, is she okay?

Just get away from us.

Sorry, my brother doesn't realize how strong he is—

You're obviously not sorry.

What? He didn't mean—

He's noisy and dangerous and he shouldn't be out in public. Now get out of here before I call the cops.

Okayyy ...

Suppressing the urge to strangle this bitch.

My brother has a brain disorder. What's your excuse, lady?

No pasa nada, hermana, no pasa nada. ¿Cómo sigue el tratamiento? ¿Algún progreso?

We're rebuilding his brain neuron by neuron. It's going to take some time.

What flavor you want?

Peesh!

Say it better.

Peesh!

Peach.

Pee-chuh!

At least he's trying. We've got to see that as a step.

Por supuesto, por supuesto. He's fifty percent there, which is more than a lot of folks, right?

I guess so.

Here you go, Jeremías.

What do you say?

Ah! Ah! Aah!!

Okay, okay, take it easy.

He's kind of loud today.

Yeah.

He likes going to the park?

He likes going anywhere.

You two go everywhere together, don't you?

Sure, we go everywhere together.

But who will take care of him when I'm gone?

And to those privileged, posteverything academic theorists who talk about the *prison-house of language*, all I've got to say is, I dare you to look my brother in the eye and tell him that language is a prison.

I mean, compared to what? Huh, smart guy?

∿

I come home to find our apartment buzzing with do-it-yourself political activity. Jhimmy's making a giant banner and protest signs in anticipation of the upcoming March for Peace with a dozen scruffy activists who managed to eat everything in the fridge except for some five-day-old vegetables, and left the sink piled high with dirty dishes. There's also a black-and-white kitten wandering around loose who left a puddle of piss in a corner of the kitchen that I guess I'm supposed to clean up as my contribution to the cause.

As for dinner, I make do with a small bowl of stir-fried five-day-old vegetables, but the combination of chemical smells from the magic markers, the glue, the paint, and the solvents is too powerful to ignore, and soon my head is throbbing where that rake's metal teeth left a permanent depression in my cranium. I open up a couple of windows, but the breeze disturbs the sheets of poster board, blowing them around, and Jhimmy insists that I reconsider my flawed "open window" policy and go around and close all the windows. A stalemate ensues. We put it to a vote, and I'm outnumbered twelve to one, with one abstention.

Property may be theft, but democracy can kind of suck, too, sometimes.

CHAPTER TWELVE

Ruth

Hazot Na'omi?

The women of the city stared at Naomi as if she were dressed in men's clothing. Where was her fine woolen cloak? Her shimmering Persian slippers? Her loyal maidservants?

Naomi turned from the charred ruins of the Temple and faced the women of Jerusalem.

"Al tikrena li Na'omi, kerena li mara," she said. Don't call me Sweet-Woman. Call me Bitter-Woman.

"But Naomi—"

"I said call me Mara."

The women's eyes widened in shock.

"For the hand of Yahaweh has gone out against me, and He has filled my cup with bitterness."

"No, no, no," they said. The Lord may turn his face from us, but he would never completely forsake his people, no more than a woman can forget her baby or disown the children of her *rekhem.*

"Shaddai has removed the blessings of the womb," Naomi said. "I went away full, but came back empty."

There was a certain glee at Naomi's plight. *She was lofty, now she's brought low.* Some of the townspeople seemed to be enjoying the spectacle of the landless elites reduced to begging for a place to lay their heads for the night in a strange city.

Ruth's heart was still pounding from the climb up the rugged rock face. She surveyed the ruined wasteland, from the charred stones of the Temple Mount to the crumbling fortifications of the Upper City a thousand yards to the west. The defensive wall was useless. Why hadn't they rebuilt it in nearly *five decades*?

Her stomach ached from emptiness. The soaring rooftops of Babylon were still fresh in her mind, their glazed yellow bricks shining like gold in the sun. *The ruins of Nineveh are bigger than this trash heap.*

"How many of you are returning from Babylon?" the women asked. "Is this all?"

"More are coming," Ben-Isaiah declared.

"Where is everybody?" Ruth asked.

It took a while for the women to make sense of her strange accent.

"Are the streets always this empty?"

"It's the time of the wheat harvest."

"Of course, the wheat harvest!" Ben-Isaiah exclaimed. "Blessed is the Lord, who bestows His bounty on the beloved children of Israel."

Ruth finally caught her breath and looked past the ruins to the fields north and west of the city. The men and women of the land were returning from their day of labor, singing snatches of harvest songs as they streamed past waves of ripened wheat, converging wearily on the road to the fallen archway of the North Gate, their baskets brimming with freshly winnowed grain.

Ruth ignored the ache in her stomach. The hour of the evening meal was approaching, and surely someone would offer the band of returning exiles some food before nightfall.

A six-man unit of Persian cavalrymen galloped into the square, raising a cloud of dust as they halted before the convoy's Persian guards, the lead horse's mane aflame with silver bands and bosses, its tail artfully braided with silver ribbons, befitting its rider's rank as a leader of the occupying forces.

He hailed the Persian guards, who saluted and addressed

him as their *hazarpatish*, a commander of thousands. He ordered Manukka to come forward.

"What is your will, my lord?"

"Is there among your charges one Ga'al son of Eved?"

"There is, my lord."

"So. You are to place him in irons and set out with the rising sun to return him to his master Yoshiyahu in Babylon."

The shock rippled through the crowd as Manukka scanned their faces and tried to apologize to Ruth with his eyes.

"By whose authority?" Ga'al demanded, and before he had time to draw his last free breath he found himself struggling to break free, sweat dripping from his forehead as the guards wrapped iron chains around his neck and looped his wrists together.

"By order of Prince Sheshbazzar himself," the commander of thousands said, "as the duly appointed governor of the district of Yehud in the *kh'shatrapavan* of Beyond-the-River."

"*Kh'shatra*-what?" said one of the exiles, grabbing Ruth by the elbow and dragging her forward.

What about the commandment not to give up a runaway slave to his master? Ruth wondered. But now that all eyes were on her, she needed to say her piece quickly and melt back into the crowd.

"It's a Medic word meaning *Protector of the Kingdom*," she said. "A protectorate," she clarified.

"Yes, that's the word," said the commander. "A *protectorate*, a vassal state wholly subservient to the empire."

"Know what that means?" Ga'al said, rattling his chains at the exiles. "It means you're *all* slaves of King Cyrus of Persia."

"We are his *servants*, not his slaves," said the commander.

"What's the difference?" said Ga'al.

The commander called on Manukka, who ordered Ruth to translate.

"I do not know the Yehudit words for *servant* and *slave*, my lord," Ruth confessed.

"That's because they're the same word," said Ben-Isaiah. "*Eved* means both *servant* and *slave*. The commander is making a distinction that is not found in the language of Yehudah."

"Attend to your orders, Manukka, Commander of Ten."

"Yes, my lord," Manukka replied, his face full of regret. And the heavy *clank* of the shackles as he dragged his prisoner away seemed to tear a piece out of Ruth's heart. What if her own status as a free woman was just as provisional and could be just as easily revoked?

"There goes your protector," Mesha taunted her.

"I can serve as my own protector," she said, gripping the handle of her double-edged dagger.

Mesha took a step toward her, his hands on his belt. "How come you speak the language of our overlords so well?"

"Yes, I think you've said enough for one day," said Naomi, yanking Ruth's arm and steering her away from the confrontation.

∼

The night air wasn't that cold, but Naomi was so weak from hunger she complained about the chill in her bones until Ruth arose and wandered among the refugees, offering to pay full silver for a spare crust of bread for her mother-in-law, but none of the refugees had a spare crust of bread.

When a devout and kindly man named Oved came by distributing handfuls of toasted grain to the refugees, Ruth offered him a fine pair of ax-heads in exchange for food and shelter for herself, Naomi, and the itinerant prophet. He invited them to stay under his roof until they could find a means of supporting themselves.

"May the Exalted One repay you seven times for letting us eat at your table," Ruth said, bowing low.

"Don't thank us yet. And we don't have a table."

It was a long way down through the rocky Central Valley and up the eastern ridge of the Upper City to the terraced farmland that Oved and others like him had been working since the terrain was abandoned by fleeing exiles.

But it was a roof and a place to spread their cloaks for the night, a patch of earth between four walls that would not buckle or bend in the wind.

~

Ruth was startled awake by the shrill wailing of women's voices scattered throughout the hills.

A young mother named Tzillah gestured to Ruth and commanded her to do something. *Come, grind.*

"Do they wail for Tammuz here, too?" Ruth asked, rubbing the sleep out of her eyes.

Tzillah nodded in recognition of the word *Tammuz*. She repeated her command, *Come, grind,* making the motions of grinding flour with a make-believe rock.

"You want me to help you grind flour?"

Tzillah had sun-darkened skin, full shapely lips, and a nose that came to a point like an eagle's. She held out her hand and helped Ruth to her feet.

They put on their sandals and stepped out into the pale morning light. A wind flowing east from the Great Sea blew gently over the hills of the Upper City.

Tzillah handed her a millstone of black basalt, and they knelt on the rocky ground to transform a measure of barley into the morning meal. The stone was porous and hard to grip, and after laboring to grind a few handfuls of grain, Ruth's whole body ached, especially her lower back and arms.

Tzillah said something about the she-goats milling about in the pen. Ruth questioned her with her eyes, so Tzillah pointed to the goats and mimicked the act of milking.

Ruth held up her hands, fingers spread wide. "I have no idea how to do that."

Tzillah shook her head in disbelief and pointed to a

pair of earthenware pitchers and told Ruth to go fetch some *mayim*.

The words weren't that different, but Ruth's head was light from hunger, so Tzillah got off her knees, grabbed a juglet from inside the house, and poured a few drops of water into Ruth's hand.

"*Mayim*."

"Oh, like *maya*."

"Right. Now go fetch some *mayim*," Tzillah said, pointing north along the terraced hill.

Ruth nodded enthusiastically. This was something she could do. But she was used to the sacred springs of more fertile lands and rivers that reliably flooded the fields every year. So when she got to the communal cistern, it was a bit of a shock to find a gigantic hole in the earth more than thirty cubits across and twenty cubits deep, with narrow steps carved out of solid rock spiraling down along the damp inner walls to a pool of brackish water at the bottom. Fetching water regularly from this stone-walled collection pit was going to be hard labor indeed.

~

Tzillah set three earthenware dishes on a woven mat in the middle of the dirt floor—a platter of flat barley bread and two small bowls containing bits of goat cheese and olives.

Oved took a disk of thin, flat bread, tore off a piece, and held it up before Ruth's eyes and said, "*Lekhem*."

"*Lekhem*," Ruth repeated. *Bread*. It was *lakhma* in Aramite.

Despite his wrinkles and a bushy beard the color of salt, Oved was still a vigorous man with a deep, resonant voice. He carried the bread over to the hearth and said, "*Kadosh*."

"*Kadosh*," Ruth repeated. That was an easy one: *holy*.

She sucked in her breath when Oved pulled back a thin curtain to reveal a niche in the wall topped by a crescent moon and stars, dedicated to the goddess.

Lit by the glowing fire, a small female figure with a torso that changed into a tree trunk stood cupping her breasts in her hands, the tendrils springing up from her pubic triangle sprouting into a seven-branched tree of life above her head. The whole arrangement resembled a leafy passage to the source of all life, the ultimate symbol of fertility.

This humble shrine couldn't compare to the magnificent effigies Ruth had bowed down to in the lands of the moon-worshippers of Ur, the Medes, and the Persians, but it was still the goddess, She-of-the-Womb, no matter what size the image.

Ben-Isaiah recoiled at the sight of the thing.

Oved led the family in prayer, offering the first taste to the Lady of Life by throwing a piece of bread into the fire beneath her feet. Ruth prayed silently to the Mother of All Things, seeking her guidance and protection.

Oved sat on the floor, looked Ruth in the eye and said, "*Kabod*." *Honor*. He offered the plate of bread to his elderly mother, Nekhamah, who took a piece, then he offered the plate to Naomi.

And so they broke bread together, eating out of the common bowls until it was safe to ask the returning exiles their names and make sure that there were no blood-feuds between their families and clans.

"See how God has smiled on us?" said Oved, gesturing toward Tzillah's husband, Zuriel, a fine-featured man with a youthful beard clinging to his pointy chin, and their daughter, Tabitha, a four-year-old with a short, wide nose and wiry black hair tied back with a piece of thick red yarn.

"And what about you dusty-foots?" said Oved, using a local term for desert nomads.

Ben-Isaiah spoke first. Of course the family knew of his namesake, the great prophet Isaiah, and they nodded with faint recognition at the mention of Naomi's husband, Elimelekh of Beit-lekhem.

Then it was Ruth's turn. They all recognized that her unnaturally short hair was a sign that she was recently widowed. Ben-Isaiah explained that she was not just a widow but a *yevamah*, a widow whose husband had died leaving her childless, which was far worse—a pitiable state.

"Looking to find a nice Yehudi master-of-the-marriage-bed?" said grandma Nekhamah, with a sly smile.

"Why, you know someone?" Ruth replied. Maybe she would be smiled upon by the God of the Yehudim, and perhaps someday the right man would bury himself in her delights once more, tilling the rich soil of her vineyard and plowing her dewy-wet fields.

"Where are you from?" Tabitha asked innocently, as Ruth wiped her fingers on a rag.

"I'm from the north."

Even Ben-Isaiah looked startled.

"Nothing good comes from the north," said Tzillah's husband, Zuriel, his nostrils flaring like a devil's.

Ruth shook her head as if correcting a minor slip of the tongue. "I mean the northern part of Aram between the Rivers."

"Which gods do you pray to?" asked Tabitha.

Ruth took a deep breath before answering. "It is the custom of my people, when we marry outside the tribe, to cleave unto the gods of our husbands."

"So what *are* you?" asked Zuriel.

"She is a *ger toshav*," Ben-Isaiah said, using a term the family would understand. "A resident alien who has chosen to follow our Lord Yahaweh's commandments."

"You want to be accepted into the tribe of Israel, is that it?" Zuriel asked.

"With all my heart and soul."

"Good. You can start by grinding flour for the evening meal," said Tzillah, clearing away the dishes.

"I'm really not that good at grinding flour."

FROM SUN TO SUN

"So I noticed. Then you can help me spin a bolt of raw wool into yarn to weave a new cloak for my husband."

"I am not very well practiced in the art of spinning and weaving."

"How about sewing?"

"I'm not much good at sewing, either."

"Brewing?"

"Sorry."

"Baking?"

"You're asking the wrong person."

"What kind of wifely skills *do* you have?"

"Well, I'm really good at sharpening weapons."

A stunned silence fell over the room so swiftly that Ruth could practically hear it go *thud.*

"I mean, you must have some tools that need sharpening. Knives, wool shears, sickles—"

"So you're handy with a sickle, are you?" said Tzillah. "Good. You can reap a few *z'rathim* of emmer and winnow out the grains, then we can split the grinding."

"I will do as you wish."

When they finished cleaning up from the meal, Tzillah led Ruth to a small patch of land behind the family's four-room farmhouse where they had planted barley, emmer wheat, and a variety of vegetables and fruit trees.

"My God, look at this soil!" Ruth dropped to her knees, clutching handfuls of the deep-red earth.

"By all that is holy," she said, filling her hands with the reddish clay and squeezing it through her fingers. "It's so rich with iron!"

"What on earth is she doing?" said Zuriel, sticking his head out the door to stare at the stranger's bizarre behavior.

"It's like blood!"

"She says the soil is so red it's like blood."

Zuriel shook his head and went back inside.

Tzillah handed Ruth a terra-cotta sickle and told her to get to work.

"What's this?" Ruth said, turning the crude instrument over in her hands. Its teeth were broken and worn, and she wasn't about to saw through a field of wheat when she could slice off an armful of stalks in one stroke with a *real* sickle.

"Can you ask my mother-in-law to bring my belongings?"

Tzillah shrugged and went inside.

A moment later Naomi came outside with Ruth's sack and warned her not to mention her metalworking skills, that her craft was not considered "women's work" in Yehudah.

"Are you kidding? Have you seen this? This sickle is made of *baked clay*," said Ruth, holding up the crude object, more like a child's toy than an actual, working tool. "Get me the curved dagger."

Naomi dug around in Ruth's sack. "You brought a sack full of dried date pits?"

"Not that sack, the other one."

"I know, but dried date pits?"

"We can use them for fuel."

"Under what conditions? In case we need to make our own arrowheads?"

Ruth turned away and set about cutting wide swaths through the hardy wheat stalks with the curved dagger, until Tzillah came running outside to stop her.

"What are you doing?" said Tzillah. "I told you to reap a couple of *z'rathim*."

Ruth straightened up, curved dagger by her side. Tzillah's eyes grew wide at the sight of the deadly weapon.

"What is *z'rath*?" Ruth asked.

"A span," Tzillah said, holding up her hand with her thumb and pinky spread apart. "One *zereth*, two *z'rathim*."

"One *zereth*, two *z'rathim*," Ruth repeated. "Got it."

Naomi pulled Ruth aside, trying to contain the damage. "And your habit of flashing iron weapons like some Kanaanite war goddess is going to get both of us into a lot of trouble." Naomi held out her hand. "Now hand it over."

After a moment, Ruth relinquished the curved dagger, and Naomi stuffed it back in the sack.

"So how are we going to eat?" Ruth asked.

The two women stared at each other, wordlessly.

They heard the blast of a *shofar* some distance off to the north.

"What's that?" Ruth asked.

"Those are the big estates beyond the North Wall," Tzillah said. "It's harvest season, and the law says that they must let the widow, the orphan, and the stranger come and glean in their fields."

"Well, I'm all three of those things," Ruth said, turning to face her mother-in-law. "I'd say it's a good idea for me to go and glean in the fields."

"You'll need to borrow an apron," said Tzillah.

But Naomi had the last word:

"Go, daughter, go."

～

Ben-Isaiah fell in beside Ruth as she strolled past the shells of the luxurious houses of the Upper City with a freshly sharpened dagger tucked into her waistband.

"I've been meaning to ask you why you sometimes call the God of Israel Yahaweh and sometimes you call Him Elohim."

Ben-Isaiah marched along the rock-strewn roadway, breathing heavily, and told her that the two names reflect different aspects of God that are needed to sustain the world, that He is called *Elohim* when He sits upon the throne of justice, and He is called *Yahaweh* when He displays the qualities of divine love and mercy.

You mean, when he acts like a goddess.

Ruth kept that thought to herself.

The sun had barely risen above the old city, but the hills were already shimmering in the dry heat.

"Let me ask you something else," she said, since he seemed to be in a receptive mood. "Why can't I talk about my past as a metalsmith's assistant?"

He answered her question with a question: "How do you say *metalsmith* in the tongue of Aram?"

"*Kainaya*," she said.

"And who was the first smith whose name is recorded in the annals of the people of Israel?"

"The first metalsmith in the land of Israel? I don't know—"

"Adam and Khava's son Kayin." He nodded as she recognized the name. "Humanity's first murderer, indelibly marked by God and sent out into the world as a wandering coppersmith, reviled but untouchable, forever without a home. Ancestor of the Kenites. Now do you understand?"

"But surely they have metalsmiths in Yehudah."

"None of them apprenticed with the master smiths of the tribe of the *Keni*."

His eyes spoke silently, adding, *as you have done.*

Ruth's gaze dropped to the edge of the path, where the dusty yellow flowers of a stunted acacia bush wilted in the morning sun. This was her reward for pledging herself to the God of the Yehudim? To be forbidden from producing anything truly useful ever again? What was she supposed to do—grind the flour and milk the goats all day long?

Surely the God of the Yehudim would find a way to open a path for her, and the goddess Asherah would give her the strength to tread upon it.

And if not, then she would just have to take up a scythe and do it herself.

They reached the remains of the North Wall and stepped over some piles of rubble that might once have been a three-chambered gate. Round a bend in the road, masses of poor folk converged on the vast fields of wheat spread out before their eyes.

"Looks like I'm not the only one who thought of this," Ruth said, tying the apron around her waist.

"Be careful," Ben-Isaiah counseled her. "Keep to yourself and preserve your womb or you will damage the cause of your mother-in-law, for whom you have already sacrificed so much."

"Thanks for the advice."

Now get in there and glean, girl.

~

"Where I go?" she asked the overseer.

"Over there, with the rest of the *nashim nokhriot*," said the overseer, unmoved by Ruth's effort to speak Yehudit.

Ruth joined the group of foreign women stooping to grab every stalk, every loose bit of grain left behind by the reapers. There wasn't much left by the time she passed over a newly harvested section of the field. The corners of the field were reserved for the worthy poor of Jerusalem, widows and orphans whose husbands and fathers had been men of some standing.

Ruth took a moment to admire the strapping young reapers, their bodies slick with sweat as the day heated up. And she couldn't help envying the female servants gathering the sheaves into bundles and carrying them to the storage sheds—at least they got to move around and spend a moment in the shade, while Ruth was rapidly learning that she was not cut out for stoop labor under the broiling sun.

Some of the women made a point of hiking up their skirts and bending over to pick up the grain to encourage the harvesters to drop a few extra stalks in their paths. But Ruth had to keep her prospects intact.

One essential skill Ruth had learned over the years was how to keep men from forcing themselves on her. She knew exactly how and where to hurt a man, but this country farm-ing stuff was already testing her endurance.

She stood up to give her back a rest and wiped the sweat from her brow. To her critical eye it appeared that the reapers would be able to work faster with sharper tool blades. Of course she couldn't say that out loud. God forbid a woman should display her knowledge.

She certainly didn't have to pretend to be clumsy about gleaning. Slivers of wild wheat stalks lodged under her fingernails and pricked the palms of her hands like thorns, and the freshly sheared-off shafts sticking up from the ground kept stabbing her toes through the straps of her sandals. It took her most of the morning to gather a few handfuls of grain, which were still attached to their stems, so after husking she'd be left with practically nothing to show for all those hours of back-breaking labor. And like the rush of superheated air from a furnace, she was overwhelmed by the crushing possibility of failure, of being unable to fulfill her vow to Naomi, to the memory of her husband, and to her husband's God. Surrounded by acres of ripened wheat, she felt like a helpless insect scuttling about under the wilting heat of the midday sun in a futile search for food. An organ-ized colony of insects had the collective means to store food for the winter, but what can a lone insect do?

The worthy poor gleaning in the corners of the field were already lounging in the shade and helping themselves to the master's grapes. Others were singing harvest songs or sharing jokes in the *sukkot*, the makeshift huts set up during harvest season for the master's servants and slaves to take a break from the burning hot sun.

Some of the women were rubbing olive oil on their hair and skin to protect themselves from the sun's rays, but Ruth hadn't felt right about asking Tzillah for a juglet of oil, at least not until she had repaid her family's generosity by bringing home something for their cooking pots.

Such modesty seemed foolish now, as her skin baked like a water-skin held over a smoking fire till the leather becomes dry and cracked. She could practically feel the moisture evaporating from her very bones.

A wave of dizziness swirled inside her brain as she became aware of a sound, buried amid the free-spirited laughter of the young women flirting with the men: the soft high-pitched peals of a child in distress. Near the western edge of the field, a sad-eyed girl around eleven years old was struggling to glean among the sheaves while faster, stronger boys kept snatching the stalks away before she could get to them and even ripping the stalks she had already collected from her hands and sneering at her weakness. The girl was so flustered she stumbled on the rough terrain and collapsed in the dirt.

Ruth broke away from the pack of foreign women and cut across the field to the rocky ditch where the girl sat hunched over her sack, empty save for a few flakes of chaff and bran, sobbing. Ruth knelt in front of her, reached out, and raised the girl's chin so she could wipe the tears from her cheeks and the stringy snot-and-teary mess dripping from her nose.

The girl, whose name was Keturah, said that her mother was dead, her brothers had gone off to join the Persians' mercenary forces, and her father was sick in bed, and they would both starve if she didn't bring some grain home. She started sobbing again.

"You just sit right there and dry your eyes," Ruth said. She got up and went leaping over the furrows after the mischievous group of boys, who tried to dodge her and get away, but she seized one of them by the elbow and spun him around.

"How dare you bully a defenseless girl?"

The boy spat in the dirt and said something in Yehudit that sounded like, "Any woman who gleans in the fields by herself is a harlot."

Ruth smacked him across the mouth before the last syllable was spoken.

Eyes wide with astonishment, the boy cursed Ruth's mother and threatened to have her sent back to Babylon where she belonged, then he whistled for his friends, who converged on the spot where they stood, facing off.

Ruth checked a move to grab her dagger, and simply planted herself in the soft earth, daring the boys to make good their threats. Her heart was pounding, her breath like the hot wind feeding the bellows in the City of Copper. If she could have transformed herself into a seven-headed fire-breathing *litanu*, the boys would have been reduced to cinders.

Witnesses dispute what happened next. Some say she merely grabbed the boy's ear and dragged him across the furrows toward the rocky ditch, but one of the landowner's servants swears he heard Ruth tell the boy to take back his curse or she would crack open his skull and drink the blood straight from his fractured cranium.

Maybe it was just her tone of voice.

But somehow Ruth browbeat the crestfallen boys into marching to the edge of the field where Keturah sat on a pile of rocks, and directed each of them to reach into their sacks and hand over a measure of grain—enough for the girl and her father to eat for a week.

Keturah ran laughing all the way home and Ruth never saw her again.

In another part of the field, the elderly landowner, whose name was Boaz, had just returned from visiting his cousins in the village of Beit-lekhem.

He called to his reapers with a heartfelt *Yahaweh be with you*. Leaning on their scythes, they responded, *Yahaweh bless you*.

Boaz signaled to his overseer.

"Welcome back, my lord," said the overseer, bowing his head.

"It's good to be back," Boaz replied. "Tell me, whose girl is that?"

The overseer turned to see which girl he meant.

"Oh, her. She's the Moabite girl who arrived with the exiles yesterday. She's been working all morning without a break, but she hasn't gathered more than an *omer* of grain."

"Yet she gives three *omer*s of grain to that little urchin, Keturah," said Boaz, stroking his shaggy white beard.

"That is true, my lord."

After listening to the overseer's report, Boaz issued a series of instructions, then set out across the field, stepping carefully around the uneven furrows which had been trampled by so many feet. He approached the group of foreign women, who bowed and said *May Yahaweh bless you* even as they schemed about how to parlay his attention into something more. Their calculating smiles dropped when they caught him eyeing just one among their group, that lucky Moabite girl.

Boaz said to Ruth, "Listen to me, *biti*."

Ruth was taken aback by his presumption of familiarity. *Who are you calling daughter, old man?*

"You are not to glean in another field or any other place," he said, the skin around his eyes crinkling in the noonday sun. "Stay near my girls behind the first row of reapers, and gather what sheaves you can in abundance. I have told my men not to harass you in any way."

"That's very kind of you, my lord," Ruth said, with a perfunctory bow.

"How are you holding up? Are you thirsty?"

"Very much so, my lord."

"I'll have my men draw you some water right away, and tell them that you may drink whenever you get thirsty."

Ruth couldn't believe what she was hearing. Could it be? Had the God of the Yehudim finally heard her pleas and sent a man of substance who acts as Yahaweh commands by showing true kindness to the stranger? She threw herself at his feet, collapsing facedown in the dirt, and blessed him again and again in the name of the God of the Yehudim.

"Why have I found favor in your eyes, that you should take notice of me, my lord, seeing that I am a *nokhriyah?*"

Off to the side, one of the foreign women grumbled, "Cripes, a simple *Thank you m'lord* would have been enough."

Boaz spoke again to Ruth, who remained on her knees before him: "I have been told and told again of the burdens you assumed on behalf of your mother-in-law since the death of your husband. How you left the land of your birth and the gods of your mother and father to become one with a people you did not know before."

Against her will, usually as strong as tempered iron, tears welled up in her eyes and she couldn't hold them back this time. They broke through her weakened defenses and fell in fat wet drops, moistening the dry soil inches from her nose. It felt as if she had been pushing a boulder up a mountainside and someone finally said *Here, let me help you with that.*

Then he said something that sounded like *May Yahaweh pay your wages in full shleymah.*

Ruth sat back on her heels and looked up at the old man. "What is *shleymah?*"

"It means, 'May Yahaweh God of Israel *fully reward* you for seeking shelter under His wings.'"

"Your words speak to my heart, my lord. Let me find favor in your eyes, even though I am lower than one of your slave girls."

"I don't have any slave girls. You must mean my *shifkhotekhah.*"

Ruth didn't recognize the word.

"My *'amahot*," he said, trying to clarify.

"Your maidservants?"

"My handmaids."

Ruth was not at all sure of the distinction. But no matter.

"Then I am truly your *shifkhah*."

"Surely. Now come and break bread with us."

He held out his hand and helped her to her feet. She wiped her eyes, brushed the dirt from her knees, and followed the elderly landowner through the rows of wheat stalks, bent low and heavy with grain, to a shady spot where the reapers had gathered to eat their midday meal. When Ruth held back, he motioned for her to sit with them, and told his servants to give her a cup of water, which she drained in an instant, and serve her a portion of bread.

Ruth said a quick blessing and sank her teeth into the bread, tearing off a huge piece with an animal sound that drew stares from some of the workers.

Boaz cleared his throat. "So tell me, how long were you in the wilderness?"

"Couple months," Ruth said through a mouthful of bread.

"Well then, you must taste what you've been missing. Come and dip your morsel of bread in this *khomets*." He signaled to the reapers to pass her a bowl of what he called *vinegar*, which was really a tangy mixture of olive oil and sour mash made from turned wine.

Ruth tore off another piece of bread and sank it in the bowl, sopping up so much of the oily red marinade it dripped through her fingers and ran down her arm as she crammed the bread into her mouth.

The bitter juices shocked her weary taste buds, and she shivered with delight.

"Wow." She coughed as the vinegar fumes went up her nose, spewing a few wet crumbs of partially chewed bread on the ground. She covered her mouth and suppressed the cough, red-faced, for bread was a precious thing that was not to be wasted.

"Um, quite," said Boaz.

Ruth licked the red stuff from her fingertips, and almost

licked it off her arm, too, but too many eyes were upon her, so she wiped up the drips with the corner of her apron instead.

Her nostrils fairly quivered as wisps of smoke wafted past bearing the tantalizing aroma of toasted grain. She glanced over at the female servants who were roasting bound sheaves of grain over an open fire. Boaz stood close by, directing them to serve out the portions, and when he came back he handed her a dish loaded with roasted grain. It was more nourishment than she had seen in one dish in a long time. She fell on her food like a rabid hyena and ate till her heart was replenished and her strength returned. It was so much food she pushed the plate away with a fair portion still left on it, untouched.

Boaz insisted that she wrap it up for later.

When she got up to go back to work, she felt revitalized. Boaz commanded his young men, "Let her follow directly behind you and glean among the sheaves, and let some of the stalks fall to the ground as well, and leave them for her to pick up. And nobody lays a finger on her. Is that clear?"

"Quite clear, my lord," they answered.

And so Ruth gleaned in the field until the light began to fade with the setting sun. Then she beat the sheaves with a flail till the dull ache between her shoulder blades condensed into a sharp, stabbing pain, but she kept swinging that flail until the pain became nearly unbearable.

Some of the workers were amazed at her strength: "A whole *ephah* of wheat!"

"Nearly forty pounds!"

"Sure wouldn't want to arm wrestle with *her*."

While the other harvest workers celebrated the end of a day spent reaping the earth's bounty, Ruth scooped up the grain in her apron and carried the whole blessed burden back along the winding road to the Upper City as the indigo skies faded into the starry black of night.

Naomi leapt to her feet, amazed, when Ruth burst in

the door looking like she was carrying a set of twins to full term in her belly.

"Where on earth did you glean today? In the king's fields?"

But of course there was no king in Yehudah.

The whole family rushed to Ruth's aid and led her over to a chair. They brought out a bunch of mismatched storage jars and set them on the floor between Ruth's legs to catch the grain spilling from her bulging apron. When they were done, the wheat kernels filled up five one-gallon jars.

Ruth unwrapped the unfinished portion of roasted grain from her midday meal and handed it to Naomi, who gobbled it up.

"Where did you get this much grain?" Naomi sang. "Blessed is he who has delivered us from hunger by letting you glean in his fields."

"I worked in one of the fields just beyond the North Wall. The old man who owns the place is called Boaz."

"Bo'az," said Ben-Isaiah. "*In him is strength.*"

"He didn't look that strong to me."

"Perhaps he is strong in the Torah."

Naomi said to her daughter-in-law, "May he be blessed by Yahaweh, who has not failed to show kindness to us! For that man is a kinsman of my husband Elimelekh—a *redeeming* kinsman."

"He must be the *nearest* kinsman as well," Ben-Isaiah said. "Of the line of Peretz."

"We can help with that," said Oved. "The kinship ties in these hills can get pretty tangled."

Maybe he has a nice handsome nephew, or a wise grandson, Ruth thought as she massaged the knot between her shoulder blades. "He even told me to stay close to his *ne'arim* until they finish the harvest."

"His male servants?" Naomi said, startled. "Surely he told you to stay close to his *na'arot*, his *female* servants. For you still must wait *one full cycle of the moon* without coming near a man

215

before any man of substance would be willing to consider marrying you. Do you understand?"

"I—I must have misspoken, for surely he said his *na'arot*."

"Surely he did," said Oved, patting Ruth on the head. "And surely our guest can be forgiven for making an innocent mistake in the language of Yehudah, which she has only begun to learn." Ruth let him run his fingers through her short, spiky hair.

"But she must be aware that a misspoken word can have dire consequences," Naomi said.

~

After the evening meal, Ruth went out back to wash her cloak, for the nights would soon be growing cold in the highlands of Yehudah, and she would need a clean, dry cloak to keep her warm while she slept.

Alone.

She scrubbed away the dust and dirt from their march through the wilderness and wrung out the cloak till the pain between her shoulders burned like a branding iron. Only her husband knew of the mark on her back. The mark of the yoke. The mark of the Rekhavim. And he was the only man who could make the pain go away, whispering soft words about how she was no longer a captive, she was a free woman, because the Yehudim were a free people. And he would bathe the spot with fresh water from the canal, and when they had wine to drink he'd pour wine on it and lick it off her, then he'd massage the tight spot between her shoulder blades as he purged her tormented flesh of the pain of being enslaved.

And now he was gone.

But now, God be praised, she would find a nice young kinsman who could redeem them all, if she played her part well.

~

Ruth slipped through the shadows to Nekhamah's bedside and gently nudged the old woman out of the arms of sleep.

"I need to see a dream reader," Ruth explained. "Don't tell my mother-in-law Naomi."

Nekhamah opened a bleary eye, blinking away bits of stringy film gluing her eyelids together. "If you must see a dream reader, seek out the wise woman whose name is Az-mawet."

Az-mawet. Death-is-strong. Or maybe the reverse, Strong-as-Death. Either way, a name signifying great strength.

"She's a real mistress of the art of reading signs and portents," Nekhamah said. "She'll tell you what they mean."

Signs and portents. Just what Ruth needed.

"I have a fine sword—a short stabbing sword I can trade for one of your goats," she said, checking to make sure no one was listening. "Tell me where to find the lady Az-mawet."

CHAPTER THIRTEEN

Ruth

Silver trumpets rang out across the valley after a royal messenger reached the city gates bearing a letter from King Cyrus granting the people of Jerusalem permission to rebuild the Temple of their God, and directing the keeper of the king's park to supply Nehemiah the military engineer with timber for the roof.

Ruth barely heard the songs of jubilation as she dragged an uncooperative nanny goat up the craggy hills jutting skyward from the lifeless valley of Hinnom. By the time she reached a cleft in the rocks, the guilty pounding of blood in her ears felt like God's own footsteps, reminding her that the Torah forbids consulting with sorcerers and inquiring of ghosts and spirits.

Ruth tugged on the rope, but the goat refused to follow. So she picked it up and carried it bucking and kicking through the narrow walls of the pass till she came to a spot where a thin stream of smoke marked the location of the lady Az-mawet's lair.

She set her squirming burden down and assessed the terrain, making sure the wise woman had plenty of time to look her over as she approached the cave, dragging the goat behind.

"And who might you be?" said the old woman, her sunken eyes peering suspiciously from a pair of deep crevasses in her sun-dried face. Her iron gray hair was tied back in a loose ponytail and she wore a dirty brown shawl over several layers of tattered clothes.

Ruth untangled the rope and tried to plant her feet on the rocky soil, but the goat kept tugging her off balance as she announced, "I seek the lady Az-mawet."

"That's a given. Now answer my question."

Ruth gave the rope a sharp tug and brought the goat to heel.

"I am a poor widow whose spirit aches for the soul of one that is dead."

The wise woman answered as the law requires: "It is forbidden to call upon the spirits of the dead." She turned away and ambled toward the mouth of the cave.

"But you do have the power to speak with the souls of the dead?"

The woman stopped. She turned to face Ruth. "Indeed, I cannot help it, for I was born with this gift, and so I am condemned to live outside the city, beyond the accusing eyes of men."

"Surely you don't have to live in such isolation."

"There is no place for me inside the walls of the city, for I am a Mistress of the Pit. And what is your name?"

"My husband gave me the name of Ruth."

"And what name did your *mother* give you?"

"Why do you ask?"

"Because Ruth is a Yehudi name and you're obviously not a Yehudi, and I need to know your *real* name."

Ruth hesitated. Revealing her true name would make her vulnerable to malevolent spirits, but the spells wouldn't work otherwise. So she pried open the locked gate of her identity and let a tiny piece of her past slip out.

"It's Rewayah," she said.

Az-mawet nodded. "What do you want from me?"

"You said something about a … pit?"

Az-mawet invited Ruth inside. Ruth ducked her head, but found she could stand up once she entered the cave, its walls illuminated by the flickering fire.

"And stop fussing with that damn goat." Az-mawet directed her to a thick post half-buried in the earth where Ruth could tie up the animal.

"The law is like a finely woven net that occasionally allows tiny, insignificant creatures like ourselves to slip through," said Az-mawet, groaning as she lowered her aging bones onto a blackened animal hide. "According to the wise men we call the *rabonim*, drawing on the creative energy of God's divine power to help heal the world is permitted, depending on which wise man you ask."

Az-mawet spooned some herbs into a couple of mismatched earthenware cups, took the kettle off the fire and poured, then offered Ruth a cup of the steaming hot liquid.

"Now you must tell me exactly what you seek," said Az-mawet. "Do not speak with two hearts, or the spirits will be angry and make a bad star shine on you."

"Let my right eye be darkened if I stray from the path of truth," Ruth swore. She tried to take a sip but the tea was too hot, so she cradled the cup and let the rising vapor bring relief to the dry membranes of her nose and mouth. And she told Az-mawet about the dream with the snake coiling around her husband's neck, and the powerful sensation gnawing at her that as long as his blood remains uncovered, his spirit will not know peace. "May the wind drive away the evil dream I have had," she said.

"So be it." Az-mawet took a big gulp of tea, swallowed it, and asked, "Any children?"

Ruth sat silently gazing at her ankles, crossed in front of her on the shaggy goatskin rug. She took a sip, but the tea was still too hot for her.

"The truth, *biti*."

Ruth looked up. "The truth is I must bear a son to pacify his spirit and carry on his name."

"And you find yourself in the uncomfortable position

of asking your dead husband's spirit for advice on how to attract a man." Az-mawet held up her hand to stop Ruth's protest.

Ruth took another sip. The tea was bitter, but it warmed her insides a little.

"It is as you say," Ruth confessed. "And if I can't solve the riddle of my husband's death or locate his closest kinsman, I am left with nothing."

"Do not let your hands become weak," Az-mawet said, eyeing the nanny goat nibbling on the rope. "But tell me, if you have so little, how did you come by the goat?"

"I made a promise."

"To do what?"

"Whatever they ask of me."

"So the matter is not yet settled, and you owe them a debt." Az-mawet didn't wait to hear Ruth's answer. "Very well. As long as the animal is truly yours to give, we may proceed."

Ruth felt a spark of hope for the first time in weeks.

"But I must caution you," the sorceress warned. "The news from the dead is not always good."

Ruth took a moment to consider. *How does a spirit feel about being called upon?* Does it disturb them to leave the realm of the dead? Is it painful to be summoned into the jangling, chaotic world of the living, like a newborn babe yanked from the womb? Like a block of stone chiseled from the earth and dragged across the floor of a granite quarry? Did it sully them to be among us? Did we disappoint them? Or did we just make them sad?

"It is my most heartfelt desire that you hear my solemn vow and witness the pact I wish to make."

"As you wish. But you must finish your tea first."

Ruth drained the cup and set it aside, a warm feeling spreading through her limbs.

"Now in order to begin, I need something that belonged to him."

Ruth stroked the amulet around her neck. She pulled the necklace over her head and offered it to the wise woman, who took the amulet and held it close, examining its contents by the firelight.

"That is all that I have left of him."

"We only need to use a tiny bit," Az-mawet said, her joints creaking with the effort of rising from the floor of the cave. Ruth was on her feet in an instant, helping the elderly woman up.

The gray-haired sage took a moment to steady herself, then tottered over to an animal hide stretched across what appeared to be the back wall of the cave. She turned and stood in profile, pausing for effect, her back straight and her eyes sharp, all traces of her previous frailty gone.

"*Hinei*," she said. *Behold.* She pulled aside the animal skin like a curtain, revealing that the cave went much deeper into the earth than first appeared, branching off into unknown realms of darkness, the flickering shadows obscuring a gaping hole in the cave floor, a deep pit that could easily become a death trap for the unwary visitor.

"*Emeth mey'eretz titzmokh*," Az-mawet said, quoting the psalm. *Truth shall spring from the earth.* She held up her hands in a gesture of blessing, then yanked the protective cloth from a crudely shaped grindstone, a rough chunk of shiny black stone honeycombed with holes and bubbly protrusions.

Ruth recognized the features immediately.

"Iron from the gods!" she said, forgetting to censor her speech in her excitement as she explored the surface of the celestial object. The stone was riddled with sharp-rimmed craters, yet worn completely smooth in places, as if it had been subjected to extremely high temperatures at some point in its trajectory, like most of the iron from the sky she had seen made into ritual implements and magical objects. It had a silvery sheen in the firelight that suggested significant traces of nickel as well. "It's one of the largest specimens I've ever seen."

"In our land they come from the region of Beit-El, and so we call them *beit-elim*, stones with souls."

"All stones have souls," Ruth said. "I mean, uh—" She fumbled for the right words.

"You mean that our father Jacob knew what he was doing when he set up a standing stone at Beit-el and anointed its head with holy oil," Az-mawet prompted her. "For surely Jacob was no idolater."

"No, surely not. Precisely."

It was time. Ruth untied the rope and dragged the unwilling nanny goat over to the magical stone. Az-mawet made the slice with a sure hand and Ruth collected a bowlful of blood for the summoning. But first they had to burn the choicest parts because *the fat belongs to Yahaweh*.

The cave filled with greasy black smoke that made Ruth's eyes water and left her clothes smelling of roasted goat meat, so her vision was a bit blurry when Az-mawet removed a sample from the amulet, sprinkled the rusty brownish flakes into a copper kettle filled with fresh goat's blood, and placed the kettle over the fire, stirring continuously till the faintest wisps of acrid vapors arose.

"Say the incantation with me," Az-mawet said.

To my right, Mikha-el, she chanted, calling upon the archangel to act on their behalf.

To my right, Nergal, Ruth chanted, slightly behind the beat like a dark echo.

To my left, Gavri-el.

To my left, Ninib.

Before me, Uri-el.

Before me, Shamash.

Behind me, Rafa-el.

Behind me, Sinn.

Az-mawet paused and reminded Ruth that no spirit rises

from the underworld unscathed, and asked once again if she was sure that she wanted to go through with this. Ruth nodded emphatically.

And so Az-mawet called on the angels of destruction. She conjured them by name—*Negef, Segef, Agaf*—Ruth felt the weight of each syllable in the pit of her stomach. She covered her nose and mouth to keep the spirits from entering her body but the names slipped through her ears and down her throat like molten lead—*T'azbun, Lrbg, Thrgar, Ylrng, Zmrchd*. Ruth tried to shield her ears as Az-mawet wrapped the goat's carcass in a dull white cloth while chanting *Bind, bind, bind!* Lady Strong-as-Death held the blood-drenched bundle over the flames until the cloth ignited. She made some signs and dropped the flaming carcass into the pit.

The fiery bundle seemed to fall forever without hitting bottom, as if the thick smoke had distorted time itself, and Ruth didn't think of uncovering her ears until pale fingers of smoke rose seductively from the pit.

Az-mawet's face appeared to float within the gauzy veils of smoke, cupping her hands and coaxing the smoke to rise ever thicker from the pit.

"Hold on … I'm getting … a feeling …"

A shadow was forming on the wall of the cave behind her.

"Your husband's name … was it … M … Ma … Ma …"

"Makhlon, yes!" Ruth said, her voice echoing off the cave walls. From out of the fog, a pair of smoky arms reached out to her.

"He's making … a declaration …"

Ruth could feel his presence, hovering tentatively between two worlds, as close as the blood pulsing in her neck. *It's him. Yes, it's him.* She could feel him, so close to her heart she could smell him, taste him … and then the smoke thinned and drifted toward the light, the mouth elongating in a silent scream, and the shadows dissipated. Ruth shook herself, tears of joy in her eyes from having felt the warmth of his touch once more, however briefly.

"Prepare yourself, daughter, for I have a message from the spirit world," Az-mawet said, her eyes watery from all the smoke. "Your husband did not die a natural death."

Ruth recoiled from the words, an icy chill chasing away the warm glow of her reverie. "It was a snake bite. I recognized the symptoms."

"Did you see any signs of a snake near his deathbed?"

"I—" she began, dead certain, but no, she had only inspected the outside walls.

"I ... I was too distraught to take notice."

"But you already suspected it, or you wouldn't have come to me." Az-mawet hobbled closer. "Perhaps you didn't even realize it at the time, but some part of your soul did, for your souls are still connected. The spirits do not lie. Your husband was poisoned."

"By whom?"

"That I cannot say. You must find out for yourself."

"Are you sure of this, O Wise One?"

"The spirits can be fickle, but they do not lie."

"It's not just my husband. This means *two* men were poisoned. Possibly three."

"Then you must seek the cause, for their blood cries out, and the land will lie fallow."

Ruth lifted her head and swore that her husband's killers would curse the day that she became his blood avenger.

"You have become the redeemer of his blood as well."

"And my husband's spirit shall know that his redeemer lives," Ruth vowed through gritted teeth.

"Then you'd better protect yourself."

"How?"

"We must dip our blades in the blood of the sacrifice."

"Done."

They took up the bowl of goat's blood. Az-mawet drew her

sacrificial blade, and Ruth pulled out her double-edged dagger, and they dipped their blades in the sacred sisterhood of blood.

Ruth called out to the departed spirit, vowing to seek out his murderers, and that nothing short of death would stop her.

Az-mawet stayed Ruth from turning away. "You must drink the blood for the charm to work."

Ruth looked at the pool of blood congealing on the blackened stone. She swallowed. One of the strictest commandments in the Torah was, *You shall not eat the soul of flesh, which is its blood*. "Can't I just swear on it?"

"It is not binding without the bond of blood for blood, for it is Yahaweh who shall judge the shedder of blood, but *you* must raise up the name of the dead, for the dead lack the strength to do it themselves."

Ruth listened to the words of Az-mawet, and knew that they were true.

"May I end up like this animal if I go back on my word," Ruth said. She tipped the blade into her mouth and let the ferrous taste of blood drip onto her tongue and slide down her throat. And she felt its forbidden powers surging through her body, running down her tingling arms to the hand holding the knife.

And she swore that she would become a truth-seeker of the Lord and drive the spillers of innocent blood into the gaping jaws of She'ol, down to the deepest part of the Valley of Death in a field of thirst surrounded by the shades of the uncircumcised and those that are slain by the sword.

"For whoever sheds a mortal's blood, by a mortal shall his blood be shed," Ruth vowed.

Az-mawet sealed the vow with a word Ruth didn't recognize.

"And now, go."

Luley Yahaweh shehoyoh lonu, b'kum oleynu odom
Azay khayim b'lo'unu, bakharoth apom bonu

The language was archaic and hard to follow.
Were it not for the Lord … they would have swallowed us alive
… and the seething waters would have swept over us …

The *rav* stopped chanting and asked his students, *What is meant by this?*

The students fidgeted on the wooden benches, and when pressed for an answer, they admitted that the passage was vague, the imagery mixed and confusing, the poetic syntax challenging.

But Ruth caught the references to being *swallowed alive* amid *seething waters* and being *ripped apart by their teeth*. It didn't sound vague or confusing to her. It sounded like a psalm written by someone with firsthand knowledge of the man-eating reptiles of the Great River in Egypt. She spoke up and told them so.

The *rav* raised his eyes and looked in her direction.

"What are you doing here?" he said.

"I want to learn the Teachings."

The students glanced at each other, suppressing giggles.

"I need to know the surest way to locate the nearest kinsman to redeem a husband's name, and also, what is the punishment for murder committed outside the land of Israel?"

The *rav* ran his eyes over her, appraising this brazen servant girl out shopping for bread on Baker's Lane, and said, "If you want to be worthy of eavesdropping on our discussion of Torah, keep silent in our presence and don't come back until you've solved the riddle of Kiryath-arba."

Ruth's face burned with fresh humiliation as she hurried through the clogged streets to the Valley Gate and sought the prophet in the hills. She found him sitting hunched over on a rocky outcrop high above the valley, staring into the abyss.

She called to him, but he was lost in thought, so she

marched up and grabbed him by the shoulder, and when he raised his head to look at her, she said, "Teach me what I do not know."

Ben-Isaiah smiled weakly. "That could take a while."

"I want you to teach me. Now. What is Kiryath-arba?"

"It is the ancient name of the city of Hebron."

"What does it mean? Is it a sign of some kind?"

"The name? It means the City of Four."

"Four *what*?"

"Well, that's the riddle, isn't it? Where did the name come from? What does it mean? Some say Arba was a great man among the Anakites, and some say it means the four giants who built the city in the olden days when giants ruled the earth, but nobody really knows."

In other words, the *rav* had given her an impossible task.

～

The caravan of exiles finally arrived in Jerusalem—fifteen hundred people spilling across the vast area of the Temple complex and nearly doubling the population of the city in the space of an hour. The Scribe of the Annals records that the welcoming feast lasted well into the night. Musicians made a joyful noise with flutes, harps, and cymbals as the priests set up the giant lampstand, and as the wine flowed, the men of substance returning from exile hungrily eyed the young Yehudi women from the local landowning families.

～

Zuriel swung the hoe at a thick thorny vine, but the iron struck rock and the old, rusty blade broke in two. He flung the useless tool into the thorn bushes and stormed off, cursing the fate that forced him to scratch out a living in this rocky landscape.

The voices of military engineers calling out measurements

drifted up from the Central Valley, carried along by the dry westerly breeze.

"Now what do we do?" said Tzillah, retrieving the broken blade from the freshly tilled earth. Bits of burnt-orange rust flaked off in her hands.

Ruth said, "I can fix it for you."

"But Naomi says—"

"Naomi says for me to keep quiet about my metalworking skills or they'll say I'm a harlot who's totally unworthy of redeeming my dead husband's name. If she's so worried about my reputation, she can come with me. The smithies will think I'm just another farmer's wife with a tool that needs fixing. And while I'm there I can ask if any of them knew a swordsman by the name of Elimelekh of Beit-lekhem."

Tzillah handed Ruth the rusty piece of iron. "I hope you know what you're doing," she said.

~

Good wine, good wine, eight shekels a jar. Get your good wine here.

Date wine, date wine, the finest date wine under the sun, my good lady. One shekel.

A ram for the sacrifice. Firstborn male, utterly without blemish. Two shekels, mister.

Take your pick, ladies, one measure of fine flour or two measures of barley flour, all yours for just one shekel.

The rams and goats are two shekels apiece. The donkeys run up to thirty. That ox right there? I can let you have him for twenty-five.

Yabruhim, ladies, fresh from the King's Gardens. Chase away those demons with the finest mandrake in the land.

The Hebrew slaves are fifty shekels apiece, my lord.

No, no, Hebrew slaves are much too headstrong. Don't you have any Hittites?

Right this way, my lord. We've got some mighty fine-looking slave girls to please the eyes. Hard workers. They make fine breeders, too. The tall ones cost a little more. You want one that can read?

Those are sixty shekels apiece, my lord. That one? Fifty-seven-and-a-pim. And you only have to pay her three shekels a year. All right, fifty-five, but that's my final offer. Sold.

Even the money is coarse and crude, Ruth thought, as the misshapen shekel weights changed hands. Just unfinished lumps of silver, really, some with sharp, nasty edges. Nothing like the refined gold and silver *staters* minted by King Croesus of Lydia and stamped with his image. Yes, *that* King Croesus.

She and Naomi squeezed through the crowd of barterers and hagglers and found themselves face-to-face with Yiskah and Hanokh. Little Asher looked plump and well fed, giggling and cooing in his mother's arms as Ruth stroked his downy cheek. But Naomi's jaw tightened, her arms remaining stiffly at her sides as Yiskah introduced a heavyset older woman with too many pearls dangling from her shawl as her mother, Asnat.

Asnat held out a limp hand to greet Ruth.

"Much pleased I am to meet you," Ruth said, attempting to speak in formal Yehudit.

"I see that you've been working in the fields," said Asnat, smiling with satisfaction as she felt Ruth's callused hands against her own soft, silken palms.

Ruth's hair had grown out a bit since the end of the wheat harvest, nearly covering the scar above her temple, but her skin was darkened from long hours in the sun, her chapped hands latticed with dozens of lacerations from the work of gleaning and grinding wheat and barley by hand.

"Most grateful I am for the right to glean in the fields," Ruth replied, awkwardly. There was a hidebound resilience in Asnat's grip that belied her fine clothes and manners, and Ruth sensed that this woman had struggled mightily for every pearl and tassel on her brightly dyed shawl and for every stitch of fine linen in her possession.

"If you need to fix that," Asnat said, nodding at the broken hoe Ruth held in her hands like a shepherd's crook,

"I suggest you go to the *khuts ha-kharashim*," she said, jutting her chin out like a prideful potentate and sashaying toward the southeast corner of the square.

"The what?" Ruth asked.

"Blacksmith Lane," said Hanokh, his eyes cast down as his wife and mother-in-law went on ahead. "Northeast end of the market, that's where all the iron chiselers—I mean, the metalworkers' stalls—and, you know, the shops are. They can help you with that." He turned to go, trailing after the women.

~

The old geezer gripped a pair of soot-encrusted tongs and pulled the clay crucible from the furnace. Ruth could hardly bear to watch him pouring the refined copper into a star-shaped mold, his knobby knuckles trembling as he guided a thin, wobbly stream of molten copper into the top-hole.

At the next stall, a master and his apprentice fed the fire of a beehive-shaped furnace with a wheezy hand-operated fanning system. The whole process was so primitive—from the thin clay shields protecting the lips of the blowing tubes to the ponderous stone molds they used to cast the iron tools—compared to the two-person hand-and-foot-operated air pumps and the sleek, heat-efficient furnaces in Luristan where the Medes and the Saka turned out peerless ax-heads and sword blades decorated with impossibly delicate images of dancing animals, their legs and antlers gracefully intertwined.

One after another, they turned her away.

Eli—who?

Never heard of him.

No iron to spare, miss.

We're melting it all down to make hinges and sockets for the new gates to the city.

And pulleys and chisels and grappling hooks for the construction of the new Temple.

We only sell iron ingots to the Persians, ma'am. Because they're defending us, in case you haven't noticed.

~

"Any luck finding the nearest kinsman *yet*?" Ruth asked, trying to keep the desperation out of her voice, but Oved just shook his head, his eyes on the floor. "We need to consult the Torah to see what else we can do."

Tzillah heaved a sack of unsifted grain into her arms, saying, "No bread, no Torah. And take Tabitha with you."

~

Ruth scooped a handful of wheat from the sack and sifted through it, removing bits of dirt, twigs, and pebbles, depositing the clean kernels in a large storage jar.

She leaned back on her elbows and let the sun's rays caress her face a moment.

"Hard to believe the Assyrian army had to bake lumps of clay in a special oven to use as slingstones," Ruth said, feeling around for the rock that was digging into her back and tossing it aside. "There are enough rocks in these hills to supply sixty armies."

"Grandma Nekhama says that when God was making the world, he gave two huge sacks of stones to his angels to spread over the whole entire earth," Tabitha said. "But as they were flying over, one of the sacks ripped open and half the stones fell on the land of Yehudah."

"That explains a lot," Ruth said, picking up a clod of dry, powdery earth and crushing it to dust with her fingers.

Across the valley on the Temple Mount, the men of God were moving great stones around, setting up a crude temporary altar.

Tabitha banged a couple of pebbles together. "How come you can't use tools of *barzel* on God's altar?" she said, using the Yehudit word for iron.

"It's probably because iron is a weapon of war, and God's House is a place of peace."

"How do you say *barzel* in your language?"

"It's *parzel* in Aramite, but that's not my language."

"What's your language?"

"You're full of questions today."

Tabitha's dark silky hair hung down past the nape of her neck, and her skin was still as soft as a baby's. Her eyes were hungry for wisdom, but her innocent questions only heightened Ruth's sense of the vast distance between this patch of flat, dry grass and the lush, verdant land of her birth.

"My mother tongue is a northern cousin of the Persian language," Ruth said, gazing toward the horizon.

"How do you say *father* in north Persian?"

"*Pitar.*"

"How do you say *daughter*?"

"*Dokhtar.*"

"How do you say *princess*?"

"*Dukhshish.*"

"How do you say *I come from Persia?*"

"*Irani-am.*"

"*Irani-am*," repeated Tabitha, pulling the petals off a dry thistle. "What's it like there?"

Ruth pictured the vast expanse of dark blue sea, magnified by her childhood memories till it stretched from one edge of the world to the other.

"There was water everywhere. Not a bit like the parched highlands of Yehudah."

"Why did you leave?"

Because I was the only one left alive when the men of Rekhav carried me off and sold me to a metalsmith who had no son, because among the tribe of the Kenites a man must have a son to pass on his knowledge to, and if he has no son then he must adopt a girl and raise her as a son, with no special consideration for the fact that she's a girl. That's why.

"Because I married Makhlon son of Elimelekh of Beit-lekhem."

"Why did you marry him?"

Across the valley, a team of surveyors crept along the edge of the City of David, inspecting the breaches in the old defensive walls and recording their observations.

Ruth had seen what warfare did to men, in body and in spirit. But not her Makhlon.

"Because he wasn't like other men of war. He was kind. He always said when you set out to make war on a city, you should always try offering peace first. And because his Torah commands the people to love the stranger that is in their midst."

"Are you a stranger?"

"Not anymore."

"Does your dead husband appear to you in dreams?"

Ruth's heart froze for an instant, then decided to go on beating.

"Not lately," she said. "But I wish he would. I need his guidance."

"Grandma Nekhamah says Grandpa Zimran speaks to her in dreams all the time."

"That must be very comforting." Ruth dug into the sack of grain but came up with mostly chaff.

"What do *you* dream about?" Tabitha asked, doing her part to sift the dirt from a few specks of raw wheat kernel with her tiny hands.

Water. I dream of a land of mud and reeds and abundant water.

"Well, last night I dreamed of a *kurukku*-bird feasting on the carcass of a donkey."

"Ewww, gross."

"No, it means we will find a safe haven."

"It does? Why? And what's a *kurukku*-bird?"

"A large bird of prey."

"What kind?"

"I don't know the Yehudit for *kurukku*-bird," Ruth said, reaching into the sack.

There sure were a lot of bug parts in this batch, especially near the bottom. She was picking out the dried carapaces of a couple of insects when tongues of fire rose from the temporary altar, and a great blast of horns and pounding of drums set the air alight.

"Looks like they're getting ready to make a burnt offering," Ruth said.

"Why do they burn the offering?"

"So the smoke will rise to the heavens and—" *feed the gods.* "So that God will take note of it, and listen to our prayers."

Tabitha watched the distant wisps of inky black smoke tracing mystical letters in the air.

Ruth dumped what was left in the sack into a chipped earthenware bowl and ran her fingers through it, feeling for the last precious kernels of grain in a pile of dried-up husks. And she told the child a tale of when the world was young, and a piece of the sky fell into the great eastern sea, raising a giant wave that flooded the earth all the way to the land of the Kushites to the south and the eastern hills of the land of Ugarit, nine hundred miles from the ocean.

The sack fluttered loosely in Ruth's hands as the breeze carried away the chaff.

The smoke rising from the temporary altar drifted across the Central Valley, carried along by a hot, dry wind from the east that seemed to echo her barren widowhood. She certainly couldn't go trawling the hills from here to Beit-lekhem searching for a suitable husband. She had to seek the assistance of a man, and there was only one who was up to the task. She would have to convince the prophet to help her gather testimony and present the proofs to the elders of the city. And she would walk through the deepest valley of darkness, facing down demons and whatever terrors lurked there, even to the gates of She'ol itself, in her quest for such knowledge.

~

"May Yahaweh be praised on this momentous occasion," declared Prince Sheshbazzar, his bejeweled arm sweeping through the air in a broad arc.

Cries of *Ya-huuuuu!*—God lives!—filled the air as attendants brought forth a golden bowl full of lamb's blood as a peace offering. The attendants raised the bowl and tilted it to the east, west, north, and south, then they dashed the blood against the charred stones of the ruined altar.

The crowd's thunderous response shook the foundations of the crippled old buildings, loosening rocks and chunks of plaster.

"And now we'll hear from a leader of the scribes," said Prince Sheshbazzar, extending his fleshy fingers toward Ezra.

Ezra the Scribe smoothed out his impossibly clean white robe and took his place before the assembled masses. He called for his scribes to write down his words in the languages of Yehud, Aram, and Persia, and to prepare a copy for the royal archives in Babylon.

"I am Ezra son of Serayah, son of Azaryah, son of Khilkiyah, son of Shallum, son of Tsaddok, son of Akhituv, son of Amaryah, son of Azaryah, son of Merayoth, son of Zerakhyah, son of Uzzi, son of Bukki, son of Avishua, son of Phineas, son of Eleazar, son of Aaron the first *kohan*."

Either he ran out of breath or that was as far back as the list of names went. Ruth couldn't imagine inheriting such a legacy and carrying the weight of it with you at all times. She didn't even know her father's name.

With great solemnity and purpose, Ezra's slaves brought out a newly revised and edited version of the Torah prepared in the land of Babylon. They held the scroll aloft for all to behold, then unrolled it to the passage Ezra had selected for the first public reading, a long list of names of the families who came up out of the land of Egypt to the land of Israel:

Khanokh, Eliav, Yakhin, Ozni, Korakh, Peretz, Makhir, Zevulon, Bekher—the list went on for so long, Ruth gave up and went searching among the sellers of roasted chickpeas and nuts, when a familiar voice cut through the air.

"What do we need a king for?" Ben-Isaiah said, arguing with a group of bargain hunters as a pair of watchmen on patrol eyed him warily. "It was the *kings* of old, *not the people*, who did evil in the eyes of the Lord and hastened the destruction of Jerusalem."

The country folk nodded in agreement, but the merchants grumbled that this would-be prophet was chasing away their customers.

"Look at the faces of the Persian elites who rule our land. Look into the eyes the Persian warriors who have conquered our territories, and know that we are no longer the nation of Israel."

One of the merchants signaled to the watchmen, who moved in to seize the loudmouth in the torn cloak.

"No, my friends, we are no longer a nation. But we are a people," Ben-Isaiah went on, as the watchmen pushed through the crowd. "How long will they rule, your line of kings?" he taunted them. "See that young woman over there?"

He pointed to a raven-haired woman in a plain woolen cloak. A handsome young warrior stood by her side, his arm wrapped around her waist. Ruth felt a jolt of recognition: the prophet was addressing Miryam and Yedidyah the Nazirite, their companions on the trek across the wilderness.

"She's going to have a baby," Ben-Isaiah declared, though Miryam had barely begun to show. "And she shall name him *God is with us*, because by the time that child is weaned and learns to tell good from bad, our prayers will be answered and we will have no need of a king."

The watchmen halted, looking at each other.

"Other nations can be corrupt and unjust," Ben-Isaiah continued. "Their ways are like the uncleanliness of a *niddah*."

Ruth felt a flame extinguish inside her as if it had been doused with a bucket of water. She had a deep, abiding love of certain aspects of the Yehudim's culture—with their fierce hatred of captivity and resistance to imperial authority, they practically worshiped the ideal of individual freedom. But their priests and prophets continually used the ways of women as a metaphor for all that is vile and corrupt, as if a woman's monthly song of blood were the foulest and most unclean thing imaginable.

One of the watchman warned: "Watch your words, prophet, or I'll charge you with putting a curse upon a ruler of the people."

Ben-Isaiah lashed out at them: "The *kohanim* inherit the priesthood from their fathers, and the judges are elected by the council of elders, but *the prophet is chosen by God alone*. Do you really believe that God prefers your bloody sacrifices to righteous deeds? Or that he prefers your burnt offerings to observing His commandments?"

"Whoa, slow down," said a local scribe, trying to keep up. "I want to get down every word of this."

⌒

Raisins and almonds for the wedding party? I'll give you a good price, madam.

Why do you want to marry that girl, anyway? Her family's got no money.

Two minas of plain wool for a shekel. You want the purple dyed wool, that's going to cost you. That purple dye comes all the way from Tyre, my friend.

But I did all that you asked, my lord.

And I said I can't pay you today. Come back tomorrow.

But—

I said come back tomorrow.

So you see, if you marry the other girl, your offspring will inherit both *estates.*

*But there's already a family of peasants living on the property.
You just leave them to me.*

*Sweet milk for drinking, sour milk for yogurt and cheese, step
right up, ladies and gentlemen, step right up.*

*What do you mean you have no records of your bloodlines? You
must prove that your lineage is pure Israelite to retain title to the land.*

But we've lived on that plot of land for three generations.

Tell you what, just sign here and we'll take care of everything.

~

The old clay oven was charred and cracked. Ruth fanned the
flames till her arms were sore and the fire burned hot enough
to melt lead. But it still wasn't enough. She yanked open the
pouch she had carried across the wilderness and dumped
the collection of dried date pits onto the glowing red coals.

She and Tzillah took turns fanning the fire, the flames
waxing bright orange and the skin on their forearms glowing
from the heat of their labor as the temperature rose more
than a thousand degrees, hot enough to melt bronze, silver,
and gold, but still a long way from the melting point of iron.

"I haven't sweated … like this … since my wedding night,"
Tzillah joked, her shirt sticking to her back as she toiled like
a beast of burden.

Ruth nodded curtly. She had endured every possible
combination of remarks on the connection between shoving an iron tool into a blazing hot oven and—well, you know.

"Can I … ask you … something?" Tzillah said, her breath
coming in short spurts.

"Sure."

Here it comes.

"Did your tribe practice … uh … group … I mean …
communal …"

"Wild, orgiastic fertility rites?"

Tzillah nodded, sucking air through her gaping mouth.

"Isn't all lovemaking supposed to be a little wild?" Ruth

said, pleased that her stamina was holding up better than Tzillah's.

The blank look on Tzillah's face said it all. *Someone's marriage has lost the magic*, Ruth thought. For nothing will cool the fires of passion quicker than hunger and poverty.

Yet Ruth sensed that, in some remote part of their brains, men secretly wished to return to the unleashed passion of rutting animals through fertility rites that were older than the knowledge of working in copper. She could feel it in their eyes, the way they stared, the burning desire emanating from them like the heat from an oven.

Tzillah's arms gave out and she collapsed against the wooden cooling racks.

"Our *rekhamim* are so desirable that most men would give anything just to fit a little piece of themselves back inside it," Ruth said.

Tzillah grinned at the thought, panting for breath as Ruth finished stoking the fire to the height of its orange-yellow fury.

"Tell me … you've traveled through many lands," Tzillah said, licking the sweat from her upper lip. "Is there really such a difference in the way that little piece of manhood is distributed among the nations of the earth?"

Ruth bobbled the crucible full of molten metal. She cursed in a foreign tongue as errant drops of scalding hot ore spilled into the ashes.

"There is much variation, even among brothers," she said, the hair on her forearms practically igniting as she tried to correct her mistake. "But overall the pale men of the northern tribes are less generously endowed than the Shemites."

She didn't want to be distracted by thoughts of such pleasures as she labored to fuse the broken pieces of the wrought iron blade. How she craved that intimacy. That touch. Those sensations. Just the two of them, cuddling in the darkness.

She blinked away hot tears as she pulled the glowing blade from the fire, placed it on a bed of ground charcoal and pressed down with all her strength. At Ruth's command, Tzillah sprinkled the rest of the coal dust on top, covering it completely.

At long last, Ruth allowed herself to smile with satisfaction.

Now they would see.

Now they would see what she could do.

A man suddenly cleared his throat behind them.

Ruth twisted around and beheld Nehemiah the military engineer standing astride the ash sweepings, arms crossed over his leather-clad chest, his manly air contrasting with his youthful beard. Further down the hill, the crew of military engineers surveyed what was left of a thousand-foot stretch of King Hezkiyah's Wall.

"Hardening the blade through red-hot contact with a bed of powdered charcoal," he said, a glimmer of a smile on his lips. "That's a hell of a lot of work to put into a lousy hoe for turnips and carrots. Where'd you farm girls learn *that* trick?"

Ruth extracted the hoe from the ashes and plunged the still-glowing metal into a bucket of waste water with a steamy hiss. When it cooled, Nehemiah yanked the hoe out of the water and examined the shiny new blade. The once rusty surface was transformed into a bright silvery layer that needed some filing around the edges, but the seam was as strong as the rest of the blade. Nehemiah tested the blade with his finger.

"My, my. You could slaughter a dozen men with this," he said, admiring the work. "So I'm going to ask you once again, where did you learn this forbidden art?"

"From a master craftsman," Ruth replied, looking squarely into the engineer's deep black eyes.

"Does this master have a name?"

Ruth reached for the hoe, letting her hand hang in the

air. Nehemiah was content to make her wait until she yielded and said, "He's not my master anymore."

He let her wrest the tool from his grasp.

"Well, whoever he was, he didn't teach you much about smithing. You girls were making so much noise, I could hear you clear across the valley."

"No, he never taught me the finer points of working with silver and gold. He was too busy working me half to death."

"Rode you like an ass, is that it?"

Ruth's eyes widened, her grip tightening around the hoe's wooden shaft.

"It's just an expression," Tzillah muttered, her face going pale. "It just means—"

"I can figure out what it means," Ruth snapped.

Nehemiah's sly grin grew even broader. "But he never let you see the best part, did he? The part requiring genuine skill? No, he had you stoking the fire and minding the air pumps."

Ruth swallowed the impulse to take the hoe and force-feed him some hot coals.

"Of course you picked up some of his secrets just by observing him," Nehemiah continued. "But he could never let on with the customers, since no warrior in the land would touch a weapon that's been handled by a woman."

He turned to Tzillah: "Bad luck, you know. Robs the sword of its power. Especially if she's a *niddah* whose touch will dull its blade."

"That's nonsense, and you know it," Ruth said, snatching her bag of tools and tossing it on the workbench where the local women prepared the bread every morning. She ignored Nehemiah's gaze, selecting a pair of files—a coarse one and a fine one—and channeled her pent-up fury into filing down the flash around the edges of the hoe blade.

Shouts rose from the valley below. Something urgent that the chief engineer needed to see right away.

Nehemiah signaled to them, and went back to watching

Ruth's arm muscles ripple and flex as she filed away the blade's rougher patches, creating a clean edge.

"Not bad, not bad at all," he said, nodding. "But I'll wager the old Kenite was content to have you hovering in the background, wiggling your little *takhat* to help push a sale along."

Ruth looked up sharply.

"And if the haggling wasn't going his way, he'd tap his foot three times and that was the signal for you to bring a nice cool drink of fermented pomegranate juice for the male clientele, making sure to bend low as you poured it for him."

Ruth lowered her gaze. "My Lord is clearly experienced in warfare, and the ways of the camp followers. Perhaps I could be of assistance—"

"Too bad there's no work for a female metalsmith's assistant in Jerusalem."

"I don't mean making weapons. I could help make plow blades, picks and shovels, knives—"

"We don't need plow blades. We need able-bodied men to help us rebuild the city's defenses. The wall is crumbling, the gates have burned to the ground, and the city is as vulnerable to attack as a wanton woman who wanders the streets at night alone."

Ruth set aside the coarse file and switched to the fine one.

"Then let the women of the city help rebuild it."

Nehemiah shook his head at her folly. "They told me you have the forwardness of a street woman, and it's true. You refuse to be ashamed."

Ruth felt the blood rising to her face once more. "You're charged with rebuilding the wall before the rainy season comes, so you don't have much time, do you?" she said, redirecting her anger into honing the blade. "You need to recruit the daughters of the land, or do you want the sons and daughters of strangers to rebuild your walls?"

His wooden smile was all teeth and no warmth. "I see

that you've been listening to that crazy prophet again. Do us all a favor and weave him a new cloak, will you? The ratty thing he's wearing smells like a dead mule."

"I have no skills in the art of weaving," Ruth said, angling the file just right to produce an earthy grating noise.

"Do you want our enemies to laugh at us and say that our warriors have become like women?"

Ruth paused and tested the blade with her finger. "Doesn't the prophet Shemuel tell of the wise woman who saved the whole city of Beit-ma'akhah with her quick thinking?"

She turned to Tzillah and asked her to fetch a length of rope and hand it to the military engineer.

"Now, Master Nekhemyah, if you would be so kind as to set your fists about two *z'rathim* apart—like so—and hold the rope as tightly as possible. A little tighter. Tighter. There."

Nehemiah held the rope taut while Ruth tested the handle's weight and balance, and when she was ready, the sharp new blade swished through the air and sliced the rope clean in two. Tzillah squealed with the sudden release of tension.

Nehemiah was left with two lengths of frayed rope dangling from his tightly clenched fists, doing the calculations in his head.

After an unusually quiet moment, he said, "Let me make some inquiries, and if it please the king, I will let you know."

~

They came from all over—the sons of Hasenah, Uriyya, and Meshezavel; the men and women of Tekoa; Shallum ben-Halokhesh and his daughters; the men of Giveon and Mitzpah; and the villagers from dozens of daughter-towns around Jerusalem.

They gathered by the Valley Gate, where the wall was in such bad condition Nehemiah could break off pieces of it with his bare hands. His plan was to restore the fortifications as far as the Broad Wall, but with most of the city's resources diverted to rebuilding the Temple, even a scaled-back plan would require a tax increase and a levy on grain that would fall most heavily on the poorest people in the district.

The people of the land assailed Nehemiah with bitter complaints: *We're being pressed into service on this wall when we live in the surrounding country! What good is it to us? Why should we pay for it? We're being pressed to the limit as it is.*

Nehemiah heard their pleas and agreed to enact measures to forgive the worst of their debts, and to redeem the children they had sold into slavery to pay those debts.

"What about letting us stay on the land we've been working for three generations?"

"We'll look into that," he promised.

～

Nehemiah told the men of Giveon and Mitzpah: You're charged with securing the entrance to the water shaft near the Gihon Spring. It's a crucial source of water that lies outside the city walls, and it's one of the weakest links in the city's defenses. I need you to block access to the shaft by fitting it with iron bars that allow the water to pass through.

As the men laid out their tools, he turned to Ruth: "You gather the kindling."

When she opened her mouth to protest, he cut her off: "You see this cliff?" he said, tilting his head up toward the sheer rock face above their heads. "No enemy has ever breached the defenses in this part of the city. When the invaders come, they usually attack from the north, which is why the people of Jerusalem have such a strong distrust of anything that comes from the north," he said, glaring pointedly at her.

Ruth gathered the driest kindling she could find and offered several suggestions about how to build the most efficient fire.

"Get me the *makkebeth*," one of the men barked at her.

She jumped at his command, rushing to grab a heavy metal hammer.

"Not that one, the other one."

"Which other one?"

"That's a forge hammer, you fool. I said get me the *makkebeth*."

Nehemiah tapped the heavy wooden mallet with the toe of his sandal, grinning at her discomfort.

The fire crackled to life easily, thanks to a steady breeze blowing through the valley. The men measured the entrance to the water shaft and began chiseling holes in the rock to secure the iron bars.

Ruth inspected the lumps of raw iron they were planning to stretch into bars, pointing out their poor quality—they might contain pockets of gas that could explode under pressure—when Nehemiah told her she wasn't needed near the forge and to gather more kindling.

Eyes rolled when Ruth tossed an armful of kindling at Nehemiah's feet, grabbed a shovel and set about examining the strange and remarkable jumble of soil types exposed by the excavations, including several feet of dark gray ash in some places, which supported the prophet's claim that in the days of old a nearby city had been destroyed by fire and brimstone.

After probing and prodding with the chisel, and some digging and sifting by hand, she came up with some fascinating samples.

"What could you possibly find of interest poking around in a hole in the ground?" said Nehemiah.

Ruth showed him a broken piece of glazed earthenware pottery, saying its glassy surface meant that it had been subjected to extremely high temperatures, nearly as hot as the hottest smelting furnaces in all Luristan, meaning at some point the region must have withstood a devastating earthquake that released molten lava from deep within the earth, which ran through the valley engulfing everything in its path.

"Now, look at *this*."

She showed him what looked like just another charred lump of glazed earthenware.

"But it's not earthenware, it's a mixture of stone and sand," she told him.

Her listener seemed unimpressed.

"Stone and sand that's been turned to *glass*."

Nehemiah examined the object with some skepticism.

"No furnace on earth can melt stone like this," she said. "Nothing earthly burns that hot. Only fire from the sky can do something like this."

Could it be? he wondered. *Was this border-crosser holding physical proof of God's wrath in her filthy, callused hands?*

~

The men of Giveon let out a collective gasp of astonishment as several feet of blackened earth gave way, revealing a cache of charred debris that had clearly once been part of a library of some sort that must have tumbled down the hillside during the city's destruction. The parchment scrolls had been reduced to cinders, but the clay seals that labeled them were intact, baked to a durable hardness by the raging fires. The seals identified various clumps of ash as the remains of legal decisions, business transactions, and sacred texts belonging to the royal archives, which were burned to the ground by the armies of Babylon on that awful day when God turned His face from His people and the Temple went up in smoke.

Nehemiah scooped up a handful of ashes, wondering what priceless literary artifacts had been lost forever as the winds from the east scattered them to and fro.

"Now what do we do?" said the merchants.

"We cart away whatever's beyond hope and sift through what's left."

"Those old scrolls could have God's name written on them—"

"They're supposed to be given a proper burial."

"Very well," said Nehemiah. "We'll give the ashes a proper burial in the valley of Hinnom."

"I'm not touching that stuff. Tell that Moabite girl to do it."

~

It was dirty, unrewarding work that left her face and arms streaked with soot. Cooking fires dotted the hillside, and some of the upper-class slaves shook their heads at the Moabite slave girl hauling cinders past the dung heaps while they climbed the hill to the ivory palaces near the Temple Mount carrying eighty-pound amphorae of wine, olive oil, nuts, and *naphtha*.

When she returned to the Gihon Spring, one of the men sweeping out the bottom layer of ashes called out as he felt something heavy and sharp.

The others flocked around him.

"What is it?"

The man held up a heavy triangular arrowhead in the Saka-Irani style used by the armies of Nebuchadnezzar, greenish- tinged with corrosion, the point still sharp to the touch.

It could have been forged by the same hand as the polished arrowheads Ruth had given the Persian commander in the desert.

Her heart jumped when Nehemiah called sharply to her.

"What is it, my lord?"

"What does that say?"

He pointed to the wedge-shaped characters incised in a ring around the base of the arrowhead.

"I cannot read Akkadian writing, my lord."

"Yet you know enough to identify the writing as Akkadian."

"I … recognize some of the characters."

"I can see that. So what does it say?"

"The figures are worn and … unfamiliar … but this part appears to say *arrow of pkd*."

"What is *pkd*?"

"I don't know. Probably the warrior's name."

"What kind of name is *pkd*?" one of the men scoffed.

"Maybe it's short for Pakudu."

"Sounds like a Babylonian name to me."

Well, yeah, it's a Babylonian weapon.

The men cast accusatory glances at Ruth's soot-smeared face until Nehemiah told her to hurry up and cart away the last of the ashes.

But as Ruth grasped the cart's wooden handles, she felt an ominous low rumbling that rapidly swelled into a clamorous uproar as the combined forces of three hostile nations swept down from the north, spilling into the valleys flanking the City of David like a pair of smoking hot pincers. She dropped the cart and leapt into the spring feet first, splashing toward the hole in the rock face and squeezing past the slick, mossy stones into the tunnel. The others followed, wading after her and climbing about fifteen feet up the water shaft, pressed together in the darkness, Nehemiah cursing the whole time that they were outnumbered and unarmed, before the rank odor of death filled their nostrils as the invading armies met at the southern tip of the Siloam Pool and hacked and stabbed and thrust and slew until the waters of the pool blossomed with red. Arrows severed arteries and spinal cords, slingstones shattered bones and amphorae, and bleeding men slid down the hill on slick streams of glistening green olives until the river of olive oil reached the cooking fires and ignited. Amphorae of oil and *naphtha* exploded and a wall of yellow-white flame rose up hot enough to carbonize clay jars and melt the porous surfaces of mud bricks.

Cowering in the water shaft, Ruth found herself praying in the tongue of Yehud: *Mima'amakim k'rosikho Yahaweh, Adonai shim'oh v'koli.*

Out of the depths I call to You. O Lord, hear my voice.

CHAPTER FOURTEEN

Felicity

The white Lexus LX sparkles in the sun, its shiny mesh grille gleaming like a beluga whale with a mouthful of diamond fillings. This set of wheels retails for about ninety grand, and it looks like it has less than a thousand miles on it, which is a shame since there's a substantial dent in the left rear fender alongside a shattered tail light, with flecks of the other car's paint embedded in the ridges around the point of impact.

I stroll up the semicircular driveway on this day of record warmth and ring the bell. The thick oak door is alive with beveled glass reflecting the midmorning sun, breaking my image up into a riot of refracted glimpses of my dark gray business suit: conservative below-the-knee skirt and matching blazer, charcoal-gray blouse, black stockings, black ankle boots, and a suede shoulder bag that's midway between a purse and a briefcase. Everything the professional female PI needs to be taken seriously in this upscale part of Long Island, just off the Vanderbilt Parkway.

Most of the cars in the neighboring driveways are high-end suburban status machines with brand names like Lamborghini, Ferrari, and an angular, black, armor-plated monster that looks like it swallowed a jet engine—each one sitting on enough horsepower to quicken the pulse of the auto racing enthusiast who bankrolled the original Vanderbilt Parkway.

A shadowy figure drifts into view on the other side of the glass, solidifying into the outline of a hunched, round-shouldered woman.

"Mrs. Lowry?" I ask, as she opens the door about six inches and blocks my entrance with her short, wide frame, which I'd describe as *matronly*, since it sounds better than saying her body is shaped like a mini-fridge. She's wearing a bright floral print dress that clings to her squat body from her neck to just below her knees, leaving very little breathing room.

"Yes?" Her hair is a glossy blond curly-do that looks like it's been frozen in place since 1998, and her light brown eyes are lit with the glow of reflected sun, but her fleshy face is tinged with gray around the edges, as if she's still recovering from the shock of a distracted driver in a gunmetal-gray Toyota barreling into her brand-new SUV.

"I'm Felicity Ortega Pérez. May I come in?"

"What's this about?"

"I called you about the accident, remember?"

I reach into my bag and hand her a business card. She holds it closer to get a better look.

"I thought you said your name was Peretz," she says, squinting at the card.

"No, it's Ortega. My mother's name was Pérez. Sorry for the confusion."

"So you're not Jewish?"

"Uh, no. Sorry."

She gives a shrug and opens the door, but I can't help feeling she's a bit disappointed in me.

The Lowry home is as pristine and airless as a museum of fine art. The living room is furnished with mid-twentieth-century modernist touches, the bone-white walls providing a silent backdrop for an array of modern takes on the ancient symbols of her family's Jewish heritage—a heavy brass menorah, a copper-colored relief of the tablets of the Ten Commandments in Hebrew fixed in amber, a framed document with a colorfully illustrated border, also in Hebrew as far as I can tell, a Chagall lithograph, and a bookcase neatly lined with every major work of Jewish American fiction, nonfiction, and reference from the past fifty years. The bottom shelf is crammed with oversized books on Israel, the Holocaust, and a slew of kosher cookbooks bearing the stains of years of devoted use.

Mrs. Lowry invites me to have a seat on the eggshell-white Scandinavian couch. A pair of silver-framed photos stare back at me from either side of the coffee table. On my left is a black-and-white studio portrait of a young couple taken sometime in the mid-1960s—a tall, robust "man's man" with a confident grin and dark wavy hair, and a gorgeous 5'2" blond with a plunging neckline, before time worked its magic and transformed her short and shapely body into a rusty old heap with the dimensions of a dishwasher. The other photo is a color headshot of a junior executive type in a power suit and tie, with a cocky Mona Lisa smile on his slightly pudgy face, as if he's sitting on a piece of insider information the Feds missed during their last sweep.

Mrs. Lowry sets out a tray of coffee and pastries. I take my coffee with milk, no sugar, she takes hers black with two artificial sweeteners. She stirs hers with a silver spoon, takes a sip, and says, "So can you help get justice for my son?"

I take a sip of pale brown coffee, which buys me a few seconds to come up with a better answer than *Huh?*

"I'm just trying to get background information before the case goes to trial," I say. "Was your son a witness?"

"May you never witness such things, even if you live to a hundred and twenty. My son wasn't a witness. He was a *victim*."

My eyebrows embark on a collision course.

"The police report didn't mention any serious injuries."

"Because there were no *injuries*. People either made it out alive or they didn't."

I tilt my head slightly, trying to realign myself with the geometry of her remarks.

"Buried under tons of wreckage," she says, her eyes glistening with unformed tears.

Okay, hold it right there. I put down my cup of bland decaf and start to explain that I'm here to interview her about the car accident, not—

I finally realize what's lying in plain view right in front of my face.

No wonder the place feels like a mausoleum.

Because it is one.

Oh, Christ. I'm going to have to recalibrate and take the long way around.

"So when I got your call, I was hoping Michael's claim finally went through," she says.

I take a deep breath and say it quickly: I'm not an investigator from the insurance company. I'm trying to find the woman who plowed into her Lexus, but I'm sorry for her immeasurable loss and the daily heartache it must bring.

"Oh. Did you lose someone on 9/11?" she asks.

"We all lost someone," I say.

Mrs. Lowry insists that I try the pastry.

I nibble on a tiny chocolate éclair, and tell her my dad was one of the volunteers, digging with hand tools at first, trying to find a living soul in those terrible days after the attack, a survivor, a sign of life, anything, and coming up with nothing but bits and pieces—a shoe, a wallet, a two-dollar bill singed at the edges, a bent subway token, a crushed FDNY helmet. All covered in thick white dust.

She nods knowingly, lips trembling as if she's saying a silent prayer. "I knew right away," she says, her gaze falling on the framed photo of her son. "Whenever Michael was running late, or if something came up, he would always call or text me to let me know, so I wouldn't worry. That's how I knew—" She can't go on.

I take her hand and gently squeeze it to let her know it's okay.

"I just knew …" she says, wiping away a tear with her other hand before it gets a chance to fall.

"I'm sure he tried to reach you …" I grope for the right words. "He was probably too busy helping others."

"Yes, that would be just like him," she says. "I still talk to him. Every day."

My turn to nod.

"I tell him how his nieces and nephews are doing in school," she says. "I tell him about the rookie pitcher who just signed with the Mets. About a new recipe I tried. Little things. Everyday things. You understand."

"Of course."

"You want to see his room?"

Not really, but go ahead if it makes you feel any better.

She leads me down a narrow hallway and opens the door to a hallowed space. She waves me toward the bed that hasn't been slept in since the 1990s, the shelf unit full of neatly folded underwear and socks, the closet where his favorite teenage band T-shirts and hoodies still hang, empty.

"I can't bring myself to give his clothes away to charity. I know that's what he would have wanted me to do, but I just can't. I know I should, but …"

I assure her it's all perfectly understandable.

She directs my gaze to the knickknacks crowding the shelf over the bed, from a pair of 1986 New York Mets bobble-head dolls to a set of vintage 1980s action figures in their original packaging.

"Everything that was precious to him, every little *tchatch-keh*, went from being just an object to a sacred thing no one was allowed to touch."

After a moment of respectful silence, I ask, "Have you ever talked to someone about this?"

"You mean his collection of Star Wars action figures? It's not for sale."

"I mean like a grief counselor or something."

"*Counselors*. What good are they? Can the counselors bring my son back?"

I don't have an answer for that.

She seals the door to the frozen diorama of Michael Lowry's childhood bedroom, leads me back to the living room couch and offers me more coffee.

My fingers have gone cold, so I cradle the cup for warmth and sit there listening as she says, "For the longest time, I couldn't even tell someone my son was a good boy, because it meant … it meant saying he *was* … you know … not he *is* … but he *was* …"

I nod. *Was* is not *is*. Words fail me, yet again.

"When I finally got up the strength to visit the 9/11 Memorial, those heartless bastards wanted to charge me *twenty-four dollars* to look at my son's final resting place."

"He's buried at Ground Zero?"

"Part of him, since the little bit they found for us could have fit in a shoe box."

That means most of his remains probably ended up in the Fresh Kills Landfill on Staten Island. She doesn't need to hear that right now.

"What did you do?"

"What else could we do? We buried the shoe box."

"I mean, what was it like going back there?"

"How else could it be? It was awful. Listening to that fat fuck from New Jersey talk about honor and sacrifice just one day after he blamed the cops, firemen, and teachers for turning his state budget into a complete disaster."

Whoa. Her language may be at odds with her genteel manner, but it's clear these emotions run deep and raw.

"I can't even turn on the news without hearing some of that *mishegas* about how the Jews knew about it ahead of time, and were warned to stay away on 9/11. Do you know how much it hurts to hear that?"

"I can imagine."

"Can you? Can you really?"

"Yes, ma'am. As you noted earlier, I'm Latina. We know all about offensive stereotypes."

I try to steer the conversation back to the accident and its repercussions. "I'm curious about the name Lowry. It doesn't sound very, uh—"

"Jewish? It's not. We changed it from Loewy."

I'm still at a loss.

"It's the old Czech form of Levi," she says. "Even a *shikse* like you must recognize the Jewishness of a name like Levi."

"One of the twelve original tribes, right?"

"More or less, depending on how you count. You sure you're not Jewish? You look a little—"

"I'm sure," I say. "So did you happen to exchange insurance and contact information with the driver of the other vehicle?"

"She wasn't insured."

"Figures. How about an address?"

"Yes, I've got it written down on a piece of paper."

~

I smooth out the note and take a photo of it with my phone: 27 Lombard Street. Plus the cell phone number that no longer works. It certainly looks like Kristel's handwriting, but I'll have to wait till I'm back in the office to compare the two samples side by side. Mrs. Lowry clutches my hand and gives me a goodbye squeeze, then I hop in the company car and crank up the *bachata* music on my dad's boom box to drown out the endless stream of toxic sludge from the radio.

I ride the wave of pulsing Latino soul music until I'm about a block away from Lombard Street, just off Jericho Turnpike in a town called Syosset, a dead end street behind a Chipotle franchise and a dentist's office.

I turn down the music and roll to a stop three houses down from number 27.

No Maseratis in these driveways. More like a rusty

Toyota Camry, a ten-year-old Honda Civic, a lovingly restored 1970s-era Harley-Davidson chopper, and a spotless Dodge Ram Rebel with a pair of FURSTEN FIRST bumper stickers adorning the rear panel alongside stickers of the American and Confederate flags.

No sign of the 1992 Toyota Corolla registered to Kristel Santos, but I still approach the house at number 27 with caution. It's a sorry-looking one-story dwelling, more of a bungalow than a house, the cracked stucco buried under a network of hairy-rooted poison ivy and untended shrubs. The perfect place to hide out and take stock till you figure out your next move.

The windows are dark, and the tall grass surrounding the splintered wooden walkway is so overgrown it's swaying in the breeze like hay. None of it looks freshly trampled, though. There's a pile of mail on the crumbling door mat. I slip on a pair of clear vinyl gloves, crouch down, and sift through the mail, checking the senders and postmarks. Mostly junk mail, and some of it looks like it's been here since the last Bush administration. Not an encouraging sign, unless someone *wants* the place to look abandoned. There's even a thin coating of dust on the mail slot, suggesting that even the US Postal Service has given up on the place. I ring the bell anyway and knock several times, telling the unresponsive doorway in English and Spanish that I'm looking for Kristel Santos and I'm here to help.

None of the window curtains appear to rustle in the slightest. Time for some unorthodox procedures. Taking care not to disturb the dust, I push open the mail slot with a vinyl-gloved finger and take a sniff of the air inside the house. It's pretty musty, with a trace of mold, but at least I don't detect the sickly-sweet odor of decaying flesh. I creep along the stucco wall around the back, on the lookout for the print of a woman's size-nine shoe, a trampled blade of grass, or some other sign that anything human passed this way recently, until my path is blocked by an intact spiderweb stretching from the sagging roof gutter to the brown needles on the nearest branch of a dying evergreen. The web could have been spun within the past hour by an enterprising spider, but it sure looks like nobody's been this way in a while. I duck under the web and keep going toward the back of the house. The broken screen door creaks open on rusty springs, and the back door is as unresponsive to my entreaties as the front.

I stop punishing my knuckles on the worn wood, and in the sudden silence I hear the distinct tread of human weight on distressed wooden boards. Coming from *outside* the house. I stop and listen, and realize I can't really distinguish anything because of the constant whoosh of traffic on Jericho Turnpike, a short distance away through the scrubby pine trees. Maybe I imagined it. I turn and find myself staring into the wide black barrel of a Kel-Tec 9mm pistol.

"Caught you!" says a grimy-faced white guy with a five-day growth of beard and a black wool watch cap pulled low over his eyebrows. He's wearing black woolen gloves with the fingertips cut off. So probably not a professional assassin.

My hands fly up to chest level, fingers spread wide, before he even finishes barking the order: "Show me your hands!"

"Take it easy, buddy, I'm just—"

"Don't move! Do *not* move! You got that?"

He keeps the gun leveled at my chest while he pulls out a cell phone and dials 911.

"*Second Precinct. What is your emergency?*"

"I caught someone trespassing."

"*Trespassing?*"

"Yes, ma'am."

"*Where are you located?*"

"Twenty-Seven Lombard Street in Syosset. We've had some break-ins recently, and she's acting all suspicious, creeping around this abandoned property."

"*The suspicious individual is a female, sir?*"

"Yes."

"*Is she white, Black, or Hispanic?*"

"Hispanic."

"Actually, we prefer the term *Latina*," I say.

"Shut up!" The gun rises toward my face.

"*Are you sure of that description, sir?*"

"Definitely. I heard her speaking Spanish."

"*Can you describe what she's wearing?*"

"Look, she's standing right in front of me. I'm holding a gun on her."

"*Okay, we don't need you to do that, sir.*"

"How soon can you get an officer over here?"

"*Is she threatening you in any way?*"

"I just told you I caught her trespassing."

"*Are you the owner of the property, sir?*"

"No, I'm a member of the neighborhood watch committee—"

"*All right, sir. What is your name?*"

"My name? What the hell do you need my name for? Just send a damn patrol car before I—"

"*Do you live in the area, sir?*"

"I just said—"

"*Is this individual responding to your request to leave the property?*"

"Yes—I was just leaving," I say loudly, leaning toward the phone.

"Shut up, you."

"*What number are you calling from?*"

"Are you fuckin' kiddin' me? You clowns don't have Caller ID?"

"Byyyye! I'm leeeeaving!" I call out, my voice pitched high and sing-songy to further defuse any tension with the local police, whom I really should have called sooner to let them know I was going to be working their patch today. Lesson learned.

"*Sir, there's nothing we can do if it isn't a case of criminal trespass and the individual willingly vacates the premises. Feel free to call us again if she does anything unlawful.*"

Click.

End of transmission.

My hooded assailant levels his eyes at me with a look of such pure hatred I feel it twisting in the pit of my stomach.

"I—caught—you—trespassing," he growls, fingers tightening around the pistol grip.

"Right. And the cops could charge you with second-degree assault for holding me at gunpoint, which'll get you *way more* jail time than a lousy misdemeanor trespassing charge."

He looks at the 9mm in his hand as if it never occurred to him that waving his precious possession around so flagrantly could possibly cause him more trouble than it's worth.

Now would be the perfect moment to swing both arms up and swat the gun out of his hand, kick him in the balls and grind his face in the dirt while cursing his offspring unto the seventh generation. But I sort of promised the police I would leave the area peacefully. And it would muss up my job interview clothes. So I give my assailant a bit of advice instead:

"And since you're not the property owner, technically, we're *both* trespassing."

"Okay, so you got me on a technicality. Then why were you spying on me?"

Oh, Jesus. This asshole points a gun at my chest and then bitches about a *technicality*? With my patience threatening to burst at the seams, I carefully explain that I wasn't spying on him, I was looking for the previous resident of number 27, a lady by the name of Kristel Santos.

"Fuckin' nut job hasn't lived here for at least a month," he says, hocking up a grayish wad of smoker's phlegm and spitting it in the dirt.

Right. *She's* the nut job.

"*Damn.*"

"Yeah, life's full of disappointments. Now get in your crappy little bean-burner and don't ever come back."

"Mister, I can't get away from here fast enough."

~

Brakes screech to a halt.

Empty lot.

Nothing but gravel and broken glass from here to the chain link fence blocking access to the train tracks.

Six-pack of empties left by the curb.

Perfect.

Hi-yaaah!

First empty beer bottle clears the fence and hits a concrete railroad tie with a resounding shatter.

Hi-yaaaah!

Second beer bottle bounces off springy section of chain link between the poles, falls to the pavement with a dull crack.

Hi-yaaaaah!

Third bottle pings off fence top, goes spinning harm-lessly into the sand. Complete dud.

Hi-yaaaaaah!

Fourth bottle kisses the steel rail dead-on with a spec-tacular burst of shards.

Beautiful.

Hi-yaaaaaaah!

Fifth bottle smashes into the chain link hard enough to send bits of broken glass spraying through the air like the fireworks in Monte Carlo.

Hi-yaaaaaaaaah!

Sixth bottle is a high pop-up, easy out, but the shortstop can't get to it and it slams into the pitted blacktop and shat-ters to end the inning.

The pitcher jogs back to the dugout.

What?

Oh, like *you've* never had to pull over, let out a primal scream, and smash some bottles.

~

I roar down Jericho Turnpike blasting industrial-strength New York rock so loud the Statue of Liberty can hear it way out in New York Harbor. I swerve onto the Route 106 cloverleaf so fast I nearly hit Cedar Swamp Road riding on two wheels. I race past the Jericho Jewish Center and an upscale supermarket, floor it in the stretch and sail over the Long Island Expressway, nearly going airborne on the overpass. I finally hit traffic at the Broadway Mall in Hicksville and I have to switch off the warp engines and crawl the rest of the way on primitive internal combustion technology.

I'm approaching a populated area, so I have to lower the volume on the boom box just as the song reaches Lou Reed's cynical twist on Emma Lazarus's earnest words of welcome:

Give me your hungry, your tired, your poor ... I'll piss on 'em.

Rest in peace, Lou.

I drive under the LIRR tracks, past a donut shop with a flock of seagulls surveying the passing cars from atop the streetlamps and scavenging from the trash. A couple blocks to the south, and I pull up across from Tommy Ard's place.

I use the company phone to call the Second Precinct and tell them I'll be working this stretch of their turf today, in case someone calls in to report a suspicious vehicle with a sultry "Mexican" femme fatale lurking behind the wheel.

This time I stay in the car awhile, watching the subject mow his lawn with an old-school gas mower so loud and obnoxious it deserves its own reality show. Ard is wearing a pair of camo cutoffs and a sweat-stained Marine Corps T-shirt that says MESS WITH THE BEST, DIE LIKE THE REST. Ard's pumped-up arm muscles are full of tattoos, his light brown hair about three weeks past a regulation crew cut, grown out and teased a teensy bit. He's working with a sense of purpose usually reserved for helicopter rescues on the high seas. He doesn't just cut the grass, he *manicures* it with a savage intensity, and when he's done polishing and buffing it, he gets out the weed whacker and makes some noise with that till the street edge of the lawn is so perfectly uniform you could bounce a billiard ball off it. Just when I think he's done, he gets out the leaf blower—can't forget the leaf blower, now, can we?—and another quarter tank of gas burns up in the atmosphere, just so he can rid the curb of every single offending blade of fresh-cut grass.

I wouldn't necessarily call it an obsession, but let's just say that if it doesn't burn gas, oil, or electricity, Tommy Ard is not interested.

He finally stows the power tools in a handyman's shed and enters his home through a side door. I figure he needs time to wash up and change, but a moment later he comes out the front door with a can of domestic beer in his hand, sits on his front step, pops the top, and sucks down half the beer in one shot. Okay, let him finish his beer and survey his handi-work. I want to approach him when he's in a receptive mood. He drains the beer can in less than five seconds, goes back inside, and comes right out with a fresh can whose contents he demolishes a bit more slowly this time. He leans back, lights a cigarette, fills his lungs, and exhales. I guess it's now or never.

Ard's eyes narrow to pale blue slits and follow me as I smooth out my skirt, cross the street to the ribbon of concrete bisecting his lawn into perfectly equal halves, and, in the absence of a clear signal not to, step onto his property and walk up to greet him.

"Mr. Thomas Ard?" I begin.

"Yeah. And who the fuck are you?"

"Fair question," I say, flashing my temporary ID, which I've altered to say that my name is Felicity DiMaggio. Yeah, I did my homework on Mr. Ard. "How about this heat, huh?"

He squints at the Cadmium Solutions logo embossed on my credentials and curls his lip as if I'm offering him a half-eaten hamburger I found in the gutter three days ago, takes a drag on his filterless cigarette, and blows the smoke off to his right.

"Certified document examiner and CFA? What the fuck's that mean?"

"It means I've gone over the reports of your unit's actions in Baghdad and I need your help filling in some of the details and clearing up any issues that could otherwise end up costing the company money."

"So you're a glorified legal assistant," he says, unimpressed.

"More like a glorified accountant, really."

My humor fails to disarm him.

"Should I be bowing down and kissing your ring right now?" he says between puffs. "Or some other part of you?"

"Could we talk inside?" I suggest.

"What's wrong with here?"

I make a show of smoothing out my skirt.

"I just think we could talk more comfortably on the living room couch than on the concrete steps."

"Why should I talk to you?"

"I'm just here to clear up some details so the case can be settled in a favorable manner. It's entirely up to you."

He takes one last drag on the cigarette, grinds it out on the shady side of the concrete steps, then field strips the butt, scatters the leftover bits of tobacco in the dirt, and rolls the paper into a tiny ball. He stands up and goes inside without a word, leaving the door open, which I guess counts as an invitation for me to enter.

I take one step inside and remain there, taking in the surroundings as Ard heads to the kitchen to toss the tiny ball of paper in the garbage. The kitchen table and chairs date from the polyester-fueled 1970s, but look sturdy and well taken care of. The front room appears to have been furnished primarily with garage sale and thrift store purchases—the couch, TV, coffee table, easy chair—all kind of beat-up, but matching, or nearly so. A couple of cigarette burns on the coffee table, but there's no leering, green-eyed escapee from an old Fu Manchu movie lurking under the couch with a stiletto clamped in his teeth, ready to pounce.

The most striking feature of the room is the dim bunker-like atmosphere—the shades are down, the curtains drawn against the daylight—and on the rear wall an enormous display case of handguns and rifles.

The whole place smells of cigarettes, beer, and oil-soaked rags. And I have exactly three seconds to find common ground of even the flimsiest kind, while he lights another cigarette, comes back to the front room and blows smoke at the ceiling. I guess that counts as chivalry in his book.

His home, his playbook, though the only book gracing his shelves is an armed forces field manual with a camouflage cloth cover.

There's a lean and efficient black metal pistol at eye level in the display case with some squiggly writing on the barrel and a gold medallion the size of a nickel on the grip near the trigger.

I scoot over to it like a fifth grader on her first trip to the dinosaur exhibit at the Museum of Natural History. The squiggly writing resolves into an Arabic inscription.

"Oh, my God. You have a genuine Tariq pistol? My brother would *kill* for one of those!"

"Your brother, huh? Where'd he serve?"

"Baghdad, Karbala, and Babylon. The motor pool."

He snorts. "Didn't see much action then."

"He saw enough," I say.

Hosing out the insides of Humvees torn apart by RPGs and IEDs. Washing away the blood and hair and bone fragments, all that was left of his friends. Dealing with the knowledge that the roof gunner was decapitated by the blast.

"Yeah, whatever." Ard shrugs. "It doesn't have the magazine capacity of today's semis, but it can take a beating and still fire accurately under desert conditions. Saddam had a whole line made up special for his private police force."

I act all impressed and fluttery as his rank machine-oil smell fills my nostrils, and he tells me how Saddam Hussein also had gold-plated models of the Tariq pistols made to give away to his "special" friends.

I'm scanning the collection looking for the next conversation piece.

"Holy shit," I say. "Is that a Glock 18?"

"You got a good eye," he says. "Lot of people think it's a regular semi. I'd love to see the look on an intruder's face when he finds out it's a fully automatic machine pistol with a capacity of twelve hundred rounds per minute, heh." He chuckles at the thought.

"Nice fucking gun," I say, mirroring his manner of speech.

And totally illegal for anyone to possess except active military and law enforcement personnel.

"Which one's your favorite?" I ask, like a total groupie.

"This one," he says, pulling a short-barreled square-nosed monster from his rear waistband and waving it in my face.

Yikes. Did not see that coming. Bad tradecraft, girl. Bad, bad tradecraft.

I force myself to stay poised and memorize the make, model, and specs.

"The Taurus Millennium 9mm Luger subcompact," I say, nodding with approval.

"With a polymer grip. Perfect for concealed carry, and let me tell you, it really puts the ammo downrange. They make a .38-caliber model with a pink polymer frame for girls."

"Yeah, but it only has a six-round capacity."

"*Seven* rounds, sweetie. Six in the magazine and one in the chamber. That extra round could make all the difference."

I shiver with excitement at the prospect of squeezing off that seventh round.

"Now, this one's got *twelve* in the magazine and one in the chamber," he says, twirling the gun by the trigger guard and stowing it in his rear waistband.

"The paper-pushers at the VA are supposed to help me find a civilian job, right?" he says, unlocking the display case and removing a distinctive weapon from the rack, some kind of exotic high-end single-shot target pistol that I don't recognize. He grabs an oily leather pouch and invites me to sit on the couch.

"Know what those clowns did? Tried to set me up at one of those cheap chain stores, like I'm supposed to put on a blue vest and greet shoppers for fifteen fucking dollars an hour like some kinda faggot. Doesn't exactly match my skill set, know what I mean? Why you think they call 'em *chain* stores, anyway? Heh."

"So what job matches your skills? Were you in communications? Intelligence? The bomb squad?"

"Think I'd tell you?"

He lays the target pistol across his knee and places the pouch on the coffee table, snapping it open to reveal a set of tools for cleaning and maintaining a firearm.

"You know, the Bible says it's okay to punish race mixers," he says, breaking the pistol open and checking to make sure the chamber's empty. "And the war's already started," he adds, expertly dismantling the target pistol piece by piece, including the extra-thin barrel and flash suppressor. I bet he could do it blindfolded.

"A white people's war," he says, eyeing my deceptively light skin.

"Hey, don't look at me," I say. "Some of my best friends are white."

"Heh. That's a good one," he says.

Even in the eerie dimness, there's a weird light in his eye. I'm not sure I can keep up the pretense much longer.

"Mind if I get us a couple of beers?" I say, trying to project enthusiasm.

"They're in the door," he says, nodding toward the kitchen.

I get up and head for the fridge. I remove a couple of cans of beer from the door, and take a quick peek at the vegetable bin and freezer. No body parts of dismembered victims. Not even a head of lettuce.

Well, that's a relief, anyway.

My phone goes *ping* as I head back to the couch. I hand him his beer, and under cover of checking my messages, I tap the camera icon and hit RECORD. I'll worry later about squaring this with New York State law.

"Did you at least get to squeeze some terrorist's balls in a vise?" I ask. "I mean, come on, that's basic stuff. Gotta squeeze their balls a little, right?"

"Joke all you want, girlie," he says, spreading the disassembled target pistol's parts out on the coffee table, along with an oily rag, a spray bottle of gun cleaner, a plastic bottle of bore cleaning gel, and an economy-size can of gun oil. "America's still on top of the heap."

Yeah, it's a heap all right.

He spritzes the metal parts and the wooden stock with cleaner and reams out the barrel with a rod and cloth.

"This baby can put a bullet between a raghead's eyes at two hundred yards," he says, wiping excess goop from the mouth of the barrel. "Up to a thousand with the scope in position."

"Not much use for a fine-tuned weapon like that in Iraq, I imagine."

"Hell no. When you're stopping a threat, you got no time to figure out who's an insurgent and who's a civilian. Just light 'em up and sort 'em out when the smoke clears."

"Like you did during that ambush at the Ishtar Hartley?"

"You know about that, huh?" he says, squirting the rag with the hypermasculine scent of gun oil.

"Not much," I admit. "The file's pretty thin."

"Fuckin' place was a hideout for terrorists," he says. "That why you're here?"

"I'm here because I'm trying to find a missing scroll."

"A missing *what*?"

"A rare, ancient Hebrew manuscript written on lambskin parchment."

"How'd it go missing?" he says, rubbing oil on the firing and trigger mechanisms with expert precision. "Somebody lose it in a poker game?"

"As near as I can piece it together, just before the American invasion, Saddam ordered his men to raid every synagogue in the country and seize valuable Jewish books and manuscripts, which were transferred to a bomb shelter in western Baghdad for safekeeping."

"Why the fuck would Saddam's troops spend time rounding up a bunch of Jew books instead of preparing for the invasion?"

"Maybe he figured he could use them for leverage or something. Maybe one of his advisors told him the Israelis wouldn't bomb the palace if they thought a bunch of priceless Torah scrolls were stored in the basement."

"That's a lot of maybes," Ard says, stroking the long, thin barrel with the oily rag.

"Yet a renowned archaeologist, Professor Patricia Woolley, said that some of the most valuable items in the Baghdad Museum were left unprotected near a back exit."

"Don't talk about her," Ard spits. "Bitch told the press we should have done more to stop the looting of all those *precious antiquities*. Like we're supposed to shoot a bunch of dune coons for stealing a piece of freakin' parchment that feels like the skin of your hundred-year-old granny."

So you know what the scroll feels like. You've touched it with your own hands.

Ard wipes oil off the flash suppressor and remounts the barrel, screwing it back into the hardened steel threads of the black metal frame. He deftly reassembles the pistol in under a minute, and tests it, pulling the trigger so the hammer strikes with a dry *click.*

"Nobody seems to understand that the Baghdad Museum isn't a single building. It's a complex spread out over eleven acres," he says, wiping up a couple of wayward drops of gun oil. "We're supposed to secure all that with five guys and a Humvee?"

"The report states that a detachment of *seven* Silver Bullet contractors was assigned to guard this particular shipment of antiquities."

"Sure, it's seven if you include the women."

"Are you saying the women aren't worth counting?"

"Look, the head of the museum's antiquities unit was a conservative Moslem woman who wouldn't speak directly to our guys besides a quick *hello* or *goodbye*. So yeah, we needed a woman's touch with that," he says, putting away the rag, tools, and cleaning supplies.

"Well, that must have—"

"Having a couple of chicks in the Humvee was a distraction that led directly to the deaths of two members of the team."

"I thought the Humvees were heavily armored."

"Is *that* what it says in that file of yours? 'Cause let me tell you, girlie, that's a bunch of bullshit."

"So what happened?"

"What happened is the media turned that mousy little pipsqueak Megan Bishop into a war hero, even though she wasn't worth *shit* in combat. No use at all. She'd have rather been back home duck hunting. I had to save her ass a couple of times."

"From what?"

"Heard her screaming her head off in that filthy hospital room as they ripped her shirt off, and charged in there and stopped them from sexually assaulting her. Or worse. Way worse."

"Wow. That was so brave of you. You literally *saved her life*. I mean … Wow. Do you know where I can find her?"

I'm expecting a typical Ard-esque response along the lines of *How the fuck should I know*, but he simply says, "Lost touch with her."

"How about Kristel Santos?"

"Fuck no."

"Phone records indicate that she called your number on August twenty-fifth."

"Yeah? Well, she didn't leave a message."

"The records show the call lasted nearly one minute twenty seconds."

"So maybe she sat on her ass listening to the busy signal. Who the fuck knows what that crazy broad was thinking? Why do you care about all this? What's in it for you?"

"Hey, this just a temp gig. For all I know, my last day is Monday."

"I got news for you, babe. These days, *everybody's* last day is Monday."

"True indeed, Mr. Ard, true indeed," I say, reflecting his statement. "Anyway, it would go a long way toward reestablishing Cadmium's credibility with strategic foreign governments if we could locate and return the missing scroll."

He considers this, scratching his cheek with the pistol's front sight.

"You could try Sergeant Dawson."

I don't recall seeing that name in the file.

"Who?"

"Sergeant Duwayne Dawson. He might know."

"He might know *what*?"

"What happened to your precious little scroll. He was one of those *Abraham-was-a-Black-man* type guys, you know?"

"So ..."

"So maybe he took the scroll and returned it to its rightful owners, the Black Hebrew Israelites in Harlem, heh."

"Sergeant Dawson worked for Silver Bullet in Iraq?"

"Different unit, but yeah."

"Do you have any reason to believe that he might have been in contact with or know the current whereabouts of your former associate, Kristel Santos?"

Oops. The professional tone in my voice is a dead giveaway.

"You'll have to ask him yourself," he says, putting on a smug what-you-gonna-do-about-it grin.

"Any idea where I can find him?"

"You're the expert, you tell me," he says, the shit-eating grin intact.

"I'm not an expert, I'm just trying to—"

"Probably find him at the Mt. Hermon Scrapyard in West Babylon. But you better hurry if you want to catch him."

I gather up my things while he locks the target pistol in the display case. He shows me to the door, and I have to shade my eyes to venture out into the bright light of day.

Just as my ankle boots hit the concrete walk, he says, that smirk still glued to his face, "You ever think maybe somebody stole that scroll as a joke just to piss off the Jews?"

"Yeah, that would be a riot."

~

Back in the car, I raise the phone to my lips, identify myself and recite the date, time, and location, and declare, *I give permission to record this conversation.*

Ass officially covered, I take a moment to run a quick check on Sergeant Duwayne Dawson. Then it's a twenty-minute ride—thirty with traffic—to the Mt. Hermon Scrapyard on Industrial Road.

Ah, Industrial Road. It's just as picturesque as it sounds. The area is surrounded by cemeteries, so there's plenty of parking on the street. A three-man crew in garbage-stained coveralls stops unloading scrap metal from a flatbed truck as I stroll through the big, wide gate, staring at me as if they haven't seen a living, breathing woman in six months. I'm still wearing my business-neutral gray and black ensemble, but the unfiltered intensity of their gazes makes me feel like I'm a half-naked fashion model strutting down the runway in fishnet stockings and a black leather bustier.

Their names are stitched above the chest pockets on their coveralls: Suárez, Corrao, Gieszewicz. Suárez is a short guy with the shiny, roasted-coffee-bean skin of a native of the Central American *sierra madre*, Corrao is an Italian American kid with a splotch of machine oil smeared across his cheek like a pro football player, and Gieszewicz is a huge mountain of a man who glares down at me as I approach, the whites of his eyes glistening in the ample space above his downcast pupils.

Suárez has a visible Cadmium Solutions bull's eye logo tattooed on his wrist, partly obscured by a pair of work gloves he's using to grip a tightly coiled length of pristine copper cable bearing the state seal and bar code.

The other guys close ranks with Suárez and press forward, surrounding me with a wall of hostility.

"Gee, that looks like the same batch Tweety had," I say.

The guys look at each other.

"You know Tweety?" says Corrao.

"Sure."

"How's he doing?"

"Good. Just saw him last night with a load of copper pipes from the projects, and some of that stuff, too." I make a vague gesture toward the snakelike coils of contraband copper.

"He still driving that rattletrap pickup truck?"

"You bet."

And just like that, the tension melts away like a popsicle

on hot asphalt. I ask if they know where I can find Sergeant Duwayne Dawson. They say he went home with a nasty chest cold.

Can they tell me where that is?

"Sure."

"Anything for a friend of Tweety's."

~

"So you're an ex-Marine?"

"No such thing," says Sergeant Dawson, savoring a mouthful of hot-and-sour soup despite his watery eyes and sniffles.

"Right. I forgot."

The cramped kitchen reeks of camphor, menthol, and eucalyptus oil from a jarful of ointment he's been rubbing on his chest since I showed up on his doorstep with a couple of quarts of wonton and hot-and-sour soup.

So what was it like working for the same outfit as Tommy Ard? Is my unasked question, since it would probably trigger a visceral response that I don't need to deal with right now.

HISPANICS DON'T EXEMPLIFY FAMILY VALUES!

I spin toward the TV, drawing a bead on a bowtie-wearing policy analyst at the neutral-sounding Center for Immigration Studies.

"Mind if I turn this down?" I say, not waiting for his reply. "It's kind of distracting."

I mute the sound just as they cut to BREAKING NEWS that a precision-guided Hellfire missile has just killed Al-Qahol's number two man in Zabul Province.

Sergeant Dawson blows his nose, wipes his eyes, and tosses another wad of tissues at the garbage, falling about a foot short this time.

"So what kind of gun you carry?" he asks, like it's a hobby we share.

"I don't carry a gun."

"Why not?"

I've seen too much of the damage they can do.

"Because sometimes the greatest strength a warrior can show is when he puts down his weapon and learns to make peace."

I pepper him with questions about whether he's had any contact with Kristel Santos and what he knows about the looting of precious metals and other objects from Iraq.

"Man, the only precious metal I saw over there was brass shell casings, solid copper hollow-point bullets, and Saddam's motherfucking chrome-plated AK-47 with a pearl grip on it. Otherwise it was just blood for oil, blood for oil."

I tell him it sounds like something Herman Melville wrote back in the days when folks lit their homes with whale oil: *For God's sake, be economical with your lamps and candles! Not a gallon you burn, but at least one drop of man's blood was spilled for it.*

"Dude knew what he was talking about," Sergeant Dawson says. "Next war, I want a nice, cushy desk job as a legal proofreader."

I ask him for the seventeenth time about any contact with Kristel Santos. He deliberates, weighing the options as if he's finally taking my request seriously.

He gets up, disappears into the bedroom, rustles around a bit, and comes back holding a metal key with a cylindrical orange plastic handle imprinted with the code number: C407.

He tells me it belongs to a storage locker near the Port Authority Bus Terminal.

"Ain't seen the Santos girl in months," he says, handing over the key. "But the last time I saw her, she said if anything ever happened to her, or if she ever went MIA, she wanted me to have this."

"And you're giving it to me?"

"She must've dug herself in pretty deep, or else you wouldn't be coming round here. I figure you're in a better position to help her dig herself out than I am. This needs a woman's touch."

"I guess."

My eye is drawn to the TV's flashy colors of a new video of Sheza Hogg pole dancing while wearing very little besides tattoos and sweat.

"Thanks for the soup," he says. "You mind putting the sound back on?"

I turn up the TV as I leave.

~

UP NEXT: SHOCKING REVELATIONS THAT GIRL SCOUT COOKIES HAVE BEEN HIJACKED BY THE RADICAL HOMOSEXUAL MOVEMENT!

Ah, Christ. My head's so full of conflicting narratives I forgot to turn on the music first. I pop one of my dad's vintage Fania All-Stars cassettes into the boom box and enter a 1970s time-warp of funky Latin soul as I head back to Midtown.

~

The overpowering smell of bus exhaust, piss, and rat shit clouds the air in the storage locker area. I fit the key into the lock and I have to work it a bit to get it to turn. The dented metal door catches, then swings open. Inside is a glossy black nylon duffel bag. I slip on a pair of clear vinyl gloves and examine the heavy duty zipper for signs of a tripwire leading to a detonator. Seeing none, I gently probe the bag's exterior with my fingers, checking for anything that feels like it might be an antipersonnel mine or something of that sort. More or less satisfied that it won't explode if I disturb it, I grab the canvas handles and lift.

Oof! It's a heavy sucker. It feels like it's full of rocks or something equally dense clunking together.

Back on the street, I consider the options. I should really

take the bag to the eleventh floor of the Schneerson Building and have the security personnel X-ray it before I do anything foolish, like opening it up right now and potentially taking out half the block. But then I'd have to bring them into this, and I'm not ready to do that yet.

Fuck it. I heave the duffel bag onto the car's trunk and carefully pull the zipper partway down. When nothing happens, I use both hands to spread the bag open. A lot of heavy objects wrapped in newspaper and black cloth. I give them all a gentle squeeze checking for wires, batteries, sharp metal edges, anything. Everything's rock solid, except for one bundle that feels like a bag of cylindrical pebbles, as opposed to, say, a bunch of ball bearings wired to an explosive charge.

It suddenly hits me: Why am I taking all these precautions when I'm less than fifty feet away from one of the greatest free-trade zone bazaars in the world? I scout the terrain and walk into one of those discount outlets on Eighth Avenue that's got everything from imported bonsai trees to racks of movies like *Hot Wet Sluts* 7 on DVD. (People still watch porn on DVD?) The security guard is a trim and fit olive-skinned *soltero* with a slick black mustache—a military cut that follows the line of his mouth and stops at the corners, which could mean he's a city cop moonlighting at his second job. The nametag says SALDÍVAR.

I lug the duffel bag over and slide it onto the counter in front of him.

"*Hola, guapo.* Can you do me a big favor?"

His eyes flit to my boobs for a microsecond, but otherwise he maintains visual contact with those soft brown eyes.

"Possibly," he says.

Nice smile, too.

"Can you give this thing the once-over with that magic wand of yours?"

Now his eyes shift to the black bag with the heavy metal zipper. Then back to mine.

He milks the moment, fingering the wand's foam-rubber grip.

"*Claro que sí.* Anything for a lovely lady."

Wow. Didn't think he'd buy into it with such conviction.

He runs the handheld metal detector around the sides of the bag, slowly at first, taking his time going over the tiny folds of fabric near the end seams, softly stroking the outer curves of the bag, staying away from the zipper cleaving it down the middle. A few quick passes around the perimeter, then he places his thumb and forefinger on the pull tab like a lover plucking a flower from his beloved's garden, and slowly undoes the zipper, guiding it along the soft mounds and hollows running the full length of the bag. He pauses in anticipation, then gently parts the fabric, opens it wide, and eases the wand in, tenderly poking and probing among the mysterious shapes and packages in a carefully controlled frenzy of license and libertinage before he pulls the wand out, zips the bag closed, and runs the tip of the wand along the zipper's thick ribbed metal teeth till it lights up bright red. He raises the wand, the light sensor changes from red to green, and it's over.

"It's clean," he says. "The only thing metal is the zipper, *mi amor.*"

"*Gracias, señor Saldívar.*"

He brings the tip of the wand to his lips and blows on it like a gunslinger at a Saturday matinee back in the day.

As satisfied as I'll ever be—I mean about the bag being safe to open—I slide the duffel bag onto the front seat of the car, climb inside, and shut the door. Only now do I reach in and heft the biggest, heaviest bundle. Definitely no moving parts. I carefully unwrap it. It's a figure of some Mesopotamian god. No, wait. It's got long hair and breasts that have been worn smooth over the centuries. So it's a goddess.

Twenty minutes later I've got a front seat full of archaeological treasures, from a collection of stone cylinder seals to fragments of an imposing sculpture of some strange and forgotten god, and a 1.5 inch-wide swatch of something that sure as hell looks like a fragment of an ancient Hebrew scroll on sheepskin parchment. All this stuff points straight to Kristel Santos, and makes her look guilty as hell. I bet her fingerprints are all over it.

Then why does the interior of the bag smell of gun oil, cigarettes, and camphor?

~

My brain's on fire, singing with the electrical hum of a thousand high-tension wires.

Ard.

Mr. Thomas Ard.

When Ard told me how useless Megan Bishop was under fire, he didn't say, *She should have been back home duck hunting*; he said, *She'd have rather been back home*, which sounds like she might have actually expressed that desire in a moment of vulnerability or just plain honesty. It's a mighty thin thread but it's all I've got.

I take the bridge back to Queens, driving with the windows open to clear out the smell of camphor and gun oil, but the fetid air rising from river chokes the life out of that idea.

I zip over to Corona, where I use my office computer to run a search of a database that hadn't previously occurred to me concerning a seriously reclusive woman. It only takes a few minutes to find a current address for Megan Bishop a few miles southeast in a quiet part of Queens. Practically right under my overly sensitive nose.

It's still early evening, and she's not that far away. Thirty minutes, tops.

This time I call ahead and explain who I am and what I want. I stand there listening to a whole lot of silence on the other end of the phone until she finally says, "Okay. But just you. Nobody else."

"Just me."

~

"It wasn't what I thought it would be like," says the unassuming woman living in the shadow of her own legend, this diminutive warrior who would prefer to melt into the autumn mist and never be heard from again.

"I guess you're just not a killer at heart," I tell her.

She survived the ambush at the Ishtar Hartley Hotel in Baghdad but ended up with her right arm and wrist broken along with a couple of ribs, a fractured left arm, and a shattered left ankle. She walks with a cane, yet insists on pouring two steaming cups of herbal tea for us from a cute little cream-colored glazed ceramic pot, placing a dish of Scottish shortbread cookies between us on the narrow table in her hideaway in the uncharted reaches of darkest Queens.

It would all be so nice and cozy if it weren't for her visibly scarred hands, trembling with neuropathy, and a couple of antique wooden duck decoys and a modern shotgun mounted on the wall along with the outlines of other guns, now missing.

"You mean I'm not a real man like Tommy Ard?" she says, her Queens accent and attitude undamaged.

"That nut job? He's not a man, he's a bundle of symptoms pretending to be a man."

"You see the tattoos on his back?"

"Just the ones on his arms—"

"Tombstones. One for every man he killed over there. Sugar?"

Her whole face brightens when she says it. Like cops and nurses, war vets can flip effortlessly from tranquil domesticity to gut-wrenching horror and back like a toggle switch.

And this particular war vet, with her short round nose, pale skin, and washed-out strands of auburn hair held back with a red plastic clip, looks like a cross between a midwestern preacher's sensible daughter, an adorable Audrey Hepburn–type gamine, and a bored, second-string cheerleader with a mean streak who just might decide to bury an ax in your brain.

I don't take sugar. Ms. Bishop shovels a few teaspoons into her cup, her unsteady hands scattering sugar crystals across the red-checked plastic tablecloth.

"Relax," I say, squelching the urge to give her trembling hands a reassuring squeeze. "My method of asking questions is much easier on the body than what you're used to."

"There are lots of ways to hurt the body," she says, sweeping up the spilled sugar with the side of her left hand. Her good hand.

"So the mission didn't exactly live up to its name," I say.

"You mean Operation Enduring Freedom?" The words drip from her tongue like nitric acid. "More like Operation Endless Fuck-Ups and Mind-Numbing Violence."

"That was actually the original slogan, but it didn't test well with the focus group."

She allows herself a wan smile.

"We made enemies *every time* a convoy went out," she says, sweetening her bitter words with a sip of sugary tea. "The guys drove like they were playing *Grand Theft Auto*, sideswiping anything that got in the way—donkeys, taxis, traffic cops, ice cream carts, children playing ball, you fucking name it."

I keep my mouth shut and just let her talk.

"And of course the regular army guys hated us for stirring up the locals with our hotdogging and leaving them to deal with the blowback. And if any of our guys ever got caught in a bad shooting, the project managers would just pull them from the duty roster and send them home on the next company jet. You can imagine how much the enlisted men and women appreciated that."

"So *everybody* hated you."

"Yeah. The Iraqi civilians, the American troops, and every guy on my team, who went around waxing anything that moved with 50-cal machine guns, even looters digging through building rubble—*fucking rubble*—then planting weapons to make it look like they were armed—"

"Gee, I thought only the NYPD could do that."

"—dumping white phosphorus and depleted uranium munitions in the Tigris, as if that open sewer they call a river wasn't polluted enough after we knocked out the water treatment plant with an errant missile."

She's clenching her fist to keep her hand from shaking.

I reach for a shortbread cookie just to give my mouth something to do.

"And the fake, misleading reports," she says, biting savagely into a cookie. "We didn't use weapons to kill people, we used *assets* to *service the target*. We weren't training mercenaries, we were *assessing civil contractors*—"

"Since it's illegal for a private corporation to train foreign mercenaries."

"Yeah, Fursten's such a lying asshole. So, you work for him?"

"Monday's my last day."

"Lucky for you. I'll never be free of this shit. You ever seen what white phosphorus does to a person?"

"It melts your flesh till it adheres to your clothes and turns your face into something that looks like what happens when you put a Barbie doll in a microwave—except that there's a skull and some teeth under the melted flesh."

I swear her pupils widen like she just bit into the fruit of the Tree of Knowledge.

"How did you know that?" she asks.

"My brother served, too. He … sent me pictures."

"Not exactly the kind of stuff you show a guy on your first date. Unless he's a fan of horror movies."

She gazes silently into her lap.

"Gone on any dates lately?" I ask, taking another bite of shortbread.

She stares into the vortex of her lap like a battle-weary woman warrior trying to decide whether to keep marching or to wander off the trail and get swallowed up by the jungle.

She nods.

"How'd it go?" I say, nearly coughing up a mouthful of cookie crumbs because my throat's gone inexplicably dry. I try to chase it, but my tea's gone cold, and Ms. Bishop insists on getting up and limping over to the microwave to warm it up for me.

It's hard to believe that a woman who appears so fragile can be so strong and resilient, that this ephemeral creature who belongs in a fairy tale prancing through the greenwood has been through the worst that life can throw at her and come out the other side, battered but breathing, with fire in her belly.

"Everything was going fine," she says, pushing the buttons on the microwave. "We were laughing and driving along, until we hit a pothole and I totally freaked."

I don't say a word as she places the freshly warmed cup of tea in front of me with her quivering hands. I just cradle the cup, warming my hands on its delicately glazed surface.

"And there are a *lot* of potholes in this neighborhood," she says, gripping the wooden arms of her chair and slowly lowering herself into her seat.

"You ever tell anyone about this?"

"How 'bout I ask *you* a question for a change?"

I take a sip of hot tea, sit back, and await her question.

"How'd you find me?"

I nod in the direction of the shotgun mounted on the wall.

"Your state-issued hunting license."

She chews on her lower lip and nods as if acknowledging a venial sin.

"Funny thing is, I haven't touched it since I got back," she says. "Haven't even dusted it off. Used to love duck hunting with my dad, but … well, you know …"

"You don't have to justify anything to me," I say, seeing my chance to crack open her shell a bit.

"They brainwashed us," she says so tartly you'd think she's been drinking raw vinegar instead of herb tea.

"I don't know if I'd call it brainwashing, exactly."

"Oh? What would you call it?"

"I'd say you were *conditioned*—by your society, by your role models, by the grand myth of American exceptionalism itself."

"Yeah, you could say."

I press on: "You have to be tough but not in a way that threatens their fragile masculinity, pretty but not a distraction, smart but not smarter than them, and diplomatic enough to mediate between the occupying forces and the local women but not be the weak link in the chain."

"You're either a mind reader or you know someone who was there real well," she says.

"I face the same crap every day at my job, minus the incoming mortar fire. That's why I like working with documents. They never try to belittle me, pinch my ass or grab me by the pussy, or try to burn me to a crisp with white phosphorus, which happens to be a war crime."

She stares intently into her teacup, as if she's trying to read her fortune in the tea leaves, only there ain't no tea leaves for her to read.

"How close were you with the other women on the team?" I ask.

"Look, we both know the only woman on the team you're interested in is that damn squirter, Santos. So why don't you just come right out with it? What do you want to know about her?"

"Why do you say she's a coward?"

"'Cause when shit got real, she freaking booked and left us exposed to direct fire."

"You mean during the surprise attack at the Ishtar Hartley?"

"The only people *surprised* by the attack were the dumbass journalists staying at the hotel."

"I thought the hotel was a terrorist hideout."

"Where'd you hear that? The place was full of foreign journalists. That's why it was such a soft target."

"I see."

"What's that mean?"

"So if the rocket fire didn't come from the hotel, what was the point of origin?"

"Shit, girl. Those rockets travel three times faster than the speed of sound. Someone fires an 85-mil Katyusha at you, you don't hear it till the blast wave knocks you flat."

"Is that what happened to you?"

"All I know is one minute I was joking with Tommy and Trane, and the next minute I was flat on my ass, covered with rubble and broken glass, and blood was gurgling out of a gaping wound in Trane's chest. I'll never forget the sound of those slurps, like a baby sucking milk from its mother's titties."

I take a moment to recover from the images summoned by her disturbing metaphor.

Failing that, I simply press on: "And that's when Tommy Ard rescued you?"

"I didn't need to be *rescued*. The other members of the team rushed me to the nearest hospital. Place was an absolute shithole. I'm talking floors slick with blood and piss from the overflowing toilets, no antibiotics or anesthetics on the shelves and no way to sterilize the instruments. But the doctors were doing everything they could. My arm was broken in three places and I had two broken ribs, and yes, I screamed in pain as they cut off my fatigues 'cause I had some bone sticking out of my arm and it hurt like hell. But they were *helping* me. Then Tommy Ard bursts in like he's fucking Chuck Norris in *The Delta Force*, firing multiple rounds at the ceiling and threatening to light up the lead surgeon's ass if he didn't fix me up right away."

"If your arm was broken in three places, how'd you empty your clip?"

"How the fuck should I know? I'm sorry …" She buries her face in her left hand for a pin-drop quiet moment, then slowly begins massaging her brow. "It's like … my mind has blank spots … that I step into sometimes."

"You don't have to apologize to me—"

She jerks her head up. "I'm *not* apologizing!"

"Okay, okay." I try to placate her. "It's just that there are, well, conflicting accounts of what happened that day."

"Uh, *yeah*," she says. "I told you that shit was for real. Next you're going to ask me if I got the serial number of the rocket they fired at us."

Damn, this thing is spinning out of control. I'd better grab the wheel and steer us back onto the highway.

"Look, I need your help, okay? I need to find her before anyone else does because she's clearly being set up for a ton of shit she didn't do, and I've got a duffel bag full of incriminating evidence that's supposed to seal the deal on her guilt, yet I can't seem to locate anybody who can give me a single bit of intel I can actually *use*. You were in the same unit, you had to get to know her just a little. It was only a six-person team that day. You probably know more about her than anyone I've spoken to in the last week."

"You know, I'm getting kinda tired of being everybody's punching bag. It's *depressing*. Seriously depressing. Look, what's the point? Why do you even give a shit?"

"Okay, okay, cards on the table. Okay?"

"About fucking time."

I reach into my shoulder bag and remove a clear plastic evidence bag containing the 1.5-inch fragment of parchment I found in the black duffel bag.

"Have you ever seen this before?"

"No."

"A scroll or a bit of parchment or anything that looked remotely like this?"

"No."

"Are you sure? Take a good look."

"I already said no. What's the big deal?"

I explain that Cadmium Solutions is particularly interested in locating a rare Hebrew scroll that they have reason to believe was smuggled out of Iraq by Kristel Santos. "Is there anything you can tell me that might corroborate those reports?"

She thinks about it, eyes roving from the honey-colored ring at the bottom of her teacup to the shotgun on the wall—which, if Russian playwright Anton Chekov has anything to say about it, will *have* to be fired sometime in the next thirty minutes or so.

"The only time I can think of is when they put me and her together transporting a bunch of old books and papers to safety before the looters could carry everything off."

My pulse quickens, but I try not to let it show.

"Can you tell me more about that?"

"There's nothing to tell. By the time we got to the library, the looters had already taken everything of value—furniture, carpeting, lighting fixtures—but I guess they didn't give a damn about a moldy cardboard box full of five-hundred-year-old manuscripts."

"The scroll is much older than that."

"Look, we were just hauling boxes of old books from one place to another. We didn't stop to read the Library of Congress Cataloging-in-Publication Data."

"And ... ?" There's something she isn't telling me.

"Like I said, the mission was strictly routine, till we pulled up in front of the Hartley."

"And?"

"And *what?*" she says with an edge in her voice.

"It's okay, you can tell me."

"Tell you *what*?"

"What happened after you got to the Ishtar Hartley Hotel?"

"What do you mean, what happened? What do *you think* happened?"

"I think someone wants me to believe that what's in that duffel bag proves that Kristel Santos brought a bunch of stolen artifacts back to the US illegally to deflect the blame from their own incompetence and criminal acts. But everyone's telling me a different version of the story to cover their own asses—"

"That's *not* what happened!" She brings the teacup to her mouth so abruptly she nearly chips a tooth on it. My tea's gone cold again.

"Okay, then why don't you tell me exactly what happened?"

Before she can protest, I stand up, pry the tea cup from her hand, and place it in the microwave for a few seconds.

"There, that'll soothe your nerves," I say, handing her the freshly warmed cup of tea.

She takes a few sips and suppresses a shudder.

I slip the evidence bag containing the scroll fragment back into the inner pocket of my shoulder bag. She takes another sip while I clear the dishes off the table and carry them over to the counter. I return the uneaten cookies to the package.

Ms. Bishop tosses back the last of her tea, pushes herself to her feet and limps over to join me at the sink. She pours the dregs from the teapot down the drain while I rinse off the dishes, running the water till it's warm enough to wash them with a soapy sponge.

She watches as I scrub the dishes, and when she's ready, she tells me about the attack on the Ishtar Hartley Hotel.

She woke up to the sight of dead and wounded, their gear covered in blood. *Everything* was covered in blood. The damage was so bad she could see clear through the armor plates on both sides of the vehicle. That's over five inches of metal, torn clean through. The force of the projectiles ripped one of her buddies in half.

"It felt like my uniform was bleeding when they laid me on the operating table, pools of pink water forming on the floor," she says. "I saw my own blood getting sucked down the drain in the middle of the floor, swirling round it and turning lighter and lighter till the stream ran clear."

Her eyes have reddened around the edges, as if some part of her is still circling the drain in that OR in Baghdad.

"How did we ever get into this mess?" she says.

"You mean, why did we go with *private security* in a war zone?" I say, rinsing the dishes in clean, clear water while she dries them. "Because the military are actually accountable, at least a little bit, anyway. Your guys weren't."

"No, I mean the whole damn mess," she says, stacking the saucers with a delicate plinking of fine china. I pass her the serving plate.

Ms. Bishop contemplates her distorted image in the plate's glossy sheen like a tormented lover seeking answers in a crystal ball.

"I wish we could take it all back," she says, putting the plate away and closing the cabinet. "But some things you can never take back."

"Yeah, and one of them is bullets." It just pops out of my mouth. She looks at me like I'm either crazy or that I understand her dilemma better than anybody.

"Sorry."

"I struggle with this shit every day," she says, gripping the counter for support. "I keep finding myself saying, Is it Tuesday or Wednesday? October or November? 6:00 a.m. or 6:00 p.m.? Did I leave the oven on? Is the toaster unplugged? Is the toaster wired to an IED? Am I on the right line at the post office? Am I even in the right *building*? Did I take my meds? Will I ever wake up from this shit?"

She yanks open a silverware drawer, sending a half dozen plastic medicine bottles rolling forward with an angry rattle. The labels warn that some of the antidepressants may have dangerous side effects, including suicidal thoughts.

"I still have to tell myself it's all right to sit on the back porch. That there probably isn't a sniper on my neighbor's roof getting ready to paint the wall with my brains."

She slams the drawer shut.

"And the guys who rushed us into that mess are all on TV crowing about their million-dollar book deals," she says, shaking her head at the impossible odds of evening out the disparity, even a tiny bit, in her lifetime.

"They should be on trial for war crimes in The Hague," I say.

"Whoa, let's not get crazy now. No need for that New World Order stuff."

"Right. Sorry."

"Can't have a bunch of foreigners undercutting American sovereignty."

"Right. Thanks for agreeing to speak with me," I say, getting my stuff together.

"You ever see a case like this get resolved in a completely fair way?" she says, walking me to the door.

"No, but I'll let you know if it ever happens."

~

By the time I get home I'm totally drained. Looks like stir-fried veggies again. Also looks like frozen veggies will have to do, since nobody else could *possibly* be expected to stop by a grocery store for fresh produce.

It's only after washing and drying the stir-fry pan that I realize my period is three days late.

CHAPTER FIFTEEN

Ruth

"Go and seek the heads of the clans and tell them to bring their weapons—lances, shields, bows, armor, anything," Nehemiah barked. "Conscript anyone old enough to handle a sword. I want every able-bodied person working on this wall. We'll work with a bricklayer's trowel in one hand and a sword in the other if we have to."

"As you command, sir." The messengers hurried off.

"We need to finish this wall before the bastards attack again."

When the smoke from the surprise attack had cleared, the people of Jerusalem found that most of the casualties had been slaves, who were replaceable, but no one had seen or heard from Prince Sheshbazzar since that day. He had evaporated like the spring rains that are long forgotten by the late summer drought.

The men set to work laying row upon row of the largest stones while the women scrambled around slathering thin, watery mortar between the ill-fitting stones, constantly checking the hills to the north for signs of impending invasion, while Nehemiah went up and down the line, inspecting the quality of the work.

Ruth slapped a mortar-laden trowel against a gap in the wall, but a large wet blob of mortar peeled away from the rock face and fell to the ground. Nehemiah picked it up and forced it into the gap with his fingers.

"Can't be afraid of getting your hands dirty on this job," he said, a confident glint in his eye.

Ruth ran her hand through her spiky hair and took in the lengthy stretch of crumbling wall with thirsty eyes.

Lord have mercy, even her eyes were thirsty.

"Your name, *Nekhem-Yah*." Ruth could barely swallow, her throat was so dry. "What does it mean?"

"It means *the Lord is compassionate*. So?"

"So I need a drink of water, O Compassionate One."

The glint in his eyes faded, and when he saw that she wasn't going to buckle, he pulled the water skin from his belt and watched her drink, her throat muscles tensing and relaxing as she swallowed and wiped her mouth with the back of her hand.

She let her body absorb some of that precious moisture as the men strained to fit the top row of stones into their niches before sundown, and the women stretched up their arms to plug the holes with mortar so thin and watery it dripped down the rock face like runny porridge.

～

'Amod!

"Halt!"

"What city are you from?" the watchmen demanded.

A team of watchmen had dragged a couple of massive chunks of broken masonry into the middle of the road to serve as barriers to unrestricted foot traffic.

"Your servant hails from Kiryath-sefer," said the merchant.

"Scroll City, huh?" said the first watchman. "Is that what you've got in the bag? Scrolls?"

"It is just as you say, sir," the merchant replied.

"Nothing else?"

The merchant swallowed drily.

"No, sir." He was clearly lying.

"Then you won't mind if we take a look, will you?"

"No, I—"

The watchman grabbed the bag and dumped out the contents. Scrolls of wisdom and prophecy spilled out, rolling in the dust. Then a baked clay figurine tumbled out, its fall cushioned by the pile of scrolls.

The watchman seized the figurine and held it up for all to see—a stylized female figure fashioned in the ancient manner, with a tiny head, no arms to speak of, a huge middle section, and legs tapering to a point where her feet should have been. Ruth marveled at the figure's condition, for it was clearly quite old, its spherical buttocks augmented by a pair of deeply incised spirals emanating from their respective midpoints, swirling outward with a generative power that suggested the journey of an unformed soul through the mysterious labyrinth of a woman's womb, ready to burst forth as a human life through the miracle of birth. It was a majestic symbol of the power and beauty of the female body.

The watchman smashed the figurine against a stone barrier.

"We'll have none of your idols here, old man. On strict orders from Ezra the Scribe himself."

Soon it was Ruth's turn.

"Right. What's your business?"

"I come to hear the public reading of the Torah."

"Ezra the Scribe has decreed that only the scribes are permitted to teach God's Torah to strangers."

"I'm not a stranger—"

"Then what's this?" The watchman grabbed the amulet hanging around Ruth's neck.

"That's a gift from my sister-in-law," Ruth said, prying it from the watchman's fingers.

"Why is there a scroll inside it?"

"Because it's an amulet."

"Take it off," the watchman ordered.

Ruth undid the clasp and surrendered the amulet. The watchman snapped it open, pulled out the tiny scroll, and studied it closely. Ruth stiffened as a cluster of reddish-brown flakes drifted down to the dust.

"It's just some pagan mumbo-jumbo," said the watchman.

"You can't bring this into the holy city," said the second watchman.

Ruth admitted that she hadn't read the inscription, since it was a gift from her Midianite sister-in-law.

"You received an amulet from a pagan without examining its contents?"

"She wasn't a pagan. She married a Yehudi just like I did."

"But you accepted a gift from a foreigner without checking its contents. What if it had contained a curse upon your life?"

"Then I guess my life would be cursed, wouldn't it? Can I have it back now?"

"You can have the amulet back. We're confiscating the scroll."

Ruth snatched the amulet from their hands. "Can I go now?"

"All right, but the streets aren't safe for a woman to walk by herself, lest she be taken for a harlot."

"Better than being labeled a foreigner," she said.

～

Heavy battering shook the hills above the valley with the sounds of wood splitting, raised voices, threats, and curses, as the watchmen went house to house seeking backsliders and idolaters, rooting out the clandestine shrines to Asherah.

Ruth was tilling a dry patch of soil behind Oved's house, tugging on a particularly stubborn snarl of roots when a cohort of watchmen pounded on the family's front door and demanded access. Before she had time to act, the watchmen stormed across the threshold and violated the shrine to Asherah, dislodging the statue from its rightful position by breaking her off at the ankles.

The watchmen said, "It's just the idols. People shouldn't have idols anyway. If you've got nothing to hide, what's the big deal?"

They smashed the goddess's sacred mounds into a hundred pieces while the women screeched in protest.

A burly watchman stepped out the back door clutching one of the statue's broken legs like a trophy. When he saw Ruth leaning on a crude farming tool, her tattered shift smeared with earth, his mouth widened into the idiot cousin of an actual smile.

"Burying more idols, honey?"

"There are no idols here," she said, taking a step back, widening her stance and gripping the hoe with both hands.

"There better not be." The watchman planted his boots in the freshly tilled earth. "What about that amulet around your neck?" he said, licking his lips.

"Stay back. I'm warning you."

"Ha! You're warning me?"

He lunged forward, a hand the size of a bear claw grabbing at the silver chain around her neck, meeting the sudden swish of sharpened metal. *A piercing scream as arterial blood spurts from the severed flesh to nourish the parched earth. A gaping wound sliced clean to the bone.*

"*Ahh!* You damned banshee!"

"I warned you to stay back."

"Babylonian whore!"

"You're lucky I didn't aim for your neck."

"Run! Run for the hills, cousin! Run!" Tzillah shouts from the back window.

But Ruth refuses to run, standing her ground as the watchmen fan out and surround her on all sides, blades high.

～

She only heard bits and pieces drifting through the barred window of her cell: Ezra the Scribe calling for a great assembly of the men of Israel. He summoned the elders and the chieftains, the judges and the commanders of ten, fifty, and a hundred—every adult male belonging to *bney ha-golah*, the sons of Exile.

Ezra said to them, "In the olden days, your fathers dwelled on the other side of the Great River, and worshiped other gods. Your father was an Amorite and your mother a Hittite, but the Lord took pity and spread his robe over you. He gave you bracelets for your arms, a ring for your nose, and a necklace of pure silver, and He entered into a covenant with you. But like an unfaithful wife, you flitted about mixing with the nations. Like a harlot taking her fee in grain, you uncovered yourself on every threshing floor."

It wouldn't be the first time a woman gave herself to a man just to feed herself, Ruth thought, leaning against the limestone window sill, the hot wind from the east caressing her cheek through the bars as a sliver of sunlight crawled across the mossy stone floor, marking time. Her stomach felt queasy from the stale crusts of bread and brackish water they had left for her. She regarded the iron bars, half eaten away by rust, and thought about how easy it would be to chisel them loose—if she only had a chisel.

"For you have profaned all that is holy to the Lord by chasing after the daughters of strangers. The Lord will cut off the man that does this and leave him without offspring!"

Her stomach twisted into knots.

"Arise! Let us renew the covenant with our God to expel all foreign women and the children they have borne. Do not be persuaded by the smooth talk of these women, for as surely as silver is melted in a furnace, so shall you be melted in the fires of God's fury if you do not act. Thus says the Lord!"

And the men of Israel swore to expel their foreign wives and children.

Ruth sank slowly to the floor, the rough stone wall scraping the skin on her back.

The scribes fanned out through the crowd, marking the foreheads of the righteous with the letter *tav*, which they drew in the form of a big black X surrounded by a circle, as they swore to sacrifice a dozen rams as a guilt offering.

Ruth wrapped a scrap of woolen cloth around her shoulders, tucked her feet under her skirt, and curled up like a newborn on the cold floor, shivering in the fading light.

~

"So what'd they get you for?"

Ruth's eyes flew open and she reached for her dagger before she remembered that the watchmen had confiscated it, leaving her defenseless. Vulnerable. Naked.

The move was not lost on her cellmate, a skinny creature in a loose-fitting shift, all rags and bones, with dust on her feet and streaks of what looked like dried blood on her upper thighs.

Ruth raised herself on one arm and studied the tiny woman's mouth, which was rather wide for her delicate cheekbones, with traces of bright-red coloring from the previous night's engagements.

"Assaulting a watchman," Ruth said.

The woman's spacious mouth curled up slightly, her seen-it-all expression giving way to a subtly knowing smile.

"And you?" Ruth asked.

"Harlotry."

Ruth looked the woman over. She was severely underfed—flat-chested and skeletal, the outline of her collarbone sharply etched in the early morning light.

"Didn't know that was a crime," Ruth said.

"It's not. Doing it on Yom Shabbat is."

Ruth pushed the dish with the stale bread toward the woman as an offering. She fell on it as if it were manna from heaven.

"Goodness, where are my manners?" the skinny woman said, licking the crumbs from her fingers.

Her name was Sheva, and she had been eking out a living from the stubborn, rocky soil with a group of lowlanders until a family of returning exiles reclaimed their ancestral estate, forcing her to take up a new trade.

If you can call it a trade, Ruth thought.

"Lowlanders?"

"That's what they call us when they think nobody's listening," Sheva said. "Anyone who lives west of the Temple Mount is a *lowlander*, and anyone they want to kick off the land is a foreigner."

Ruth nodded.

The sound of tortured screeching reached their ears from the Temple Mount as the attendants blew *shofars* driving a dozen rams to the main altar as guilt offerings.

"Sounds like they're really going through with it," Ruth said, her jaw tightening.

"With what?"

Ruth kept her eyes clamped shut as an abdominal spasm roiled her insides, waiting it out, waiting for the pain to subside, and wondering what the hell she was supposed to do when the blood came in this filthy place.

"Hey, are you all right?"

Ruth shook her head, curling in on herself, rocking in place as the ram's horn *shofars* kept up their mournful cries.

The knots of pain finally loosened their grip. Relief flooded her limbs as her bowels untwisted and her breathing gradually eased.

"You should take safflower tea for those cramps," Sheva said.

"Oh, do the jailers keep a garden of such herbs?"

"I mean when you get out. Till then, I've got some rags you can use."

"Thanks," Ruth said with genuine gratitude. When she was able to focus her thoughts, she told Sheva how the men of Yehudah had taken a sacred oath to dissolve their marriages and expel their foreign wives from the land of Israel.

"What kind of man does that?" Ruth asked.

"You mean, what kind of man is eager to divorce his aging foreign wife for the promise of a young, *pure* Yehudi girl?" Sheva's mouth opened wider than a barn door on greased hinges to release a cascade of bitter laughter.

"They can't all be so piggish," Ruth said. "Surely there are *some* men who will refuse to obey this edict."

"You mean like that guy who calls himself the Scribe of the Annals? He's all right on letting you marry whoever you want, I guess, but he's as stiff as the rest of them on keeping Shabbat and stamping out the adoration of Our Lady Asherah."

Ruth emitted a mild expletive. Her loving husband had patiently taught her how to keep a pure kitchen and guard the holy day of the Yehudim, but he never stopped her from worshiping the goddess.

"But that Nekhemyah guy," said Sheva. "The one who's rebuilding the walls?"

"Nekhemyah Ben-Khakhalya of Shushan."

"That's the one."

"What about him?"

Sheva pulled back her skirt, revealing a network of knotty red-and-purple welts curving around her thighs.

"Oh, my," Ruth said, since she didn't know what else to say.

"Anyone who buys or sells on the seventh day shall be publicly whipped on his orders for engaging in trade on Yom Shabbat. And the same goes for any man who refuses to leave his foreign wife." Sheva nodded toward the cup of dirty water. "You gonna finish that?"

"No. It smells like swamp mud."

Sheva upended the cup and drained it, slammed it down empty and wiped her mouth on her sleeve.

"It's just—" Ruth stopped and took a moment to marvel at Sheva's hidden strengths.

Sheva looked at her blankly. "What?"

"How did a *scribe* get so much power?" Ruth said. "Ezra Ben-Serayah's not even a Persian official."

"He's the high priest's uncle, for shit's sake. You know how it is—grease enough palms and you could get them to raise his nephew's slave-wife to full legal status."

"There's a category called *slave-wife*?"

"Why? You planning on marrying up?"

"No. I mean, well, what girl isn't? It's just that—"

"And they say *I'm* a harlot. Who's your owner, anyway?"

"I don't have an *owner*."

"Take it easy, will you? It's just an expression. We call a man who takes a woman in marriage a *ba'al ishah*, the *owner* of a woman. But it really means *master*."

"Same thing."

"No, it's not. We call a man who makes the best beer a *master* of brewing, a man who harvests the most grain a *master* of the earth, and a man who knows how to screw his wife for more than ten minutes a *master* in bed." She chuckled knowingly.

Up on the hill, another ram yielded to the sacred blade in a shower of blood sluicing down the sides of the altar.

"So a woman who has a *ba'al ishah* lording over her is not the same as a *slave-wife*," Ruth confirmed.

"What's it to you?"

"It might prove useful to know that there's a lesser category of *wife*."

The ram's horns' dissonant bleating lasted till the sun sailed off into the twilight and the sky turned a dusky indigo.

Ruth drifted into a troubled sleep, transported to a vast field of wheat, its center blasted flat as if by a fireball from the sky, and in the middle of the blackened earth, a pool of reddish-black blood bubbling up from a wet slash in the mud, like a man's lips, murmuring in the tongue of Yehud.

The blood wasn't sinking into the ground, it was

spreading, poisoning the crops, lapping at her toes, yet she couldn't look away, for it was her husband's blood crying out to her, forming words meant for her ears alone, a disembodied soul beyond all earthly concerns telling her something he never got to say in life.

Eretz al-tekhasi dami.

She knew those words. *Eretz* was earth, *dam* was blood. What did the rest mean?

Eretz al-tekhasi dami.

Earth ... do not ... arrange? Do not ... trample?

Eretz al-tekhasi dami.

It came to her at once: *Earth, do not cover my blood.*

She jolted awake, her heart pounding, her thighs wet with blood. Her shift sticking to her, stained by the steady trickle from between her legs, forming an unsightly puddle on the filthy stones.

"Sounds like you had one hell of a nightmare, sister," Sheva said, getting out the rags to help Ruth wipe up the mess.

Ruth's dream-tormented mind was still trying to grasp a fading trace of the spirit's ephemeral energy, because something was picking at her, a message from beyond the grave. She sopped the blood from her thighs while puzzling out the riddle of why her husband's spirit would speak to her in the tongue of Yehudah instead of the tongue of Aram, which is what they always spoke together, and suddenly it was clear. Ruth didn't need a dream reader to explain it. He was telling her that she was right: the roots of this bloodcrime lay in the land of Israel.

A rough pounding on the door, and a team of guards walked in, eyes widening at the spectacle of two women cleaning up a *niddah*'s blood-flow.

"You! Ruth the Moabite!" one said, averting his eyes in revulsion.

Ruth felt exposed and vulnerable, and for a moment

refused to identify herself by the derogatory epithet. But in the end, she had no choice.

"That's me."

"You're getting out. Nekhemyah the engineer says he needs every available worker to rebuild the wall."

"*Halleluyah*," she said, wiping her hands on a rag.

CHAPTER SIXTEEN

Felicity

And the water in the river was turned to blood, and the fish in the river died, and the river became foul, so the people could not drink water from the river.

The good people of southern Queens County woke up this morning to find their neighborhoods engulfed by the stench of millions of dead fish, eels, crabs and jellyfish clogging Rockaway Inlet. All twelve of Jesus' disciples *and* Mary Magdalene could have tap-danced across Jamaica Bay on the wall-to-wall carpet of rotting bluefish, bass, and flounder after a period of unusually warm weather led to an unsustainable increase in algae, whose sudden die-off reduced the oxygen supply in the water, killing the fish.

I'm trying to fill the gaps in my knowledge of ancient Hebrew documents by setting up appointments with three leading Torah scholars in a single day, which I believe is a record of some kind, starting with Julie Zeltserman, a Torah scribe whose studio overlooks the greasy waters of Maspeth Creek.

Ms. Zeltserman shows me how she begins each session by scribbling four Hebrew letters on a scrap of paper, dunking her nib in the ink and letting a huge drop fall on the paper, obliterating the name of *Amalek*.

"The Jews are such a text-based culture that for us, the ultimate punishment is having your name erased," she says. "Every year we ask God to write our names in the Book of Life. *On Rosh Hashanah it is written, on Yom Kippur it is sealed—*"

"*And on Hanukkah it is fried in oil and eaten with sour cream,*" I say.

She cocks her head and regards me with those big dark eyes. With her pale complexion and dark, wavy hair, she could pass for a cousin on my mother's side.

"I work with a lot of lawyers and tax accountants," I say.

She nods. "The Jewish people certainly have a long tradition of legalistic wrangling and debating the meaning of biblical passages."

"Like that the Bible doesn't literally say *God hates fags* anywhere?" I ask, popping open my briefcase and reaching inside.

"The Hebrew Bible does condemn male homosexuality in a single phrase, but it *repeatedly* condemns greed, race hatred, hypocrisy, and corrupt officials," she says.

"Fuck yeah, it does."

"Um, yes," she says, turning her attention back to the glossy black letters, their wavy verticals flickering like tongues of black fire on the luminous sheepskin parchment.

"Now what can your scribal expertise tell me about this?" I say, laying the evidence bag on her drawing board with the scrap of Hebrew writing facing up.

"Where did you get this?" she says, examining the fragment.

"From a storage locker near the Port Authority Bus Terminal. Can you tell me if it's part of the Scroll of Ruth?"

"Well, the first line is a command: *kadosh l'hashem lo yimakhar.*"

"What's that mean?" I say, grabbing a pencil to take notes.

"Holy unto the Lord. It shall not be sold."

"Uh-oh. Too late."

"It's been sold?"

"Worse. What about the rest?"

"Well, it starts with the same word as the Book of Ruth, *vayehi*, but that's just a formulaic opening meaning *it happened*, or *it came to pass.*"

"What about the rest?"

She performs a quick deciphering of the fragmentary content.

"*For it happened in … of our captivity … the Lord called upon His anointed … and bade him … move against the kingdom of Babylonia … Persian engineers …* I'm not familiar with the passage, but the language is post-Exilic. The prophet Isaiah refers to King Cyrus of Persia as *God's anointed* after he frees the Israelites from captivity."

"So it's part of the book of Isaiah?" I straighten up, my neck and shoulders stiff from stress and frustration.

"It's not part of any canonical biblical text, but it bears a similarity to the language and tone of the later Isaiah."

"But … don't Ruth and Isaiah belong to completely different historical periods?" I say, giving myself a one-handed neck massage that's not terribly effective.

"Only Christian Bibles place Ruth between Judges and Samuel," she says, damping the fires of my urgency. "Most modern scholars believe that Ruth was written as a direct response to the racially exclusive language in Ezra and Nehemiah. That would date its composition to sometime after the return from the Babylonian Exile in the late sixth century BCE, making it roughly contemporary with the later chapters in Isaiah."

"What can you tell me about the Book of Ruth itself?"

A malodorous breeze ruffles a poster-sized work of calligraphy with colorful cut-paper borders that looks like the one I saw hanging on Mrs. Lowry's living room wall.

"What's the meaning of all that Hebrew?" I ask, indicating the poster.

"It's a *ketubah*."

I wait for more.

"A marriage contract," she explains. "And it's written in Aramaic, not Hebrew."

"Oh."

She lays down her quill.

"The Scroll of Ruth is the shortest narrative book in the Bible, so you're not looking for some big, fat Torah scroll."

I strike a pensive pose, the pencil's eraser touching my chin.

"There are passages that positively simmer with raw sexual energy," she says, a catlike glint in her eye. "As a widow and a foreign woman, Ruth's status is highly uncertain. Yet she's constantly idealized in rabbinic literature as being irresistibly young and fertile. There's even a passage in the *Ruth Rabbah* where Rabbi Yokhanon says that Ruth was so stunningly beautiful that every man who saw her had a spontaneous orgasm."

Transgressive merriment sputters forth from my lips.

"Now *that* is an impressive skill," I say, unable to keep a lid on the giggles.

"I gather they never taught you that particular midrash in Catholic school," she says.

"No, no, no." Muzzled laughter constricts the sinews of my throat and abdominal muscles till it sounds just like crying. I do my best to compose myself. "So is she a flesh-and-blood woman or a fertility goddess?"

"She's really a bit of both. The sexually charged scene at the threshing floor ends with her redeemer Boaz dumping a bushel of grain in her lap. You don't have to be a world-famous Harvard professor of symbology to figure that one out."

I finally get a chance to catch my breath as she goes on. "She also represents another kind of fullness that's extremely important to desert nomads—a plentiful supply of water. The Talmud suggests that the name Ruth is derived from *ra'ah*, to drink one's fill."

"Sounds like what the guys on the corner used to call *a long drink of water*," I say. "When they were being polite, I mean," which for some reason reminds me that I woke up to an empty bed for the fourth day in a row with no sign of redness spotting my sheets.

All the more reason to get back to business.

"What's so special about the Baghdad Scroll of Ruth?"

She immerses her nib in the ink. "It's supposed to be longer than the version in the Bible, with some significant variations in terms of content and tone. Some scholars have even suggested that the scroll was written by a woman."

"Based on what evidence?" I say, tapping the pencil eraser against my chin.

"Because the Book of Ruth is a female-centered story that focuses on the problems of a couple of poor, desperate women. Because it depicts the complex relationship between a mother-in-law and a daughter-in-law working together toward a common goal, despite their differences. And because God commands us to protect the lowest class of people in the social order, the widows, the poor, and the foreigners—which is exactly what Ruth is, a poor widow and a foreign woman who is prohibited by law from marrying a son of Israel."

"Hold on a sec—"

"In some cases, a woman is only fully accepted by her husband's clan after she bears a son to carry on the family name and pray for his father's soul in She'ol, though that's a later development."

"What's She'ol?"

The quill rises with a solemn flourish.

"The abode of the dead, the underworld, what the Akkadian tablets call the *field of thirst*, whose size is three hundred years' journey."

Clouds of ignorance darken my brow, threatening rain.

"She'ol is so big they don't measure it in terms of distance traveled, but the years it takes to cross it," she says.

"Sounds a bit like Los Angeles."

She gives me a pert little smile.

"The prophets Isaiah and Habakkuk describe She'ol as a kind of ravenous demon with huge, reptilian jaws that swallows kings and beggars alike."

"Still sounds like Los Angeles."

"Ruth's biggest problem is that she has no husband or son to secure her place in the social order, yet the biblical text never shows her longing for a child or crying out to God to end her barrenness."

"So what happens?"

"They bend the rules a bit and she marries Boaz of Bethlehem, and they all live happily ever after."

"Does she love him?"

She looks me straight in the eye: "Michal, daughter of King Saul, is the only woman in the Bible who is described as *falling in love* with a man."

"So who's the lucky guy?"

"A young warrior named David."

I nod, tapping the pencil on a piece of scrap paper. "Could you do me a favor and show me how to recognize Ruth's name in Hebrew?"

Without a word, she draws what looks like a curved ax-blade, a railroad spike, and a two-legged bentwood table on the scrap of paper, and hands it to me.

"That's it? Only three letters?"

"Hebrew is generally much more condensed than English, and most of the narrative description isn't very flowery."

My phone goes *ping*. It's a text from Detective Gustella. *Where are u?*

I reply that I'm getting background on the missing scroll.

Then why's the car been parked in Maspeth Creek for 45 minutes?

I reply that I need to be able to recognize the scroll when I come across it.

Believe me you'll know when you see it.

Really? I wonder how he can be so sure of that.

Professor Woolley's class is meeting in Triboro Community College's tiny science lab. She's making the lecture fun by bringing flour, sugar, cinnamon, and other ingredients and walking the students through the stages of cookie production while lecturing about how patriarchal monotheism systematically downgraded the status of powerful goddesses like Ishtar and Inanna, but that Asherah presented the biggest challenge to Israel's brand of monotheism. It wasn't enough to merely weaken her: All traces of her cult of worship had to be scrubbed from the written records *and* from people's homes, and prophets like Isaiah claim that she never existed in the first place.

One sign of her enduring popularity: when Professor Woolley's team unearthed the ruins of a second century house destroyed by Romans during the Bar Kokhba revolt of 132–135 CE, they found a cache of gold and silver jewelry that some unfortunate woman must have buried under the dirt floor before fleeing. One of those rings bore the image of a winged goddess carved into the polished surface of a precious stone embedded in the gold.

"Even at that late date," Professor Woolley declares, "in the second century of the Christian Era, the women of Israel still clung to the goddess."

A loose-knit sorority of students from twenty different countries nods in silent recognition of a lone woman's struggle to survive in a time of disastrous upheaval that they might only know from the sterile world of a Wikipedia article. Although some of them look like they might be refugees themselves, from different wars, a bit closer to our era.

"So a powerful goddess gets reduced to a relatively minor figure like the Mistress of the River, an archetype that persists for centuries in still recognizable forms such as the Lady of the Lake in the Arthurian legends. Her footsteps can still be found in the teachings of the Kabbalists and thinkers like Moses Cordovero, who affirms that Asherah lives on in the spirit of Wisdom, and Reik affirms that feminine aspects of God's essence embodied in figures like Wisdom and the *Shekhinah* are the *disguised, scarcely recognizable* remnants of the primal Israelite mother-goddess."

And a little thing called the Virgin Mary, Holy Mother of God, I'm thinking.

She takes a handful of flour, drops it on the cutting board with a silent explosion of white powder, rolls out the dough, and fills a baking pan with uneven rectangles shiny with raw egg, butter, and molasses, all of it that sunbaked reddish-brown like the figures in an Egyptian wall painting, the color of the earth the first humans were made of, according to the Bible.

Dr. Woolley shows the students how to carve their names in Akkadian in the wet, clay-like medium with a pair of wedge-shaped chopsticks.

Within minutes, the seductive smell of baking cookies permeates the lab. Gingerbread is not my favorite, but there's something exquisite about the smell of fresh-baked cookies, even if they don't contain the requisite critical mass of chocolate.

The students *ooh* and *aah* with delight when their edible cuneiform tablets come out of the oven, some gobbling them up on the spot, others attempting to preserve them by wrapping them in cheap brown paper towels.

As the students file out, Dr. Woolley approaches me with a fresh-baked cookie in her hands.

"A peace offering," she says.

I oblige, taking the cookie and biting off a corner.

"I'm afraid we got off on the wrong foot last time," she says.

"I just caught you at a bad moment," I say out of the side of my mouth so as not to spatter her with cookie crumbs.

Her bloodless lips part to form a crinkly smile.

"I brought something for you, too," I say, nudging the duffel bag at my feet.

"We can talk privately in my office," she says, heading for the exit.

I hoist the duffel bag and follow her down the narrow hallway.

"When did you switch from studying ancient Iraq to ancient Israel?" I ask.

"We'll be returning to Iraq as soon as security conditions allow it," she says, optimistically. "In the meantime, focusing on Israel during the Babylonian period was a natural switch."

The faint smell of dead fish drifting over from Jamaica Bay lingers in the hallway leading to Dr. Woolley's office.

Her shelves are crammed with books, papers, file folders, and artifacts, but one holds a place of honor on her desk: a statuette of a woman with a traditional Egyptian hairstyle and skirt, laboring on her hands and knees with a strained expression, her featureless hands permanently fused to the heavy stone in front of her.

"That's one of my favorites, too," she says. "It's from the fifth dynasty of the Old Kingdom, about 2350 BCE. This woman would have spent a couple of hours a day, *every day*, on her knees grinding flour with a heavy millstone just to feed her family. We found clear signs of arthritic deformities and repetitive stress injuries to the toes, knees, and lower backs of *every* adult female skeleton we examined from that dig."

I give the long-suffering statuette a sympathetic glance. *I know how you feel, sister.*

"Is that where you keep the *real* cuneiform tablets?" I say, noting a large metal storage cabinet with wide, shallow drawers.

"It's more of a jumble of broken pieces, I'm afraid, of no practical interest to anyone but an expert in the field."

She directs my gaze to a large color photo of a wall relief depicting a couple of Egyptian dudes in loincloths with their arms around each other, in profile. They've got identical hairstyles, too. Short, dark, and tightly curled.

"The inscription identifies them as the king's personal manicurists," she says. "So I doubt we'd find any signs of work-related injuries on their remains. They must have been very well regarded, since they received the kingdom's highest honor of being buried with the pharaoh."

"That's their idea of a great honor, huh?"

"The curious thing is, no one knows why they're depicted embracing in the manner of a married couple. Were they siblings? Identical twins? Conjoined twins?"

"Hell*ooo*, they're the royal *manicurists*," I say, flashing the universal limp-wristed sign of the flamboyantly gay man.

Dr. Woolley's pale lips pinch together in distaste.

"Now what have you got for me?" she says, tilting her nose at the duffel bag.

I use this opportunity to lay the partially nibbled cookie on the edge of her desk, and hoist the duffel bag onto a chair and zip it open, releasing a hint of camphor and cigarette ash. I step back and gesture for her to look for herself. Dr. Woolley reaches into the bag and pulls out a foot-long triangular chunk of baked clay with a sky-blue glaze on one side. The three-inch-thick slab of earthenware is broken from a larger piece, like a slice of pie, revealing the highly compressed clay inside.

"No wonder the bag was so heavy," she says, hefting the giant paperweight and examining it from all sides. "The bricks from King Nebuchadnezzar's time are generally superior to ours, denser and longer-lasting than most typically found today."

"How do you know it's from King Nebuchadnezzar's time?"

She turns the triangular chunk of brick over so I can see.

"His name's stamped on the bottom," she says.

The bottom is unglazed, with the clear impression of a lengthy cuneiform inscription pressed into the clay.

"What are those squiggles?" I ask, pointing to what looks like a child's doodling next to the dense lines of text in a dead language, frozen in time.

She leans closer to examine the squiggles.

"It's Aramaic," she says. "*Z-B-N-h.*"

"What's that mean?"

"It means that around two thousand six hundred years ago, a worker named Zabinah or Zebineh carved his name in the wet clay."

I'm suitably impressed by this information, but Dr. Woolley finds it necessary to add: "Think of it. A lowly brick worker was able to write his name on a piece of the king's palace."

I nod with recognition. "Sounds a lot like my dad."

Dr. Woolley's mouth twitches with incomprehension.

"My dad's a construction worker," I explain.

"Ah," she says, her facial muscles relaxing a bit.

She sets the brick fragment on her desk and reaches into the duffel bag, pulling out one of the heavier items, wrapped in pages torn from the Middle East edition of *Stars and Stripes*.

She carefully unwraps the ink-smeared newsprint, exposing a tarnished metal ax-head. The eye and butt of the ax are a dull smoky gray, but someone put a *lot* of effort into burnishing the rest of the blade with steel wool or something equally abrasive, because the intricate reliefs on the ax-head's cheeks are so smooth and shiny they look like they could have been hand-forged last weekend by the blacksmith at the local Renaissance faire.

"It's a ceremonial ax-head," she says. "The kind of gift a king might present to a visiting dignitary. And some idiot has nearly *ruined* it by trying to scrape off centuries of oxidation build-up. That's like trying to clean the *Mona Lisa* with chlorine bleach."

"It wasn't me." I raise my hands in a display of innocence.

She tests the newly sharpened blade with her thumb.

"This ax-head presents some important features that are characteristic of the metalwork from a region of ancient Persia known as Luristan. I couldn't say for certain without further examination," she says, peering at the unpolished design elements where the steel wool didn't reach. "But if it's genuine, it would be a remarkable find in such good condition. The blades manufactured in the province of Luristan are of such high quality that they could only have been produced by advanced artisanal methods capable of maintaining a constant furnace temperature of more than 2,500 degrees Fahrenheit for over forty hours. No one knows how they managed it with Iron Age technology."

I gently pry the ax-head from her white-knuckle grip and lay it on the desk.

"Wandering metalsmiths served far-flung communities in the Ancient Near East that didn't have the means to do elaborate work in copper, silver, and especially iron," she says. "Imagine the effect it must have had when a band of rootless nomads swept into a village bringing their strange and magical skills. Even demons are powerless against a well-wrought implement made of iron and flame."

"You make them sound like a badass biker gang or something."

For once, she doesn't bat it back at me.

"The comparison is not entirely unwarranted," she says with a bemused twist of her dry lips.

Stop the presses, boys! I think we struck funny bone!

"The Kenites were a tightly knit group with their own code of behavior, jealously protecting their trade secrets as they roamed the hill country of Kanaan. What else have you got in there, anyway?" She yanks open the duffel bag and paws through the contents, but she's too much of a pro to risk further damage to the contents, and after the initial flurry of righteous indignation, she commences a slow, meticulous examination of the broken pieces of fallen idols, the displaced gods and goddesses, their names forgotten, their powers unrecognized, their features worn smooth by the shifting sands of time.

She lets out a sudden burst of outrage when she opens the burlap pouch full of cylinder seals and spreads them out on her desk, and while she's poring over them, I finally get the chance to explain that I'm trying to locate a scroll that went missing during the madness of the war.

"Why come to me?" she says, holding up a cylinder seal the size of her pinky, carved from reddish stone. "We've hardly done any fieldwork in Iraq since the first Gulf War."

"I have reason to believe a former student of yours knows where the scroll is."

"Which former student?" she says, turning the cylinder this way and that in the light to gauge its translucence. There appears to be a flaw beneath the surface, a razor-thin crack cutting right through the soft stone.

"Kristel Santos, remember? She's on your roster—"

"She never attended class," Dr. Woolley says, abruptly.

"Oh?"

"*What?*"

"Well, it's just that the last time we spoke, you told me she hadn't attended class since the second week of the semester."

"What difference does it make? I can't be expected to remember every—"

"Do you recognize this?" I silence her protest with a wave of my hand, the plastic evidence bag dangling from my fingers.

"Where did you get this?" she says, reaching for the plastic bag.

"It was in the duffel bag along with everything else."

"*Ick!* What's this stuff?" Her fingers come away covered with black powder.

"Fingerprint powder. Sorry, some of it got on the bag."

"You dusted a priceless artifact *for fingerprints*?" she says, seething.

"You told me this was a forgery."

"No, I said the Baghdad Scroll is a forgery," she says, saliva gathering at the corners of her mouth.

"So this *isn't* a piece of the Baghdad Scroll?"

"I couldn't say without examining it under laboratory conditions."

"Either way, the prints on the back of the scroll fragment match the prints in the company's personnel file for Kristel Santos. A near-perfect match. A bit too perfect, actually."

"What do you mean?"

"I mean that the other objects in the bag are covered with hundreds of smeared or partial prints, which is normal for objects that have been handled by so many people, while this scroll fragment—the only *document* in this cache of stolen treasures—has a couple of near-perfect prints of Kristel Santos's right thumb and index finger. No smearing whatsoever."

"And just what does that mean?"

"It means someone's trying too hard, like when the signature on a forged document is absolutely identical to an existing signature."

"What's wrong with that?"

"Nobody signs their name *exactly* the same way twice. It's a standard beginner's error."

"And you'd like me to look at this and give you some answers?" she says, reaching for the scroll fragment again, but I keep it out of reach. "If you want my assistance, you have to leave it with me."

"Sorry, I can't allow that."

"Then how am I supposed to examine it?"

"Got a photocopy machine in the office?"

"Don't be ridiculous."

"You can take a picture of it with your smartphone—"

"I need to examine the original."

"I understand that, but I can't let it out of my sight."

"Why not?"

"I need to establish an unbroken chain of evidence."

"Evidence? Of what?"

"Just take a quick look at it and tell me what you think."

I let her pluck the evidence bag from my hand and lay it on her desk. She flips on the desk lamp and slides open a drawer, pulls on a pair of white cotton gloves and grabs a pair of tweezers, which she uses to carefully remove the scroll fragment from the polyethylene bag.

She rolls her chair an inch closer to the desk and adjusts the lamp, redirecting its cone of light toward the brittle heart of the dried scrap of parchment. She drags over a large magnifying glass secured to a metal clamp and embarks on a thorough examination of this precious sample of specially treated hide, gliding over each dip and dimple of its craggy terrain with rapt attention.

"The calligraphy is roughly similar to samples from the Dead Sea Scrolls," she says, gazing through the glass at the long-tailed letters bobbing along like a fleet of crooked-masted sailboats on rough seas. "If you let me take a small sample I might be able to analyze the genetic fingerprint and tell you whether this is lamb or goatskin, or even identify the particular goat it came from. We might even be able to match it with other fragments from the same scroll."

"So it's definitely part of a larger scroll?"

"I couldn't begin to answer that without further data, but it's the most likely explanation."

"I mean, what kind of clues lead you to that conclusion?"

She raises her head. "Oh, that's right. You want *clues*. Because you're a detective of some kind."

"A certified document examiner," I correct her.

"Oh, a *certified* document examiner. How impressive. Did you sign up for the three-week correspondence course or did you take the full *six* weeks?"

Okay, now she's just being a bitch.

I explain that certification requires several years of full-time training with a certified forensic documents examiner (FDE) or a recognized document laboratory, and passing written and oral examinations administered by the American

Board of FDEs, adding, "And by the way, it's time to update your put-downs. All the fake diploma mills are online now, not correspondence courses."

The room is silent for a moment.

"Well, that's entirely appropriate," she says, pursing her lips in a passable imitation of contrition.

"Fine. Now tell me more about why you believe this fragment is part of a scroll."

I let a few seconds of dead air go by as she examines the specimen.

"Hmm. The lines of text are nearly parallel and the calligraphy looks like the work of a professional scribe," she says, "while the language is consistent with the formulaic openings of historical and prophetic texts in the style of Chronicles or Isaiah."

"Nothing about Ruth?"

"Why do you keep going on about the Book of Ruth?" she says. "It's a minor text, a simplistic fable of little historical interest."

She keeps redirecting the conversation *away* from the Book of Ruth, but there's a crack in the foundation somewhere, some rot in the support beams. I can smell it as surely as I can smell the powdered ginger in those fresh-baked cookies.

She plucks a shiny steel lancet from the tool drawer, along with a glass specimen jar, and carefully slices through a few millimeters of the upper right corner of the scrap of parchment, then makes a perpendicular cut and removes a tiny sample with a pair of tweezers, dropping it in the specimen jar and sealing it with a flick of her wrist.

I slip the parchment back into the evidence bag as she hefts the ax-head and lays it under the magnifying glass.

"I once spent a *very* hot summer in the Judean foothills investigating the extent of the Assyrian campaign of 701 BCE," she says. "We found evidence of catastrophic destruction, including a layer of burnt debris that was *eight feet deep*. The

Assyrian king had ordered the captured leaders to be stripped of their clothing, tied down and skinned alive, and had his court artists commemorate these atrocities by carving them in stone for wall reliefs in the palace at Nineveh."

"I'm getting the impression that the Assyrians were kind of like the Klingons of the Ancient Near East."

She's put off by my *Star Trek* reference, frowning as she reaches into the tool drawer for a curved metal pick that looks like it belongs in a dentist's office.

"There was no shortage of savagery in the region, if that's what you mean. During the first Jewish revolt, the Roman general Ptolemy, angered by the rebels' deliberate withdrawal to strategic positions surrounding their village, ordered his men to butcher the remaining women and babies, cook their flesh in huge pots, and pretend to eat some of it to convince the Jewish fighters that his men were flesh-eating cannibals and terrify them into surrendering."

"Yeah, we'll kill the women and children and chop up their bodies *to give the impression* that we're ruthless and bloodthirsty. Right."

She grips the dentist's tool in one hand and scrapes a few flecks of greenish crud from the ax-head onto a microscope slide for closer examination. She pushes the big magnifying glass aside and yanks the plastic dust cover off the binocular microscope on the far edge of her desk.

Her hands betray a slight tremor as she struggles to secure the slide to the stage under the microscope's lens. Maybe it's stress. Or nerve degeneration. She takes so long adjusting the focus knobs, I find my attention wandering to the storage cabinet against the opposite wall.

"This is rather odd," she exclaims, peering through the dual eyepieces.

"What's odd?"

"The ax-head itself is remarkably free of rust, which suggests that it wasn't a weapon of war."

"Right. You already told me it was a ceremonial gift."

"I said it was *probably* a ceremonial gift—"

She rises from her chair and I hear a little *pop* like a piece of chalk breaking in half. She cries out, crumpling over as her hand flies to her left knee.

"Are you okay?" I say, gripping her arm to steady her.

"No, I'm *not* okay," she says, clearly in pain. "It's an old injury that flares up from time to time. A heavy-handed Army Ranger slammed the metal door of his Humvee on my leg while they were evacuating us during the first Gulf War."

I'm thinking, *Sucks to get old, huh?*

But prudence prevails.

"Can I get you anything? A glass of water?"

"Water, hell, I could use a good stiff drink," she says, massaging her knee. "In the ancient world, beer and wine were often safer than the local water supply because the alcohol killed the bacteria in the water. It helped women earn a living, since they considered it women's work to brew and sell beer, but the laws were strict. In King Hammurabi's time tavern owners who overcharged their customers were punished by being tossed into the river. They called it *going to see Judge River*."

"This Judge River sounds like a very even-handed jurist."

She flexes her left knee, testing its elasticity. I guess it passes the test.

"At least tribes like the Saka were egalitarian," she says. "The burial mounds in northwestern Iran confirm that male and female warriors were interred with their horses and war chariots, along with amulets that may have functioned in a similar way as what the Israelites called *bati ha-nefesh*, or *houses of the soul*."

"I gather this has nothing to do with Motown Records."

"Certainly not."

"Stax? Atlantic?"

"They were likely worn by women who believed they housed the soul of a loved one." Her face brightens as some of her stamina returns. "We found just such an amulet at a dig in Jerusalem containing traces of a man's blood mixed with an extremely potent snake venom. If I'd found it in Babylon or Nineveh, I'd have figured its owner for a pagan priestess or a shaman. Either way, she must have been a hell of a woman to mess with."

My phone buzzes with an emergency alert: CONTACT ADULT DAY CARE FACILITY

Oh, shit.

"I've got to take this," I say, slipping the parchment fragment into its plastic slipcase and into my bag. "Are you sure you're feeling all right?"

"I'm fine."

I leave her with the contents of the duffel bag to examine, identify, determine the provenance of, and, if stolen, contact the original owners, if they're still walking the earth. I'm rushing out the door when she calls me back to remind me that I haven't finished my gingerbread cookie.

I run outside and call the facility. I ask them what's the emergency.

"He ate a Band-Aid!"

Aw, Jesus. That's the emergency? Because my brother eats vinyl examination gloves—whole. Sometimes worse. Sharp metal objects, strips of plastic torn from his mattress protector that can block his esophagus, foam rubber ear plugs that go clear through him and end up floating in the toilet bowl or clogging the septic system.

They give me the whole bit about how they gave him plenty of water to ease the Band-Aid's passage and they're monitoring him closely, and I'm like *Yeah, yeah, yeah. Thanks.* While all the time I'm thinking, *Don't do that to me, you frigging morons.*

CHAPTER SEVENTEEN

Ruth

Then came the dreaded *khamsin*. The hot, dry wind from the east moved in and made itself at home, extracting every atom of moisture from the air till the grapes withered on the vine, the olives shriveled on the branches, and the grain in the fields crackled dryly, begging for water. First the leeks and cucumbers vanished from the stalls in the open market, then the figs and pomegranates, and finally the lentils, till there was nothing left but the stiff papery coverings of onions and garlic bulbs drifting about in the hot breeze. The flour reserves dwindled till the breadmakers dampened the fires on Bakers Lane, and not a crumb remained in the larders, from the grimy hovels hard by the Dung Gate to the dirt floor farmhouses on the western hill.

And the hirelings from the proud manor houses swarmed across the valley and stripped the western ridge of twigs and branches to keep the hearth fires burning, while the people of the land scrambled about uprooting the thorny vines that etched networks of unruly red lines across their arms and hands. And after they burned through the supply of thorns, they went out to gather dried goat turds. And when they burned through those, they emptied out the privies and spread the contents in the sun, and threw together whatever crumbs were left in the jars—all the broken, mouse-chewed kernels of wheat, barley, millet, spelt—and baked thin, brittle cakes over fires fueled by dry human shit.

And as the wells ran dry, the people dug up the dry

streambeds and wadis, expending three measures of labor to recover half a measure of silty water.

And every prophet from Beit-shemesh to Jericho converged on the city, crying out *Halilu!*

Howl! For the day of the Lord is near
For the light has gone out of the sky
The earth is screaming like a woman in labor
And every river runs dry

The women of the land were told to burn any remaining idols and scatter the ashes to the wind as the law commands. But their devotion to Asherah was so deeply rooted in their souls they took their beloved figurines of the mother goddess and buried them beneath the floors of their homes or in the nearby fields.

By the time Ruth trudged up the hill, shaking off the dust of prison, Oved's livestock had dwindled to a pair of listless goats, bleating weakly, the nearby fields picked bare.

Tzillah was too weak to grind the coarse barley meal into flour, having spent the afternoon kneading the last bits of straw into the manure cakes to bind them together and laying them out to dry.

"I'll do it," Ruth said, and Oved smiled and thanked her.

Ruth found Naomi in the back room tending to Nekhamah, and together they helped the creaky, white-haired matriarch rise from her sickbed and shuffle to the dining area.

"How are you feeling today, grandmother?" Ruth inquired.

Naomi muttered, "While you were picking fights with the watchmen, I was laying hot compresses on her limbs and emptying her piss pot."

"It feels like there's sand in my joints," Nekhamah said, her voice hoarse.

"Sounds like you could use some *levonah* to help relieve the inflammation. And maybe some *yabruhim*," Ruth said.

"*Levonah?*" Naomi scolded her. "Incense from the kingdom of Sheba? Where are we supposed to get the silver to buy a measure of pure Sabean incense? And what on earth is *yabruhim*?"

"It's a root—"

Nekhamah lowered herself noisily to a sitting position. Next to her sat poor Tabitha, her once glowing apple cheeks now sunken and taut over her cheekbones.

Oved invited Ben-Isaiah to join them. "Come and lead us in prayer before we break bread. Or at least we call it bread," he said, indicating the undercooked gruel cakes that Tzillah was bringing from the foul-smelling hearth.

Ben-Isaiah took his place near the serving dish and offered up this prayer: "O Lord, hasten the day when those who are lost in the lands of Assyria and Egypt shall bow down to You on the holy mountain in Jerusalem. And on that day, the mountains will drip with sweet wine, and the hills will flow with milk, and all the rivers and streams of Yehudah will flow with water, and a fountain will go out from the House of the Lord."

Must he use such lush imagery? God, it's agony.

"And on that day, they shall beat their swords into plowshares and throw their shields into the sea. Nation shall not lift sword against nation, and they shall not know war again. Amen."

"Amen."

The bread was lumpy and raw in places, with a faint smoky aftertaste of human excrement.

"One more week of this and we're going to have dig up the bones of the dead and grind them for meal," Tzillah said bitterly.

Tabitha let out a tiny squeak of horror.

"Don't worry, no one's going to dig up the dead," Ruth said, patting the little girl's bony hand.

Zuriel chewed a hunk of this poor man's bread, his sunken cheeks swelling and shrinking like a lizard's, his eyes radiating such resentment at Ruth he might as well have tattooed the message on his forehead: *We barely have enough for ourselves. Why are we feeding you?*

"Mother Nekhamah," Ruth said, fishing around in her sack. "The good Lord has left me with one last treasure I can trade for the medicine you need, and some food for the little one."

She placed the curved dagger in her upturned palms and held it out, its damascene blade glinting in the pale light of the sputtering oil lamp.

Nekhamah managed a feeble smile. "We're almost out of lamp oil as well."

"I will do what I can," Ruth promised.

"Why are you doing all this for them?" Naomi said, when they were clearing away the dishes.

"Because there is a time for healing and a time for slaying, and that time is coming soon."

~

Ruth and Ben-Isaiah spent hours laboring to convince reluctant farmers and suspicious housewives along the high road to the west to speak with them, with no luck.

"We'd better turn back before we have to forage for food."

"How do you know the guilty ones are in the land of Yehudah and not in Babel, where the deaths occurred?" Ben-Isaiah asked, slipping on some loose pebbles as they worked their way down the narrow, winding path.

"Because the bloodguilt has poisoned the land of Yehudah."

"Ruth—"

She stopped in her tracks. It was the first time he had called her by name.

"How do you expect to uncover the truth about your husband's murderers? It could be anybody. The heart of man is devious. Who can know it? Only the Lord can know a man's heart."

"Some evil deeds are not so deeply hidden as all that, Mr.

Prophet," she said, passing beneath the rock-cut graves looming above. The ancient cemetery had been well maintained in the olden days, but now the marking stones were toppling over, the untended graves spilling out of the denuded earth.

They took the cobbled roadway up to the Valley Gate, trudging past the dark, lifeless houses whose families had mortgaged their children to acquire the land, then mortgaged the land to pay off the creditors, and had finally chosen slavery over a lifetime of poverty. At least slaves got regular meals.

"I've been thinking about what you said about how the nations shall beat their swords into plowshares," she said.

Ben-Isaiah's eyes fairly twinkled with pride. He was particularly fond of that turn of phrase.

"But you can't really beat a sword into a plowshare. You'd have to melt it down and recast it."

Ben-Isaiah cocked an eyebrow at her, then shrugged. "Very well, I'll change it. How about, *They shall throw their shields into the sea, and melt down their swords and recast them into plowshares. Amen.*"

"Amen," Ruth responded.

The streets were nearly deserted, except for the most desperate souls begging for relief.

A sunken-eyed harlot threw herself at the prophet and clung to his cloak, offering her mouth, her breasts, or any part of herself with such rabid intensity that she didn't seem to notice that Ruth was standing right there.

Ben-Isaiah peeled himself away from the half-mad harlot like a shaggy-haired ram freeing itself from a thorn bush.

Other women hurried past, shame written across their faces as they fled from the storehouses, averting their eyes and cradling tiny pouches of unmilled grain or whatever was left at the bottom of the storage jars. Ruth could tell they weren't true harlots—they were wives, daughters, widows, and foreign women like herself, bargaining with the only asset they had left.

The market was eerily quiet, except for the northwest corner of the square, where a colorful array of women stood in ranks like a platoon of warriors ready to march to the sea.

Could it be? Were there truly women warriors in Yehudah?

Ruth scurried over, hoping one of them would be interested in purchasing a beautiful curved dagger. But as she drew near, the noble commander of fifty reading their orders aloud from an ornate scroll underwent a swift metamorphosis into a slimy flesh merchant confirming the delivery instructions for an order of forty tall, pretty women in exchange for a three-month supply of food and water.

Ruth's heart sank when she saw what was happening.

Payment in women.

And of course they had to be tall and good-looking to command a high price on the foreign market. No wonder she took them for foot soldiers.

These poor, nameless women.

She wanted to know who they were. She wanted to summon a scribe and pay him to make a list of their names, so their names would not be erased. Like hers would be, unless she could find a man to take her.

Once the bill of sale was signed and sealed, the female cargo were marched out of the square, and the dust settled once more on the paving stones.

Ruth and Ben-Isaiah searched the desolate streets for food and fuel, until a merchant with a vacant look in his eyes said there was no olive oil left in the whole city. They were down to their last drop of the sesame oil, too.

"Well, someone's got cooking oil," Ruth said, noting the smoke rising from the chimneys of the wealthy homes on the hill.

Even the harlots walking the streets of the wealthier precincts looked more shapely and well-fed than the spindly-legged wretches plying their trade further down the hill.

Through the marble archways of a gated mansion, they glimpsed a pair of house servants slaughtering a fatted calf, enough to feed fifty people, a hundred if you stretched it. The beast's warm blood flowed through a channel into the gutter, and Ruth was gripped by a powerful craving for the strength she could draw from it, despite the Torah's severe and unambiguous prohibition: *Anyone who consumes blood, that soul shall be cut off from his people.*

But she was already cut off from her people.

They headed to Blacksmith Lane, where the sole merchant open for business that afternoon offered to buy the curved dagger for a fraction of its true value.

Sold.

But there was no food, clean or unclean, to be had at any price, so they scoured the fancy shops on the hill for medicinal herbs and cooking supplies, then headed back down toward the valley. As they passed under the eaves of a newly expanded manor house, a woman who appeared to be another high-class harlot approached them. Ruth hardened her features to keep the harlot at bay, and quickly recognized the judgmental sneer of Asnat, mother of Yiskah, who puffed up her chest and paraded past them without a word.

Yet there was something of the professional in her walk. After a few paces Ruth slowed, knitting her brow in thought.

"What is it?" asked Ben-Isaiah. "Surely you don't care what that preening old peacock thinks of us."

"Never mind her. I've got an idea."

～

They sought out the cluster of tiny houses where the married infantrymen live with their wives and children.

Miryam's belly was huge, the child due any day now.

"It's going to be a boy," she told them, rubbing her slightly pointy abdomen. "Just like the prophet said."

"The child you carry is proof of God's blessing," Ben-Isaiah replied, his words grating on Ruth's spine as he described how easy it is for certain woman to get pregnant, that even a speck of dust floating on the breeze may be enough to plant the seed, if the womb is fertile and ready to receive it.

"I need to speak with your husband," Ruth said, cutting short the pleasantries.

Yedidyah was perched on a stool out back, shirtless under the blazing sun, trimming his long, nappy hair. As a Nazirite, he was allowed to do this once a year at the time of the grape harvest.

It took him a moment to recognize her.

"You've lost a few pounds," he said by way of explanation.

He pulled up a stool for her, his muscles gleaming with sweat.

"The men-at-arms are well fed from the city's stores, I gather," she said, taking a seat.

"Our rations are fairly generous," he admitted, sitting back down in the afternoon sun.

"The infantry never lacks for supplies," Ruth said. She unclenched her fist and let the shiny silver shekels spill into the open palm of her other hand. She fiddled with the half-ounce lumps of metallic ore, as if gauging their silver content with her bare hands.

No one spoke, till Ruth filled the silence: "And I only have a couple of these misshapen lumps of silver—excuse me, *shekels*—to buy food for the family I'm staying with. That is, if anyone had some food I could buy."

Yedidyah snipped off the last of his wayward locks and put the shears down.

"With a hungry baby on the way?" he said, staring at the pile of hair near his feet. "Sorry."

He looked up at her.

Ruth nodded. "I understand."

Yedidyah fidgeted with the shears.

"Could you spare a drink of water, at least?"

"Of course, of course!" he said. "Miryam! Some water!"

Miryam came outside with two earthenware cups half-full of lukewarm water.

"May God repay you," Ben-Isaiah said.

Ruth wrapped her hands around the cup as if a desert spirit might snatch it away from her at any moment.

She drank it down in one gulp.

Ben-Isaiah took a sip of water, came over and poured the rest into Ruth's cup.

"You have it," he said. "You need to keep up your strength."

Ruth drained the second cup, her eyes half-closed.

"Oh, that was good," she said, shivering in near ecstasy.

Yedidyah couldn't help laughing, but it was nervous laughter.

Ruth gazed into the empty cup, wondering if there were some way to suck the last bit of moisture from the unglazed earthenware.

"But that's not the reason I came," she said.

The mercenary kept his eyes level with hers.

"How long were you employed as a soldier of fortune in the Babylonian army?" Ruth asked.

"About eighteen months, all told."

"And during that time, did you ever fight alongside a man named Elimelekh, an Ephrathi from Beit-lekhem?"

"Elimelekh the Ephrathite? Sure, I remember him. An older guy, right? He was like a father to some of the guys in the unit."

His mouth rearranged itself into a tight-lipped smile.

"Were you there on the day he was killed in battle?"

"I was there, but he wasn't killed in battle."

"He wasn't?"

"I mean, it was battle-related … but …"

"But what?"

Yedidyah scratched his newly shorn chin.

"It was the weirdest thing," he said. "We all thought he'd been hit by a poisoned arrow."

"But—?"

"But there wasn't any arrow. Or a corresponding wound. There was barely a scratch on him, except for a tiny nick on his thigh from his own sword."

"He died of a self-inflicted wound?"

"It wasn't a wound, it was a *scratch*. You don't die from a scratch."

Unless the blade is poisoned.

She asked Yedidyah to describe the symptoms.

"I told you, the same as if he had been shot with a poisoned arrow. I have seen such things on the battlefield." Yedidyah's throat tightened at the memory.

"So have I," Ruth said. "Because what you're describing sounds like the deadly poisoned arrows of the Saka warriors."

"We weren't fighting the Saka! Our unit was never stationed that far north. On that day we were fighting in Harran."

Then maybe someone poisoned his sword.

"Who else was there?"

"What do you mean, who else?" Yedidyah said, incredulous. "There were over a thousand warriors on the field that day."

There was no point in pushing any further. Ruth thanked them for the water and said her goodbyes.

"Let me know if you remember anything else about that day."

"I'm doing my best to forget it," Yedidyah said, draping his arm around his pregnant wife and holding her close.

Ruth forced herself not to be consumed with envy.

They didn't have much, but they had each other, and that was enough.

For now.

~

"Well, that was a dead end."

"Not quite," Ruth said. "Once you separate the ore from the dross, a pattern emerges."

"A pattern?" Ben-Isaiah said as they dragged their feet up the bone-dry paths of the western hill, churning up dust the whole way. "I don't follow."

"We have three men, a father and two sons, dying under similar circumstances."

"But the father and sons died more than a year apart, under completely different circumstances. That's hardly what I'd call a pattern."

"I mean the *manner* of their deaths, which is consistent with snakebite poison in all three instances."

"Dying of a snakebite isn't exactly unheard of in the Land between the Rivers, especially in a pitched battle against barbarians whose idea of warfare is launching earthenware pots full of venomous snakes into the enemy's ranks."

Ruth bristled at his words. "We'll see who the real *barbarians* are. Let me ask you something—can ordinary iron break apart iron from the north alloyed with copper?"

Ben-Isaiah didn't have a ready answer. Ruth's knowledge of metalsmithing easily surpassed his, and that intrigued him. Everybody knew that iron was stronger than copper. But what about a mixture of iron and copper? He searched for the solution until they came within hailing distance of Oved's house, and Ruth had to supply the answer herself.

"No. The answer is no," she said. "The northern alloy is tougher."

"You have to teach me more of those metalsmithing metaphors," he said, with disarming sincerity. "*Separating ore from the dross, iron breaking apart iron.* We'll have to hire a scribe to write it all down."

"I thought you didn't believe in using scribes to write down your prophecies."

The prophet sighed. "The days of the prophets are coming to an end, and my words will not be passed on unless they are written down."

"The scribes haven't taken over yet," she said, taking his arm and offering the comfort of her smile.

The western sky was darkening from the brilliance of molten gold to the dusky red glow of a clay oven.

"The sun knows when to set, my dear," he said, patting her arm.

The corners of her mouth quivered, and a warmth spread through her bones, a boundless excitement pulsating through her body, coming perilously close to igniting a wildfire that would not be satisfied till it devoured everything in its path and left her virtue a smoking ruin.

She was too inflamed by her own desires to notice Naomi standing at the window, watching it all.

CHAPTER EIGHTEEN

Ruth

Ruth pulled open the sack and let the luxury goods spill out. A half measure of *levonah* for Nekhamah's aching bones and some *yabruhim* to ease her troubled mind, and a brand-new copper pot for deep frying and stews.

"Copper distributes heat much better than baked clay pots, so you won't need to waste so much fuel," Ruth said, presenting the shiny new pot to her flustered hostess.

Tzillah ran her fingers over the gleaming metal surface of the expensive stewpot. "I've … always dreamed of having a cooking pot made of real copper," she said, stumbling over the glaring mismatch between this sparkling piece of cookware and the human shit-cakes they were burning for fuel.

"If only we had some food to cook in it," Zuriel grumbled.

"And the best part is that it's nonporous, so you can cook meat *or* dairy in it," Ruth said.

Ben-Isaiah wagged his finger at her signaling *No no no*, but Tabitha was fascinated by her dimpled reflection on the shiny surface of the vessel.

"We also found some stone-oil," Ruth said, handing Zuriel a jar of gritty black oil that a merchant had collected from the lake of asphalt. "Not for cooking, of course. For light."

"Great. Now we can watch ourselves starve to death," Zuriel said. But he took the jar and poured a bit of oil into the old clay lamp, and lit the wick to keep the darkness at bay a little longer.

Ruth ignored his bitter mood. "I've still got a few shekels left. Tomorrow I'll go search for more food."

"Why not tonight?" Naomi snipped. "After all, you seem to have the energy to go gallivanting around the city anytime you want, day or night."

Ruth felt a new level of irritation radiating from Naomi. Had she seen?

Oved busied himself stoking the hearth fire. Naomi helped Nekhamah to her feet and threw a cloak around her shoulders, and Tzillah tossed a couple of chunks of *levonah* onto the hot coals. The incense began to sizzle, releasing its curative vapors. The women held Nekhamah steady so she could raise the hem of her skirt a couple of inches to trap the sweet clouds of smoke to soothe her leg cramps, until the last bits of amber incense fizzled away, the silky tendrils drifting away into the night.

Tzillah poured a tiny bit of murky bottom-of-the-well water into the copper pot, added a few pinches of *yabruhim*, and set it on the hearth to warm.

Oved grabbed the last remaining piece of furniture in the household, a footstool, and set it before his mother.

"Are you feeling any better, *imma*?" he said.

"A bit, my son, a bit," she said, sitting on the stool unassisted. "My joints do feel a bit less creaky."

"Yah be praised," said Tzillah, bringing her the infusion of *yabruhim*.

After a few sips of the peculiar-tasting brew, Nekhamah warmed up and her face relaxed.

"Thank you, my children," she said, her voice still hoarse despite the soothing effects of the tea. "My eyes haven't beheld such a terrible hunger and since the days of the great siege."

She took a few more swallows of tea, and got a faraway look in her eyes. She closed her eyes and let her spirit take flight through the drafty corridors of time.

The lamp flickered and hissed, the flame diminished to a pale, bluish dot. Zuriel got up, his knees stiff, and snatched the jar of oil, stirring up sediment as he clumsily poured out some of the crude stone oil to rekindle the flame.

Nekhamah opened her filmy eyes and drained her cup to the last bitter drop. She shivered, the cold penetrating her bones, and drew her cloak more tightly around herself.

She rose, and the family accompanied her as she padded down the dark passage to the back room, and so to bed. The prophet followed with his persistent questions, leaving Ruth and Naomi alone in semidarkness.

The cheap black lamp oil was full of grit and other impurities, and the flame sputtered constantly, making the outline of Naomi's features vacillate between the sculpted miracle of living flesh and the sunken hollows of a vengeful spirit come back from the dead. Her eyes were closed, not in peaceful communion, but pressed tight with the intensity of fervent prayer.

Ruth sat quietly until Naomi opened her eyes.

"Daughter, we can't go on this way."

"What way?"

Naomi's mouth tightened. "You can't keep living among the Yehudim as a foreign woman, giving away your treasures for a handful of shekels when there's no bread to be had at any price," she said. "After all, I want you to be happy."

Ruth's eyebrows shot up. It had been a long time since anyone pretended to care about her happiness.

"And what do you suggest I do?"

"Ah! Your three months of isolation are finally up, and it just so happens that there is a redeemer in Yehudah who is our nearest kinsman. He is a man of wealth and standing." Naomi clapped her hands together. "His name is Boaz."

"Boaz? You mean the old man who owns all those wheat fields? *He's* the nearest kinsman?"

"I mean Boaz, who owns wheat fields and barley fields and much more besides, and who alone can redeem my husband's legal standing."

"*He's* the best you could find?" Ruth said. Oved was lurking in the passageway, a safe distance from the open flame of her rage.

"Daughter—"

Ruth reached the limit of her abilities in the tongue of Yehudah and produced a string of violent-sounding words in a strange language that nobody understood. But they didn't sound complimentary.

"Only Boaz can redeem my husband's name," said Naomi. "Don't turn your back on me now, after we've come so far."

Ruth felt the sharp *pings* of a blacksmith's hammer shooting through her skull.

"You promised. You made a vow."

"And I intend to honor my vow." Ruth's eyes bored into Naomi's like nails.

"He alone has surplus grain in storage," Naomi said. "And he's winnowing it tonight on the threshing floor."

"And how do you come to know this?"

Naomi studied Ruth's bare feet on the dirt floor. They would have to wash her feet and scrub under her toenails as well.

"We will help you prepare," said Zuriel.

"Prepare for what?" Ruth turned to face him. The whole family stood in the passageway, bearing silent witness to Ruth's vow. She tried to read the expressions on their faces, but the lamplight was too dim.

"You need to wash off all this dirt, rub fragrant oil into your hair, put on some fine clothes, and—"

"Hold on—" Ruth said.

"What's wrong?"

"Nothing—except that I have no water to wash in, no fragrant oil to rub into my hair, and no finery to cover my nakedness. How attractive do you think I am to him, anyway? Thanks to a steady diet of moldy bread and foul water, I'm all skin and bones."

The whole clan spoke at once:

"We've got a bit of water to spare—"

"I have oil, my daughter—"

"You can use one of my finest dresses—"

"Hold it, hold it." Ruth held up her hands. "You have a *selection* of fine dresses?"

"Only two," Tzillah admitted. "From when times were better. But one of them should fit you."

"I'm glad you've got everything all figured out," she told the clan.

"That's not—"

"Listen! You came to us as a stranger, and we took you in," Zuriel said, pressing the point. "And you promised to do anything we asked in exchange for giving you a healthy young goat to do whatever filthy pagan *sheketz* you did with it. Well, we're asking you to do *this* for us."

Naomi took a step closer to her daughter-in-law. "If you truly wish to be my redeemer, you must go down to the threshing floor of our kinsman Boaz. Don't let him see you until he has finished eating and drinking his second or third cup of wine, for that will put him in kindlier mood—"

"And then what?"

"And when he lies down, mark the place—"

"He's going to sleep outdoors all night next to a pile of grain?"

"He needs to personally guard the harvest," said Zuriel. "You can't leave something like that to the servants. Half the grain would be gone by daybreak."

The rest of the family nodded in agreement.

"So mark the place," Naomi continued, "and go over to where he is lying and uncover his... well, his feet... uncover his feet, and crawl into bed with him. He'll take it from there."

"I'm sure he will." Ruth scanned the grimly lit faces floating before her eyes, seeking the eyes of the prophet. But he kept his face hidden, his head bowed in prayer with his hair covering his eyes.

Ruth dropped her gaze, and there stood little Tabitha, thin and hungry, looking up at Ruth with her big dark eyes.

"Give me some breathing room," Ruth said. "I need a moment to myself."

~

"Are you there, my beloved?" Ruth looked up at the starry sky. "Is your spirit still following me?"

She thought of his manly touch, how he had soothed her with it, and let her give free rein to her desires.

"If you can hear me, I beg of you … forgive me for what I am about to do."

She laid her hands in her lap and clasped them tightly, her fingers interlocking as a sign of an unbreakable bond, her knuckles turning white, forcing the blood to her fingertips. For this was a bond of blood, and she curled her body around it and prayed that her husband's spirit would understand. After a moment of silent meditation, she broke the bond and raised her hands to the night sky, her fingers spread wide.

O stars, let my words rise up like the smoke of fine incense and guide me on my quest.

O sun, stop your singing! O Shamash, let me not walk the road alone.

O Laylah, whose name is The Night, take pity on me, look upon my empty hands and send me a message of pregnancy and childbearing.

O Ishtar, how long will your face be turned away from me? Let me no longer be a pitiable widow, begging for relief! Fill me with your fearsome strength, your defiant rage, and remove my capacity for mercy, for the blood of three good men must be avenged, and I must track down their killers and deal with them fearlessly.

And finally:

And you, Yahaweh. Where have you been?

Look at me and answer me, O Lord, my God!

For I am up to my neck in filth and my feet are slipping, and more people than I can count hate me for no reason.

O God.

Did You create me for nothing? Only the living can praise Your name and give thanks.

O God, I'm calling to You from a narrow place, from the bottom of a grave, from the belly of She'ol.

Give me children or I'll die.

And as she gazed into the starry womb of night, split down the middle by shimmering particles birthing new stars and sprinkling stardust across the heavens from horizon to horizon, she heard a voice calling out to her:

"Move it, Ruth. We don't have all night!"

∽

"Now shed your widow's garments."

"And wash and clean yourself of your past idolatry."

"Just do as I told you, and leave it in God's hands."

"I will do as you say."

"What a gorgeous dress! Like a bridal gown—"

"And such a lovely shade of green."

"I don't know, it's a bit loose and low-cut—"

"So much the better!"

"Here, wrap yourself in this shawl. And don't let anybody see you lest they take you for a harlot."

"I—"

"You look like a whole new person."

"And remember to claim kinship with him."

"I know, I know."

"Now rub some of this into your hair."

"My God, where have you been keeping that stuff?"

"Such finely scented perfume—"

Naomi pulled Ruth aside and whispered something for

her ears alone: "I'm sorry that in a moment of anger I was ungrateful and dismissive of your sacrifices on my behalf."

She clasped her daughter-in-law to her breast.

"Now go. And may a goodly wind carry you there."

And so Ruth went out into the night, the wind blowing like divine breath upon her back, wrapping her in the seductive aroma of perfumed oil, spurring her onward and guiding her up the hill to the threshing floor. And just as her mother-in-law had said, the elderly landowner was there, setting up his billet for the night and watching over mounds of freshly winnowed grain. The sight of so much wheat almost made her faint.

The old man froze, thinking he heard another living soul. But the wind picked up and after a moment Boaz shook his head and spread his cloak on the ground.

At least his hearing is still good, Ruth thought, but his sense of smell must be blunted, since the sensually arousing fragrances wafting off her went unnoticed.

Boaz ate and drank till his heart swelled with contentment, then he wiped his ragged white beard and he went to lie down behind the biggest pile of grain.

Good. Maybe no one will see us together.

He covered himself with a blanket, for the nights were getting colder as the last harvest of the year approached.

Ruth waited in the shadows, fighting off the shivers until it was safe to reveal herself. Then she crept over to where he lay and pulled back the blanket, uncovering his legs, and lay down beside him.

And it came to pass in the middle of the night that the old man trembled with cold, and reached for the blanket to cover his legs. He touched her warm body and drew back, startled right out of his sandals.

"Who are you?"

He pawed at her head to see if she was a hairless demon of the night.

Ruth slowly extracted his gnarled hand from her hair.

"I am your *amah*, your handmaid, Ruth," she said, using the magic of words to raise her status from a foreign slave-servant to an eligible bride. "And now you must spread your robe over me and pull it tight, for you are my redeemer."

"Your *what*?" he said, his face still pale. "So you're not a spirit?"

"No, I'm a woman. See?"

Ruth opened her shawl, revealing the smooth outlines of her breasts and releasing a heady dose of flowery perfume.

Boaz pulled his sandals back on.

"Are you married or unmarried?" he asked.

"Unmarried."

"Are you pure or impure?"

"Uh … it's a bit complicated."

Boaz's woolly eyebrows furrowed like a buzzard's.

Ruth quickly clarified: "I am the widowed daughter-in-law of your kinsman Elimelekh."

"Ah!" His face lit up. "What are you doing here?"

Getting a bit forgetful, too.

"Listen to the words of your servant," she said. "The seed of Elimelekh has been cut off, without a son or daughter or any close relative to redeem his name. So it falls to you, his nearest kinsman, to redeem it. And you must perform this *mitzvah* without delay. It cannot wait much longer, for my sole desire is to fulfill it."

His eyes still seemed a bit misty, so she leaned her head back and offered herself to him, arching her back and pushing out her chest like the figure of a prowling lioness curling around an ivory knife handle.

He gazed at her body, on display for him alone, breathing in the enchanting scent in her hair.

"You are blessed of Yahaweh, daughter!" he said, spittle

flying from his lips. "This act of *khesed* is even greater than the first, in that you didn't go chasing after all those young *bakhurim*, like the other flighty young maidens. Now don't be afraid, my daughter—"

Ruth steeled herself for his touch.

He continued: "I'll do whatever you say, for the elders who sit by the gates of the city must surely know that you are an *eshet khayil*."

"Wait—are you calling me a *live woman*? You still don't believe I'm a real woman?" She reached for the top of her bodice, prepared to rip it open and get this seduction—or whatever it was—over with already.

"No, no, it means a *virtuous* woman, a woman of value," he said, staying her hand. "It says so in our collection of proverbs."

"Oh. I see."

"But—"

His hand stayed protectively over hers.

"But ... ?" she said.

"While it is true that I am a near kinsman, there is another who is nearer than I."

"There *is*?"

Oh, shit. Now what?

Boaz reached up and caressed her strangely short hair.

"Stay with me now, and in the morning, we shall go and inquire if he is willing to redeem you. If he agrees, *tov!* Good! Let him do the kinsman's part. But if he does not want to redeem you, then, *khay-Yahaweh,* as the Lord lives, I will redeem you. Now lie down until morning," he said, making room for her beside him.

He saw her hesitation. "It's too dangerous for you to go walking alone in the middle of the night. Stay with me until dawn."

She felt that fire in her bones again, the itchy feeling that Makhlon was with her in spirit, worming his way under her skin, for his love was stronger than death, his need for vengeance calling to her from beyond the grave.

"I will stay with you until just before the dawn," she said, lying at his feet.

"You don't have to curl up into a little ball like that. You'll be much more comfortable if you stretch out. Don't worry, if the evil inclination comes upon me, I will restrain myself, and remain *ba'oz*, steadfast. Get it? *Bo'az* must remain *ba'oz*."

"I get it, I get it."

She lay on her side with her back to Boaz, and he lay down beside her. She noticed he had stopped calling her *daughter*.

"Aren't you cold?" he asked.

"I'm fine."

He draped his arm around her anyway, and pressed his body against hers from behind.

"You've been waiting so long, a little longer won't hurt," he breathed on the back of her neck.

And she felt his flesh become like a turnip.

A rather soft-boiled turnip.

She willed her body to remain as rigid as possible, but her flesh was still soft and pliant, and he squeezed against her till she was no more than an inch away from being legally married.

The dawn couldn't come soon enough.

～·

The hours dragged by in the old man's embrace, then she rose while it was still too dark for anyone to recognize her.

"Now be careful," Boaz said, sounding rather pleased with himself, as if he had just endured a superhuman test of his will power and restraint. "We can't let anyone know that a woman came to the threshing floor."

"Afraid I'll spoil the seed or something?" Ruth was too hungry to care about the standards of proper female comportment.

So she was caught off guard when Boaz suddenly spoke up and commanded her, "Hold out that shawl you are wearing, young man."

As if that would fool anybody.

"Like this," he prompted her. "Spread your arms out like this."

She gripped the shawl by the fringes and spread her arms while he scooped up six measures of grain, one for each hour they had spent together, and filled the shawl till it grew too heavy for her. Then he sprinkled a handful of grain onto her head and playfully mussed her hair, spewing seeds onto her face and down the front of her dress. Her hands were full and she couldn't do anything to stop him without spilling the grain. Then he helped her tie it into a bundle and strap it on her back so she could carry it more easily.

The fabric dug into the old wound between her shoulder blades, but the weight was evenly distributed and she soon fell into the rhythm of a beast of burden, lugging more than six *se'ahs* of grain over the ridge and begging God for the strength to bear the load.

Ruth swore that she would rather have one measure of grain and some *real* lovemaking than six measures of grain and *restraint*.

And as the morning chased the starlight away, it was as if she was seeing the city's radiant skyline for the first time.

Naomi saw her coming and met her at the door of the farmhouse.

"*Mi at, biti?*" she asked. Who are you, my daughter?

Ruth pushed past her mother-in-law, dropped to her knees and unstrapped the bundle. A bushel and a half of grain spilled out across the floor.

The family gaped at the sprawling heap as the loose grains rolled to a stop near their feet. Tabitha plucked a kernel from the dirt, popped it in her mouth, and bit down.

"It's *shever!*" she said, using a word Ruth didn't recognize.

The Yehudim had more than a dozen words for various stages of grain—standing, fresh, heaped, parched, crushed, ground into meal and flour, a different word for each condition.

Nekhamah hobbled forward. She bent low, took up a handful of grain, and let it sift through her fingers. It was of good quality, free of rot and parasites.

"You came to us a stranger," Nekhamah said. "Yet you have done this for us. What could we possibly give you in return?"

"You have already given it, *imma*," Ruth said, her shoulders sagging.

She felt a bit like a kernel of wheat herself, after it's been crushed beneath a heavy wheel to remove the husk.

Naomi knelt and rested her hand on Ruth's shoulder and repeated her question, "Who are you, my daughter?"

"Still unmarried, for now."

Naomi's hand flew to her mouth, and she bit down on her fingertips to keep herself from wailing.

"Your plan worked perfectly, except for one little unforeseen detail," Ruth explained.

And Ruth told them about how Boaz had dealt with her, saying, *Do not go empty-handed to your poor, widowed mother-in-law, but go back full.*

Tzillah smiled gratefully as she crouched down and swept a cupful or two of grain straight into a flat pan without bothering to wash the grain first, and put the pan on the fire to toast.

"Well done, lass," Oved said, grinning from ear to ear as he and Zuriel whisked up the grain and filled the storage jars, while Tabitha performed the very serious duty of gathering the far-flung kernels that had rolled across the dirt floor with her tiny fingers. "I'd say your debt is paid."

Only Ben-Isaiah looked askance at the heap of grain, as if Ruth had earned it on the threshing floor like the desperate harlots offering their bodies in exchange for a fistful of raw barley that in normal times would be used as fodder for donkeys.

"Time to get you out of these, um, revealing clothes and into something more modest," said Naomi. "You need to dress appropriately when you stand before the council of elders, for our kinsman Boaz will not rest until the matter is settled."

"I'd rather eat first," Ruth answered.

"Of course, of course." Everyone agreed.

"Then I need to wash this awful perfume out of my hair."

~

The sun was high overhead by the time the council of elders took their seats, and Ruth was already perspiring under the clothing that at Naomi's insistence covered her from head to foot, like a bride on her wedding day.

Boaz asked the crowd of onlookers to keep a respectful distance, for they would be acting as witnesses, and he would pay them in grain for their services. The people readily agreed, eager for something, anything, to distract them while they awaited their next taste of bread.

He explained that the ten elders, all men of wisdom, were needed to affirm before the people of the Holy City that, despite recent statements to the contrary by certain highly placed individuals, the Torah clearly allows a member of the community of Israel to marry a Moabite woman.

All eyes turned to Ruth, who was doing her best to appear modest as the sweat dripped down her back.

Boaz presented his argument in earnest: "I have come before the council of elders on this day because our kinswoman Naomi, who has returned from exile in Babylon, must sell a parcel of land that once belonged to our kinsman Elimelekh, from the town of Beit-lekhem."

Ruth looked sharply at Naomi. This was the first she had heard of Naomi having a claim to a disputed plot of land.

That's the kind of thing people get killed over.

"And I am offering to redeem it for her," Boaz said. "If there is another kinsman present who is closer, and is willing to redeem it, let him speak now."

A shuffling of feet cleared the way as a group with a special interest in the case pushed through the crowd.

"There is one who is closer," said an overbearing woman with a voice like a ram's horn.

Naomi let out a gasp.

Asnat and Hanokh stood before the assembly with Yiskah by their side, holding their son, Asher. The child had grown quite a bit during the months since Naomi had last seen him. And now she saw quite clearly that the boy possessed the features of her dead son, Makhlon.

CHAPTER NINETEEN

Felicity

"*Vat* did you say your name *vas*?" the elderly man asks, cupping a shaky hand to his ear.

"Felicity Ortega Pérez," I say, enunciating as clearly as possible as I hand him my business card.

"Peretz?" he says, studying the card through wire-framed glasses nearly half an inch thick. "*Dat* name has a noble lineage, *mine* dear child," he says with a Yiddish accent so thick it sounds like it's been marinated in a barrel of pickles and slathered with *shmaltz*. "Peretz son of Judah is the forefather of Boaz and King David, and therefore of the Messiah himself."

Dr. Menashe Greenberg is one of the last Yiddish-speaking Jews left in Brighton Beach, on a block that's practically all Russian now, far enough from the environmental disaster unfolding in Jamaica Bay to keep the rotting fish smell at a distance, and near enough to Coney Island to get a whiff of Nathan's Famous when the trade winds blow in from the west.

"No messiahs in the family, as far as I know, and it's *Pérez*, not *Peretz*."

"Really?" he says, scanning my facial features through his thick eyeglasses. "Are you sure? Because—"

"May I come in?"

"Of course, *mine* dear." He steps aside, keeping a hand on the doorknob to steady himself. He's wearing a faded white buttoned shirt and dusky gray pants held up with a pair of worn suspenders. His back is hunched and his unkempt hair has gone white, but his face still has the ruddy glow of a man who spends his afternoons strolling along the boardwalk.

It's a fairly small apartment, made even smaller by the piles of books and papers crammed onto the sagging, dusty shelves, as well as on the tables, chairs, and any other available surface, including the kitchen counters, the oven, and from what I can see, the toilet tank lid in the bathroom.

"I would need ten lifetimes to read all the books I vish to read," he says. "Now, come sit. You vant I should make some tea?"

"Only if you're having—"

He sits me at a small card table with just enough room for a couple of mugs of tea and a sugar bowl, between a towering pillar of books and the couch, which is sagging listlessly beneath four huge, swaying stacks of newspapers and journals.

My phone pings with a message, and I *swear* I silenced it. Damn smartphones. It's from Jhimmy: *Big planning meeting @our place 2 nite*

Oh, great. Just what I need after a long day running myself ragged in the outer boroughs. Why not just reroute the Number 7 train through our kitchen? Or would you rather run it through the bedroom?

"Julie Zeltserman sends her regards," I say, as Dr. Greenberg sets a couple of chipped enamel mugs of tea on the table.

"She told me already you were coming. So you're interested in the Book of Ruth?"

"Yes, I—"

"Which version you vant to discuss? Hebrew or Yiddish?"

"There's a version in Yiddish?"

"Give a listen," he says. "*Un es iz geven in di teg vos di shoftim hobn gehersht, iz geven a hunger in land.*"

"That's the opening verse about how *there was a famine in the land*, isn't it?"

"Ah, you see? You got it from that last bit, *iz geven a* hunger *in land.*"

It's not the short *u* of the English *hunger*, but a darker Gothic sound, *hoonger*, that lands like a punch in the gut, giving a physicality to the gnawing emptiness of hunger that is definitely lost in translation.

"There are more than a dozen famines in the Bible," he says.

"Yeah, we should contact the marketing team and tell them the Bible would sell a lot more copies if they included some recipes in the back."

"But you didn't come here to joke vit me about biblical recipes," he says. "Your real question is, *Vhy* is Ruth so important? *Vhy* is her story in the Bible in the first place?"

"I guess."

"You don't guess, you *know*," he says, banging the card table with the flat of his hand so hard the swaying mountain of books nearly comes tumbling down.

"Smell that?" he says, abruptly changing course.

"What?"

He tilts his head up and takes a great big swig of air, his nostrils flaring.

"Smell it?"

I take a moment to be a bit more mindful of the scents carried along on the easterly breezes.

"Ocean spray … wet sand … and … umm … frying oil?"

"They just put in the french fries," he says, winking at me rakishly with what I take to be paternal affection, because this ninety-year-old man couldn't possibly be flirting with me, right?

"In a few minutes, you'll smell the fresh knishes from Ostropolier's Deli," he adds, as if he's reserved a table just for the two of us. "Now vere vas I?"

"The importance of Ruth—"

"There is a kabbalistic reading of Ruth," he says, splaying

his fingers like a high priest blessing the congregation. "The night before God destroyed Sodom and Gomorrah in a hail of fire and brimstone, an angel visited Lot and placed a holy seed in him, a divine spark that gets passed down through his oldest daughter to seven generations of Moabites until it is implanted in Ruth, who through her own bravery and sacrifice redeems the entire nation of Moab. And from this we learn that God alone vill not bring about our redemption, mankind must *vork* for it as vell."

"Then I guess we're screwed, aren't we?"

"You're too young to be so bitter." He tries to recapture the magic like a fortune teller caressing the air around a crystal ball. "From the spark in Ruth's womb, the line of King David springs forth in an unbroken chain, all the vay down to the Messiah, which is vhy it's so important for her to produce a male offspring."

"Yeah, what's up with that?"

"It's an ancient prejudice," he admits, his face aglow. Must be all this talk of seeds and wombs and offspring.

"Many ancient cultures believed in an afterlife in a dreary underworld whose monotony can only be relieved briefly by a son or another male descendant who offers sacrifices in the name of the deceased. When we dig deeply into Torah, we often end up learning something very different from vat we originally set out to learn."

"Sounds a lot like my job."

He nods, gravely, rubbing his white-stubbled chin. "Such knowledge does not always lead to joy."

Yeah, just ask Eve. She'll tell you all about it.

"You're a very smart girl," he says. "Your parents must be proud of you."

I lower my eyes, gazing at my lap.

"Is something wrong?"

"Well, yeah," I say. "First, I'm not a girl. I'm a woman."

"Oh, I—"

"And second, my mom died when I was six years old."

His suntanned face pivots toward me, the thick lenses magnifying his bloodshot eyes till they look like giant, watery oysters. He blinks away some of the wetness and says, "So you've been tested in the fire and come out stronger."

"I don't know about that—"

"The Jews are no strangers to such testing."

He hunches a little closer to me as if he's sharing a guilty secret.

"The Torah teaches us that the three most important people on the Exodus out of Egypt all die vithout reaching the Promised Land. Moses's sister Miriam is buried in the vilderness of Zinn, near the place where God instructs Moses to strike the rock with his staff, and cool vater miraculously springs—"

"I know. It's my mother's name."

"Your mother's name is Miriam?"

"Well, her name was María, but my great-aunt used to call her Miriam when I was a kid. I always thought it was like a nickname or something."

"Because it's a Jewish name."

"Yes, but—"

"Hold on. Your mother is Miriam Peretz?"

"For the last time, my name's not *Peretz*, it's—"

"Not *the* Miriam Peretz?"

"I—what?" Something tickles the back of my throat. "What do you mean, *the*—"

"No *vunder* you remind me of her."

"You knew my mom?"

"Everybody knew—" A shadow falls across his face. "Then you don't know?"

"Don't know what?"

His tongue grows heavy with dread, like a cold lump of iron, his face going slightly ashen beneath the suntan.

The temperature in the room drops twenty degrees.

The blood in my veins freezes solid.

The ghost of Franz Kafka comes waltzing through the peeling wallpaper, swinging an ax at the frozen sea inside of us as Dr. Greenberg pushes himself to his feet, groaning with the effort, and shuffles over to his writing desk.

His big desktop computer is a clunky old dust magnet with an outdated operating system that takes way too long to load the image on a vintage CRT monitor. Then suddenly there it is. A mugshot.

It's her.

Not a cousin who happens to look like her, not a long-lost twin sister with better teeth and bigger boobs, not a total stranger who bears a passing resemblance. It's *her*.

It's my mom.

It's María Pérez.

The date of her arrest matches the official date of her death, the day she disappeared from my life.

I unceremoniously push past the old man so I can get to my phone. I feel like the blood is being squeezed from my head as I plunge between the stacks of papers toward my bag, the one fixed point in a world spinning out of control. I fumble ineffectively with the stubborn zipper, tunnel vision, shock, ripping my bag open and seizing the phone in my uncooperative hands.

Greenberg keeps up a running commentary while I'm searching, swiping, tapping with trembling fingers, reading, tapping, reading, gaping in wide-mouthed astonishment, and reading some more.

"The name Peretz means a *breach*," he says, his voice a thousand miles away down a mineshaft. "Because he forces his vay out of the womb past his twin brother, Zerakh."

Charges of unauthorized antigovernment activity and lending material support to radical leftist and indigenous terrorist groups. Sentenced to thirty years.

"It can also mean a *break* with tradition, or vith the past, vich certainly seems to apply in your case."

She didn't die suddenly of some unexplained disease while visiting family twenty years ago. She died of exposure and malnutrition in Peru's notorious Montenegro Prison, high in the Andes, twelve years ago, and was buried in an unhallowed plot of land just outside the prison walls, a tiny cement marker bearing her federal inmate ID number. I search for a number to call.

Country code, city code, province. Hundred-year-old switchboards, downed lines, static. Yelling to be heard.

They put me on hold for a century or so, then a contemptuous voice confirms it: "*Sí, esa puta está allí. Donde aquellos judíos jodidos pertenecen.*"

Yeah, that bitch is there all right. Where all those fucking Jews belong.

Screen shattered.

Circuits overheated.

The smell of burning plastic.

It wasn't a big trial. Not important enough make headlines over here. She was small and powerless against the apparatus of the state during a period of heightened antiguerrilla hysteria. There were appeals, but the US government claimed no knowledge, then later admitted that they did know but chose not to intervene.

She didn't die suddenly. She was thrown into a cell and slowly succumbed to the cold, harsh conditions in total isolation, and the US government did *nothing*. Not Bush. Not Obama. And certainly not the worthless fuckos who came after.

"So I'm part Jewish?"

"Actually, according to our tradition, if your mother vas Jewish, you're Jewish. You're one hundred percent Jewish."

"I've got to be somewhere," I say, shoving my worthless devices back into my bag. "Sorry."

"No need to apologize. You have been done a great disservice, mine child. You've been deprived of your heritage, of your identity, of the knowledge of who you really are, and this is a great calamity, for with knowledge comes visdom, and so it is written, *You shall not forsake the teaching of your mother.*"

"Gotta go."

"Just make sure you grab a knish from Ostropolier's Deli on your vay out."

~

I try texting my dad over and over: *Why didn't you tell me???*

No reply.

Whose ashes did we scatter across Flushing Bay? Or was it just an urn full of newspaper ash?

I've got half a mind to race right over to the job site and confront him.

No, no. Got to calm down.

I try to contact Jhimmy. I call and text and email. I even log on to FriendSpace and send him an urgent message via that service's outmoded platform.

He does not respond.

Switch to manual override.

Ever notice how manual override never works?

I've *got* to talk to somebody about this.

I've just got to.

~

"So what does it mean to be part Jewish?" I say, slipping around the crowd of hungry commuters queued up at the empanada truck in front of Atlantic Terminal.

"First of all, from what you've told me, technically you're *all* Jewish," says Professor Shulevitz.

"I'm still trying figure out what that means."

The late afternoon sun caresses the Williamsburgh Savings Bank, bathing its clock tower in liquid bronze. I got ahold of Professor Shulevitz just as he was leaving the TCC campus and asked him to meet me, said *Yes, it's an emergency*, then sped up Coney Island Avenue blasting my dad's worn-out salsa and merengue tapes to drown out the self-critical mantra playing repeatedly in my head: *How could I have been so stupid? How could I have been so fucking stupid?*

A steady stream of cars flows down Flatbush Avenue from the Manhattan Bridge, its hulking steel suspension tower looming over the Brooklyn skyline like a gap-toothed prizefighter grinning at the prospect of knocking you flat.

We're both in business clothes, carrying nearly identical shoulder bags like a couple of wolves of Wall Street heading to our private lair in one of the brash new steel-and-glass high-rises sprouting up all over the neighborhood like silver daggers aimed at the sky, daring the clouds to get close. But not too close, buster.

"You could say that being Jewish is about adapting, no matter how bad things get," he says, his energetic strides eating up so much sidewalk I have to hustle to keep up.

The red-and-white-striped awnings of Junior's Restaurant are calling to me from the next intersection. I resist the impulse to calm the swelling seas of my identity crisis by eating my weight in chocolate cheesecake.

Calm the seas? More like blot out the trauma of learning the truth about my mom's disappearance and her death, not when I was six, but when I was fourteen, old enough to understand the awful situation she was in and try to do something about it—start a social media campaign, stage a hunger strike in the middle of ninth grade lunch period, hijack the president's plane, *something*.

A couple of kids zoom by on skateboards, sporting T-shirts declaring their allegiance to nearby Fort Greene.

Professor Shulevitz suddenly breaks left and cuts across Flatbush Avenue. I stay on him like a point guard for the Nets as we head west on Fulton. A middle-aged Black man with a neatly trimmed salt-and-pepper beard, a beret and a pair of horn-rimmed glasses is heading into Junior's. God, I envy him.

"So what's it like being a private investigator?" he says.

"It's not as glamorous as it looks on TV, Professor Shulevitz," I say, stepping around a Black dude in a red hoodie checking his phone. He rejoins me on the other side.

"Call me Aaron, please."

"Felicity." It feels weird saying my name in English. I can't explain why, but it's like I'm hearing my mom's voice calling my name. My real name. The name she gave me.

"*Felicidad* in Spanish."

"Aaron. *Harun* in Arabic," he says, with a sparkle in those dark, velvety eyes. "I'm sure your mom would be proud of what you're doing. Ecclesiastes warns that we will find injustice everywhere, that *one high official is protected by a higher one, and both of them by still higher ones*."

"Wow, there really *is* nothing new under the sun, is there?" I say, scurrying past an electronics store with a solid wall of TVs tuned to WWTF News.

"But the mystical tradition teaches us that tiny shards of primordial creative energy are embedded in all that is evil. And it's up to us to peel back the layers to retrieve those divine sparks and heal our divided world."

"You're just trying to make me feel better about working for an evil corporation." I step aside as a young Latino with an aerodynamic helmet flies by on a bicycle.

"Some of the more fervent believers even tie a white sash around their waists before praying to symbolically divide the lower, earthly part of our bodies, the part that needs to piss and shit, if you will, from the upper, spiritual part."

"So the birth canal is considered down and dirty?"

"I'm afraid so. Location, location, location."

A B38 bus grinds its gears pulling away from the curb, stirring up a cloud of grit and blowing hot exhaust fumes into my face. I cover my nose and mouth a bit too late and the particle-laden exhaust provokes a coughing fit so severe it feels like someone's driving a steel spike into my abdomen. I nearly collapse in the professor's arms.

"Jesus," he says, grabbing my biceps to steady me. "This city is not a good place for someone with multiple chemical sensitivities."

"Yeah, if I worked in a coal mine, I'd be the one warning the canaries about the gas leak."

He grips my arms tightly, and I've got to confess it sure feels good to have a strong man support me right now. I can feel my pulse beating where his fingers grip my flesh.

But still …

I pull away slightly.

"You okay?" he asks.

No. I feel like dropping to all fours and barfing in the gutter till I purge the taste of bus exhaust from of my mouth, but that would probably be considered unfeminine behavior.

"Okay," I say, recovering enough to notice the huge display of lace bras and panties hanging in the gigantic store window behind us. "How am I supposed to make sense of all this?"

"I've got an answer, but you may not like it," he says, the peekaboo bras and black lace panties fluttering seductively in the store window.

"I asked, didn't I?"

"Okay." He needs a breath of air, too, before continuing. "Near the end of the Torah, God tells Moses that he has reached the end of his time on earth, and that after his death, the people he's been leading will go *whoring after other gods*, and they will break their covenant with God, and so God will abandon them. *I will hide My face*, says God, turning away from his people and leaving them to their own devices. And so we are separated from God's intimate involvement in our daily lives very early on. We're left to figure things out for ourselves."

And there it is.

Abandonment. Loneliness. Death.

Each word hammering at me until something cracks open and my eyes well up and somehow I end up pressed against Aaron's chest, dampening his nice woolen tie with my tears.

He holds me tightly, without a trace of awkwardness as the raw emotions come gushing out of me.

"You've been through a lot," he says.

"Why bother?" I say, my voice muffled, my mouth buried in the woolly wetness. "What's the point?"

"Mazl tov, you're officially Jewish," he says, handing me a tissue so I can dry my tears and blow my nose.

"That's nice of you to say," I reply, pulling back.

I can't take my eyes off the fishnet pantyhose, swaying in the breeze.

"Mind if we keep walking?"

"Sure."

Now here's the weird thing. Clinging to this man I barely know felt like a healthy, natural release. And a welcome one. It's the separating that feels awkward. We stand there like two kids at the junior prom, unsure of where to put our hands, so we busy ourselves smoothing out the wrinkles in our clothes and blotting up the slick wet spots I left on his shirt and tie. And we set off again in the direction of Boro Hall, where a fiery red glow is setting the tree-lined streets ablaze, while legions of violet-brushed clouds amass in the upper atmosphere like an invading army.

"Nice sunset," I say.

"Yeah, too bad those beautiful sunsets are caused by all the light-scattering particles in the air pollution over New Jersey."

"Boy, you sure know how to drain the romance out of something."

"Romance? Who's talking romance?"

I face him.

"What is this?" he says, bewildered. "What are we doing?"

I look into his eyes, his full lips, and—my phone buzzes. Damn it, I fucking *swear* I silenced it. I take it out to shut it the hell up, and see the alert:

THREE-STORY BUILDING ON GLENMORE AVENUE IN EAST NEW YORK COLLAPSED DURING RENOVATIONS. ONE CONFIRMED FATALITY.

I make my excuses and tear myself away from this warm, caring man and run all the way back to the company car, clawing at my phone, trying to call my dad. I call and text at least six or seven times. I'd send up signal flares if I could. Nothing. Not even voicemail.

Nothing but silence and static.

I come close to breaking the land speed record for a conventionally powered vehicle, gunning it down Atlantic Avenue for five miles straight using a series of highly illegal moves, and I know I've hit East New York when the rotting fish smell grows thicker, more vomitous. I leave some rubber on the curb as I run a red light to make the turn onto Linwood, forgetting that Glenmore is one-way going east to west, so I have to circle around, the teeth on that old metal rake biting into my skull with every beat of my pulse.

I stomp on the brakes and the car screeches to a halt, engine smoking. It's like a scene from a war zone. Emergency vehicles, flashing red-and-blue lights, beat cops setting up a yellow-tape perimeter, and I'm fighting to get through, not explaining myself well, until I let out a shriek upon seeing my dad squatting in the dirt, his clothes covered with blood and soil and the ghostly white dust of pulverized sheetrock, holding Eloy's crushed, lifeless form in his arms like the Virgin Mary cradling the broken body of her son.

They finally let me through and I dash over to him, wiping blinding tears from my eyes as I fall to my knees and hug him close, rocking back and forth as he wrestles with the words, barely distinguishable from a groan. "We *told* the boss the foundation was unstable, but he made us keep digging and digging—"

So undocumented immigrants are taking jobs from Americans, huh? How many of you would have taken this crappy job?

"I stayed with him to the end," my dad says, each leaden syllable stamped with the mark of agony, each wheezy breath a cry of pain, his face streaked with blood and tears. "One of the cops gave him his last rites. Then I shut his eyes. *Le cerré los ojos*," he says, as a couple of responders approach, radios squawking. "*Que Dios tenga piedad en su alma*."

I automatically make the sign of the cross.

I look up at the cops standing around in a semicircle, their individuality blurred, their faces grim with the helplessness that comes with confronting the finality of death.

Strength in numbers doesn't work on Mr. Death.

Oh, sure, you can put up a big defense, but Death only has to score once.

One of the younger cops—a big, athletic gal with the name KARAM etched on her nameplate—lowers herself to one knee, memo book in hand, and requests, almost apologetically, "Uh, sir? We need to get a statement. Could I get your name again?"

Amid the deepening shadows and the stroboscopic effect of the emergency response lights, I'm the only one who notices that my dad's having trouble breathing.

So I answer for him.

CHAPTER TWENTY

Ruth

And like a thunderbolt loosed by the storm-god himself, Ruth knew that she was looking into the faces of her husband's killers.

Her fingers curved around the handle of her dagger, but she remembered her husband's words, *When you set out to make war on a city, try offering peace first*, and she held off, waiting for Boaz to argue her case before the council of elders.

"We are gathered before you to prevent *ha-karet*," said Boaz, describing the worst fate imaginable, the dying out of a man's lineage. "We seek *l'hakim shem*, so that the name of Elimelekh shall be called in Israel. And we seek it through *khalitzah*."

Ruth already felt lost in the sea of unfamiliar legal terms, but she was sure of one thing: Hanokh was *not* of the line of Elimelekh. He couldn't be. He wasn't even circumcised till Ruth performed the rite herself.

The foremost elder, a wizened old man named Shelomo, asked to see the evidence that little Asher was the nearest kinsman.

"The answer is right before your eyes," Asnat said, with a boldness that made Ruth uneasy. "As you can plainly see, my grandchild bears a distinct resemblance to Makhlon, son of Elimelekh."

"That's not possible," Naomi said. "Both my sons were at war at the time that child was conceived."

"Do you have any witnesses to support that claim?" said Asnat.

"The only witnesses are back in Babylon or conveniently dead."

Asnat pretended to be struggling with her own heart, before spinning a convoluted and not terribly convincing tale that many years ago, one of Elimelekh's cousins sired a son named Shelef. She swore that Shelef lay with her daughter Yiskah and was the true father of Asher—the *only* surviving male descendant of Elimelekh's nearest kinsmen—and when Shelef died suddenly, Hanokh was good-hearted enough to marry Yiskah and become the child's stepfather.

"What did he die of? A snakebite?" Ruth asked. "That seems to happen to anyone who gets in your way."

"How do we know your husband wasn't killed by your own evil ways?" Asnat said. "Why else would your own mother-in-law tell you and your idolatrous sister-in-law to go home *to your mothers' houses?*"

"Where did you hear that?"

"From me," Yiskah said, bearing witness. "When they parted, I heard her mother-in-law say those exact words."

Ruth stared at Yiskah, wide-eyed.

"Moving on," Boaz addressed the council. "When a man dies without a son, it is our solemn duty to find a home for his wandering spirit so that he can complete his earthly mission."

"Fine," Asnat declared. "My son-in-law Hanokh, acting as a proxy for my grandson Asher, can marry this foreign woman and produce a child in the name of Elimelekh."

Damn, I should have screwed the old man when I had the chance, Ruth thought. *At least I'd be his wife instead of being up for grabs like this.*

Naomi tried to help, testifying that when Ruth married Makhlon, son of Elimelekh of Beit-lekhem—she stopped herself from saying her *master*—her *guardian* let her choose seven choice weapons as her dowry. But in her hour of need, she has been compelled to trade away all but one.

"She traded a polished iron blade fit for the king's garden

to buy a poor family a measure of *levonah* from the land of the Sabeans for their aging grandmother and a jar of stone-oil for their lamps."

Some of the people expressed admiration for Ruth's selfless act of *khesed*. Everyone knew how expensive those medicinal remedies were.

"I don't know why we're even debating this," Asnat said, "when our leaders have ordered the true Yehudim to separate themselves from all impurities in our midst."

"And I suppose you think we're the impurities," Ruth said, grabbing the hilt of her double-edged dagger.

Ben-Isaiah gripped her arm and addressed the multi-tudes. "There is no blanket condemnation of intermarriage in the Teachings," he said. "Thus says the Lord: *I will gather still more from the nations of the world to those already gathered.*"

He paused to let the words sink in.

"So I ask you, people of Jerusalem, shall we turn away this worthy woman, who has freely chosen to turn to the God of Israel?"

"There. You've said it yourself," Asnat said. "She's not one of us."

Ruth faced the council with her hands pressed over her food-starved belly. "I have treasured the words of God's mouth more than my daily bread, for He commands us to treat each other with *khesed* and *rakhamim*, and not to oppress the poorest among us but to seek justice for all, and not think in our hearts of doing evil against one another."

"Baah!" Asnat jeered. "She claims to be one of us—let her prove it."

"Did you not hear?" said Ben-Isaiah. "She just summed up the whole of the Torah in one breath."

"And with enough coaching, she could probably do it standing on one foot," Asnat replied. She turned to elder Shelomo. "Test her the way your namesake was tested by the queen of Sheba."

Elder Shelomo held up his hand for silence. "It is a reasonable request that we test the petitioner's knowledge of our ways, since her appeal hinges on whether or not she can claim the right to be treated as a full-fledged member of the community. What say you, elder Boaz?"

"Even Abraham had to petition the Hittites to hear his plea," said Boaz, bowing to the will of the elders. "I accept the council's terms."

"Then it's settled. Elder Yokshan, you may begin."

A balding old man with a pinched face and crooked teeth stirred to life and beckoned to Ruth with a crooked finger.

"We'll start with an easy one," said elder Yokshan. "Who can extract purity from impurity?"

Almost too easy, Ruth thought. *A metalsmith, a milkmaid, a midwife*—there were a hundred ways to answer this riddle. But she chose the answer they probably wanted.

"God."

Asnat rolled her eyes at the old fool's easy question.

Elder Yokshan nodded succinctly, acknowledging Ruth's answer, and sat back.

"Elder Tzohar," said elder Shelomo.

An elder with a drooping nose and poor eyesight squinted at Ruth, barely making out her blurry outline, and Ruth swore she heard Asnat's teeth click together in a fiendish grin.

"One came from Terakh, one came from Akhaz, one came from Amon, and one came from the nations. What does this teach us?"

Ben-Isaiah and Ruth exchanged glances. She knew there was a connection between the three names. *Terakh* was Abraham's father, an idol worshipper from the city of Ur of the Kasdim, so the question was about fathers and sons.

Akhaz. The name sent a shiver through her, since it belonged to a man who did great evil in the eyes of the Lord.

No, not just a man—a king. And not just any king, the

one who bowed down to the king of Assyria and said, *I am your slave.*

Yet his son, Hezekiah, was a good king.

So.

The riddle was about bad fathers producing good sons.

Amon.

Whose father was he?

Someone exemplary, presumably. The only other decent king in a long line of awful ones.

Ruth closed her eyes for a moment and the name came to her.

She opened her eyes, and spoke with such assuredness even the judges were impressed. "Terakh begat Abraham, Akhaz begat Hizkiyah, Amon begat Yoshiah, and the nations of the world begat the people of Israel."

"And what does this teach us?"

"This teaches us *not to hate the stranger*, because the children of Israel are themselves descended from the people of many nations."

"What else?"

"It teaches us not to oppress the children of a wicked man, because they can grow up to be righteous leaders of men."

By the time she finished, some in the crowd were nodding along with her.

Elder Tzohar's eyes twinkled brightly, suggesting that she might have some unspoken allies on the council.

"Elder Shimon," said elder Shelomo.

Elder Shimon's features were surprisingly smooth, his skin reddened but not wrinkled by the sun. But his tone was sharp, even a bit hostile: "King Yarov'am brought a calf to life with it, and Daniel brought the calf low by removing it. What do we learn from this?"

Ruth felt the ground giving way beneath her feet.

Take it slowly, she told herself. *Try breaking it down into pieces.*

Elder Shimon must have been referring to the golden calves that King Yeroboam set up in Beth-el and Dan, but she didn't recall anything in the prophetic teachings about him bringing the idols *to life*.

She definitely would have remembered that.

But she did remember a tale her newly wedded husband told her by the campfire one evening as the army marched toward the plains of Babylon, a tale of an evil king who ordered his priests to carve the name of God on the forehead of a golden bull, and *Lo, the bull began to speak in the holy tongue*. The details were a bit fuzzy, but somehow a man of God named Daniel, pretending he wished to worship the idol, approached the golden bull and removed the word, and the idol fell to the ground stone dead.

"From this we learn of the *only situation* when it is permitted to erase the holy name of God."

There was a great intake of breath from the crowd as elder Shimon accepted her answer with a dull wave of his hand.

"Elder Zimran," said elder Shelomo.

There's more? Ruth thought. In all the trials she had ever heard of, the hero only has to answer *three* questions.

Elder Zimran was so frail his thick woolen cloak practically swallowed him up like a tortoise shell. And when he leaned forward, the wrinkled skin on his neck completed the resemblance.

Ruth had to approach even closer to hear him.

"She married two, and gave birth to two," elder Zimran said, stopping to catch his breath. "Yet all four had one father."

Thank God this was an easy one.

"Tamar the Amorite married Er, son of Yehudah," Ruth answered. "And when Er died she married his younger brother, Onan. And when Onan died, to preserve the line of their father, Tamar contrived to bear two children, Peretz and Zorakh, to Yehudah, who was thus the father of all four."

The elders nodded and seemed satisfied.

"Elder Avima'el."

Elder Avima'el had only a few wisps of wavy white hair clinging to his skull, but his eyes were still bright with wisdom.

"How can you say that a stranger who studies Torah is entitled to the same treatment as a son of Israel?" he challenged her.

Ben-Isaiah sensed Ruth's panic and calmly advised her, "Just tell them *where it is written*."

Ruth flashed the merest hint of a smile at him.

"Um … it is written in the Scroll of the Priests," Ruth said. "The Lord speaks to Moses and says, *The man who keeps My laws shall live by them*. It does not say the *king*, or the *kohan*, or the *son of Israel*. It says anyone. Any man. Any *mortal*."

Elder Avima'el nodded once. "That is correct."

Hushed praises sprang from mouths of the men who found themselves admiring Ruth's wisdom and the women who had hated her at first and found themselves coming around to her cause.

"Enough," said Asnat, reaching into the folds of her beaded robe. "If you're so good at adopting the ways of your Yehudi relatives, then how do you explain *this*?"

Asnat whipped out a short-bladed dagger and held it up for all to see.

It was the copper-hafted dagger that had disappeared from Ruth's sack one night in the wilderness, the one with the ivory handle bearing the image of the goddess Inanna and the strange inscription in the language of the Kasdim praising the god of smiths.

"Do you recognize this?" she said, flinging the question at Ruth.

"I recognize it."

"You see?" Asnat addressed the fickle masses. "She admits that this knife used for pagan sacrifices is hers!"

"She is making false witness against me. That knife has never—"

"Do you deny that you traveled widely across many lands with a metalsmith of the Kenite tribe?"

"I do not deny it."

"Was he your husband?"

"He was my master, I was his apprentice."

"Did you live together as man and wife?"

"I was his *servant*, not his *wife*."

"Same thing," someone said, since everyone knew a female slave's principal duty was to increase the master's household by producing a slew of slave children. It came with the job.

Frankly, it *was* the job.

"You should have seen her unchaste behavior on that march through the wilderness," Asnat testified. "Chasing after that so-called prophet and lifting her skirts for any mercenary who happened to be passing by."

"That is an accursed lie, you—you—" Ruth couldn't think of an effective curse in Yehudit.

Asnat's smile revealed two rows of sparkling white teeth.

"You weren't even there!" Ruth said. "How would you—?"

The words stuck in her throat.

Ruth whipped around to face Hanokh, who looked like he was ready to crumble. And so she turned her eyes on Yiskah, whose once soulful eyes may as well have been carved in black onyx. And in that moment Ruth knew the identity of her true betrayer.

"You accuse me of being unchaste," Ruth began. "But you are guilty of far worse—the crime of polluting the land with blood."

"We have shed no blood in the land of Yehudah," Asnat sneered.

"Because you shed blood in the land of Babylon."

"Where is your proof? Where are your witnesses?"

"I witnessed my husband's death by poisoning with my own eyes."

"Too bad that the word of a single witness isn't admissible for an offense of any kind, much less the capital crime of premeditated murder."

"There is another witness," Ruth said, and for a fleeting instant, signs of worry streaked Asnat's brow. "The God of Israel."

Asnat's brow smoothed again. "Moabite women are not to be trusted as witnesses, even when they call on the God of Israel."

"For the last time, I am *not a Moabite*."

"What are you, then?"

"A daughter of Adam, just like you."

That confident smirk broke out again. "Isn't it written that *no idolater shall have a share of a Yehudi kinsman's property?*"

Asnat's words won over a fair portion of the crowd, forcing Ruth to resort to an argument she abhorred: impure lineage.

"Your appeal to redeem Elimelekh's property should be denied for another reason," Ruth said.

"And what's that?" Asnat said.

"Your offspring are ineligible, for it is written in the Scroll of the Chieftains, *You shall inherit no portion of our father's wealth, for you are the son of a harlot.*"

There. She had launched her scorpion bombs, had emptied the cauldrons of flaming *naphtha* on the heads of her besiegers.

To no effect.

"Go ahead and call the child's grandmother a harlot," Asnat replied. "A Yehudi harlot is worth more than a foreign slave-wife."

"Who are you calling a slave?" Ruth shot back. "*I am a free woman.*"

"Oh, where do I begin?" said Asnat, as if the task of enumerating the evidence was too burdensome to contemplate.

"First, it is the custom among the Kasdim to say *Go home to your mother* when they free a slave from their obligations," Asnat explained. "Naomi was heard speaking these words to her daughter-in-law before numerous witnesses. Second, on the road through the wilderness, she consorted with a runaway slave named Ga'al. Who but a fellow slave would do such a thing?"

"Lots of people *consorted* with him, including your son-in-law—" Ruth began.

"Third, she gashed herself and shaved her head after the death of her husband, a pagan practice that is strictly forbidden under our laws. She did this in front of numerous witnesses."

Asnat's supporters broke out in a chorus of *ooooooohs*.

"Shaving your head is a sign of mourning, not servitude," Ruth said. "I cut myself by accident because I didn't have a mirror—"

"We know exactly what you were doing." Asnat countered. "Now, you claim that your husband was a Yehudi warrior—"

"I do not *claim* it, he—"

"Because according to King Yoshiyahu's code of law, if a Yehudi warrior sees a woman he desires among the prisoners of war who have been taken captive, he brings her to his house, and she must cut off her hair, trim her nails, and wear sackcloth for a month—all things that this woman did in front of dozens of witnesses. Are these not the actions of the lowest and most wretched class of person—a slave woman whose body is nothing more than the spoils of war?"

"I ... I ..." Ruth's head felt empty, her energy depleted. She had openly performed those actions, unaware that the tribal law code defined them as proof of a servile state.

Ben-Isaiah saw her struggling and came to her aid. "What you say is true," he told Asnat, "but that same passage goes on to say that if those conditions are met, then the captive woman becomes the soldier's wife—in other words, she has full status as the *wife* of a Yehudi warrior, just as any righteous stranger who accepts the *mitzvot* shall be considered a Yehudi."

"Except for one problem," Asnat replied. "Their marriage was never valid, because her so-called husband didn't legally marry her; he acquired her from her previous master."

"That's not true," Ruth hissed.

"What's not true? The part about him not marrying you or the part about him acquiring you?"

"He brought me out of servitude."

"You mean, he brought you out of *slavery*."

"He paid the bride-price for me."

"How much?"

"*What?*"

"How much did he pay for you?"

Ruth turned to the men sitting in judgment, scanning their faces.

Elder Shelomo nodded once and said, "I'll allow the question."

Ruth's shoulders sagged as if her arms had turned to lead, her head drooping.

"How much did he pay?" Asnat pressed.

Ruth addressed the ground beneath her sandals in a small, thin voice.

"Forty pieces of silver."

"A little louder, please," elder Shelomo prompted.

"I said, forty pieces of silver."

"*Forty* shekels?" said Asnat. "That's quite a bargain. The standard bride-price is fifty shekels."

Ruth kept silent.

"But it's about the right price for a hard-working female *slave* like yourself. You already said you were that Kenite metalsmith's assistant. I'm sure you were worth a lot to him."

They weren't shekels. There were Babylonian units. Nearly a pound of silver. He paid for my freedom. And I loved him for it.

Asnat pressed on. "During the first public reading of the Torah, in the square just below the Temple, this woman referred not to her *parents*, but to her *guardians*. She spoke these words directly to me and she shall not deny them now."

"That was just my rudimentary Yehudit. I was still learning the language—"

"Well, you've been here long enough to speak the language properly by now, which leads to my next point: Last night, during a secretly arranged meeting between her and Boaz on the threshing floor, this woman referred to herself as his *slave*, not his handmaid—"

Ruth's mouth dropped open.

"How on earth would you know what I said? What kind of—"

"—or his bondmaid. But certainly *not* as the widow of his nearest kinsman who is entitled to a levirate marriage."

Ruth was speechless at the audacity of the lies, but her anger swiftly found its way to her tongue.

"Handmaid, house-slave, son-of-a-slave, bondswoman—why do you people have so many words for different forms of servitude? Yet you use the *same word*, *eved*, whether you're speaking of a skilled indentured servant or a captive slave whose primary role is to let her master do *pakad* to her, which is *not* among the standard duties of a metalsmith's apprentice."

Some of the crowd sucked in their breath, shocked by Ruth's rough language.

Asnat faced the elders. "The council will note that she does not deny that she referred to herself as a *house-slave*." She turned back to Ruth. "And you've been living here long enough to know the difference by now."

"So that's your proof? That I don't know the exact meaning of every word in your language?"

"There is one final bit of undeniable evidence," Asnat said, leering at Ruth. "*The mark of the yoke.*"

Ruth swallowed her next utterance.

Asnat's leer grew as wide and sharp as a sickle.

No ... I ... I ... but ... how ... ?

Only her husband knew about it.

Asnat was moving her lips, addressing the council, but her words got lost in the giant *whooshing* sound funneling through Ruth's brain.

The next thing she knew the elders were nodding and the watchmen were seizing her and holding her still while one of them clumsily nicked the back of her neck with the point of his sword as he slit open the thin fabric of her tunic and a pair of watchmen pulled in opposite directions, ripping the cloth in two, exposing to all the fibrous scar tissue between her shoulders, the damaged places her husband had kissed with such tenderness.

Ruth finally had her answer.

When the women bathed me ...

After I faced down the storm-god in the wilderness.

Everyone was staring at the whorl of puckered flesh in the indelible shape of an iron harness ring, now dripping with fresh blood.

"You see?" Asnat reveled in her triumph. "The sign of the god Rakkab-El, whose symbol is a chariot yoke. Proof that she is a slave to another god."

"I—" Ruth bit off the words, fighting back tears. She did not want to give these two-legged serpents the satisfaction of seeing her cry.

"What was that?"

"I said I *was* ... I *was* ... enslaved by the Rekhavim."

"And to their god."

"I ... it ..." Her strength was failing. She looked to the prophet, pleading with her eyes.

Ben-Isaiah came forward. "They *made* you do it, didn't they? They made you serve their god, isn't that right?" he said.

Ruth nodded. "To live among the Rekhavim, you must follow their ways."

Ben-Isaiah turned to the elders. "You see? Surely it is no sin for her to have followed their ways under such duress."

"Except for the sin of idolatry," said elder Shelomo. "That is unforgiveable under *any* circumstances."

"It is forgivable when one's life is in danger," Ben-Isaiah said. "They would have killed her had she refused."

"Such things happened before my eyes," Ruth murmured as the afternoon shadows lengthened around her.

"Speak up, woman," elder Shelomo instructed.

"They threatened to pull us apart with their horse-drawn chariots if we didn't bow to their gods."

"Us?"

"Me and the other … captive women."

"*Slave* women," said Asnat.

"*Captive* women," Ruth insisted, feeling as much of a captive as at any time she lived under the yoke. A prisoner of their laws. On display before the whole community. Exposed.

Ruth took a deep breath, and said, "Enough. It's true I was once a pagan and a slave. Just as you were once slaves in the land of Mitzrayim," Ruth said. "But didn't the people of Nineveh change their ways when the prophet Yonah told them to cease their evil behavior or the city would be destroyed?"

Some of the elders glanced at each other, eyebrows raised. This strange woman certainly knew her Torah and Prophets.

"Even the father of the tribe of Yehudah changed his ways when he understood what he had done to his daughter-in-law Tamar, and he established the line of Peretz, from which my suitor Boaz is descended."

Heads nodded among the onlookers. The elders conferred, agreeing that it would be hard to rule that Ruth was unworthy because she was ignorant of the ways of the Yehudim.

Elder Shelomo ordered the watchmen to release her, and gestured for Ruth to approach.

Ruth steeled herself and approached the bench, swatting away any assistance and insisting on holding her torn tunic together with her fist, ignoring the warm trickle of blood caused by the watchman's wayward blade.

"Speak the truth to me now," elder Shelomo cautioned her.

"I shall do as you say."

"Good," he said. "Now tell me. What is the true name of the tribe you were born into?"

Ruth chewed on her lower lip, then she raised her free hand in the manner of an oath and said, "I was born into the Aryan tribe of the Saka, whom the Akkadians call the Ashguzai. But I believe the Yehudim call us by another name."

"What name is that?"

Ruth lifted her head and said:

"The Ashkenazim."

~

The council deliberated till the setting sun turned the western sky blood red, when they finally reached a verdict:

"*Hakeshiyvu, hikeshiyvu!* We find that this child, Asher Ben-Shelef, holds the right of the nearest kinsman to redeem this woman, Ruth the Moabite, through marriage. Since he is but a babe in arms, the right transfers to his stepfather, Hanokh Ben-Abba."

Asnat gloated like a fly buzzing around a jar of honey.

Ruth swore she felt her cervix contract as she pictured this thorny hedgehog of a man lying with her and claiming ownership of their children.

Hanokh turned seventeen shades of pale as elder Shelomo addressed him, saying, "Are you willing to take this woman and become her master, even though she is a childless widow with no dowry?"

Ruth bristled at the word *master*, while Hanokh glanced fretfully from his wife to his mother-in-law.

"I ... you see ... uh ..." Hanokh groped for the words.

"It's just that ... well ... if our firstborn child is a boy, then he won't be considered *my* son, but the son of Makhlon of Beit-lekhem. Right?"

"Right. So?"

"So what's in it for me?"

Ruth's toes were tingling as if she were teetering atop a narrow roof beam.

"And ... also ... uh ... I wouldn't want my ... uh ... children ... to be tainted ... with ... foreign blood."

If looks could kill, Hanokh would have been dead thrice over, with Asnat's angry gaze joining Ruth's piercing death stare. And Yiskah wasn't exactly showering him with love either.

"And ... uh ... clearly ... this ... uh ... this woman's first husband died for his sins ... for ... you know ... marrying a foreigner ... and all ... I mean ... any man who touches her ... dies ... am I right?"

A number of men agreed that Ruth and Naomi must be dangerous women, whose *rekhamim* possessed some kind of demonic power that destroyed every man who uncovered their nakedness.

"So what if the same thing happens to me?"

Beards wagged here and there, and heads nodded.

But Hanokh folded under his wife's withering gaze, saying, "I can't risk ... uh ... damaging the ... uh ... peace and harmony of our ... happy little home ... by taking a second wife."

And just like that, with a few words from this sniveling worm of a man, Ruth was liberated from the obligation of becoming his second wife.

"Duly noted and recorded," elder Shelomo declared, before clearing his throat. "And now, Boaz Ben-Etzioni, it is up to you. After all the testimony that we have heard, do you still intend to redeem this woman?"

"I still intend to redeem her," Boaz said.

"Then you must perform *khalitzah* with your kinsman."

"You have my word on it," said Boaz, eyeing Hanokh for any signs of weakness or deception.

"Very well," said elder Shelomo. "The parties shall approach the bench and perform the *khalitzah* in front of the council and the community of Israel."

"That's it?" Ruth objected. "What about charges of murder? What about payment of blood for blood?"

Ben-Isaiah advised her to withdraw her objection, *For it is He who hears the cry of the afflicted. And it is He alone who avenges bloodshed.* He took hold of one of her hands, which was surprisingly cool and damp, a sure sign of her distress.

The *kohanim* pushed through the crowd, dragging a reluctant heifer into the public square, its eyes bound shut with a red cloth.

"If you say so …"

"That's my girl," said Ben-Isaiah, leading Ruth to a spot directly between Hanokh and Boaz as they took their places for the *khalitzah* ceremony.

"Now, repeat after me," he said.

Ruth spoke the words he whispered to her in the fading daylight: "My husband's nearest kinsman refuses to perform the duty of a redeeming kinsman to me."

Ben-Isaiah prodded Hanokh, who mumbled something in response.

"Louder, please," Shelomo instructed him.

"I said, *I reject her*," Hanokh said, keeping his head down.

Following the ways of the Yehudim, Ruth knelt before Hanokh, placing her left hand on his lower leg, and used her right hand to loosen the straps of his footwear. Then, in a surprisingly intimate gesture, she lifted his leg and pulled off his sandal, exposing his bare foot.

Ruth stood up and displayed the sandal that was supposed to be filled with Hanokh's flesh.

Now, the sons of Levi say that the woman is supposed

to spit on the ground in front of the kinsman who refuses to redeem her, but Ruth spat into his sandal and said, "Thus shall it be done to the man who refuses to rebuild his kinsman's house and restore his name."

"And so you agree to give this woman to another?" said elder Shelomo.

"I give her to another," Hanokh said, as Ruth handed the spit-smeared sandal to Boaz.

"And you will acquire her?" elder Shelomo addressed Boaz.

"I will acquire her," Boaz said, clutching the sandal in his knobby fist.

And Boaz said to the elders and to all the people, "You are witnesses on this day that I am taking Ruth the Moabite, widow of Makhlon, as my wife, to raise up the name of the deceased, so that his name may not be cut off from his kinsmen. You are witnesses today."

And the people at the gate answered, "Witnesses!"

And so a compromise was forged.

Ben-Isaiah explained the procedure: "If a man is found slain, and the murderer remains unknown, the town elders must defray the bloodguilt."

They made Ruth go through the motions like a wanderer in the land of dreams. The *kohanim* took the heifer and held it so that the *kohan gadol* could plunge a dagger into its neck. And as the blood streamed forth, they made Hanokh smear some of it on the palms of his hands. They had to prompt Ruth to hold out her hands so Hanokh could grasp them in his wet, sticky hands and thereby form a primitive bond of blood.

Then they made Hanokh and Ruth wash their hands over the bloodstained corpse, while the *kohanim* declared: *Our hands did not spill this blood, and our eyes did not see it done. Be merciful, O Lord, and do not charge your people Israel with the blood of the innocent, but absolve us of bloodguilt.*

"Absolved? Are you kidding me?"

"It's better this way, trust me."

Ruth ignored the prophet's advice and plunged into the crowd to confront the unholy trio that had plotted to destroy everything she loved.

Asnat smiled that serpentine smile of hers, and Ruth was seized by the urge to fix those perfect teeth with the dead weight of a blacksmith's hammer. Hanokh couldn't even bring himself to look Ruth in the eye.

Yiskah had no such conflict, standing tall, her posture rigid and severe, her stone hard gaze challenging Ruth to raise an objection, to condemn her motives, to make a distinction between them.

Ruth's hot young blood seethed with unspoken thoughts: *And to think that I risked my life for you. I faced the demon of the whirlwind to protect your child.*

Ruth locked eyes with each of them in succession—the conniving mother-in-law, the hapless stepfather, the protective mother—and cursed them all: "You may be absolved by the council of elders, but not by me."

Asnat turned away, and the others followed. They didn't have to listen to any more denunciations.

"May the Lord strike you with the pox of Mitzrayim, with boils and scabs and an itch that never heals. May the God of all things make your skies as hot as iron and your earth as hard as copper so that no plow can break it and may your seed be scattered like salt!"

Ruth went after them, but powerful hands held her back, so she directed her final curses at the napes of their necks: "May your name be cursed in the city and cursed in the country! May dogs devour you in Jezreel and whores bathe in your blood!"

She unleashed a barrage of curses, struggling against the men restraining her. "Let me go!"

"No." Boaz's voice. "You've said quite enough already."

CHAPTER TWENTY-ONE

Felicity

They file in by the hundreds, their smoky silhouettes as dark as the seven-ton bronze statue of Atlas glowering in the noonday sun across the avenue. They doff their hard hats as the standing room only crowd inside St. Patrick's Cathedral edges aside to let them through, many still wearing their steel-toed work boots and reflective safety vests, straight from the job.

My dad is curled up into a ball of anguish on the seat next to me, devastated by the loss of his *compañero*.

Rows of firefighters in dress blue uniforms lower their heads in remembrance as Cardinal O'Donoghue addresses the gathering in his scarlet-and-gold vestments, his voice echoing through the PA system:

"It was these men, and others like them, who answered the call when our city was grieving." Cardinal O'Donoghue makes a sweeping gesture toward a velvet rope–enclosed section where twenty-six empty chairs have been set aside in a place of honor before the altar, each bearing the scuffed hard hat of a construction worker who died this year in a work-related accident.

In an unusual move, the cardinal steps aside and defers to a Latino priest in a long black cassock named Father Moreno, who starts off by quoting the Psalms:

"*Do you judge uprightly, O you sons of men? Do you really decree what is just? No, in your hearts you work wickedness.*"

It's an odd choice for a funeral oration, and there's some nervous rustling in the pews when he starts haranguing the politicians and business leaders who showed up to pay their obligatory respects for giving the construction boom the go-ahead in the first place:

"The day after 9/11, we were told we must rebuild New York or the terrorists win," says Father Moreno, his amplified voice rattling the stained-glass windows. "But how patriotic is it to cut corners and build as fast as you can if workers get killed in the process?"

Mayor Gatti looks like he'd rather be chained to a rock somewhere in the Caucasus.

A camera crew that isn't supposed to be here turns their blinding lights on a contingent of construction workers clutching battered helmets in their hands, unaccustomed to the bright lights of TV. Even that orange-haired ass clown who leveraged half of Atlantic City looks like he'd rather be anywhere but here.

"Where were you when the chain securing an eight-hundred-pound steel girder at a construction site in Sunset Park gave way and the girder came crashing down, crushing Arturo González's chest?" Father Moreno asks the self-proclaimed masters of the universe.

My dad's muffled sobs sharpen to a wail as he clutches my arm for support, his callused fingers digging into my tender flesh like iron hooks.

"Where were you when a six-ton support collar came loose and a crane collapsed on East Fifty-First Street, leaving seven people dead? Where were you when a cracked turntable that hadn't been inspected in *six years* failed and the top of a crane broke away and fell twenty-three stories onto Ninety-First Street, killing two workers? Where were you yesterday afternoon, when the workers on Glenmore Avenue in East New York were digging through the rubble by hand, desperately trying to reach their brother Eloy Sucushñay before it was too late?"

My dad stuffs his fist in his mouth to stop the high-pitched whine from escaping at full volume.

"I'll tell you where you were: You were at City Hall, lobbying against the New York State Laborers Union's proposal to hire more crane inspectors, arguing that it's bad for business, that it's bad for the bottom line, that a crackdown on safety is causing *too many costly delays*, even though we only have *four* crane inspectors for the entire city. But what about the cost in human life? How much is a man's life worth to you?"

Waves of shock and indignation ripple outward from the pulpit, marked by gasps of outrage, expletives, hands flying to mouths. My dad tries to block it all out, covering his ears with his hands and burrowing into my side. Angry tears fill my eyes in spite of my goal to remain stoic in front of the VIPs.

"*Better the meager resources of the righteous than the obscene wealth of the wicked, for the wicked are never satisfied,*" Father Moreno castigates the real estate tycoons in the fourth row. Great quote, but I don't recognize the source. I'll have to look it up later.

"Let us now honor the fallen," Father Moreno says, his words landing heavily on the polished marble floor.

The construction workers raise their hard hats in tribute as the iron church bell tolls twenty-six times while labor union representatives read off the names of the twenty-six workers who lost their lives doing the work of rebuilding the city, brick by brick, building schools and hospitals, bridges, and subway tunnels.

My dad's eyes are squeezed shut and his forehead feels a little feverish. I give him a nudge as he starts shaking. I'm patting his cheek saying, *Papi, Papi, tienes que respirar,* as his face is turning red and I cry out *Papi!* and slap him hard enough to make heads turn and he finally expels the air in his lungs and a torrent of words comes spewing out of his mouth—a droning rendition of a dozen Hail Marys and an Act of Contrition, ending with *God forgive me.*

God forgive me, says the man who buried the truth about

my mother because he says he wanted to protect me, because it might have harmed his application for citizenship.

God forgive me, you lying bastard.

~

"That was some pretty fancy driving the other day," says Detective Gustella, stepping into my cubicle with a spiral-bound report on the latest crime statistics.

"Oh, you heard about that, huh?"

"Everybody heard about that."

Oh, great.

"I'm going to need the car for another day or two."

"Don't know about that, honey," he says, flipping open the laminated cover with the bull's eye logo on it and skimming the first paragraph of the report. "Mr. Fursten wants you working at your terminal so he can track your progress in real time—"

"You can tell him I'm *this* close to locating Kristel Santos."

"What's taking you so long to find her?"

"The bullshit smokescreen surrounding everything else about this case."

"Sounds like someone's gonna be working late tonight."

I shrug.

Detective Gustella pays no attention to the noise issuing from the TVs, shaking his head at the report's concluding paragraphs.

"Here we are trying to sell our line of premium security packages," he says, "and all the statistics show that violent crime is *decreasing*. People just aren't stealing as much as they used to."

"Sure they are, but no one's going after the white-collar criminals, Detective."

The WWTF News crew runs a clip of Mayor Gatti on the steps of St. Patrick's Cathedral, giving what passes for a measured response to Father Moreno's sermon:

KEEP IN MIND THAT CONSTRUCTION IS A
DANGEROUS BUSINESS AND YOU WILL ALWAYS
HAVE FATALITIES. ELIMINATING THE BUILDINGS
DEPARTMENT AND REPLACING IT WITH A PUBLIC
CORPORATION WILL DO MORE TO PROTECT THE
SAFETY OF THE PUBLIC, AS WELL AS CONSTRUCTION
WORKERS, THAN MOST OF THE BILLS SUBMITTED TO
THE CITY COUNCIL!

Translation: *He wants to privatize the Buildings Department.
Jesus, they want everything, don't they?*

"And writing the reports is such agony," says Detective
Gustella, closing the cover and jamming the report under
his arm.

"You know something, Detective? *Reading* your reports
is agony, too."

He laughs at my joke and leaves me tethered to the
computer terminal.

The WWTFers are telling me to stay tuned for a live
debate between presidential candidate Rick Fursten and
acting Secretary of Blocking Legislation (I believe that's his
title) Julian Rendón, and suddenly I have an urgent need to
flee to the ladies' room, seek out the stall farthest from the
TVs, slam the metal door and lower the toilet lid so I can sit
fully clothed, lean my head against the cold metal walls, and
listen to the steady drip of the third faucet from the right
echoing off the tile walls.

Plip … Plip … Plip …

My period is five days late, with no word about when
it's coming. My period can be *so* inconsiderate sometimes.

And still the faint audio reaches me like poison gas seeping through the cracks in the walls and windows. I bury my
head in my hands, trying to block it all out.

But it doesn't go away. None of it goes away.

And then—

IN LOCAL NEWS, ANOTHER WORKPLACE FATALITY, THIS TIME ON LONG ISLAND. THE BODY OF LEONIDAS SUÁREZ WAS RECOVERED FROM A DUMPSTER AT THE MOUNT HERMON SCRAPYARD IN NORTH BABYLON.

What? The metal door bangs open as I rush out to catch the story.

SURVEILLANCE VIDEO SHOWS THAT SUÁREZ WAS WORKING IN A RECYCLING BIN WHEN A CRANE OPERATOR DUMPED TONS OF SCRAP METAL INTO THE BIN, CRUSHING SUÁREZ TO DEATH. A SUPERVISOR AT THE SCRAPYARD DECLINED TO COMMENT. SERVICES FOR SUÁREZ WILL BE HELD TOMORROW AT THE SAVARESE FUNERAL HOME IN BRENTWOOD, LONG ISLAND.

Fucking hell. I was just talking to him a few days ago and now … Jesus …

Looks like I'm going to need the company car after all.

Flashy graphics and punchy theme music tell the world that it's time for the live debate.

My throat's as dry as sandpaper. I find the vending machine and have to steady my hands just to feed the bills into the slot. I press the buttons and a bottle of factory-fresh water drops into the well. I unscrew the plastic cap, tilt the bottle, and down most of the contents without stopping for breath.

I seek out the divine Ms. Tori, Keeper of the Keys, and tell her I need to take another look at the FinkBerg file.

"What file?" she asks, her eyes wide as headlights.

"FinkBerg Incorporated."

"Who?"

"*FinkBerg.*" I spell it out. All that gets me is a blank stare. "One of Silver Bullet Security's biggest subcontractors in Iraq."

"Oh." Tori disappears into the file room, leaving me at the mercy of the TV monitors.

"Not there," Tori says upon her return.

"What do you mean, not there? Did someone check it out or something?"

"You can't check out a file. This isn't a lending library."

"Sign out, borrow, examine, whatever you want to call it. If it isn't in the file drawer, where is it?"

"I don't know. It's missing."

"But I was just looking at it a couple of days ago—"

"What was that company name again?" she says, sitting down at her computer.

"*FinkBerg Incorporated*. They had a contract with Silver Bullet worth $70 million."

She types in the information.

"So they were subcontractors?"

"*Yes.*"

More typing.

"What type of services did they provide?"

"Designing and building living quarters, showers, toilets—"

The typing stops.

"Silver Bullet only subcontracted out nonstructural services such as laundry, catering, and gasoline delivery."

"*Gasoline* delivery?"

"The CPA authorized Cadmium Solutions to truck in gasoline from Kuwait and Turkey—"

"You're telling me the Coalition Provisional Authority paid Cadmium Solutions to *deliver gasoline* to the country with the second-largest oil reserves in the Middle East?"

"Not to Cadmium directly, but—"

"How much?"

"I'm afraid that information is classified."

Young Miss Tori seems to have gotten quite an education since I last spoke with her.

"Just round it off for me."

"I'm afraid that's—"

"Thousands? Tens of thousands? Hundreds of thousands?"

Tori's index finger edges sideways and hovers over the red security button on the intercom's keypad.

"*Millions?*"

Tori's got a big decision to make now.

Oh, fuck it. I'll figure it out on my own.

I do an about-face and head back to the cubicle, barely nodding at Maylita as she shuffles by with her cart of cleaning supplies, working the late shift again.

I can't believe I have to talk Detective Gustella into convincing the bosses to authorize my use of the company car for one more day.

"Kristel Santos was part of the same crew as Suárez, Detective. I'll give you four-to-one she turns up at his funeral."

"Make it five-to-one and I'll give it my best shot," he says.

"You're on."

I finally feel like I'm closing in on some answers. And I've got the rest of the afternoon to get ready for tomorrow's expedition to the suburban ghetto of North Babylon, Long Island.

Okay, time to rethink all my assumptions—starting with *Noticiero-Zaragoza*'s online article detailing the deadly attack on Silver Bullet's team of contractors at the Ishtar Hartley Hotel. I was so hungry for answers that I pounced on the information in that piece without fully vetting the source. It passed all the preliminary tests, but it's time to dig deeper.

I'm trying to bypass the firewall and verify the source of the article, which is proving to be rather difficult. That alone should send up a red flag: Since when does a puny online news agency require a greater level of protection than the Department of Defense?

MR. FURSTON, YOUR REBUTTAL?

I THINK WE JUST NEED TO REMEMBER THAT GOD'S

WATCHING *OVER* OUR TROOPS! AND THAT WE
SHOULD BE *ONE* HUNDRED PERCENT UNITED IN
PRAYING FOR *THEIR* SAFETY AND THE SUCCESS OF
THEIR MISSION!

God, if you're listening, I'd just like to say that you can
stop spending so much time watching over the troops, that
your time might be better spent if you came over here and
gave our leaders the wisdom to avoid war in the first place.
Sound like a plan?

I keep banging my head against the firewall protections.
I try sneaking around them, tunneling under them, boring
a hole straight through them. Damn, this is a tough sucker.

People are walking by, shaking out their rain-soaked
umbrellas, the only visible indication that there is still a big,
wide world out there beyond the black hole of cyberspace.

I think I finally found a weak spot. I just need to hammer
away at it.

Jesus, it's like opening a can of radioactive glow worms.
There are more intricately knotted malware threads than I've
ever seen in one place, with multilevel IP address spoofing,
heavily cloaked URLs, encrypted server-to-server traffic, and
so many backdoors it'll take me hours to untangle this mess.

Detective Gustella glides into my cubicle and makes a
big deal of clearing his throat.

I look up.

He dangles the car keys in front of me. "You're on,
Speedy," he says, with a big fat grin on his face.

～

I turn away from the screen, giving my eyes a break. Too
much data to absorb in one sitting, too many numbers neatly
aligned but still not adding up.

I head back to the women's bathroom and stare at my
sleep-deprived face in the mirror as I'm washing my hands,

wondering if it's still raining outside. I might as well be working in an underground bunker, right next to the six-month supply of canned peas and beef jerky.

I get back on the computer and keep hacking away for another hour or so until I finally make some headway, tracing the source of the online article to a defunct email address that was deleted from a decommissioned website but not thoroughly wiped from the server. The old Morse Techtonics website. Before they changed their name to Silver Bullet, an affiliate of Cadmium Solutions.

It's the same creepy realization that caps off the classic ghost story told around a million campfires and sleepovers: *It's coming from inside the building.*

I text Jhimmy that I'm working late but I should be home in time to make dinner, if he doesn't mind eating a bit later than usual. He responds with a thumbs-up emoji, texting that he's with a group of activists from the community center, putting the finishing touches on the signs and banners for tomorrow's big antiwar protest.

I dive back in to the cold, black heart of cyberspace, trying to isolate the sender's computer. I'm orbiting a massive unidentified object, zeroing in, and I've almost got it in my sights when a voice disturbs my circles.

"*¿Señorita Felicidad?*"

God damn it. What is it now?

"*¿Qué?*" I ask without looking up, annoyed by the interruption.

"*Creo que debería ver esto.*"

"*¿Ver qué cosa?*" I say, not even registering the switch to Spanish.

I look up. Maylita's holding a green plastic recycling bin full of interoffice memos and pink and yellow copies of old shipping receipts. We continue in Spanish.

"What's all this stuff?" I say, getting up from the terminal and stretching my arms.

"It was supposed to go into the shredder, but I think you should see it first."

"And why's that?" I say, peering into the recycling bin.

She doesn't answer, so I reach in and pull a couple of random documents from the pile.

Jesus H. Christ.

The first item is a spreadsheet showing that Cadmium Solutions overbilled the CPA by $60 million, charging nearly $100 million for construction work that actually cost around $40 million. Sample item: a helipad near Falluja. Cost: $790,000. Invoiced: $1,570,000. And a line indicating that during a single four-month period, Cadmium Solutions was paid more than $1.5 *billion* for gasoline deliveries from Kuwait and Turkey.

A mischievous smile scampers across Maylita's face, her cheeks glowing with pride.

I paw through the recycling bin, yanking out document after document, mostly mundane blathering about mission statements and the cost of replacing the filters in the air duct system, but some of the more incriminating items were plainly torn up by hand by someone who *still* hasn't learned that if you really want to eliminate a paper trail without starting a bonfire in the break room, use a crosscut shredder, dumbass.

I spread the puzzle pieces out on the desk, and the two of us set to work taping them together. It's almost fun to see the pieces falling into place. The first document we restore reveals that Silver Bullet's subcontract with Cadmium Solutions violated the provisions of Cadmium's parent contract with the Pentagon (a big no-no). The next one details the shoddy construction work done on the barracks in the Green Zone, including air pockets in the cement foundations, crooked walls and support beams, structures built out of square, and in one instance an explosion that injured two US Marines when a subcontractor dropped a tank of acetylene down a flight of concrete steps.

"Any more bins like this?" I ask.

"No, but I've been saving all the papers I thought might be important," she says, opening a compartment in her custodial cart and presenting me with a sheaf of documents.

They might as well be on a silver platter.

Even a cursory examination makes it clear that the information buried in these documents could do some serious damage to the company. The first ten pages alone include a draft of a report on the US Army private who was electrocuted while showering in one of the barracks built by FinkBerg Incorporated, but also reviews *seventeen similar fatalities* due to ungrounded or poorly maintained heating equipment and substandard electrical wiring. Cadmium Solutions middle management are suggesting a simple line of defense: The US military never specifically requested that the company fix the faulty wiring.

"You rescued all these from the shredder?"

I practically throw my arms around her, but I have to stop myself and do a look-left-look-right rubbernecker like a small-time hustler casing the slot machines in Atlantic City to make sure nobody's watching. Surveillance cameras hang from the ceiling at regular intervals like a strange species of bat with unblinking eyes, and I don't want anyone watching the monitors to realize how excited I am.

I make myself sit calmly at my desk and speed-read document after document till my eyebrows start smoking. The worst are the before-and-after pages stamped DRAFT FOR COMMENT ONLY, which provide a detailed record of the editorial changes the senior staff made regarding crucial matters like the rules of engagement. In one case, the original language was clearly intended to rein in the lawless cowboy spirit of Cadmium's force protection personnel:

> Company policy does not tolerate the targeting and deliberate killing of civilians and noncombatants.

> Any action intended to cause death or serious bodily harm to civilians or noncombatants shall be treated as an act of terrorism.

Then some asshole reversed the passage's meaning with a few quick strokes of a blue pencil:

> Company policy does not tolerate the targeting and deliberate killing of civilians and noncombatants *by terrorists*. Any *such* action intended to cause death or serious bodily harm to *others* shall be treated as an act of terrorism.

So now it says that a terrorist committing a terrorist act constitutes an act of terrorism. Glad we cleared that up.

The handwriting looks familiar, but it's not Detective Gustella, Velda Renko, or VP Haggard. Fursten? I'm about to sift through the case files when I tell Maylita she better keep moving or the security guards are going to get suspicious.

"*Bueno*, but you'll tell me what you find?"

"Absolutely."

She unlocks the wheels on her cart and pushes it to the next cubicle, stopping to pull on a fresh pair of blue vinyl gloves.

"Wait a second," I say.

"Yes?"

"That was some damn good investigative work, Maylita."

"Just beginner's luck," she says, spraying a rag with cleanser and wiping up the coffee stains on the computer table.

Beginner's luck. The words stick in my head.

I know I should back off, but you might as well tell a trained foxhound on the scent to stop chasing that darn fox.

I put together some minimal cloaking and dive head-first into the cesspool of the Cadmium Solutions internal messaging system. I isolate the entry point for Gustella's account, and go at it with the soft, light touch of an amateur cracksman deftly handling a set of ivory-handled picklocks that his dear old grandad passed down to him before the war.

Gustella's account is protected by a nearly impregnable shield, like a walled fortress shrouded in mist, but there are some vulnerabilities. My crude assault on the castle walls is probably triggering alarms that lead right back to this terminal, but I'll just have to pray for rain and cover my tracks later.

I'm not interested in his damn emails. I'm after the files stored on his computer.

But you can hardly expect me to ignore a series of emails to mfink@finkberg.com with multiple-megabyte attachments.

I crack a few open.

It's standard stuff, at first. The State Department is threatening to cancel Cadmium's contracts in Iraq and Afghanistan due to cost overruns and their reckless *yee-ha!* tactics, but when Cadmium promises to subcontract out most of those duties to companies with somewhat less troublesome track records, the DOS grants an extension to a subsidiary of the company formerly known as Morse Techtonics.

The next attachment lays out the bare facts about the armored vehicles Cadmium Solutions deployed outside the Green Zone, affirming that they did *not* have "five inches of metal armor" protecting them as indicated in their contractual agreements and numerous public statements. More like a half inch at best.

But the next one strips the bark right off me: undeniable proof that Silver Bullet's subsidiary, Bighorn Industries, supplied the US Army with body armor for nearly 250,000 troops in Iraq and Afghanistan that failed to meet Bighorn's own testing standards, including defective helmet armor that broke apart under fire, sending splinters into the wearer's brain, which is exactly what happened to Specialist Jeremías Ortega Pérez, motor pool operations, Babil Province, Iraq.

The worst part is that they knew.

They *knew* their body armor wasn't up to standard. And they went ahead and did it anyway.

Jesus …

What should I do?

Almighty God, tell me what to do.

It'll take months to do this properly, to get all the necessary warrants and subpoenas and whatever else we need to expose this … this … *crime against humanity.*

Giving them all the time they need to expunge the evidence.

And then there's the matter of explaining what on earth I was doing inside Gustella's corporate email account. I should really just turn around and tiptoe away from this.

That's my rational side talking.

My irrational side wants to hunt down the perpetrators and slowly torture them to death. (Death of a thousand cuts? Gradually lowering them into boiling oil? I'm still torn.)

The Bill of Rights only protects you from unreasonable searches and seizures conducted by agents of the US government. Anything a private citizen finds during an illegal search is admissible, folks.

I kick down the door to Gustella's computer files and ransack them for evidence. It doesn't take long to find a folder with my name on it. I break the seal and summon the beast with seven heads: They've got records of all my movements, all my phone and email activity, including street-level security camera and satellite images of my GPS-tracked location in the company car. That's how they knew every detail, every brake-pad-grinding inch of my little stunt driving act yesterday.

I commit a flagrant violation of the intellectual property clause in my contract by deleting my files from Gustella's hard drive and purging them from the server, taking care to leave the empty shell of the folder intact as a decoy. Then I gather everything I can vacuum up, and download it to a set of USB drives I keep in my shoulder bag for just such emergencies. I can't risk emailing this stuff to my office in Queens because that would open me up to all kinds of nasty criminal charges in addition to the ones I'm already flirting with. But I can burn the trail to this terminal pretty effectively.

First, I take the company-issued cell phone, stick it in a half-open drawer, and accidentally slam the desk drawer on it, shattering the screen. When I try to remove the phone to prevent further damage, damned if it doesn't get caught in the drawer and I end up breaking the phone in half. God, I can be *so* clumsy sometimes.

Now it's time to plant a self-destruct feature in the network. Although maybe it's just a defect in the system. One that the company that sold you the computer network knew about but went ahead and sold it to you anyway.

You know how that can happen.

I do my best to leave a smoking crater of Detective Gustella's computer files and throw them off the scent by planting a series of tiny cluster bombs at the entry points to five other terminals, including this one, while reciting the ancient biblical curse, *May your name be erased from all storage and retrieval systems in perpetuity throughout the universe, forever and ever, Amen.*

Sometimes you've just got to throw the damn money-changers out of the temple.

~

I pick up a bagful of red and yellow bell peppers for stir fry, and some dark chocolate chips for baking, because a tray of warm chocolate chip cookies fresh from the oven is a guaranteed crowd pleaser, even among the disparate special interest groups at the community center—except for the vegans, who will insist on cookies made with vegetable oil and blended organic flax seed instead of butter and eggs. I'll have to make a separate batch for them, but it's a small price to pay for a little goodwill.

Some people actually make cookies without *chocolate*.

Or so I've heard.

But my plans for a nice quiet dinner and some well-deserved downtime with Jhimmy get shot to hell the instant I walk in the door. The furniture has been pushed against the walls so Jhimmy's anarchist friends can use the floor space to make giant papier-mâché puppets of a billionaire arms merchant in a top hat with dollar signs where his eyes should be, an unflattering effigy of Mayor Gatti getting ready to shine the billionaire arms merchant's shoes, and a green Statue of Liberty whose seven-spike crown has been replaced by seven nuclear-tipped missiles. At least they spread out some old newspaper and drop cloths, because that DIY papier-mâché paste can get awfully messy. They're also painting antiwar slogans on poster board and large banners. I only recognize about half of the people invading my living room and spilling paint on the floor. A couple of the others look at me in my professional clothes and give me some major *Who the fuck are you?* attitude.

Jhimmy comes over to hug me hello, but he's got fresh paint on his work shirt, so we settle for a quick peck on the cheek.

"I thought you were doing this at the community center, not in the middle of our living room," I say softly, for his ears alone.

"They said the project's too politically biased," he says. "And the Center doesn't want to go through another funding battle with Mayor Gatti."

"Working for *peace* is a bias?"

"It is when your protest signs make fun of the mayor."

Two of the women smile and wave at me, Rayna Ziegler and Vanessa Lopez-Estrella, from a spot in the middle of the floor where the dining table usually sits. They're tearing a pile of rags into strips to tie the banners to the heavy duty cardboard tubes laid out in front of them because the police won't allow the protestors to hold up their signs with wooden slats or broom handles, which can be turned into weapons, they say.

I smile and wave back.

I exchange brief, strained pleasantries with a few of the activists who have taken over our apartment: Jailene García, an oval-faced Latina studying political science at Queens College–CUNY; Zekiya Thompson, a dark-skinned African American gal who's long on attitude but still coming to grips with her own suppressed history; Faatma Khan, the bright, dutiful daughter of Pakistani immigrants who's got nerves of steel under that demure façade; and Samuel Kondey, a soft-spoken immigrant from Ghana who's hoping to get into the nursing program at Hunter College.

"That better be water-based paint," I say to the pair of activists who are painting the puppet billionaire's clothes black, and dripping black paint all over the wooden floor through the many holes in the drop cloth.

One of them, a Latino with short dark hair and a dark complexion, holds up a jar of black paint, his face solemn and unsmiling: "Tempera paint's water based, right?"

"Yes, it is." I nod, but somewhere beneath the vaguely raw-egg-and-wet-dog odor of tempera paint is the unmistakable smell of linseed oil.

I direct my olfactory sensors to a guy on his knees, painting a sign that reads: WERE SICK OF CRUMBS. He's got a scruffy white-boy soul patch and a tattoo on his left bicep of the word CHAOS with a circle around the A forming the anarchist symbol. Mismatched paintbrushes and squashed tubes of oil-based paint lie scattered on the floor around him.

I grab a couple of rags from Rayna and Vanessa and quick-step over to the guy. He sits back on his heels and watches me nearly trip over the empty beer bottles cluttering his work area. I hand him the rags and tell him to make sure he cleans up the paint he's spattering all over my nice wooden floor.

"Yes, ma'am," he says, mock saluting me.

I look at the message on his sign.

"What's that mean?"

"It means the one percent keep trying to feed us crumbs from the table, and the ninety-nine percent are saying, *No, thanks. We're sick of the crumbs. We want the whole feast*."

"You might want to go with a simpler message."

"What's wrong with the message?" he says, barely concealed hostility rising to the surface.

"I'm just saying it's pretty hard to fit all that on a sign," I say, turning away. "And there's an apostrophe in *we're*."

"Hey! Where you going?"

"To change out of my work clothes, okay?"

I nearly break my neck trying to step around a jumble of tarps that turns out to be camouflaging a couple of buckets of congealing papier-mâché paste.

I hear Jhimmy telling the guy, "Zack, my man, some women simply don't appreciate that the floor is just a really big shelf."

I try not to slam the bathroom door as I make a much-needed visit.

Oh, fuck. One of the guys has dribbled piss all over the toilet seat and the floor, as if this were a public restroom, and I have to wipe it up with a wet paper towel before I can sit. I'm on my knees reaching around the toilet's white porcelain base to get at the last few drops when I realize the wallboard's damp with misdirected piss as well, and it's already soaking in.

Jesus, there's no way I'm cleaning all this up without a bucket of soapy water and a pair of rubber gloves.

The phone's ringing but nobody's answering it.

Somewhat relieved, I retreat to our bedroom to shed my Wall Street plumage and put on a pair of worn jeans and the blue-and-orange Mets sweatshirt my dad gave me for my fifteenth birthday.

Zack's going on about how the CIA is planting computer chips in people's heads to control their thoughts, or some such conspiracy theory nonsense.

"We don't need CIA mind-control chips, dude," Jhimmy says. "We already have mind control. It's called corporate media."

"Then let's go after the media!" Zack says. "Let's go down to the TV studios on Avenue of the Americas and smash some windows!"

Avenue of the Americas? Who the hell says that? Everybody I know calls it Sixth Avenue.

"That's playing right into their hands, dude," Jhimmy says, diplomatically. "That's all anyone remembers about Seattle or Davos. We could have a million people turn out for a peaceful protest, and all it takes is a couple jerks breaking windows and the headline's going to be: VIOLENCE MARS PEACE PROTEST."

"That just proves my point," Zack says. "That's the only language they understand!"

I slip past on my way to the kitchen, carefully avoiding the piles of shredded newspaper and paste stains on the floor while Jhimmy and his comrades get sidetracked into a debate over the proper response to the monolithic power of corporate media.

I grab the bag of peppers and carry them to the sink, which is full of dirty dishes with half-eaten food still stuck to them.

"*Viva la revolución*," I say as I scrape the uneaten food into the compost bin, rinse off the plates and put them in the rack to dry. And I still need to clear some counter space.

I put the dirty glasses in the sink, sweep the apple cores and banana peels into the compost bin, chase the roaches away from the half-eaten loaf of bread that's been lying on the cutting board since God knows when, and pick up the half-gallon milk container, thinking it's empty, but there's a heavy sloshing in the bottom. It's about a quarter full and warm to the touch. I open the spout and take a sniff. *Bleahh!* The milk has turned sour, beyond redemption.

I spit the foul lingering taste of it into the sink, rather noisily, making no secret of my disgust.

"*¿Qué te pasa?*" Jhimmy says, appearing in the doorway.

"The bread and milk have been sitting out since *this morning.*"

"Oh yeah, I was going to put them away, but I got distracted," he says, turning away.

"Yeah, the sun came up," I grumble as I pour the spoiled milk down the drain. I rinse out the container, stomp on it, and stuff it in the recycling bin.

I wash the peppers, cut them in half, and remove the seeds. Then I chop them up and toss them in the pan with some sliced onion and garlic, add some sliced tomato and cilantro and stir them till the juices start to bubble.

"There is one thing I do not understand," says Samuel, in his endearingly soft spoken postcolonial British West African accent. "The US is the wealthiest nation in history. How is it possible that the people are so uneducated?"

"Because the main objective of our system is turning out a bunch of obedient cogs in the machine," Jhimmy says. "They prefer indoctrination to education because education *makes people think.*"

That's my Jhimmy.

But it's a pretty sad commentary on our times when it's a radical act to state that the purpose of education is to make people think.

"That's such a bourgeois argument—" Zack starts in.

It only takes a few minutes for the tomatoes to cook down and the sauce to thicken. I stir it around and turn the heat down to simmer.

"Stir-fried vegetables again?" Jhimmy says, venturing into the kitchen.

"Yes, but it's not the same dish," I say, coquettishly. "The last three nights I stirred the vegetables in a *clockwise* direction, while tonight I'm stirring them in a *counter*-clockwise direction. Can you taste the difference?"

I hold up the wooden spoon for him to taste. He brushes his hair out of his eyes and blows on the steaming sauce, then puts the smooth wood grain to his mouth, closes his eyes and takes a slurpy, sensual taste, getting thick red sauce on his lips.

"Oh, yeah. Completely different taste."

He opens his eyes and smiles. I smile back.

"Let's go Mets," he says, giving my sweatshirt a tug before rejoining his comrades.

I get out the chocolate chips, the baking soda, the sugar, the butter, the salt. I grab the flour tin, which barely weighs a couple of ounces—wait a minute. There's supposed to be five pounds of white flour in here. I open the tin. It's empty.

I go through the cupboard looking for the sack of flour I *know* I bought a few days ago, flinging the cabinet doors open and slamming them shut with increasing ferocity. I pick up the empty tin in a completely irrational gesture, as if I need to double-check and make absolutely *sure* that the flour's missing before I fly completely off the handle.

"Where the hell did all the flour go?" I shout to the kitchen-gods.

"We needed it to make the paste for the papier-mâché," says Jhimmy, leaning against the doorjamb.

I turn to him.

"You used all of our flour to make the *paste* for your giant puppets?"

"Could you keep your voice down?" he says. "First, they're not *puppets*, they're political satire, and second, they're great for attracting media attention—"

"And nobody thought of going to the store to buy more flour?" I whisper harshly.

"It wasn't a priority."

"Didn't your mom teach you *anything* about sharing domestic responsibilities?"

"This can wait till later," he says, shoving himself away from the doorjamb. "You know, I didn't have a nice comfortable upbringing like you did."

"At least you had *two parents*."

"What the fuck is that supposed to mean?" he says, turning on me. "Is this just one of your crazy mood swings? Look, I'm sorry you can't indulge your chocolate craving—"

I'm about to blurt out a nasty retort when a heavy thud rattles the dishes in the rack. Jhimmy and I lock eyes for a brief moment of *What the—?* followed by another heavy thud as a police battering ram breaks down the front door to our apartment and a tidal wave of black-clad riot cops in full strike force gear floods the living room. They're wearing riot helmets with face shields, obscuring their identities, and so much tactical body armor they look like an army of Robocops as they fan out, cuffing people and ripping up the tarps and banners like they're searching for a mad bomber in a suicide vest.

Jhimmy rushes into the fray and is immediately slammed to the floor by a couple of riot cops with hard plastic knee pads, which they jam into my immobilized boyfriend's kidneys. I take a step toward him and a big, burly storm trooper shoves me back into the kitchen.

"We got bottles and rags for making Molotov cocktails," one cop announces, pulling a bunch of heavy duty clear plastic evidence bags from a pouch in his black Kevlar vest and filling them with Zack's empty beer bottles and the rags Rayna and Vanessa were shredding into strips.

"We got puppet-making materials," says another, yanking the tarp off the buckets of leftover papier-mâché paste.

"Looks like we got the makings of some pepper spray in here," says the big, burly cop, shoving me aside and staring at the peppers simmering on the stovetop as if I'm cooking up a batch of uranium oxide.

Before I can stop him, he yanks the frying pan off the fire and dumps our dinner into the sink.

"*Whoa! Whoa! Whoa!*" I launch myself at him. "What happened to knock-and-announce?"

"Don't mean shit if we hear evidence being destroyed," he says, nodding toward the mess in the sink, which is now clogging the drain.

"Evidence *of what*?" I shout over the confusion. "Where's your warrant?"

"You've obviously forgotten 9/11," he says.

Oh, have I?

"Yo, Sarge!" the burly cop shouts over his shoulder. "Little Miss Trotsky here wants to see the warrant."

He pivots *exactly* ninety degrees sideways like some kind of cyborg so I can squeeze by. The Robocops are everywhere, dumping armfuls of books and papers on the floor and trampling them with their riot boots, ripping the sheets off our bed and tossing the contents of my underwear drawer on the floor, dropping the toilet tank lid onto the tiles where it shatters so they can shine their heavy-duty Maglites into the water tank looking for contraband, yanking the cables out of the desktop computer, and bagging Jhimmy's laptop as evidence. They've neutralized the opposition, forcing most of the activists to their knees in the middle of the floor and hog-tying them wrists to ankles with plastic handcuffs. The few who remain free are filming and texting madly, ignoring repeated orders to surrender their phones, as the cops go around grabbing the phones and stuffing them into five-gallon evidence bags.

The cops are also seizing the protest signs and banners, so Rayna quickly scribbles the words, WE LOVE YOU, PRESI-DENT KINNEY on some poster board.

"Is this one okay?" she asks, before a cop rips the poster out of her hands and threatens to shove a Flash-Bang grenade up her ass. I didn't even notice the grenades on their belts in all the mayhem. At least they didn't use *those* on us.

A pair of heavily armed riot cops stand side by side, legs apart, blocking the front door with their military grade assault rifles angled toward the floor, 40mm tear gas canisters and other nonlethal projectiles swinging from their belts.

Then a cop who must be the squad leader assumes a triangular stance, pointing a sixteen-round Glock semiautomatic pistol at my chest, dead center.

It's all rather intimidating.

Especially when you know that the Police Department–issued pistols don't have safety catches.

The burly cop shoves me toward the squad leader, who raises the angle of his pistol slightly, so he's not aiming it right at my heart, but he could take my ear off with it if he wanted to. He disengages his left hand, reaches into his vest, and pulls out a piece of paper folded in thirds that he shakes out with one harsh movement and holds up for me to read.

It's a legal warrant all right, authorizing the seizure of all electronic devices with operational storage and retrieval systems (computers, tablets, smartphones), any printed matter (newspapers, books, pamphlets) suspected of containing subversive content, and any clothing that might be used for unlawful purposes (ski masks, gas masks, gloves). All that's missing from the list is a pair of black low-heeled pumps with retractable, poison-tipped stiletto blades concealed in the toe like the enemy spies used in *From Russia with Love*.

"Looks kind of vague and overly broad to me," I say.

"Standard Operating Procedure when we're investigating ties with terrorists."

"Ties with terrorists? Are you kidding me?"

"You gonna come quietly or do we have to use force?"

"That isn't much of a choice."

"You want freedom of choice? Fine." He gives a nod and the cop behind me grabs my wrists and jerks them behind my back and up, practically pinning them to my shoulder blades.

"Ow! That fucking hurts, asshole."

The cop behind me jerks my wrists even higher, even though a Criminal Court judge recently upheld the people's right to curse at a police officer.

The squad leader reaches into a pouch on his belt and holds out two types of plastic restraints.

"You want the white one or the yellow one?" he asks.

"So the only freedom you're willing to grant me is the freedom to choose what color handcuffs you put on me."

"White it is," says the squad leader.

"What you're doing here is totally illegal," I protest as they cuff my hands behind my back. A pair of riot cops grab my arms, one on each side, and lead me out the door and down the stairs.

The cop on my right helpfully informs me that if I genuinely believe I am the victim of an improperly executed warrant, I am free to exercise my right like any other citizen to hire a lawyer and bring a civil complaint against the NYPD.

The cop on my left snorts loud enough to hurt my ears.

They drag me out the front door of the building and into the street, hurling me headlong into a surreal scene of hellish mayhem. Hundreds of police have blocked off the street, outnumbering the arrestees by twenty to one. A pair of police helicopters hover overhead, sweeping the area with high-powered searchlights. They've parked six armored police vans two-by-two nose-to-tail at right angles, creating a three-sided corral so we can all be rounded up behind orange plastic netting while some of our concerned neighbors film what's going on with their smartphones until they're chased away by the cops maintaining the perimeter. The glint of light on metal catches my eye and I look up. There are snipers—*snipers*—on the roofs, glaring through their scopes at us.

Half a dozen riot cops surround the corral armed with 40mm grenade launchers packed with beanbag projectiles that they're supposed to be aiming at our legs, but which are in fact aimed at throat level.

They jam me into the holding pen and tighten the noose around us as the burly cop exits the building cradling my stir-fried bell peppers in a couple of double-strength evidence bags.

The squad leader gets on the horn, and after a blast of earsplitting feedback, orders us all to sit down in the middle of the street. We comply just to get our heads below the brain-rattling sound waves. He then announces that we're all under arrest for blocking traffic—which he just ordered us to do—and the cops begin processing us one by one, letting us out of our orange plastic cage and into the waiting police vans one at a time. They process Rayna, Vanessa, and Jailene, but when they get to Zack, he leans in close and whispers something, and the cop at the gate tells his partner, "Yo, Vinny, he's under."

An undercover cop?

Of course. The guy who was agitating for more violence.

One of Jhimmy's comrades—I think his name is Chad— blurts out, "You fucking snitch!" and lunges at Zack. "Is that even a real tattoo?" he yells, and claws at Zack's CHAOS tattoo, scraping some of it off with his fingernails. "I knew it! You fucking rat—!"

But in a second, poor deluded Chad is knocked to the ground and pummeled by five cops at once. Zekiya films the whole thing with a smartphone they obviously missed and when they come after her she tosses the phone over the plastic netting to a bystander, who runs east with about a dozen cops chasing her toward a tiny square presided over by the green-patinaed statue of a Civil War hero that this crowd would just as soon melt down and use for bullets.

The detainees struggle to their feet, pressing against me

so tightly I can't move as a riot cop aims his grenade launcher at my head and I try to raise my hands to protect myself but *oh, right* they're cuffed behind my back, so I try to duck but I'm pinned in place by the press of bodies and there's a loud *pop* and something hits me in a flash of blackness.

CHAPTER TWENTY-TWO

Felicity

"Yo, Pérez!" a fellow detainee yells.

The sound strikes my eardrums, but my brain refuses to respond.

"Check it out, you're famous."

I open my eyes and a splash of pain radiating from a golf-ball-sized welt on the right side of my cranium makes me regret the decision. My brain feels like it's been scrubbed with Comet. I try to prop myself up on my elbows, but some unseen force has shackled my shoulder muscles to the hard metal bench.

A Latina with a shaved head and tribal tattoos snaking around both arms is pointing excitedly to a patch of graffiti-filled wall on the other side of the cell as if the hand of God just tagged the wall in flaming letters.

It takes a moment for my eyes to focus on the message scrawled in bold black marker:

¿TAS JODIDO? LLAMA A
FELICITY ORTEGA PÉREZ

Followed by my office number in Queens.

"Great. I'm holding-cell graffiti."

I lie back down, my stomach doing backflips.

"Come on, *chica*, this is like one of those celebrity endorsements! You gonna get a lot of business outa this. All you gotta do is put your website up here, too. Anybody got a Sharpie?"

My mind spirals back to the woozy hours in the middle of the night—the bare room, the wobbly chair, the smell of burnt coffee and sweat, the police detectives standing over me for endless hours of wild accusations with all the flourishes, walking in with reams of official-looking folders and claiming they know everything about me, batting away my denials and telling me they found my DNA on admissible evidence even though it usually takes two to three months to get DNA results, trying to get me to name names in exchange for a nice, cool ice pack to press against the swelling on my bruised skull, and even stooping to the old con job of claiming that my comrades already rolled over on me so I might as well come clean, while I just sat there holding on to the precious grain of knowledge that if they had any real evidence against me, they'd be using it, instead of going for the full-court press.

There's a bottomless pit where my stomach should be as I sink back into oblivion, but in the blink of an eye I'm summoned back to the drab reality of this noisome holding cell:

"Hey, Perez!"

A female officer bangs on the bars with a metal baton.

"Get off your ass and follow me. You made bail."

~

"How come you came instead of my dad?" I ask, my head still throbbing.

"You're welcome," says my elderly neighbor, Mrs. Perel, as we walk past a deli with a bright pink ham hanging in the window. The mere sight of it make me nauseous.

"Sorry, I'm just one of those people who's not fully human till I've had my morning coffee."

"I went without coffee for six years during war," she says, stopping and facing me, the front window of the deli looking like a giant TV set tuned to that new hit reality show about watching salamis age. "You need coffee?"

"What I need is an ice pack."

"What for you need ice pick?"

"Not an ice *pick*, an ice *pack*."

"For head wound?"

"Yeah, but how'd you know about—?"

"How bad is it? Let me look."

I incline my head so she can sweep her fingers through my hair and examine the wound.

"Ow!"

"Stop moving so much. Hmm. Is not so bad as it looks."

"Oh, you're an expert on head wounds?"

"Have you been checked for internal bleeding? Did they give you CT scan?"

"They wouldn't even let us use the bathroom."

"Well, you're still standing here making smartass remarks, so you must be all right. You're lucky it was just a glancing blow."

"It didn't feel all that *glancing* to me."

"Trust me, you'll be fine. If it had been direct hit you'd be unconscious or dead by now. But we should get some ice for that."

I follow her inside the deli, tottering unsteadily on swollen feet. Thank God there are a couple of empty chairs at a tiny round-topped table. I slump down in one and cup my hands to my face, trying to block out the sounds and smells, to no avail. My head's spinning.

People are rushing to work, ordering fried egg sandwiches, tuna melts on whole wheat, and in one case the cross-cultural delicacy, "*Un bagel por favor, con shmear.*"

Just listening to the cracking of eggs, the sizzle and pop as they're deposited on the steam table next to the hash browns simmering in bacon grease, is enough to make me feel the hot sticky sweat of acute motion sickness.

Mrs. Perel returns with a large coffee, a cup of herbal tea, and a clear plastic cup full of ice that I press to the side of my head like a wide receiver for the New York Giants pinning a thirty-two-yard pass to the side of his helmet.

"Start with herbal tea. Work your way up to coffee," Mrs. Perel recommends.

I oblige by taking a sip of hot peppermint tea.

"Everything's so expensive now," she says. "Tea, coffee, everything."

"What do I owe you?" I ask, blowing on the tea.

"For tea and coffee? Don't be silly."

"I mean for bail."

"Then you don't know?"

"Don't know what?" I say, my chest seizing with fear. There's a rat's maze inside my skull full of tiny critters trying to claw their way out, and I'm not up to answering a bunch of questions.

"They were ready to charge you with inciting riot and resisting arrest, then video of you getting shot in head goes viral on social media. All charges dropped."

"Hooray for cell phone cameras," I say, taking another sip of tea with one hand while I hold the makeshift ice pack in place with the other. Cold condensation is dripping into my ear and down my neck, but I'm beyond caring.

"What about the others?" I croak.

"Most were released. Some not."

"What about Jhimmy?" I ask, though I'm pretty sure I know the answer.

Mrs. Perel lets out a sigh.

"They're still holding him. Because he is ringleader, they say. Your comrade Chad is in worse position. They are charging him with two counts of aggravated assault against police officer, which carries—"

"A sentence of up to thirty years," I say, my family's deeply ingrained fatalism rearing its ugly head.

"They set bail at one million dollars."

"Shit."

I take a couple of swallows of peppermint tea, and push the cup away from me.

"I'm ready for the coffee," I declare.

She slides the coffee over to me.

"You'll fight it, of course," she says.

"Yeah, but not today. I've got some unfinished business on Long Island."

She eyes me skeptically. "You are going to work today?"

"I'll be fine. I just need—"

"To have your head examined."

"Yeah. How come you know so much about head wounds?"

"You need more ice?"

"No, I'm good."

We sit there amid the grind and hiss of buses, the blaring of car horns, the harmonic convergence of customers ordering breakfast in a dozen different languages, and the talking heads on TV chattering nonstop about the inevitability of war in Zabul Province.

"Would it surprise you to learn this eighty-eight-year-old woman once carried rifle and fought with partisans?" she says, even though she knows the answer is *No, not a bit*. "We ambushed patrols, laid land mines on tracks when troop trains are passing through. I only wish we had killed *more* of those Nazi bastards."

The years have been rough on her. Her youthful figure long gone, her face wrinkled, her body shriveling up. Yet she sits ramrod straight in defiance of the weight of those years.

"You're a tough old bird, all right," I say. "We should talk more."

The sky outside is cloudy and overcast, with more rain on the way.

I suddenly have to pee. Must be all the liquids I'm consuming.

"In spring of forty-three, we even had a Seder," she says. "Can you believe? A Seder, in forest northwest of Minsk! We had no *karpas* or *zeroah*, but plenty of bitter herbs."

"I didn't know you were observant."

"Not so you'd notice."

"Do you fast on Yom Kippur?"

"I fasted enough in Buchenwald."

~

I rush into the drugstore, searching for the aisle marked FAMILY PLANNING, and grab the first Early Pregnancy Test I can lay my hands on. There's a line for the cashiers but I can't wait that long. My head's splitting open and I've *really* got to pee so I set my sights on the employees' bathroom. I push past a teenager pricing a carton full of shaving cream canisters and barricade myself behind the metal door marked EMPLOYEES ONLY. The place smells like a box of used cat litter, that special mixture of piss and shit and ammonia and moldy cement with no ventilation at all, and I nearly bust a seam trying to work open the brass stud button on my jeans. I tear the EPT carton open and fish out the plastic wand, which is vacuum-sealed in a plastic bag that I have to rip open with my teeth so I can unzip, yank my jeans down, and assume the position, pissing all over the clean white fibers protruding from the tip of the wand, which turn a reassuring yellow just to let me know my kidneys are still working properly after last night's abuse.

Someone bangs on the door.

"Hey, you can't be in there."

The piss stream subsides, and I hold the tester in one hand while trying to wipe myself with the other, but they've installed one of those enormous, heavy spools of cheap institutional toilet paper that are *impossible* to rotate through the tiny slit in the plastic housing with one hand, and I keep tearing off half sheets of coarse, thin butcher paper and I want to know what execrable asshole came up with the design for a fucking *toilet paper dispenser* that manages to mess with you by *not dispensing toilet paper* when you're trying to wipe yourself, for fuck's sake.

The knocking gets louder, more insistent.

"Move it, babe. You're not supposed to be in there."

I'm standing in this windowless toxic waste disposal unit with my jeans around my ankles and a few drops of unwiped piss dripping down my leg, holding the pregnancy test and waiting for a sign from God, from Odin, from Aphrodite—seriously, I'll take a sign from *any superhuman deity* at this point.

The metal door shakes on its corroded hinges, and the pounding reverberates off the cold cement walls with brain-rattling effectiveness.

"Yo, hurry up, it's an emergency."

"Ma'am, we need you to exit the bathroom."

"Yo, hurry up, yo!"

The blue line is starting to form.

I'm pulling up my jeans one-handed and fumbling with the zipper. Only now do I notice all the empty pregnancy test boxes spilling out of the garbage onto the floor. I'm clearly not the first woman to come in here desperate to know the truth, even if she has to resort to shoplifting.

"Ma'am, if you don't open up right now, we're going to have to call the police."

One blue line. That's all. No cross piece. Well, not really. Faint traces of one, but definitely not a plus sign, right? That means it's a negative, right? No equivocating now, give it to me straight. That's definitely a minus sign, right?

"Ma'am—"

"Okay, okay, just a damn minute," I answer, zipping up my jeans and opening the door.

"Is there something we can get for you? Something we can do to help?"

"Sure. You got a screwdriver and some pliers?"

"Try hardware. Aisle six."

⁓

I pull the company car over just before the ramp to the Manhattan Bridge, double parking on a major thorough-fare. But this should only take a moment, and I am the very essence of corporate cool in my dark gray business suit and skirt. I release the seat belt so I can slide over and duck my head under the instrument panel, just beneath the satellite radio permanently tuned to WWTF News, which also sends out a GPS signal giving my exact location to my bosses and anyone else with access to a decent Wi-Fi network.

It's a bit of a pain in the neck in this position, but I find a plastic seam, slip the screwdriver in, and pry the panel open just wide enough to allow me to shove the long-nose pliers in and grab a couple of wires, but it's an awkward fit and I tug till my hands are slick with sweat and my wrists howl in protest, and I finally rip the wires out. Way too much work. Should have gone with wire cutters instead. Next time.

I get out and do a quick sweep of the car, checking the undercarriage until—*jackpot*—I recover a tracking device planted inside the right rear wheel well.

Fortunately, I'm headed over the deep, fast-moving water of the East River, and no one's going to see this little device again in this lifetime.

～

The slashing rain muffles the sound of cars swishing by on Sunrise Highway. It's a pretty small turnout, with Suárez's friends and relatives barely fitting under a handful of wind-whipped umbrellas in this dreary little corner of North Babylon Cemetery.

I'm parked a short distance away with the window part-way open, trying to stay dry, if not warm. I think I disabled the heater along with the radio, but a silent radio is a fair trade-off. At least the stabbing pain from my head trauma is down to a dull ache.

The priest is reading from a Spanish prayer book about

how *if you obey the Lord your God, and faithfully observe His commandments, blessed shall be the fruit of your womb, and blessed shall be your fruit basket and your kneading bowl.*

Suárez was a combat veteran, so he's being buried with full military honors—a team of pallbearers in dress uniform, a prerecorded rendition of Taps, and an honor guard salute consisting of three soldiers in white ceremonial gloves firing three successive rifle volleys into the limitless aether.

It also means the creatures have come out of the woodwork. One hundred feet from the cemetery's entrance, the minimum distance stipulated by a recent court order, two dozen members of the Axminster Sovereign Citizens Church freely express their hatred of most of the people who live in this country while a contingent of rain-soaked Suffolk County cops keep them in line behind light blue sawhorses.

"DEPORT ILLEGAL ALIENS! DEPORT ILLEGAL ALIENS! GOD HATES FAGS! GOD HATES FAGS!"

A dark-skinned Latino with the funeral cortege is wearing a rain-dampened sweatshirt that says WE DON'T LIKE YOU, EITHER.

The priest continues:

You shall not abuse a poor and destitute laborer, whether a fellow countryman or a stranger who is in your land. You must pay him his wages on the day you hire him, before the sun sets, for he is needy and his life depends on it; Let him not cry to the Lord against you, for it shall be a sin on your head.

A cluster of hawks circles high overhead. At least someone's showing respect for the dead. The noise from the demonstrators makes it hard to meditate on the tragedy of Private Suárez's death, much less contemplate one's own mortality.

A distant rumbling comes rolling down the highway, the kind you don't even hear at first, you just feel the earth thrumming beneath you, then the sensation travels up your legs and tickles your groin, as the rumbling swells with deep bass notes that make my red corpuscles vibrate in sync with the thunderous roar of a squadron of Harley-Davidsons at full throttle. And what an earth-shaking scene it is as more than a hundred members of the Patriot Knight Riders come *roarrring* off the highway and swerve onto Livingston Avenue, braving the dead zone between the protesters and Private Suárez's final resting place with their gleaming wet hogs, revving their V-shaped cylinder-head assemblies till smoke rises from the exhaust pipes and streaks of rubber are burned into the blacktop.

Two members of the military honor guard perform the ritual of removing the flag from the coffin and snapping it into a tight, starry blue triangle to present to a woman who's too absorbed in her grief for me to determine if she's Suárez's sister or his girlfriend, or what.

The woman cradles the folded flag in her arms as she hugs the people close to her and exchanges a few words with the priest before walking out the gate, past the row of bikers, her eyes fixed on the glistening black tarmac beneath her feet. I can't tell what she's feeling, what she thinks about the bikers, but I imagine there must be some relief in the cathartic roar that so effectively drowns out the intruders on this sorrowful occasion.

I spot Kristel Santos leaving the cemetery and climbing into a dented, iron-gray 1992 Toyota Corolla.

～

The fifteenth Station of the Cross ought to be *Jesus Attempts to Drive on Long Island*. The old man in front of me shouldn't even be driving. Well, technically, what he's doing *isn't* driving. He's puttering along at 10 mph below the speed limit and soft-pedaling the brake every twenty feet or so. Jesus, does he have a shipment of nitroglycerine in the trunk or something?

Plus he's got a bunch of bumper stickers telling me FUCK YOUR FEELINGS; NUKE THEIR ASS AND TAKE THEIR GAS; and WARNING: I VOTE PRO-LIFE, among others. But if he really

wanted to be helpful he'd have one that says WARNING: I
DRIVE LIKE SHIT.

When he *finally* turns onto a side street I do my best to
close the distance between the crippled company car and
Kristel Santos's rust speckled Toyota without causing a five-
car pileup on these slick, wet roads. She bears right onto
Commack Road, giving me a chance to catch up when she
hits a long light at Bay Shore Road. When the light changes,
she heads north, leaving Babylon behind and takes a right
onto Long Island Avenue.

Traffic slows to a crawl near the entrance to an industrial park. A rough patch of sandy soil across the street from
the LIRR parking lot serves as the gathering place for a
couple dozen day laborers milling about and trying to stay
dry while a pair of enterprising middle-aged Latinas help
ease the men's misery by selling them home-cooked meals
of *arroz con pollo* and *empanadas* out of the trunk of their car.

Which is why I'm stuck in the eastbound lane when a
police cruiser in the westbound lane gives a warning blip of
the siren and rolls up on the group. The two police officers
hop out, ticket books in hand, and start questioning the
women about their off-the-books operation.

Damn. They're going to get hit with vending without
a license, failure to collect state sales tax, and maybe even
health code violations. I wish I could help, but I can't risk
losing the tail.

Handcuffs? Seriously?

Oh, shit—they're *arresting* them. *And impounding their cash.*

"Yo, what the fuck?" I'm unbuckling my seat belt, ready
to jump out of the car when the traffic starts moving again.

"Sorry, señoras," I tell myself as I strap myself in and step
on the gas. "A gal's gotta eat."

I've been told that if the Brentwood cops are in a particularly playful mood, they'll confiscate your shoes and make
you walk home barefoot from the precinct house.

Kristel Santos's Toyota turns into the industrial park. I follow her onto a drab strip of asphalt some wiseguy named Executive Drive, past the Suffolk County Probation Department, a tool and die manufacturer, a wire and cable company, and a uniform supply warehouse, and I've got to say it takes a rather mordant sense of humor to name a couple of featureless access roads Wilshire Boulevard and Rodeo Drive. We pass a loading dock lined with shipping containers before turning onto—*oh, shit*—a long, straight featureless road through a barren stretch of wilderness leading to the ruins of the old Pilgrim State Psychiatric Hospital, and Kristel Santos would have to be legally blind not to spot me in the rearview mirror on this deserted road. We snake through a warren of streets with colorful names like A Road, G Road, and F Road before passing the Michael J. Grant Campus and Funeral Home—at least that's what I *think* the sign said—and ending up on a quiet street in the shadow of the Long Island Expressway just as the rain starts letting up.

The Toyota pulls to the curb in front of a house that looks like a ranch until you notice the first floor is mostly hidden below ground level. It must be some kind of basement apartment. The exterior is pretty well kept, like the rest of the block, except for a mildewy queen-size mattress lying half on the lawn, half in the street that the trash collectors apparently refused to collect. The back yard is overgrown with scrubby pines and thorny greenbrier, nature's own barbed wire, going all the way back to the noise abatement wall dividing the Expressway from the rest of humanity.

Kristel gets out of her car and faces me, leaning against the car door with her arms crossed like she just *knew* that someone was going to pick up her tail if she went to that funeral.

There's no point in pretending. I pull up behind her and get out. I can tell right away from the smell in the air that her neighbor's doing a dryer load of laundry that was washed in a heavily perfumed detergent.

We eye each other like a couple of wrestlers sizing up an opponent while the crowd screams for blood. She looks like she could use a few hot meals and some sun.

"You know the hardest thing about living on Long Island?" she says.

I wait for the punchline.

"You can't flush used condoms down the toilet like you can in the city. They'll fuck up the septic system."

I nod, my eyes cutting to the basement apartment. My next question is put on hold by a black Dodge Charger cruising by with blacked-out windows, chrome wheels, street-hugging suspension, and earth-shaking bass booming out of its thousand-watt sound system.

"Mind if we talk inside?" I shout over the heavy bass notes, which aren't doing my headache any good.

She gives a defeated shrug, as if I'm a black-hooded hangman asking if she wants her noose made of coarse hemp or the more expensive fine hemp, and leads me down the steps to a cramped one-room apartment with about as much natural light as an underground prison cell. Just the place for a person who's isolated, depressed and borderline suicidal, but who just needs one more little push.

Heavy black curtains cover a pair of tiny windows high up in the front wall, blocking out all sources of illumination except for the pale, sickly light seeping through a filth-encrusted transom over the door.

She has few possessions, yet the place feels cluttered. She's living out of a couple of duffel bags and an army-green backpack. Her clothes are scattered around the room, a relatively clean pile lying near the backpack, the rest tossed about the length and breadth of a shit-brown shag rug that smells of spilled beer and forty-year-old bong water. There's probably enough aging pot residue in the old shag fibers to turn on a busload of hardcore stoners. Junk food wrappers drift aimlessly around the edges like tumbleweeds, amassing in the corners. A thoroughly defeated twin bed mattress lies on the floor, its spirit crushed, no bed or box spring, the sheets gray with age.

Due to some unfathomable quirk of my physiology, the strong chemical smell of artificially scented laundry detergent will give me a debilitating headache within minutes, but forty-year-old bong water is just a ripe, tangy smell.

And despite the mess, nothing in here smells one bit like camphor, gun oil, or cigarettes.

I scan this uninviting living space, searching for a common point of reference, my eyes drawn to the only decoration in the place—a golden plastic crucifix hanging all by itself in the middle of the dark wood veneer wall paneling.

"You know what this place needs?" I say.

"What? Granite countertops? A fancy espresso machine? A chandelier?"

"It could use a bit more light, yeah."

Kristel turns on a lamp housing a seven-watt Christmas bulb that gives off precious little light.

"Happy now?" she asks.

I shrug. What am I supposed to say to that?

I take a couple of steps toward the gilt plastic Jesus. I study the physiology of the corpus, which is quite realistic, except for the plastic seam running down the side.

"So who are you, anyway?" she asks.

I hand her a business card.

"I'm a friend of a friend."

Kristel pulls off her winter jacket and tosses it on the floor, giving me a glimpse of the sacred heart tattoo on her upper arm peeking out from her T-shirt sleeve.

There's nowhere to sit and have a comfortable conversation or even to make a cup of nice, soothing chamomile tea. My eyes land on the pile of relatively clean laundry.

I pick up the first article of clothing on the pile, an extra-large polo shirt with a word that in the dim light looks like

FASCIST stitched over the left breast in shiny red thread, but a second look affirms that the letters form the acronym FASCC, whatever that means. Either way, it's two sizes too big for her.

I shake the wrinkles out and fold the shirt into a neat rectangle and place it in the empty backpack.

"So what are you doing here?" She looks at the card. "What does a certified document examiner want with me?"

"I'm here because you had the bad luck to be deployed with a bunch of guys who were all gung-ho about killing anything that moves," I tell her, reaching for the next item, a faded green T-shirt. I fold it neatly and drop it on top of the polo shirt. "Including Iraqi police officers they were supposed to be working with."

She comes closer, her eyes flitting to the transom over the door, as if a sniper's bullet might shatter the glass at any moment.

I finish folding the relatively clean laundry.

"You got a garbage bag around here somewhere?" I ask.

"Roger that," she says, digging around in the pantry for a box of thirty-gallon garbage bags that must be from a previous tenant.

I pull one out, find the drawstring loops and shake the bag out to its full size.

"Here, hold this for me," I tell her.

She holds the garbage bag open and follows me while I crawl across on the floor in my knee-length skirt gathering up all the junk food wrappers and stuffing them into the bag.

"I talked to your old bunkmate, Megan Bishop."

The garbage bag gives a sudden shiver in her hands. I grab an empty Cheetos bag and toss it in with the rest of the garbage.

"She said the bad boys in the unit even targeted looters who weren't threatening anyone, just digging through rubble."

"Shit, they weren't *looters*." Kristel's grip tightens on the garbage bag. "They were digging out victims of the building collapse."

"That wasn't in the report."

"A lot of things ain't *never* gonna get into those reports."

"They will if you tell me," I say, reaching the corner and gathering up a bunch of empty bags of popcorn, corn chips, potato chips, candy bar wrappers, greasy taco packaging, and several empty boxes of milk chocolate Raisinets, which pretty much count as health food in *this* pile of processed junk.

"Tell you what?"

"What really happened that day at the Ishtar Hartley," I say, my voice as flat as an electrocardiogram hooked up to a dead man.

She doesn't answer, and I keep my head down, taking an inordinate amount of time to clear the last of the candy wrappers from this corner of the room.

"Probably still gives you nightmares, doesn't it?" I say, as blandly as possible. "No matter how hard you try, the faces of the dead just keep popping into your head—"

"Stop it," she says.

"Like when your buddy steps on a tripwire and loses half his abdomen—"

"Stop it, God damn it! Stop it! Just fucking stop it!"

"All right," I say, sweeping up the crumbs till this part of the room is completely garbage free, then I start working my way along the back wall toward the opposite corner. "Then why don't *you* tell me what happened?"

She doesn't say a word as we fill a second garbage bag.

"We need a couple more garbage bags," I say, getting up and dusting off my knees.

"Why?"

We're standing ankle-deep in a river of dirty clothes and junk food residue and she wants to know why we need more garbage bags? Okay, not my place to judge.

"Those two can go down to the curb," I say, shaking out another garbage bag. "Let's make one pile of clothes to take to the laundromat and another for the clothes that can't be salvaged. Hold this open for me."

She dutifully holds the third bag open while I gather up the dirty laundry. And she finally starts letting it out, one drop at a time.

"The shit that went down that day—it wasn't a terrorist attack on our unit," she says, as I keep ferrying dirty laundry into the laundry bag as if we're chatting about whether her delicates should be washed in warm or cold water.

"They had reporters from all over the world staying on the top floors of that hotel, including guys from Al-Jazeera and shit, right?"

"Uh-huh."

"And, well, some of the guys in our unit didn't like what them Saudi journalists were saying about us, you know?"

Al-Jazeera is based in Doha, Qatar, but this isn't the moment to give her a geography lesson.

"So ... they ... launched an attack," she says. "*Our* guys launched an unprovoked attack on a group of unarmed foreign journalists. *Our* guys fired those machine guns rounds and grenades at the top three floors of that hotel."

I reach a mound of foul-smelling clothes that are stiff with what appears to be dried excrement of various vintages and consistencies.

"There was no enemy fire *at all* coming from the hotel," she says. "The only people in our unit who got wounded were hit by pieces of glazed brickwork that our own bullets blasted off the hotel's façade."

I nod noncommittally, trying not to get dried egesta all over my fingers.

"You got nothing to say to all that?" she says.

Next up is a clump of used panties stained with blood and other excretions. Jesus, chronic depression is a bitch.

"It's pretty intense stuff," I say, looking up at her. "So what happened to the two members of the unit who were killed?"

Kristel presses her lips together tightly, holding back tears.

I let out a sigh. "You don't have to tell me. I think I can figure it out."

"Yeah?"

"Yeah."

"Then why don't you say it?"

"You sure?"

"Hell yeah, I'm sure. Say it."

I unearth a pair of socks that were rolled into a ball when they were still wet with … something. They've been buried so long even the mold has mold.

Into the garbage bag.

"The report said your team that day consisted of six people in a lightly armored vehicle—"

"That's some bullshit right there, yo," she says, wiping her eyes. "There was *no* armor on that vehicle. It was *not* armored. And there were *seven* people on the team, not six."

"What? Are you sure?"

"*Fuck yeah, I'm sure.*"

"Because every other source is saying there were only six people on the team."

"Where you hear that?"

"Like I said—everyone." I lift up a crusty gray tank top and get a strong whiff of decaying flesh. A rotting mouse corpse lies on what might be a gray T-shirt, crawling with an unfamiliar species of slimy blue-gray maggots, not the more common white ones.

"You got any rubber gloves?" I ask.

"Sorry."

"Paper towels?"

"Uhhh … maybe."

"You've got thirty seconds or I'm sacrificing this tank top for the greater good of humanity."

I sit back on my heels while Kristel checks the cabinets for paper towels.

"Okay, so help me piece this together," I say to her from across the room. "It's pretty clear that at least two members of the team, you and Megan Bishop, didn't want to participate in the assault on the hotel. Am I right?"

She doesn't answer.

"Which leads me to the next assumption."

"And what's that?" she says, returning with a roll of paper towels that's down to its last two sheets and handing it off to me like a relay baton.

I take it from her and peel off the last two sheets.

"That at least one other member of the team tried to stop the assault, either by arguing with the others, or trying to seize their weapons, or by pointing his own weapon at them, or maybe even trying to block their fire with his own body. And somebody shot him in cold blood, right in front of you."

She squeezes her eyelids shut, forcing the tears out of the corners of her eyes, and nods.

I double-fold the last two sheets of paper toweling, and double them again so I can pick up the rodential remains without getting dead mouse goo all over my hands. Or maggots. (Did I mention the maggots?)

Yikes! I drop the whole origami project as Kristel's knees give way, leaping up to steady her as she nearly collapses, and ease her to the floor next to me.

"Let me get rid of this, okay?"

I pick up the festering mouse corpse and flush it down the toilet, then I wash my hands in the kitchen sink.

"Let me get you some water," I say, digging out a filthy glass. And I mean *filthy*. I didn't know it was possible to grow an inch-thick colony of furry green mold in the dregs of a single glass of beer. I wonder how long *this* little biology experiment has been going on.

I scrub it clean, then run the cold water for a good thirty seconds before filling the glass with fresh, clean water.

I hand Kristel the glass and kneel next her.

She takes a couple of swallows and stares at the hidden patterns in the shit-brown shag for a couple of minutes before she finally says, "Trane was a good guy, you know?"

I nod.

I put my hand on her shoulder, waiting to hear the grisly details of yet another firefight in a war gone bad.

"Part of his head flew right past me," she says, taking another sip of water and nearly choking on it. She coughs up the words: "I ended up on the ground—*cough*—kinda like this—*cough*—holding him—*cough*—completely helpless as the blood gushed out of him into the parking lot."

She nearly gags on the words, but recovers and takes a few deep breaths.

"It was all over in a second. No last words or nothing."

I squeeze her shoulder.

"Most of us would want to seek forgiveness after that kind of incident," I say. "Unless you're a guy like Tommy Ard."

The mere mention of his name sends a jolt through her body.

"What do you mean?" she asks, eyes wide with panic.

"I mean that when the Good Lord put together Mr. Thomas Ard, he seems to have left out the part we call empathy."

Her eyes say she needs more.

"It means I'm willing to believe that it only took two guys to do all that damage at the Ishtar Hartley. Am I getting warm?"

The earth turns on its axis for a minute or two, then she nods.

"Was there any kind of investigation?"

She lets out a bitter cackle.

"Yeah, sure," she says. "Only problem is the investigators

work for the same company as the contractors, and the same payroll department issues the paychecks. You hear me?"

"Loud and clear."

"There were no bullet holes in our vehicle, no shell casings on the scene from the AKs and BKCs the Iraqis used, and *definitely* no sign of a Katyusha rocket. Next day, the investigators came and found casings from our own M4 rifles and 7.62mm machine guns, and some of our 40mm grenade casings, too."

"Yeah, I'm familiar with the model."

"That all you got to say?"

I hold off a moment, weighing my words.

"So who was the other guy?"

"What other guy?"

"Look, we both know that Ard is a grade-A psycho. But you just told me the hotel was hit with a barrage of rifle fire, machine-gun fire, and grenade-level ordinance. So who was the other assailant?"

Kristel squeezes her eyes shut as if trying to block out the mental image, but it doesn't work any better than it did the first time.

"Did he get away?" I ask.

She seems confused by my question, so I clarify: "Is he still out there? Or did Ard kill him, too?"

When she finally speaks, it's in a low whisper, as if she doesn't want the listening devices embedded in the ceiling to pick it up and relay the message back to Central Command.

"Ard said he would kill us if we said anything, and that he would get away with it because we were in the middle of a war zone and no one could touch him. He even destroyed the hotel's security cameras and the video footage of the confrontation."

"But you're not over there. You're here now."

"Makes no difference," she says. "Sometimes I wish he *had* killed me. He shoulda shot me right then and there, then

I wouldn't've had to live through all this—this—" She chokes back tears.

"You don't mean that."

"Sure I do, I do, I do." She shakes her head, tears rolling down her cheeks. I do my best to comfort her.

"There is a way out of this," I tell her.

She turns to me with the tentatively hopeful look of someone who has forgotten what it means to be hopeful.

"But first I have to ask you about the scroll."

She jerks away, flicking my hand off her shoulder. "What do you want from me, a confession? I never *touched* that damn scroll."

"But your fingerprints were on it."

"Jesus, don't you know *anything*?" she challenges me.

"Apparently not. Go ahead and educate me."

She holds her hands up, fingers splayed wide like she's trying to get me to back off.

"When they hired us to work for Cadmium, they said we all had to be fingerprinted as a condition of employment."

"Yeah, they said that to me, too—"

"Only they made us do *two* sets of fingerprints, one on the regular forms, and one on some kind of sticky tape stuff," she says, wiggling her fingers like sea anemones. "So like if you ever get out of line, or threaten to expose something they wanna keep secret, they can plant your prints on *anything* they want—gun barrels, stolen artifacts, you name it."

"Documents," I say, my mouth getting dry.

She nods at me as if to say, *You're getting it now, aren't you?*

"Like I said, there is a way out of this."

"Yeah? You got some magic pixie dust in that bag of yours?"

"Something even better." I reach into my bag and pull out a tiny digital recorder.

"Oh, no. No no no," she says, pushing herself to her feet and hustling over to the sink to get more water.

I follow her.

"The place is starting to look half decent," I say, running my finger along the grimy countertop and inspecting it for dirt. "You want me to start on the counters next?"

She stands there, her face a mask of fear.

"Or would you rather I start on the microwave? That thing looks pretty filthy, too. You got some sponges and abrasive cleanser?"

"You serious?" she says.

"About this?" I say, holding up the recorder. "Hell, yes."

"So you want me to, like, make a confession?"

"I just want you to give me your recollection of the events, in your own words, just like you did a minute ago."

She clams up.

"Choose wisely, sister," I say. "Because if you don't, they're going to pin the theft of that scroll and by extension every one of their bloody crimes on you—which is exactly what they're doing, isn't it?"

She lets the blood leave her heart and circulate around her body for a minute or so, but eventually her conscious mind catches up with what she already knows is true, and she agrees.

"Okay, let's do this," I say, clearing a space on the counter and pressing RECORD.

I begin: "This is Felicity Ortega Pérez. I'm a private investigator employed by Cadmium Solutions regarding the matter of former Silver Bullet employee Kristel Santos. The witness has not been paid or coerced in any way, so the statement she is about to make is of her own free will and is a true description of the circumstances exactly as she remembers them."

I give her a look that says, *Ready?*

She nods.

I give the date, time and location, and Kristel is just about to say her piece when a loud knock rattles the front door, the knob turns and a pair of Suffolk County cops walk right in, followed by a couple of security personnel from Cadmium Solutions who might as well be wearing matching jumpsuits labeled Thing One and Thing Two.

"You led them to me!" Kristel yells. "I can't believe you led them to me!"

And she's right—I obviously *did* lead them to her, but saying *Yes, but I didn't realize they were following me* doesn't seem like it would help much.

"*¡Cómo me puedes hacer semejante cosa—!*"

"You're making a big mistake," I tell the cops. "She didn't do anything—"

"Save it," says one cop.

"*¡Mentirosa!*" Kristel screams in my face. My head is pounding from all the noise.

"They making her take the blame—"

"We got her prints on a boatload of stolen goods," says the other, reaching for the handcuffs on his belt.

"That's just what they want you to think—"

"Get the fuck away from me! Don't you touch me!" Kristel tries to run away, as if there's anywhere to run in this concrete dungeon. What's she going to do? Hide behind the pile of dirty laundry? Climb on top of it and hold them off like King Kong on the Empire State Building?

The cops have their hands on their guns, but see no need to draw their weapons as they corner her like a petrified rabbit. She shrinks from their grasp, cursing them as they come for her with a crazed look in her eyes. "*¡No me toquen! ¡Suéltenme!*"

"We'll get the charges dismissed, I promise," I shout over the turbulence, leaving out the unspoken qualification: *I hope.*

But she's not listening to me. Nobody's listening to me. They slap the cuffs on her and drag her up the steps. I try to follow, but Things One and Two block my path with their massive bodies.

The game is up, but I keep charging.

"How'd you guys find me, anyway?" I demand.

They get a nice, condescending chuckle out of that.

"You think the GPS unit you chucked in the river was the *only* tracking device on that car?" says Thing One. "Better do more than a quick sweep next time, girlie."

Fuck. I don't want to give them the satisfaction of watching me crumble. I still have a few cards up my sleeve.

"We need you to come with us now," says Thing Two, inviting me to climb into the company limousine idling at the curb.

"What about the other car?" I say, nodding at the wounded warrior I've been driving all over the NY metro area in pursuit of … well, not the truth, exactly. More like the truth's second cousin once removed.

"We'll send a man for it," says Thing One. "Too bad for you that by the time they deduct all the property damage you've done from your paycheck, you won't have change left for the subway."

They get a good laugh out of that, too.

I watch from the bottom step as the cops stuff Kristel Santos into the back of the cruiser.

Kristel's a good name for her—a precious thing, hard but fragile, and almost impossible to put back together once broken.

"Jesus, will you look at this dump?" says Thing One, looking around the basement apartment. "You'd think somebody might've at least tried to clean the place up."

CHAPTER TWENTY-THREE

Ruth

The women of Beit-lekhem got together and collected items for Ruth's wedding day. They lent her a shawl with blue threads woven into the fringes to protect her from demons, and made her chew on perfume-soaked herbs to make her breath smell sweet.

The *kohan* wore a robe with tiny bells stitched into the hem to provide additional protection from demons. He spoke of *kidushin*, sanctification, and pledging to honor their mutual bond before three witnesses, so that on this special day of celebration, their sins would be forgiven.

Boaz's wrinkled hands shook with anticipation, fumbling to lift the bride's veil. When a couple joins in wedlock in Ruth's homeland, the vigorous young warrior raises his beloved's veil with the point of his sword. And if the bride is a warrior herself, she lifts the flaps of his peplum with her own sword.

The procession to the wedding chamber was accompanied by verses from the *Song of Songs*: *Let my lover come to his garden, and eat its choicest fruits!*

But when Ruth was finally alone with Boaz, she found she had to work his timid flesh like a potter spinning the wheel, using both hands to raise a shapeless lump of clay into a usable vessel glistening with wetness in the lamp light.

"Come on, old man, come on," she said, trying to give life to his limp, flightless flesh.

Until finally, like egg whites beaten to a soft peak, the listless flesh stiffened slightly, and she kept at it, coaxing and teasing until he came to her like a blind worm, slithering to and fro until he collapsed, pale and spent, like a man at death's door.

He had stopped breathing, she was sure of it.

But soon the hairs in his nostrils began to sway, and his breathing gradually returned to normal.

And Yahaweh gave her a pregnancy.

~

The waters swirled inside of her, and divided into the waters of the flesh and the waters of the fluid, and the flesh began to form inside the fluid, and the spirit of life entered the flesh.

And on the tenth day of the seventh month, the people refrained from eating or drinking, washing or coupling, so they could perform what the Israelites call *kippur*, the purging of guilt. And the *kohan gadol* praised the name of the God of Israel, and the people fell on their faces and pleaded with Yahaweh, the God of Israel, saying *Put me in the Book of Life*.

And the women wept for the lack of rain till the tears ran down their faces and the Temple slaves closed the East Gate with a mighty slam. Then a Levite blew the piercing blasts announcing the arrival of the jubilee year, when every slave owner must let his Yehudi slaves go free.

And on the fifteenth day of the seventh month, the people celebrated the harvest festival, parading up the hills and returning with their arms full of olive branches, palm leaves, myrtle, and pine, and they harvested figs, and baked bread and laid it before the Holy of Holies. And they harvested the wine grapes, which in the olden days would have led to wild nights of dancing and leaping around the bonfires as rivers of wine flooded the streets, but things had changed since the olden days. Instead, the *kohanim* recited the passage from the Scrolls of Moses that begins, *Arami oved avi. My father was a wandering Aramean.*

And after seven days the wind shifted, bringing moist air from the sea, and the rains came, first in tiny droplets the people could barely feel, annihilated by little puffs of dirt as they struck the ground. Then the drops grew fatter, until the windows of heaven flew open and the waters came crashing down amid fire and thunderbolts, as if the heavens themselves were crying tears of joy. And the people rejoiced that God had not turned his face from them.

And the sons of Israel kept marrying foreign women from Ashdod, Ammon, and Moab—even though Nehemiah upbraided them and cursed them and had some of them whipped, and made them swear before God that they would not allow their sons and daughters to marry such people. He ordered the watchmen to close the city gates on Yom Shabbat, and purged the priesthood of every foreign element, and begged God to remember him well for all the good deeds that he had done.

And all the desperate childless sons of Exile hungrily eyed the daughters of Jerusalem as if they had just sprung up like the first flowers of spring, to be gathered up all dewy and sweet to adorn their homes and provide them with offspring of their own making, or through their male slaves.

And somehow, through it all, Ruth was lucky to be well fed, and her belly began to swell.

And the wild-eyed mendicant who calls himself Son-of-Isaiah could be seen wandering the streets of the city at all hours of the day or night arguing with the shadows and preaching to the deaf:

Listen, O foolish people, O heartless nation! Listen, you heads of the House of Jacob, who pervert justice and speak with two hearts, who say that darkness is light and light is darkness, who say that evil is good and good is evil, who lie awake at night plotting to cheat men out of their homes.

Send for the wailing women so they can mourn us. For the harvest is finished, the summer is gone, and we are not saved.

When the season of life finally came, Ruth's contractions were so severe she couldn't even think of God—couldn't think of the words, the prayers, the supplications. She was supposed to be asking God for forgiveness, but the pain was simply too much to bear. She asked for some *keneh bosem*, the curative sweet cane of the eastern tribes, but of course there was none.

So she sent for a scribe instead.

The midwives offered her wine spiced with myrrh to dull the pain, but she refused it. She wanted to tell her story with her mind unfogged in case she died within the hour, a very real possibility.

"Right, now what's so important that it couldn't wait till after the birth?" asked the scribe, sitting on the edge of the couch and unlatching his writing case.

"I want you to make two copies," Ruth said, gritting her teeth as her lower back burned with another contraction. "One for the keepers of the royal archives in Babylon, the other for my sister-in-law, Orpah, of the tribe of the Midianites, to be read aloud at the grave of Makhlon Ben-Elimelekh, so that he may be comforted by the news of his son's birth, and the knowledge that we have done *l'hakim shem ha-met*."

Raising up the name of the dead.

"*To my sister-in-law, Orpah*," the scribe repeated as he scribbled down the words.

"Remember me to your daughters."

The scribe cocked an eyebrow at the strange formulation, but money had changed hands so he dutifully wrote down what she said, word for word.

Ben-Isaiah's voice cut in abruptly: "Maybe I should hire a scribe as well."

The midwives hurried to cover the expectant mother with a woolen blanket, griping about the presence of men in the birthing chamber. But Ruth, breathing heavily, silenced them with a firm, "I want him here."

The scribe looked the prophet over. "What do *you* need a scribe for?"

"To help spread the word," Ben-Isaiah said, pulling a well-worn scroll from his cloak. "The people of Israel have shown the world they don't need a king to rule over them, and pretty soon they'll realize they don't need any prophets, either."

Weary from wandering the streets, Ben-Isaiah plopped down next to the scribe, nearly upsetting his inkwell. The scribe glared at him, but the prophet didn't seem to notice. He just stared at the cracked ceiling as the midwives coached Ruth in the fine art of breathing.

"I need fifty copies of this scroll on durable parchment, and I can barely afford *one* on a flimsy sheet of papyrus," the prophet lamented.

Ruth closed her eyes, her face flushed, perspiration beading up on her forehead and upper lip. The contraction slowly dissipated, and Ruth slumped back against the birthing stool, letting her abdominal muscles go slack.

"By putting so much emphasis on the Torah, I have managed to make myself obsolete, because anyone can be holy if they follow the Torah." Ben-Isaiah gave a shrug of resignation. "Now all I can do is wait for the Messiah to come."

"*Selah*," said the scribe.

Ben-Isaiah stood up and pulled on his cloak.

"Don't go," Ruth said, gulping for air.

"*Khazak w'ematz*. You must be strong and resolute, so your name will live on. And know that wherever you go, I will be with you," he said, placing the scroll of his teachings on the table. "As for me, I will leave this city, and travel throughout the land to spread the Lord's Teachings, and those who seek knowledge of the Torah shall find me."

And he walked out, letting the curtains swing back into place, covering the doorway and keeping out the noise and light.

Ruth dictated her tale to the scribe until the contractions

came so close together that the midwives finally tossed him out.

And she bore a son.

And the women said to Naomi, "Blessed is the Lord, who has given you a redeemer today! May the name of the dead be raised in Israel! For a son is born of your daughter-in-law, whose love and devotion to you has been better than seven sons. May the Lord make her like Rachel and Leah, even though she is a Moabite."

And they took the child and gave it to Naomi, saying, "A son is born to Naomi!" And they named him Oved, for he was the son of a wanderer, of the line of Peretz. And Oved begot Jesse, and Jesse begot David.

And the daughters of Israel celebrated the birth of Oved with music and dancing, and they praised God because everything had worked out so well in the end.

Ruth lay on the pallet, her faced bathed with tears.

She called for the scribe once more and told him to seal the two finished copies of the text in earthenware jars, and to tell the recipients to store them in a cool, dry place, so that they would last a long time.

But not yet. There was still more to tell.

And she said unto me, *Write.*

CHAPTER TWENTY-FOUR

Felicity

The driver passes under the Expressway, makes three quick rights, and merges with the traffic heading west to New York City.

"We know what you did," says Thing One, pressing against me on my right.

"Yet you let me take out the company car today."

"So you could lead us to Santos," he says.

"Yeah, thanks for that," says Thing Two, digging his elbow into my ribs as he adjusts his position. "Say what you like about how we handled the war, but the oil's flowing again."

"Yeah, too bad there's all that blood mixed in with it."

That stops the conversation for a good long while.

~

"It has come to our attention that you were arrested last night for disorderly conduct," says Velda Renko, holding court behind her polished oak desk, flanked by Detective Gustella and Things One and Two, whose company ID lanyards indicate that their actual names are Franza and Gaines, respectively.

"Among other charges," she adds.

"Which were dropped this morning."

"I'm sure you understand that we can't have anyone working for us whose actions can be perceived as subverting the rule of law—"

"Then you'll be pleased to learn that I'll be presenting the

US District Attorney's office with a full portfolio of evidence confirming that Cadmium Solutions deployed illegal weaponry in Iraq including but not limited to grenade launchers, white phosphorus projectiles, and soft-core bullets that our own troops are banned from using under The Hague Convention—"

"This is about that incident at the Hartley Hotel, isn't it?" says Franza.

"Because something really stinks about all this," I press on, casting each word in molten lead, ignoring my smoldering headache.

"I think we can all agree that the incident at the Ishtar Hartley was terribly tragic," says Velda Renko, her coppery hair shimmering in the cool glow of her computer screen. "But it's not the fault of the contractors. They believed they were under attack, and it's not our place to second-guess the actions of the men and women in that unit under combat conditions."

"We did what we had to do," Franza says, pointing his thick index finger at me accusingly. "In case you forgot, America's at war—"

"Wait a minute," I say, breaking in. "Did you just say *we*?"

"You better learn to shut the fuck up or we're gonna bust you down to Dumpster diving," says Gaines.

"Fine with me," I tell him. "It's honest work, and I'm used to dealing with maggots."

"This is gonna be just another case of some disgruntled former employee trying to make us look bad," says Franza, stepping on whatever Velda Renko was about to say.

"You're going to have a *lot* more disgruntled former employees when they find out Cadmium was only paying them four hundred dollars a day but was billing the US government a *thousand* a day per contractor."

"Those figures are incorrect," said Velda Renko. "Cadmium Solutions made less than twenty dollars profit per day for every contractor we had over there—"

"You realize that I've examined the books firsthand, don't you? And that I'm a certified forensic accountant?"

"Good luck getting access to those materials now that we've revoked your security clearance," says Gaines.

"Then I guess it's a good thing I made copies."

Franza and Gaines stare at each other like a couple of infielders who just let an easy pop-up fall between them for a base hit.

"You're not authorized to copy those materials under the terms of your contract—"

"I'll be sure to tell that to the prosecutors after I provide them with proof that Cadmium Solutions has been regularly overbilling the Pentagon since the 1990s," I say, my confidence building. "And that the company's been especially adept at creating shell corporations that specialize in generating reams of fake invoices for fictitious expenses relating to leasing oil rig maintenance equipment and other heavy industrial machinery. The Pentagon's going to be *really* pissed about that. The IRS, too."

And then … I feel something warm and wet, like molten goop oozing out of my uterus and sliding down inside me. *No, not now, dammit!* I mean, *Yes, thank God*, but talk about bad timing. Ugh!

"And the FBI is going to be rather displeased with you for violating the Economic Espionage Act of 1996," Velda Renko says. "Which carries penalties of up to five million dollars and fifteen years' imprisonment for misappropriating trade secrets with the intent to benefit a foreign power."

"A foreign power? That's a bit of a longshot, even for you guys."

"Nah, it'll be easy to convince a jury once we tell them all about your mom," says Franza.

An icy stiletto tickles the back of my neck, and it's all I can do not to visibly shiver.

It's an act, it's an act. I keep telling myself that these types *always* act like they know more than they really do in the hopes that you'll be only too eager to fill in the rest for them.

But the warm flush of fecundity is seriously handicapping my defensive edge right now. I've got emergency pads in my bag, like every female PI under the sun, but I can't call for a timeout now. Too bad I went to my dad's to shower off all that jailhouse scum and grab a change of clothes before heading out to Long Island—because this would be so much easier in my faded blue jeans and Mets jersey.

I steel myself and tell Franza, "Leave my family out of this—unless you want to donate some of your brain cells to my permanently disabled brother. Give me a call and maybe we can set something up."

Franza looks at Velda Renko. They exchange signs, and she nods.

"There's also the matter of the damages to company property," she says. "Your company-issued cell phone, for instance, and the car—"

"I had reason to believe that the phone's security protocols had been compromised, so I was attempting to implement a new debugging procedure, which unfortunately malfunctioned. I'm afraid it's still in the beta-stage. And there was nothing to indicate that the tracking device on the car was placed there by the company, rather than by a competitor, or I would *never* have dreamed of interfering with its operating functions."

That's the best I can do under the circumstances.

"We know all about you breaking into Gustella's account," Franza says. "And don't try to deny it, we were watching it *live* on the monitors as you did it. You really oughta keep a lid on those emotional outbursts of yours. You left a digital trail a mile wide."

The two bruisers share a snicker about that one.

"And I know all about your attempt to plant Kristel Santos's fingerprints on the looted artifacts in that duffel bag."

"Yeah, right," says Franza.

"I don't mean you personally, but here's the thing about contracting out labor that you really should be doing yourself. There's always an excuse. Am I right, Detective?"

Detective Gustella, who hasn't said a word throughout this whole proceeding, gives me a curt nod. I do my best to keep swinging.

"Oh, they knew enough to wear latex gloves so they wouldn't leave their fingerprints all over the loot. But they left a pair of used latex gloves in the bottom of the duffel bag containing traces of the wearer's skin cells, which means DNA samples, which are far more conclusive evidence than fingerprints. So you see the dilemma."

It's a complete bluff. A total head fake. But they don't know that.

Velda Renko looks at me like she's measuring me for a coffin, and makes a quick call to the bullpen. Looks like they're going to bring in the closer.

She gently returns the phone to its cradle.

"The company is willing to be lenient in this case," she says, the words sliding off her tongue like honey. "After all, you were successful in locating Ms. Santos for us, just as you were hired to do."

"Just to be clear," Franza says, interrupting Velda Renko again. "The only reason we hired you was because we knew that Santos gal wouldn't even *talk* to one of our guys."

"Yeah, we had to get a Spanish chick to do the job for us," says Gaines. "Maybe we'll throw in a bonus since you personally delivered her into our hands a couple days ahead of schedule."

"How thoughtful of you," I say, shifting uncomfortably, my panties sticking to me.

"We have clearly reached a stalemate," Velda Renko announces, unaware that a chess metaphor is wildly out of place in this high-stakes baseball game. "You claim to possess potentially incriminating evidence about certain company policies, and we allege that you committed numerous criminal acts in procuring said evidence."

Franza leans in again: "She means we're going to slap you with the biggest lawsuit you've ever seen."

Velda Renko glances at him, clearly vexed by his constant intrusions.

"Fine. I'll give the files to the presiding judge and let her decide if it's worth pursuing," I counter.

"We'll tear your credibility to shreds, girlie," says Franza, ticking off the charges on his beefy fingers. "Lying on your job application form, breach of contract, theft of services, damaging company property—"

"When we're done with you, you won't be able to get a job walking dogs," Gaines says.

I've fallen behind in the count and it's time to go for the squeeze play.

"What if I get you the scroll?"

They all eye each other like I've just offered them prime gold mining stock on one of Pluto's lesser moons, but no one wants to be the one to say no.

Franza breaks the silence: "Who gives a shit about a fucking thousand-year-old piece of paper?"

"Actually, it's more than two thousand years old and it's written on parchment, and I was hired to find it in order to clear the company of any charges that they actively abetted such looting. Those charges are still pending."

Pluto and its largest moon Charon whirl silently around each other, eternally locked in a gravitational dance more than four billion miles away.

"And you're telling us you know where it is?" says Velda Renko.

"With ninety-nine percent certainty."

"And what do you want in return?"

What do I want? How about first-rate treatment for

Specialist Jeremías Ortega Pérez at the best medical institutions in the northeast? Including physical and occupational therapy and any other rehabilitation programs that might improve his condition. Or at least move him up on the freaking ten-year waitlist for VA center treatment.

What I get is a fancy trussed-up version of *We won't tell if you won't tell*. Once we iron out the details, including an agreement to drop the most serious charges against Kristel Santos, Velda Renko says:

"Deal?"

"Deal," I say.

"Let's roll," says Franza, grabbing his coat.

"I need to stop at a drug store first."

He looks at me shakes his head.

"Women," he says.

~

Professor Woolley looks up from the pile of lab reports on her desk, the soft light from her desk lamp briefly rendering the lenses of her reading glasses opaque, like a golden shield hiding her eyes.

"Mind if I come in?"

"I'm really quite busy at the moment—"

"I'm afraid this can't wait," I say, strolling into her office.

"All right, but I can only give you a few minutes. This is the busiest part of the semester."

"Now, let's see," I say, making a big show of looking around. "When I first came here, you made a point of directing my attention to a photo of a four-thousand-year-old painting of a pair of royal manicurists."

"Four thousand *three hundred* years old. Now what are you doing here?" she asks, taking off her reading glasses, letting me see her eyes as they narrow with suspicion.

"So I'm going to turn around and look at what's on the opposite wall."

I turn and face the large storage cabinet.

"What's gotten into you?" she says, with growing alarm. "What on earth are you talking about?"

"Ah, yes. The storage cabinet. More specifically, a large metal storage cabinet with wide, shallow drawers containing what is purported to be a jumble of broken cuneiform tablets *of no practical interest to anyone but an expert in the field*, I believe you said."

She pushes violently away from her desk as I march over to the storage cabinet and try to open one of the drawers.

Locked. Of course.

"Open it or I'll break it open."

"How *dare* you come in here and speak to me like that? Now get out or else—"

"Or else I'll plant myself here till the cops can get a judge to issue a warrant and we'll open it up *their* way. No telling *what* kind of damage they might do. Or you can do it my way and walk out of here a free woman."

"I'm calling campus security—" She shoves a pile of papers aside and picks up the phone.

"Unlike Kristel Santos."

That slows her down.

"What about Ms. Santos?" she says, the phone cord dangling loosely from the receiver, as if it's as tired of life as I am at this particular moment.

"She stole it, didn't she?" I say. "What I mean is, she spotted the Baghdad Scroll in a pile of looted treasures and retrieved it for you."

Professor Woolley keeps the phone cord dangling for a few moments, then finally puts it to bed and tucks it in for the night.

"Is it stealing to steal from thieves?" she asks.

"Yeah, pretty much."

"Haven't you ever bent the rules for a good cause?"

"I've trampled on my share of rules, Professor Woolley,

but never at the expense of someone with even *less* power and privilege than I have."

Her eyes grow cloudy with doubt.

"They're making her the sacrificial lamb so that you can keep living your nice, quiet, respectable life grading lab reports," I say, unable to keep the accusatory tone out of my voice.

She's torn between hearing me out and calling security.

"I just want to see what all the fuss is about," I say, which has a greater measure of truth in it than a lot of the things I've had to say over the past few days.

Professor Woolley's hand sinks into the pocket of her lab coat, jingling a set of heavy brass keys.

She unlocks a middle drawer and there it is, rolling around in the back, amid the stray crumbs of broken tablets. It's so small, it looks like a burnt *taquito*, a corn tortilla rolled up into a cylinder no more than six inches long and about an inch in diameter and left in the oven too long. This is the big deal everyone's been making such a fuss about?

She puts on a pair of white cotton gloves and carefully unfurls it before my eyes in all its faded glory. It's the same cramped, angular Hebrew script with the elongated letter stems as the fragment in my possession. A chunk of the top right corner of the scroll is missing, having been unkindly cut off at some point during its travels. I pull the much-abused fragment out of my shoulder bag and hold it up so it fills in the gap. It's still in the evidence bag, and a little worse for wear, but otherwise it's a perfect fit. The prodigal daughter, given up for lost, has returned to her mother's embrace.

"Beautiful, isn't it?" she says. "Just beautiful."

"I'm amazed you can still unroll it."

"It was stored in a clay jar under extremely dry conditions—nearly ideal for the preservation of untanned vellum parchment."

"Who does it belong to?"

"It belongs to the people of Iraq," she says, rolling it up and placing it back in the drawer. "We found it in Babil Province, about twenty kilometers north of Najaf, near a site that local tradition identifies as the tomb of the prophet Ezekiel."

"The prophet Ezekiel is buried in Iraq?"

"As an exile in Babylon, he was the only Israelite who received the gift of prophecy outside the land of Israel, according to rabbinic tradition."

"So what did you do with it?"

"We gave it to the Baghdad Museum."

"Yet here it is in your office."

Her nostrils flare like a wild filly champing against her new harness.

"You don't seem to have any idea what it was like in the mid-1980s—before you were born, I imagine—when Saddam Hussein began a campaign of systematically persecuting the country's remaining Jewish population, one of the largest in the Middle East, raiding synagogues and looting collections that had been left undisturbed for centuries. Imagine what that feels like. The Jews had been living in Iraq for *two thousand five hundred years* but were *still* treated like foreigners."

"Believe it or not, I can relate."

Professor Woolley looks skeptical, so I get back on track:

"That explains how all those Torah scrolls ended up in the Baghdad Museum."

"Where we found them stored under such appalling conditions that many of the scrolls were waterlogged and moldy. We *rescued* them."

"So what went wrong?"

She flinches at my blunt query, gazing at the ruined landscape of broken tablets and potsherds in the metal drawer.

"We tried to save the museum's collection, or what was left of it, scrambling to pack what we could into more than two dozen reinforced aluminum trunks that were supposed to be shipped here for their own protection. But Rick Fursten and his cronies at Cadmium Solutions screwed that up with their heavy-handed tactics and unaccountable shooting of unarmed civilians."

"So you took the Baghdad Scroll as compensation for all the pain and loss that Cadmium put you through?"

"What can you *possibly* mean by that reckless accusation?"

"I mean, I'd be bitter too if the region's endless wars derailed my career—"

"Jesus, enough with the girl talk, Perez," says Franza, waltzing in with Gaines. "*Yakety-yak-yak.* Just hand over the frikkin' scroll, already, okay?"

"How *dare* you come in here and order me around?" says Professor Woolley, duly outraged.

"Save it, lady," says Gaines. "Where was the outrage when Saddam was gassing and raping his own people?"

"Yeah," says Franza. "You were just fine with that, but you had to go and bitch to the media that we wouldn't shoot unarmed looters in street clothes who weren't posing a threat, which would have been considered a war crime, by the way."

"All right, you couldn't shoot them," Professor Woolley concedes. "Couldn't you have just *scared* them away?"

"Those ragheads don't scare as easy as you do, honey," says Gaines.

"Yeah, you fled the country as I recall," says Franza.

"After someone mailed me a letter with a *bullet* inside and a note telling me to leave the country or they'd kill me."

"Enough of this," says Franza, holding out his hand, palm up, and flipping all four fingers toward himself in a commonly recognized gesture among the locals. "Hand it over."

"I'm calling campus security," says Professor Woolley, parading back to her desk.

Franza opens his mouth to spew more Queens-accented invective but, much to my amazement, actually holds off when he sees my upraised hand.

Leaving me with the unenviable task of trying to calm Professor Woolley.

"Don't worry, they'll return it to the proper authorities, along with the other looted artifacts," I say, trying to reassure her. "But *they* get to return it. You see how it is?"

"No, I *don't* see how it is," she says, leaving that poor, abused phone cord dangling in the air once more.

I do my best to explain, without sounding too much like a mob enforcer, that, basically, we can ruin them with what we know, but they can ruin us with what they know. So it's a bit of a standoff, except for the part about them not leaving till she hands over the scroll and the duffel bag full of ancient Babylonian swag.

"You imbeciles have no idea what's at stake," Professor Woolley says, flinging the words at her besiegers. "Southern Iraq is where we find the first written stories. King lists. Epic poems. Love poetry. It all started there, and *now* look what we've done to it. Bank vaults containing priceless artifacts bombed and flooded. Bronze Age villages littered with unexploded bombs. The glazed brick tiles of ancient Babylon's Processional Way broken and crushed by American tanks. You have *zero* understanding of what we're in danger of losing forever."

"We understand what *you're* gonna lose if you don't let us have the friggin' scroll, Ms. Woolley," says Gaines.

"*Doctor* Woolley," she spits. "I led the team that discovered the scroll!"

"So it's a case of finders keepers?" Gaines says.

"Do you have *any* idea how many artifacts were looted during the pointless, stupid, disastrous Iraq War? Tens of thousands, quite possibly *hundreds* of thousands."

"Yeah, we kind of had our hands full dodging RPGs and bringing Saddam to justice," says Franza. "No thanks to people like you, who never said one word about Saddam's atrocities."

"Could we not refight the war in Iraq right now, please?" I suggest.

"You mean Operation Iraqi *Freedom*?" says Franza, direct-ing some of his aggression at me. "Because that's what we brought to that pissass country. *Freedom*."

Professor Woolley says, "Your so-called freedom facili-tated the destruction of the *only* existing material records of some of the oldest urban civilizations in the world!"

The words come tumbling out of her mouth like candy from a busted piñata: "Looters were using *backhoes and bull-dozers* to rip up the landscape at nearly every major site in the region—Adab, Ashur, Babylon, Nippur, Mashkan-Shinar—"

"Oh, boo-hoo," says Franza.

Professor Woolley growls with rage.

"We're *finally* going back, the first visit by a fully equipped team in *more than twenty years*, to a previously unexplored site a few miles from Ur that was settled by a tribe of wandering nomads around four thousand years ago, when the area was mostly marshland," she says, regaining some of her compo-sure. "I keep thinking if we dig down deep enough, we'll eventually reach a layer of pure wet sand with the footprints of Adam and Eve walking side by side."

She rubs her eyes, which seem to have aged about twenty years in the last three minutes, her skin drying up like a time-lapse image of a mummified corpse in a cheap horror movie, as if she's absorbing all of society's evils in addition to her own.

"And the window will slam shut for another twenty years if we start a war in Zabul Province ..."

Franza and Gaines swoop in like birds of prey who've been waiting for the final death rattle.

Professor Woolley knows when she's been defeated. She wavers a moment before picking up the scroll, then puts it in a cylindrical protective case and, after a slight hesitation, places it in Franza's outstretched hand. I add the fragment I've been holding for safekeeping, and slink off to my ever-lasting shame, and we're done.

On the way down the stairs, Franza says, "Man, you sure are one crazy bitch."

He means it as a compliment.

I tell him, "Hey, I'm the sane one in the family. You should meet my cousin Filomena. Now *that* bitch is crazy."

~

My, my. Here it is, Thursday already and I'm *still* not rich and famous. My exploits remain unheralded in the press even though my investigative skills helped clear Cadmium Solutions of all charges related to smuggling precious Ancient Near Eastern artifacts into the country.

Although to be fair, Cadmium's been kind of busy dealing with a US government audit that uncovered more than $13 billion in charges that Cadmium was unable to justify or support with adequate documentation. Their inability to produce missing or corrupted computer files is blamed on a temporary contractor who no longer works for the company.

CEO Rick Fursten argues that *any* fines would harm the company's *ability* to protect our troops, and that as a God-fearing Christian and a loyal American, he *just* isn't going *to* allow *that*.

Fursten's lucky the state goes easier on perjury than God: He puts bearing false witness against thy neighbor right up there with idolatry, adultery, and murder.

The state is far more accommodating, and by this point Cadmium's willing to do *anything* to settle out of court rather than risk public exposure of their security breaches, until some hotshot corporate lawyer produces a cache of legal documents showing that the company's controversial actions in Iraq are covered by the Coalition Provisional Authority's Order 17, giving contractors blanket immunity from prosecution for *any* acts performed as part of their contracts or *any subcontracts thereto*, leading a federal judge to vacate all charges against the subcontractors who tried to blow the top three floors off the Ishtar Hartley Hotel.

Cadmium does end up losing one contract, to arm aircraft at the CIA's secret bases in Balochistan Province—prompting CEO Fursten to complain that *Performance doesn't matter in Washington, just politics*—but the $170 million contract to supply security in Iraq gets extended indefinitely by President Kinney's administration.

Fursten celebrates by throwing Kristel Santos to the dogs, pressing charges against her to the full extent of the law.

With all his money, you'd think he could afford to buy himself a functioning moral compass.

Or at least rewire the old one.

Nobody seems to have told Fursten about our deal, and the prosecutors going after Cadmium give up as soon as they realize that they're *never* going to get a conviction based solely on documentary evidence of the white-collar crimes, so we never learn the full story, we just know somebody sure got away with *something*.

Early the next morning, he tweets out the message: *Let Freedom Reign!*

The next day, Cadmium Solutions officially changes its name to BlueStone Industries, moves its corporate headquarters to Dubai—one of those places where you can make enormous cash deposits without having to answer all those pesky questions about where it came from—and submits a competitive bid for a $22 billion contract with the Pentagon to train Balochistan's provincial police force.

I find myself thinking how the sun is already halfway through its lifespan, and these clowns are all running around trying to vacuum up as many millions as they can before the clock runs out. But the sun's not going to care who has the millions and who doesn't when it becomes a red giant and engulfs the earth, is it?

~

As for the Baghdad Scroll, Carbon-14 testing confirms that the parchment dates from around 150 BCE, significantly later than the previously proposed date of circa 550 BCE. An Orthodox rabbinic tribunal conducts an independent evaluation of the scroll's textual content, and announces with a collective yawn that it's nothing more than an early copy of the Scroll of Ruth, with only minor differences from the Masoretic text, and therefore nothing to get excited about.

A separate group of Conservative and Reform women rabbis does their own textual analysis, and while agreeing that the text contains only minor anomalies, notably the opening invocation to King Cyrus of Persia, they argue that it should not be dismissed as simply being *a copy of a copy*, in the words of the Orthodox tribunal, but should be celebrated as evidence of the authority of the Masoretic text, and for its importance among the women of the tribe of Judah, since its very existence suggests that it passed from mother to daughter to granddaughter, from generation to generation, down through the centuries.

In response, a group of ultra-Orthodox rabbis asserts that since the Book of Ruth unquestionably dates to the time of the Judges, roughly corresponding to the eleventh century BCE, and that a woman who played such a pivotal role in the history of Israel couldn't possibly be of Persian descent, the so-called Baghdad Scroll must be a fake.

In other news, President Kinney's press secretary announces that a surprise middle-of-the-night air strike has taken out Al-Qahol's number two man in Zabul Province. Wall Street responds with a huge rally.

Assistant Secretary of State Marlene DuBois dismisses critics of Operation Zabuli Freedom, calling the bombing campaign *The birth pangs of a new tribal region*. So remember, kids, if you ever want to get away with doing something truly awful, just put the word *freedom* next to it.

A prowar rally blocks traffic in lower Manhattan, marching up Broadway with a police escort while carrying enormous painted icons of President Kinney and Governor Treplev of Balochistan Province that are evidently being held up with stout wooden poles.

And about five minutes after my contract with Cadmium Solutions expires, I receive a letter from the health insurance company denying my brother further coverage, saying that the policy does not apply to physical damages suffered because of "acts of war or terrorism," and that he really should read the fine print more closely next time.

And that's the way it is, folks. No happy ending. No golden ticket falling out of a chocolate bar into my lap.

I can't help thinking of the words of wisdom from something called the Midrash Zohar: *Whoever grudges assistance to the poor does not deserve to exist in this world, and he also forfeits the life of the world-to-come.*

Professor Shulevitz must have told me that one, and suddenly I'm overcome with the desire to speak to him right this minute. I could use a strong shoulder to cry on, and Jhimmy's arraignment isn't till Monday. I call Professor Shulevitz—I mean, Aaron—and invite him out for breakfast.

"Sure, I've got an insatiable craving for an Egg McGuffin," he says.

"*Bleah*. I haven't eaten breakfast at a McDonald's since I was fourteen years old."

"Not an Egg McMuffin," he corrects me. "An *Egg McGuffin*. It's a breakfast sandwich whose contents serve to move the plot along in an Alfred Hitchcock movie."

I groan into the receiver.

"I also need to stop at the local flower shop to pick up a ten-pound bag of *plotting soil*, which helps guard against gardener's block."

"Do these jokes work on your students?"

"Tell you what," he says. "Let's meet at Ratner's on Delancey. They're going out of business and I've got to have one last cheese blintz before they close the doors."

~

"Well, no wonder you're so light-skinned," says Professor Aaron, referring to my mother's lineage as we stroll along the East River Promenade, fresh-roasted coffee and cheese blintzes warming our insides. There's a chill in the air and the dead fish smell has *finally* faded into history.

"If you ever want to emigrate to Israel," he says, "you'd have a much easier time of it than the Eritrean refugees flooding into south Tel Aviv."

"You know, for a country founded by a people fleeing oppression, Israel sure isn't living up to its promise."

"Neither are we," he says, looking across the river at the old Domino Sugar refinery, which recently shut down production after more than 120 years and put two hundred people out of work. "We're supposed to be a light unto nations. We're supposed to be more humane, more ethical, more forgiving, more just."

"So what happened?"

"What happened is our leaders should have studied history better, and learned from a figure like Cyrus the Great, whose policy was to leave the civil and religious infrastructure of the kingdoms he conquered relatively intact, instead of forcing the Persian system on them."

I look into his eyes, and see a whole other world reflected in them.

"As opposed to every American intervention in my lifetime," I say, a cold gust of wind making my eyes water. I turn aside and blink it away. "So we've learned absolutely *nothing* in twenty-five centuries?"

"Except that all empires collapse, sooner or later."

Families are out enjoying the fresh air, from young mixed race couples with babies wrapped snugly to their chests to venerable Asian American grandmas seemingly impervious to the brisk December breeze scything off the East River, their preschool-age grandchildren running around with their arms spread out, making engine sounds like little airplanes circling in a sky that is forever clear and blue.

"Don't gaze *too* wistfully," Aaron says, catching me, "or someone might think you're desperate to have children."

"Someday," I say, crossing my fingers.

"Fingers crossed," he says, mirroring my gesture. "You see how assimilated we American Jews are? We don't think twice about doing something as patently Christian as crossing our fingers."

I shake my head. "Sometimes I feel like I'm fighting against a history that isn't even mine."

"But you can reclaim that history, or at least a piece of it," he says. "The King James version of the Book of Ruth teaches us that she was modest and submissive, but the Ruth of the Hebrew Bible is a bold and valiant woman who risks everything for her aging mother-in-law."

"If I have even *one drop* of that woman's blood in me, then I am proud to count myself as one of her descendants."

"You don't have to go back *that* far," he says. "Jesus was part of a long tradition of rabble-rousing Jews who weren't afraid to speak truth to power, without regard for the consequences."

"The Jesus they taught me about was as immaterial and otherworldly as the fairies inhabiting the Irish countryside."

Aaron shakes his head with an amused chuckle.

"What?"

"Once we became a text-based religion, we pretty much jettisoned all the lesser supernatural beings from the official canon," he says. "Though of course mystical figures like Elijah the Prophet and Lilith the night spirit persisted in Midrash and folklore. Even God stops talking to us by the time we get to the books of Ezra and Nehemiah in the mid-fifth century BCE, and he certainly doesn't come down and walk among us."

"What about the goddess Asherah?"

It's his turn to look me in the eye. "Of all the other gods and fairies, she was the last to go. She held on the longest."

"They tried to silence her," I say, returning his gaze. "And yet she persisted."

~

On my way back to Queens, I field one last call from Velda Renko before the Number 7 plunges under the river. She wants to know what I'm planning to do with the files that are still in my possession. I tell her I'm giving them to Judge River for safekeeping.

"What? Judge *who*? Wait—"

Oops. Another service interruption. They've really got to do something about the Wi-Fi connection on this line.

~

The roar of the subway gives me plenty of time to mull over how the rich white guys who own everything lost a *tiny* sliver of their power and privilege during social upheavals of the mid-twentieth century, and they've been fighting like hell ever since to get it all back, with interest, calling everything they don't like an attack on their freedom. As if freedom is a zero-sum equation, a limited commodity to be hoarded, because if some previously marginalized group *gains* a bit more freedom, that means the dominant group *loses* some freedom. But freedom isn't like that. What they really mean when they say the word freedom is *power*. But you sound like a jerk if you complain that a minority group is taking away a tiny piece of your white male *power*. But that's what they mean.

So don't be fooled.

The subway train rattles and screeches along, stoking the dull ache emanating from the welt on the side of my head. As I climb the stairs to our apartment, my feet landing heavily on each step in time with the blood hammering away at my bruised cranium, I feel the pounding of each inflamed capillary as I rip down the NYPD's yellow CRIME SCENE tape blocking the entryway and step inside the scavenged, looted wreckage of our apartment, and my simmering headache becomes a volcanic eruption.

Lord, what a mess.

Seems like I've spent my whole life cleaning up the messes that men leave behind, but they just keep leaving their trash in the middle of the floor for me to trip over.

And you can't simply change boyfriends like you're changing a light bulb, especially if the bulb isn't blown, and it doesn't want to be changed.

Oh, Jhimmy. Why do you make it so hard to love you?

But there's no use crying over spilled … whatever the fuck it is I've spilled.

I just need to get to work picking up the pieces of my wrecked apartment, and try to put my life back together.

But it's such an unholy mess, I have to sit down, overwhelmed.

I don't even know where to begin.

Appendix

And for fans of putting recipes at the end of a book, behold:
the Prophet Ezekiel's Recipe for Poor Man's Bread:

> Take thou wheat, and barley, and beans, and lentils,
> and millet, and spelt, and put them in one vessel and
> make thee bread from them.... And thou shalt eat it
> like barley cakes, and thou shalt bake it on human
> excrement.
> —Ezekiel 4:9–12

Acknowledgments

The primary inspiration for this novel came from working with feminist Hebrew Bible scholar Ilona N. Rashkow at Stony Brook University. Prof. Rashkow introduced me to a "gutsy babe" (in her words) named Ruth when I was her teaching assistant for several semesters for a course called Images of Women in Literature. The lectures focused on "re-visioning" biblical scenes in ways that undercut traditional patriarchal readings, creating a space for feminist and other interpretations.

In Ruth's case, a single line of dialogue was enough to get me started (more on that in a moment). In general, women don't have much of a voice in the Hebrew Bible, but when they choose to speak up, they make demands, and those demands are listened to.

In Western art and Christian biblical interpretation, Ruth is typically presented as the epitome of modesty, deference, and self-sacrifice (i.e., a model Christian woman). In the Middle Ages, she was viewed as a convert to Christianity and a precursor of the Virgin Mary herself; some paintings even depict her with golden blond hair. But a close reading of the Hebrew text reveals Ruth as a determined woman who repeatedly creates her own agency. For example, many translations of Ruth 2:2 depict her asking permission from her mother-in-law Naomi to go glean in the fields (e.g., the Revised English Bible: "May I go?"). But the Jewish Publication Society's translation has Ruth taking the initiative: "I would like to go the fields and glean" (1743).

In Ruth 3:4, after Naomi tells Ruth to go to the threshing floor and crawl into bed with Boaz, Naomi says, "He will tell you what to do" (JPS, 1745). But it is Ruth who tells Boaz what to do, instructing him to spread his robe over her.

But the best single example comes from one of the more famous declarations in the Hebrew Bible: In Ruth 1:16, when Naomi tells Ruth to go back to her people and her gods, many translations depict Ruth as ever so mildly resisting Naomi's request, and using future tense verbs, or else they soften the bluntness of the biblical Hebrew with flourishes of poetry, as in the King James Version (which does both): "Intreat me not to leave thee, or to return from following after thee: for whither thou goest, I will go ... thy people shall be my people, and thy God my God." Prof. Rashkow paraphrased the Hebrew text as being much more direct: "Don't tell me to go. I'm going with you. Your people are my people. Your God is my God."

Now *that's* a kick-ass woman I can write a novel about!

One challenge is that the Book of Ruth is the shortest narrative book in the Bible, with only four chapters. So I had to do a lot of research to create the foundation for a story set in ancient Israel in the year 538 BCE. The primary purpose of such research is to learn enough to build a convincing world for the story, but also to learn when you're allowed to deviate from the known. I have taken numerous liberties with the source material, compressing events from different decades into a single season or two, and especially by moving the action of the Book of Ruth from the eleventh century BCE to the end of the Babylonian Exile in the sixth century BCE. I have my reasons. I did a fair amount of research for the modern-day part of the story as well. An abbreviated list follows:

Translations and commentary on the Torah, the Hebrew Bible, and the Book of Ruth:

Adele Berlin and Marc Zvi Brettler, eds., *The Jewish*

Study Bible; Rabbi Menachem Davis, ed., *Interlinear Chumash* (Schottenstein edition); *Encyclopaedia Judaica*, 2nd ed., "Levirate Marriage and Halizah"; Tamara Cohn Eskenazi and Tikva Frymer-Kensky, *The JPS Bible Commentary: Ruth*; Richard Elliott Friedman, *Commentary on the Torah*; *The Bible with Sources Revealed*; Rabbi Elyse Goldstein, ed., *The Women's Torah Commentary*; Rabbi Hersh Goldwurm, gen. ed., *Talmud Bavli: Avodah Zarah* (Schottenstein edition); J.H. Hertz, ed., *The Pentateuch and Haftorahs* (Soncino); *The Interpreter's Dictionary of the Bible* (5 vols.); The Jewish Publication Society, *JPS Hebrew-English Tanakh*; The King James Version; Koren Publishers, *The Jerusalem Bible*; *The Midrash Rabbah: Ruth* (Feldheim); Harry M. Orlinsky, *Notes on the New Translation of the Torah*; Ilana Pardes, *Ruth: A Migrant's Tale*; W. Gunther Plaut, *The Torah: A Modern Commentary* (5 vols.); *The Revised English Bible*; Rabbis Nosson Scherman and Meir Zlotowitz, gen. eds., The Artscroll Series: *Bereishis*; *The Book of Ezra*; *The Book of Nehemiah*; *The Chumash* (Stone Edition); *Megillas Ruth*; *The Tanach* (Stone Edition); *The Twelve Prophets*; *Tehillim: The Book of Psalms* (Feldheim); Yehoash, *Tanakh* (Yiddish translation); Jacob Neusner, trans., *The Mishnah*.

Additional works:

Peter R. Ackroyd, *Israel under Babylon and Persia*; Penina Adelman, ed., *Praise Her Works: Conversations with Biblical Women*; William Foxwell Albright, *Yahweh and the Gods of Canaan: A Historical Analysis of Two Contrasting Faiths*; Lindsay Allen, *The Persian Empire: A History*; Joan Aruz, Kim Benzel, and Jean M. Evans, eds., *Beyond Babylon: Art, Trade, and Diplomacy in the Second Millennium B.C.*; Scott Atran, *In Gods We Trust: The Evolutionary Landscape of Religion*; Henry Trocmé Aubin, *The Rescue of Jerusalem: The Alliance between Hebrews and Africans in 701 BC*; Michael Axworthy, *A History of Iran: Empire of the Mind*.

Bernard J. Bamberger, *The Story of Judaism*; Ian Barnes, *The Historical Atlas of the Bible*; David Barsamian and Noam Chomsky, *Power Systems: Conversations on Global Democratic*

Uprisings and the New Challenges; Propaganda and the Public Mind; Robert N. Bellah, *Religion in Human Evolution: From the Paleolithic to the Axial Age*; Hayim Nahman Bialik and Yehoshua Hana Ravnitzky, *The Book of Legends/Sefer Ha-Aggadah: Legends from the Talmud and Midrash*; Matthew Bogdanos and William Patrick, *Thieves of Baghdad: One Marine's Passion for Ancient Civilizations and the Journey to Recover the World's Greatest Stolen Treasures*; Athalya Brenner, ed., *Genesis: A Feminist Companion to the Bible* (Second Series); Herbert C. Brichto, "On Faith and Revelation in the Bible," *Hebrew Union College Annual* 39 (1968): 35–53; "The Worship of the Golden Calf: A Literary Analysis of a Fable on Idolatry," *Hebrew Union College Annual* 54 (1983): 1–44; Maria Brosius, *The Persians: An Introduction; Women in Ancient Persia, 559–331 BC*; Steven Kerry Brown, *The Complete Idiot's Guide to Private Investigating.*

Joseph Campbell, *The Hero with a Thousand Faces; The Masks of God: Primitive Mythology*; Rajiv Chandrasekaran, *Imperial Life in the Emerald City: Inside Iraq's Green Zone*; Abraham Cohen, *Everyman's Talmud*; Georges Contenau, *Everyday Life in Babylon and Assyria*; Gaalyah Cornfeld, *Archaeology of the Bible: Book by Book*; John Curtis and Nigel Tallis, *Forgotten Empire: The World of Ancient Persia.*

Stephanie Dalley, *Myths from Mesopotamia: Creation, the Flood, Gilgamesh, and Others*; Edith Deen, *All of the Women of the Bible*; Max I. Dimont, *Jews, God and History*; Ernst Doblhofer, *Voices in Stone*; E.S. Drower, *The Mandaeans of Iraq and Iran: Their Cults, Customs, Magic, Legends, and Folklore.*

Yaron Z. Eliav, *God's Mountain: The Temple Mount in Time, Place, and Memory*; J.A. Emerton, "'Yahweh and His Asherah': The Goddess or Her Symbol?," *Vetus Testamentum* 49, no. 3 (July 1999): 315–37.

Brian Fagan, *Time Detectives: How Archeologists Use Technology to Recapture the Past*; Kaveh Farrokh, *Shadows in the Desert: Ancient Persia at War*; Howard Fast, *The Jews: Story of a People*; Vergilius Ferm, ed., *Ancient Religions: A Symposium*;

I.L. Finkel and M.J. Seymour, *Babylon: Myth and Reality*; Israel Finkelstein and Neil Asher Silberman, *The Bible Unearthed: Archaeology's New Vision of Ancient Israel and the Origin of Its Sacred Texts*; *David and Solomon: In Search of the Bible's Sacred Kings and the Roots of the Western Tradition*; Louis Finkelstein, *The Jews: Their History, Culture, and Religion*; Margalit Fox, *The Riddle of the Labyrinth: The Quest to Crack an Ancient Code*; Thomas Frank, *What's the Matter with Kansas? How Conservatives Won the Heart of America*; Ellen Frankel, *The Five Books of Miriam: A Woman's Commentary on the Torah*; Tikva Frymer-Kensky, *In the Wake of the Goddesses: Women, Culture, and the Biblical Transformation of Pagan Myth*; *Reading the Women of the Bible: A New Interpretation of Their Stories*.

T.H. Gaster, *Myth, Legend, and Custom in the Old Testament: A Comparative Study with Chapters from Sir James G. Frazer's "Folklore in the Old Testament"*; *The Oldest Stories in the World*; Carol Gilligan, *In a Different Voice: Psychological Theory and Women's Development*; Louis Ginzberg, *Legends of the Bible*; Jonathan Golden, *Ancient Canaan and Israel*; Robert Goldenberg, *The Origins of Judaism: From Canaan to the Rise of Islam*; Cyrus H. Gordon, "Belt-Wrestling in the Bible World," *Hebrew Union College Annual* 23, no. 1 (1950–51): 131–41; *The Common Background of Greek and Hebrew Civilizations*; Lester L. Grabbe, *Judaism from Cyrus to Hadrian: The Persian and Greek Periods*; Robert Graves and Raphael Patai, *Hebrew Myths: The Book of Genesis*.

James Harpur, ed., *Great Events of Bible Times*; James Hastings, ed., *Encyclopaedia of Religion and Ethics*; John H. Hayes and J. Maxwell Miller, *Israelite and Judaean History*; Chris Hedges, *Empire of Illusion: The End of Literacy and the Triumph of Spectacle*; Herodotus, *The Histories*; Elizabeth Caldwell Hirschman and Donald N. Yates, *When Scotland Was Jewish: DNA Evidence, Archeology, Analysis of Migrations, and Public and Family Records Show Twelfth Century Semitic Roots*; Alfred J. Hoerth, Gerald L. Mattingly, and Edwin M. Yamauchi, *Peoples of the Old Testament World*; James K. Hoffmeier, *Israel in Egypt: The Evidence for the Authenticity of the Exodus Tradition*; Barry W. Holtz, ed., *Back to the Sources: Reading the Classic Jewish Texts*; Philip Houston, Michael Floyd, and Susan Carnicero with Don Tennant, *Spy the Lie: Former CIA Officers Teach You How to Detect Deception*.

Louis Jacobs, *Oxford Companion to the Jewish Religion*; *JPS Guide: The Jewish Bible*.

Judith A. Kates and Gail Twersky Reimer, *Reading Ruth: Contemporary Women Reclaim a Sacred Story*; Homa Katouzian, *The Persians: Ancient, Mediaeval and Modern Iran*; Michael Katz and Gershon Schwartz, *Searching for Meaning in Midrash: Lessons for Everyday Living*; Ben Kiernan, *Blood and Soil: A World History of Genocide and Extermination from Sparta to Darfur*; Judy Klitsner, *Subversive Sequels in the Bible: How Biblical Stories Mine and Undermine Each Other*; Samuel Noah Kramer, *Sumerian Mythology: A Study of Spiritual and Literary Achievement in the Third Millennium B.C.*.

Lee I. Levine, *Jerusalem: Portrait of a City in the Second Temple Period*; James W. Loewen, *Lies Across America: What Our Historic Sites Get Wrong*; *Lies My Teacher Told Me: Everything Your American History Textbook Got Wrong*.

Jodi Magness, *The Holy Land Revealed*; Max L. Margolis and Alexander Marx, *A History of the Jewish People*; Leo Markun, *Prostitution in the Ancient World, Little Blue Book No. 286*; Victor H. Matthews, *Judges and Ruth*; Herbert G. May, ed., *Oxford Bible Atlas*, 3rd ed.; Dennis J. McCarthy, "Further Notes on the Symbolism of Blood and Sacrifice," *Journal of Biblical Literature* 92, no. 2 (June 1973): 205–10; "The Symbolism of Blood and Sacrifice," *Journal of Biblical Literature* 88, no. 2 (June 1969): 166–76; Robert W. McChesney, *Corporate Media and the Threat to Democracy*; Carol Meyers, *Rediscovering Eve: Ancient Israelite Women in Context*; Jean Murley, *The Rise of True Crime: 20th-Century Murder and American Popular Culture*.

Erich Neumann, *The Origins and History of Consciousness*.

A. Leo Oppenheim, *The Interpretation of Dream in the Ancient Near East: With a Translation of an Assyrian Dream Book*; Harry M. Orlinsky, *Ancient Israel*; David L. Owen, *Hidden Evidence: 50 True Crimes and How Forensic Science Helped to Solve Them*.

Raphael Patai, *Gates to the Old City: A Book of Jewish Legends*; *The Hebrew Goddess*; Steven Poole, *Unspeak*; Chaim Potok, *Wanderings*; James B. Pritchard, ed., *The Ancient Near East: An Anthology of Texts and Pictures*.

Katherine Ramsland, *The Forensic Psychology of Criminal Minds*; Norma Rosen, *Biblical Women Unbound*; *Leo Rosten's Treasury of Jewish Quotations*.

Heleen Sancisi-Weerdenburg, Amélie Kuhrt and Margaret Cool Root, *Achaemenid History*, vol 8, *Continuity and Change*; Jack M. Sasson, *Ruth: Commentary and Formalist-Folklorist Interpretation*; Jeremy Scahill, *Blackwater: The Rise of the World's Most Powerful Mercenary Army*; Danny Schechter, *The More You Watch, The Less You Know*; S. Schechter, "The Riddles of Solomon in Rabbinic Literature." *Folklore* 1, no. 3 (September 1890): 349–58; Rabbis Nosson Scherman and Meir Zlotowitz, gen. eds., *History of the Jewish People: The Second Temple Era*; Gershom Scholem, *Kabbalah*; Robert M. Seltzer, *Jewish People, Jewish Thought: The Jewish Experience in History*; Avigdor Shinan and Yair Zakovitch, *From Gods to God*; Maynard Shipley, *Sources of Bible Myths and Legends, Little Blue Book No. 851*; Morton Smith, "The Common Theology of the Ancient Near East," *Journal of Biblical Literature* 71 (1952): 135–47; Norman Solomon, *War Made Easy: How Presidents and Pundits Keep Spinning Us to Death*; Katherine E. Southwood, *Ethnicity and the Mixed Marriage Crisis in Ezra 9–10: An Anthropological Approach*; Stephen Spector, *Evangelicals and Israel: The Story of American Christian Zionism*; Adin Steinsaltz, ed., *The Talmud: A Reference Guide*; Menahem Stern, *Greek and Latin Authors on Jews and Judaism*, vol. 1, *From Herodotus to Plutarch*; Elizabeth Stone, "National Geographic Society's Cultural Assessment of Iraq"; "Cultural Assessment of Iraq: The State of Sites; Southern Iraq (May 2003)"; "Cultural Assessment of Iraq: The State of Sites; Northern Iraq (May 2003)," National Geographic online, https://www.nationalgeographic.com; "Patterns of Looting in Southern Iraq," *Antiquity* 82, no. 315 (March 2008): 125–38; Martha Stout, *The Sociopath Next Door*; Jacob Stromberg, *Isaiah after Exile: The Author of Third Isaiah as Reader and Redactor of the Book.*

Emily Taitz, Sondra Henry, and Cheryl Tallan, *The JPS Guide to Jewish Women: 600 B.C.E.–1900 C.E.*; Savina J. Teubal, *Sarah the Priestess: The First Matriarch of Genesis*; Joshua Trachtenberg, *Jewish Magic and Superstition: A Study in Folk Religion*; Isadore Twersky, ed., *A Maimonides Reader.*

Dvora E. Weisberg, *Levirate Marriage and the Family in Ancient Judaism*; Aryeh Wineman, *Mystic Tales from the Zohar*; Diane Wolkstein and Samuel Noah Kramer, *Inanna: Queen of Heaven and Earth*; Robert Wright, *The Evolution of God.*

Howard Zinn, *The Bomb*; Sivan Zlotnick, "Silent Women of Yehud: Notes on Ezra 9–10," *Journal of Jewish Studies* 51, no. 1 (Spring 2000): 3–18.

I also lifted a few lines from my students at Suffolk Community College with their permission, including Duane Dotson, Lizzy E., Aaron Lyautey, and Mike Sherry, and from Sharona Perel at Queens College CUNY. Other sources include Noam Chomsky, for a joke about OIF I cribbed and rewrote in my own fashion; author Barbara Paul, who, if memory serves, came up with the phrase "ass officially covered"; PM Press staffer Stephanie Pasvankias, for the story about her mom discovering that she was "holding-cell graffiti"; author George Cuomo of *A Couple of Cops* and retired police detective Al Della Penna for the line about tossing incriminating evidence into a lot of "deep, fast-running water" and how no one will see it again "in this lifetime." The text of John Bolton's amendments to a rules of engagement document are taken directly from Steven Poole, *Unspeak: How Words Become*

Weapons, How Weapons Become a Message, and How That Message Becomes Reality, p. 126. Another scene uses parts of the George Zimmerman/Trayvon Martin 911 transcript. Periodicals consulted include *Biblical Archaeology Review* and *PI Magazine*. I must also acknowledge a *New York Times* "Metropolitan Diary" item from sometime in the 1980s or 1990s for a line overheard at the deli. Yes, it stayed in my mind for more than thirty years.

And finally, thanks to Zoe Quinton, whose editorial skills greatly improved an earlier draft of this novel; and to Deborah Skolom for locating all those articles through inter-library loan; Deanna Bosché, Denise Drevis, Jarred Puig, and Barbara Young for (ahem) helping me print out large Word files; Prof. Krin Gabbard of SBU, from whom I borrowed the porn title *Hot Wet Sluts*; and my colleague at SCCC, Prof. Ginny Horan, for the duct-tape-in-the-shoes story.

And since some authors make a point of name-checking the bands who provided the soundtrack for their research and writing, I'd like to thank Sergei Rachmaninoff for composing *The Isle of the Dead*, which I blasted repeatedly while writing the storm-in-the-desert scene. You should play it while reading the scene, too.

About the Author

Kenneth Wishnia's novels include *23 Shades of Black*, which was nominated for the Edgar Allan Poe Award for Best First Novel and an Anthony for Best Paperback Original; *Soft Money*, a *Library Journal* Best Mystery of the Year; and *Red House*, a *Washington Post Book World* "Rave" Book of the Year. His short stories have appeared in *Ellery Queen*, *Alfred Hitchcock*, *Queens Noir*, *Long Island Noir*, *Send My Love and a Molotov Cocktail*, and elsewhere. His novel *The Fifth Servant* was an Indie Notable selection, a Best Jewish Book of the Year according to the Association of Jewish Libraries and the *Jewish Press*, won a Premio Letterario ADEI-WIZO, and was a finalist for the Sue Feder Memorial Historical Mystery Award. He edited the Anthony Award–nominated anthology *Jewish Noir* and coedited *Jewish Noir II* with Chantelle Aimée Osman. He teaches writing, literature, and other deviant forms of thought at Suffolk Community College on Long Island.

ABOUT PM PRESS

PM Press is an independent, radical publisher of critically necessary books for our tumultuous times. Our aim is to deliver bold political ideas and vital stories to all walks of life and arm the dreamers to demand the impossible. Founded in 2007 by a small group of people with decades of publishing, media, and organizing experience, we have sold millions of copies of our books, most often one at a time, face to face. We're old enough to know what we're doing and young enough to know what's at stake. Join us to create a better world.

PM Press
PO Box 23912
Oakland, CA 94623
www.pmpress.org

PM Press in Europe
europe@pmpress.org
www.pmpress.org.uk

FRIENDS OF PM PRESS

These are indisputably momentous times—the financial system is melting down globally and the Empire is stumbling. Now more than ever there is a vital need for radical ideas.

In the many years since its founding—and on a mere shoestring—PM Press has risen to the formidable challenge of publishing and distributing knowledge and entertainment for the struggles ahead. With hundreds of releases to date, we have published an impressive and stimulating array of literature, art, music, politics, and culture. Using every available medium, we've succeeded in connecting those hungry for ideas and information to those putting them into practice.

Friends of PM allows you to directly help impact, amplify, and revitalize the discourse and actions of radical writers, filmmakers, and artists. It provides us with a stable foundation from which we can build upon our early successes and provides a much-needed subsidy for the materials that can't necessarily pay their own way. You can help make that happen—and receive every new title automatically delivered to your door once a month—by joining as a Friend of PM Press. And, we'll throw in a free T-shirt when you sign up.

Here are your options:

- **$30 a month** Get all books and pamphlets plus a 50% discount on all webstore purchases

- **$40 a month** Get all PM Press releases (including CDs and DVDs) plus a 50% discount on all webstore purchases

- **$100 a month** Superstar—Everything plus PM merchandise, free downloads, and a 50% discount on all webstore purchases

For those who can't afford $30 or more a month, we have **Sustainer Rates** at $15, $10 and $5. Sustainers get a free PM Press T-shirt and a 50% discount on all purchases from our website.

Your Visa or Mastercard will be billed once a month, until you tell us to stop. Or until our efforts succeed in bringing the revolution around. Or the financial meltdown of Capital makes plastic redundant. Whichever comes first.

> "One of the most distinctive series in mystery fiction. Refreshingly original and complex."
>
> —*Minneapolis Star-Tribune*

23 Shades of Black

Kenneth Wishnia
with an Introduction by Barbara D'Amato

ISBN: 978-1-60486-587-5
$17.95   300 pages

Soft Money

Kenneth Wishnia
with an Introduction by Gary Phillips

ISBN: 978-1-60486-680-3
$16.95   288 pages

The Glass Factory

Kenneth Wishnia with an Introduction by Reed Farrel Coleman

ISBN: 978-1-60486-762-6
$16.95   256 pages

Red House

Kenneth Wishnia
with an Introduction by Alison Gaylin

ISBN: 978-1-60486-402-1
$16.95   288 pages

Blood Lake

Kenneth Wishnia with an Introduction by Liz Martínez

ISBN: 978-1-60486-430-4
$17.95   384 pages